DEAD TOMORROW

Peter James was educated at Charterhouse, then at film school. He lived in North America for a number of years, working as a screenwriter and film producer before returning to England. His novels, including the *Sunday Times* Number One bestselling Roy Grace series, have been translated into thirty-five languages, with world sales of thirteen million copies. Three books have been filmed. All his novels reflect his deep interest in the world of the police, with whom he does in-depth research, as well as science, medicine and the paranormal. He has also produced numerous films, including *The Merchant of Venice*, starring Al Pacino, Jeremy Irons and Joseph Fiennes. He divides his time between his homes in Notting Hill, London and near Brighton in Sussex.

Visit his website at www.peterjames.com
Or follow him on Twitter @peterjamesuk
Or Facebook: http://www.facebook.com/peterjames.roygrace

DEAD TOMORROW

PETER JAMES

PAN BOOKS

First published 2009 by Macmillan

This edition published 2011 by Pan Books
an imprint of Pan Macmillan, a division of Macmillan Publishers Limited
Pan Macmillan, 20 New Wharf Road, London N1 9RR
Basingstoke and Oxford
Associated companies throughout the world
www.panmacmillan.com

ISBN 978-0-330-54599-0

3 5 7 9 8 6 4

A CIP catalogue record for this book is available from
the British Library.

Typeset by SetSystems Ltd, Saffron Walden, Essex
Printed and bound by CPI Group (UK) Ltd, Croydon, CR0 4YY

Visit **www.panmacmillan.com** to read more about all our books
and to buy them. You will also find features, author interviews and
news of any author events, and you can sign up for e-newsletters
so that you're always first to hear about our new releases.

IN MEMORY OF FRED NEWMAN

RESPECT!

1

Susan hated the motorbike. She used to tell Nat that bikes were lethal, that riding a motorcycle was the most dangerous thing in the world. Over and over again. Nat liked to wind her up by telling her that actually, statistically, she was wrong. That in fact the most dangerous thing you could do was go into your kitchen. It was the place where you were most likely to die.

He saw it for himself every day of his working life as a senior hospital registrar. Sure there were some bad accidents on motorbikes, but nothing compared with what happened in kitchens.

People regularly electrocuted themselves sticking forks into toasters. Or died from broken necks after falling off kitchen chairs. Or choked. Or got food poisoning. He liked, in particular, to tell her the story of one victim who had been brought into A&E at the Royal Sussex County Hospital, where he worked – or rather *overworked* – who had leaned into her dishwasher to unblock it and got stabbed through the eye by a boning knife.

Bikes weren't dangerous, not even ones like his monster red Honda Fireblade (which could hit sixty miles an hour in three seconds), he liked to tell her; it was other road users who were the problem. You just had to watch out for them, that was all. And hey, his Fireblade left a damn sight smaller carbon footprint than her clapped-out Audi TT.

But she always ignored that.

The same way she ignored his moans about always

having to spend Christmas Day – just five weeks away – with the *outlaws*, as he liked to call her parents. His late mother was fond of telling him that you could choose your friends but not your relatives. So damn true.

He had read somewhere that when a man marries a woman, he hopes she will stay the same forever, but when a woman marries a man, her agenda is to change him.

Well, Susan Cooper was doing that OK, using the most devastating weapon in a woman's arsenal: she was six months pregnant. And sure, of course he was proud as hell. And ruefully aware that shortly he was going to have to get real. The Fireblade was going to have to go and be replaced by something practical. Some kind of estate car or people carrier. And, to satisfy Susan's social and environmental conscience, a sodding diesel-electrical hybrid, for God's sake!

And how much fun was that going to be?

Having arrived home in the early hours, he sat yawning at the kitchen table of their small cottage at Rodmell, ten miles from Brighton, staring at the news of a suicide bombing in Afghanistan on the *Breakfast* show. It was 8.11 according to the screen, 8.09 according to his watch. And it was the dead of night according to his mental alertness. He spooned some Shreddies into his mouth, swilled them down with orange juice and black coffee, before hurrying back upstairs. He kissed Susan and patted the Bump goodbye.

'Ride carefully,' she said.

What do you think I'm going to do, ride dangerously? he thought but did not say. Instead he said, 'I love you.'

'Love you too. Call me.'

Nat kissed her again, then went downstairs, tugged on his helmet and his leather gloves, and stepped outside into the frosty morning. Dawn had only just broken as he wheeled the heavy red machine out of the garage, then swung the door shut with a loud clang. Although there was a ground frost, it had not rained for several days, so there was no danger of black ice on the roads.

He looked up at the curtained window, then pressed the starter button of his beloved motorbike for the last time in his life.

2

Dr Ross Hunter was one of the few constants in Lynn Beckett's life, she thought, as she pressed his surgery bell on the panel in the porch. In fact, if she was honest with herself, she'd be hard pushed to name any other constants at all. Apart from *failure*. That was definitely a constant. She was good at failure, always had been. In fact, she was brilliant at it. She could fail for England.

Her life, in a nutshell, had been a thirty-seven-year-long trail of disasters, starting with small stuff, like getting the end of her index finger chopped off by a car door when she was seven, and steadily getting bigger as life took on more gravitas. She had failed her parents as a child, failed her husband as a wife, and was now very comprehensively failing her teenage daughter as a single-parent mother.

The doctor's surgery was in a large Edwardian villa in a quiet Hove street that had in former times been entirely residential. But now many of the grand terraced houses had long been demolished and replaced with blocks of flats. Most of those that remained, like this one, housed offices or medical practices.

She stepped into the familiar hallway, which smelled of furniture polish tinged with a faint whiff of antiseptic, saw Dr Hunter's secretary at her desk at the far end, occupied on a phone call, and slipped into the waiting room.

Nothing had changed in this large but dingy room in the fifteen or so years she had been coming here. The same water stain, vaguely in the shape of Australia, on the stuccoed ceiling, the same potted rubber plant in front of the fireplace, the familiar musty smell, and the same mismatched armchairs and sofas that looked as if they had been bought, back in the mists of time, in a job lot from a house clearance auctioneer. Even some of the magazines on the circular oak table in the centre looked as if they had not been changed in years.

She glanced at a frail old man who was sunk deep into an armchair with busted springs. He had jammed his stick into the carpet and was gripping it firmly, as if trying to prevent himself from disappearing into the chair completely. Next to him an impatient-looking man in his thirties, in a blue coat with a velvet collar, was preoccupied with his BlackBerry. There were various pamphlets on a stand, one offering advice on how to give up smoking, but at this moment, with the state of her nerves, she could have done with advice on how to smoke *more*.

There was a fresh copy of *The Times* lying on the table, but she wasn't in any mood to concentrate on reading, she decided. She'd barely slept a wink since getting the phone call from Dr Hunter's secretary late yesterday afternoon, asking her to come in, first thing in the morning, on her own. And she was feeling shaky from her blood sugars being too low. She had taken her medication, but then had barely swallowed a mouthful of breakfast.

After perching herself on the edge of a hard, upright chair, she rummaged in her bag and popped a couple of glucose tablets into her mouth. Why did Dr Hunter want to see her so urgently? Was it about the blood test she'd had last week, or – as was more likely – about Caitlin? When she'd had scares before, like the time she'd found a lump on her breast, or the time she'd become terrified that her daughter's erratic behaviour might be a symptom of a brain tumour, he had simply rung her himself and given her the good news that the biopsy or the scan or the blood tests were fine, there was nothing to worry about. Inasmuch as there could ever be *nothing* to worry about with Caitlin.

She crossed her legs, then uncrossed them. Dressed smartly, she was wearing her best coat, blue mid-length wool and cashmere – a January sale bargain – a dark blue knitted top, black trousers and black suede boots. Although she would never admit it to herself, she always tried to make herself look good when she came to see the doctor. Not exactly dressed to kill – she had long ago lost the art, not to mention the confidence, to do that – but dressed nicely at least. Together with a good half of Dr Hunter's women patients, she had long secretly fancied him. Not that she would have ever dared make that known to him.

Ever since her break-up with Mal, her esteem had been on the floor. At thirty-seven she was an attractive woman, and would be a lot more attractive, several of her friends and her late sister had told her, if she put back some of the weight she had lost. She was haggard, she knew: she could see for herself just by looking in the mirror. Haggard from worrying about everything, but most of all from worrying for over six years about Caitlin.

It was shortly after her ninth birthday that Caitlin had first been diagnosed with liver disease. It felt like the two of them had been in a long, dark tunnel ever since. The never-ending visits to the specialists. The tests. The brief periods of hospitalization down here in Sussex, and longer periods, one of almost a year, in the liver unit of the Royal South London Hospital. She'd endured operations to insert stents in her bile ducts. Then operations to remove stents. Endless transfusions. At times she was so low on energy from her illness that she would regularly fall asleep in class. She became unable to play her beloved saxophone because she found it hard to breathe. And all along, as she became a teenager, Caitlin was getting more angry and rebellious. Demanding to know *Why me?*

The question Lynn was unable to answer.

She'd long ago lost count of the times she had sat anxiously in A&E at the Royal Sussex County Hospital, while medics treated her daughter. Once, at thirteen, Caitlin had had to have her stomach pumped after stealing a bottle of vodka from the drinks cabinet. Another time, at fourteen, she fell off a roof, stoned on hash. Then there was the horrific night she came into Lynn's bedroom at two in the morning, glassy-eyed, sweating and so cold her teeth were chattering, announcing she had downed an Ecstasy tablet given to her by some lowlife in Brighton and that her head hurt.

On each occasion, Dr Hunter came to the hospital and stayed with Caitlin until he knew she was out of danger. He didn't have to do it, but that was the kind of man he was.

And now the door was opening and he was coming in. A tall, elegant figure in a pinstriped suit with fine posture, he had a handsome face, framed with wavy salt and pepper hair, and gentle, caring green eyes that were partially concealed by half-moon glasses.

'Lynn!' he said, his strong, brisk voice oddly subdued this morning. 'Come on in.'

Dr Ross Hunter had two different expressions for greeting his patients. His normal, genuinely warm, happy-to-see-you smile was the only one Lynn had ever seen in all the years that she had been his patient. She had never before encountered his wistful biting-of-the-lower-lip grimace. The one he kept in the closet and hated to bring out.

The one he had on his face today.

3

It was a good place for a speed trap. Commuters hurrying into Brighton who regularly drove down this stretch of the Lewes Road knew that, although there was a forty-mile-an-hour limit, they could accelerate safely after the lights and not have to slow down again along the dual carriageway until they reached the speed camera, almost a mile on.

The blue, yellow and silver Battenburg markings of the BMW estate car, parked in a side road and partially obscured from their view by a bus shelter, came as an unwelcome early-morning surprise to most of them.

PC Tony Omotoso stood on the far side of the car, holding the laser gun, using the roof as a rest, aiming the red dot at the front number plates, which gave the best reading on any vehicle he estimated to be speeding. He clicked the trigger on the plate of a Toyota saloon. The digital readout said 44 mph. The driver had spotted them and had already hit the brakes. Using the rigid guidelines, he allowed a tolerance of 10 per cent over the limit, plus two. The Toyota carried on past, its brake lights glowing. Next he sighted on the plate of a white Transit van – 43 mph. Then a black Harley Softail motorbike sped past, going way over the limit, but he wasn't able to get a fix in time.

Standing to his left, ready to jump out the moment Tony called, was his fellow Road Policing Officer, PC Ian Upperton, tall and thin, in his cap and yellow high-visibility jacket. Both men were freezing.

Upperton watched the Harley. He liked them – he liked

all bikes, and his ambition was to become a motorcycle officer. But Harleys were cruising bikes. His real passion was for the high-speed road-racer machines, like BMWs, Suzuki Hayabusas, Honda Fireblades. Bikes where you had to lean into bends in order to get round them, not merely turn the handlebars like a steering wheel.

A red Ducati was going past now, but the rider had spotted them and slowed almost to a crawl. The clapped-out-looking green Fiesta coming up in the outside lane, however, clearly had not.

'The Fiesta!' Omotoso called out. 'Fifty-two!'

PC Upperton stepped out and signalled the car over. But, whether blindly or wilfully, the car shot past.

'OK, let's go.' He called out the number plate – 'Whiskey Four-Three-Two Charlie Papa November' – then jumped behind the wheel.

'Fuckers!'

'Yeah, cunts!'

'Why don't you go chasing real criminals, right?'

'Yeah, 'stead of fuckin' persecuting motorists.'

Tony Omotoso turned his head and saw two youths slouching past.

Because 3,500 people die on the roads of England every year, against 500 a year who are murdered, that's why, he wanted to say to them. *Because me and Ian scrape dead and broken bodies off the roads every damn day of the week, because of arseholes like this one in the Fiesta.*

But he didn't have time. His colleague already had the blue roof spinners flashing and the siren *whup-whooping*. He tossed the laser gun on to the back seat, climbed in the front, slammed the door and began tugging his seat belt on, as Upperton gunned the car out into a gap in the traffic and floored the accelerator.

And now the adrenalin was kicking in as he felt the thrust of acceleration in the pit of his stomach and his spine pressed against the rear of the seat. Oh yes, this was one of the highs of the job.

The Automatic Number Plate Recognition video screen mounted on the dash was beeping at them, showing the Fiesta's index. Whiskey Four-Three-Two Charlie Papa November had no tax, no insurance and was registered to a disqualified driver.

Upperton pulled over into the outside lane, gaining fast on the Fiesta.

Then a radio call came through. 'Hotel Tango Four-Two?'

Omotoso answered. 'Hotel Tango Four-Two, yes, yes?'

The controller said, 'We have a reported serious road traffic collision. Motorcycle and car at the intersection of Coldean Lane and Ditchling Road. Can you attend?'

Shit, he thought, not wanting to let the Fiesta go. 'Yes, yes, on our way. Put out an alert for Brighton patrols. Ford Fiesta, index Whiskey Four-Three-Two Charlie Papa November, colour green, travelling south on Lewes Road at speed, approaching gyratory system. Suspected disqualified driver.'

He didn't need to tell his colleague to spin the car around. Upperton was already braking hard, his right-turn indicators blinking, looking for a gap in the oncoming traffic.

4

Malcolm Beckett could smell the sea getting closer as his thirty-year-old blue MGB GT halted at the traffic lights to the slip road. It was like a drug, as if the salt of the oceans was in his veins, and after any absence he needed his fix. Since his late teens, when he joined the Royal Navy as a trainee engineer, he had spent his entire career at sea. Ten years in the Royal Navy and then twenty-one years in the Merchant Navy.

He loved Brighton, where he was born and raised, because of its proximity to the coast, but he was always happiest when on board ship. Today was the end of his three weeks' shore leave and the start of three weeks back at sea, on the *Arco Dee*, where he was Chief Engineer. Not so long ago, he rued, he had been the youngest chief engineer in the entire Merchant Navy, but now, at forty-seven, he was fast becoming a veteran, an old sea dog.

Just like his beloved ship, every rivet of which he knew, he knew every nut and bolt of his car, which he had taken apart and put back together again more times than he could remember. He listened fondly to the rumble of the idling engine now, deciding that he could hear a bit of tappet noise, that he would need to take the cylinder head off on his next leave and make some adjustments.

'You OK?' Jane asked.

'Me? Yep. Absolutely.'

It was a fine morning, crisp blue sky, no wind, the sea flat as a millpond. After the late autumn storms that had made his last spell on board pretty grim, the weather was set fair, at least for today. It would be chilly, but glorious.

'Are you going to miss me?'

He wormed his arm around her shoulder, gave her a squeeze. 'Madly.'

'Liar!'

He kissed her. 'I miss you every second I'm away from you.'

'Bullshit!'

He kissed her again.

As the lights turned to green, she depressed the clutch, crunched the gear lever into first and accelerated down the incline.

'It's really hard to compete against a ship,' she said.

He grinned. 'That was a great bonk this morning.'

'It had better last you.'

'It will.'

They turned left, driving round the end of the Hove Lagoon, a pair of artificial lakes where people could take out rowing boats, have windsurfing lessons and sail model ships. Ahead of them, adjoining the eastern perimeter of the harbour, was a private street of white, Moorish-styled beachfront houses where rich celebrities, including Heather Mills and Fatboy Slim, had homes.

The salt in the air was stronger now, with the sulphurous reeks of the harbour, and the smells of oil, rope, tar, paint and coal.

Shoreham Harbour, at the western extremity of the city of Brighton and Hove, consisted of a mile-long basin, lined with timber yards, warehouses, bunkering stations and aggregate depots on both sides, as well as yacht marinas and a scattering of private houses and flats. It had once been a busy trading port, but the advent of increasingly large container ships, too big for this harbour, had changed its character.

Tankers, smaller cargo vessels and fishing boats still made constant use of it, but much of the traffic consisted of commercial dredgers, like his own ship, mining the seabed for gravel and sand to sell as aggregate to the construction industry.

'What have you got on in the next three weeks?' he asked.

Trusting the wives they left behind was an issue for all sailors. When he had first started in the Royal Navy he'd been told that the wives of some mariners used to stick a packet of OMO washing powder in their front windows when their husbands were away on a tour of duty. It signalled *Old Man Out*.

'Jemma's nativity play, which you'll just miss,' she answered. 'And Amy breaks up in a fortnight. I'll have her moping around the house.'

Amy was Jane's eleven-year-old by her first marriage. Mal got on fine with her, although there was always an invisible barrier between them. Jemma was the six-year-old daughter they had together, with whom he was much closer. She was so affectionate, so bright, such a positive little person. A complete contrast to his own strange, remote and sickly daughter by his first marriage, whom he was fond of but had never really connected to, despite all his efforts. He was gutted that he would be missing Jemma playing the Virgin Mary, but was long used to the family sacrifices that his chosen career entailed. It had been a major contributing factor to his divorce from his first wife, and something he still thought about constantly.

He looked at Jane as she drove, turning right past the houses into the long, straight road along the south side of the harbour basin, going almost deliberately slowly now as if eking out her last minutes with him. Feisty but so lovely, with her short bob of red hair and her pert snub nose, she was wearing a leather jacket over a white T-shirt and ripped blue jeans. There was such a difference between the two women. Jane, who was a therapist specializing in phobias, told him that she liked her independence, loved the fact that she had her three weeks of freedom, that it made her appreciate him all the more when he was home.

Whereas Lynn, who worked for a debt collection agency, had always been needy. Too needy. It was one thing to be wanted by a woman, desired by a woman, lusted after by a woman. But to be *needed*. It was the need that had ultimately driven them apart. He'd hoped – in fact, they had both hoped – that having a child would have changed that. But it hadn't.

It had actually made things worse.

The car was slowing down and Jane was indicating. They stopped, let a truck loaded with timber thunder past, then turned right, in through the open gates of Solent Aggregates. Then she halted the car in front of the security Portakabin.

Mal climbed out, already in his white boiler suit and rubber-soled sea boots, and flipped up the tailgate. He hefted out his large, soft bag and pulled on his yellow hard hat. Then he leaned in through the window and kissed Jane goodbye. It was a long, lingering kiss. Even after seven years, their passion was still intense – one of the pluses of regularly spending three weeks apart.

'Love you,' he said.

'Love you too,' she replied, and kissed him again.

A tall man, lean and strong, he was good-looking, with an open, honest face and a thatch of short, thinning fair hair. He was the kind of man colleagues instantly liked and respected; there was no *side* to him. What you saw was what you got.

He stood watching her reverse, listening to the burble of the exhaust, concerned about the sound when she revved. One of the baffles in the twin silencers needed replacing. He would have to put it up on the hoist when he got back. Also, he needed to take a look at the shocks, the car didn't seem to be riding as well as it should over bumps. Could be the front shock absorbers needed replacing.

But, as he entered the Portakabin and signed his name in the log, exchanging pleasantries with the security guard, other things were starting to occupy his mind. The starboard engine of the *Arco Dee* was coming up to 20,000 hours, which was the company's limit for an overhaul. He needed to do some calculations to pick the optimum time for that to happen. Dry docks would be shut down over the coming Christmas holiday period. But the owners of the *Arco Dee* weren't concerned about holidays. If he'd spent £19 million on a boat, he probably wouldn't be either, he reckoned. Which was why they liked to keep it working 24/7 for as much of the year as possible.

As he headed jauntily along the quay, towards her black hull and orange superstructure, he was happily unaware of the cargo that would accompany them back from his next voyage, scheduled to start in just a couple of hours' time, and the trauma it would bring to his own life.

5

Dr Hunter's office was a long, high-ceilinged room, with sash windows at the far end giving a view of a small, walled garden and, minimally screened by barren, wintry trees and shrubs, the stark metal fire escape of the building beyond. Lynn had often thought that in grander days, when this had been all one house, this office was probably the dining room.

She liked buildings, particularly interiors. One of her biggest joys was visiting country houses and stately homes that were open to the public – and there had been a time when Caitlin had quite enjoyed that too. It had long been her plan that when Caitlin was off her hands, and the need to earn money was not so pressing, she would do a course in interior design. Maybe then she'd offer to give Ross Hunter's surgery a makeover. Like the waiting room, it could do with a spruce-up in here. The wallpaper and the paint had not aged anything like as well as the doctor himself. Although she had to admit to herself that there was something reassuring about the fact that the room had barely changed in all the years she had been coming here. It had a learned feel about it that always – until today at least – made her feel comfortable.

It just appeared a little more cluttered on every visit. The number of grey, four-drawer filing cabinets against one wall seemed to keep increasing, as did the index boxes in which he kept his patients' notes stacked on the top, along, incongruously, with a plastic drinking-water dispenser.

There was an eye-test chart inside a light box on one wall; a white marble bust of some ancient sage she did not recognize – perhaps Hippocrates, she thought – and several family photographs above a row of crammed, old-fashioned bookshelves.

One side of the room, behind a free-standing screen, contained the examination couch, some electrical monitoring equipment, an assortment of medical apparatus and several lights. The flooring here was a rectangle of linoleum inset into the carpet, giving this area the appearance of a mini operating theatre.

Ross Hunter motioned Lynn to one of the pair of black leather chairs in front of his desk and she sat down, putting her bag on the floor beside her, keeping her coat on. His face still looked tight, more serious than she had ever seen him, and it was making her nervous as hell. Then the phone rang. He raised an apologetic hand as he answered it, signalling with his eyes to her that he would not be long. While he spoke, he peered at the screen of his laptop.

She glanced around the room, listening to him talking to the relative of someone who was clearly very ill and about to be moved into the local hospice, the Martlets. The call made her even more uncomfortable. She stared at a coat stand with a solitary overcoat – Dr Hunter's, she presumed – hanging from it and puzzled over an array of electrical equipment that she had not seen, or noticed, previously, wondering absently what it did.

He finished the call, scribbled a note to himself, peered at his screen once more, then focused on Lynn. His voice was gentle, concerned. 'Thanks for coming in. I thought it would be better to see you alone before seeing Caitlin.' He looked nervous.

'Right,' she mouthed. But no sound came out. It felt as

if someone had just swabbed the insides of her mouth and her throat with blotting paper.

He retrieved a file from right at the top of one pile, put it on his desk and opened it, adjusted his half-moon glasses, then read for a few moments, as if buying himself time. 'I've got the latest set of test results back from Dr Granger and I'm afraid it's not good news, Lynn. They're showing grossly abnormal liver function.'

Dr Neil Granger was the local consultant gastroenterologist who had been seeing Caitlin for the past six years.

'The enzyme levels in particular are very elevated,' he went on. 'Particularly the Gamma GT enzymes. Her platelet count is very low – it has deteriorated quite dramatically. Is she bruising a lot?'

Lynn nodded. 'Yes, also, if she cuts herself the bleeding takes a long time to stop.' She knew that clotting agents were produced by the liver, and with a healthy liver they would immediately be dispatched to cause clotting and stop the bleeding. 'How elevated are the enzyme levels?' After years of looking up everything Caitlin's doctors had told her on the Internet, Lynn had accumulated a fair amount of knowledge on the subject. Enough to know when to be worried, but not enough to know what to do about it.

'Well, in a normal healthy liver the enzyme level should be around 45. The lab tests that were done a month ago showed 1,050. But this latest test shows a level of 3,000. Dr Granger is very concerned about this.'

'What is the significance, Ross?' Her voice came out choked and squeaky. 'Of the rise?'

He looked hard at her with compassion showing in his eyes. 'Her jaundice is worsening, he tells me. As is her encephalopathy. In lay terms, her body is being poisoned by toxins. She's suffering increasingly from episodes of confusion, is that right?'

Lynn nodded.

'Drowsiness?'

'Yes, at times.'

'The itching?'

'That's driving her crazy.'

'The truth is, I'm afraid Caitlin is no longer responding to her treatments. She has irreversible cirrhosis.'

Feeling a deep, dark heaviness inside her, Lynn turned for a moment and stared bleakly through the window. At the fire escape. At a wintry, skeletal tree. It looked dead. She felt dead inside.

'How is she today?' the doctor asked.

'She's OK, a bit subdued. Complains that she's itching a lot. She was awake, scratching her hands and her feet, most of the night. She said her urine's very dark. And her abdomen is swollen, which she hates most of all.'

'I can give her some water tablets to help get rid of the fluid.' He made a note on Caitlin's index card and suddenly Lynn found herself feeling indignant. Surely this warranted something more than a sodding index-card note? And why didn't he have such things on a computer these days?

'Ross, when – when you say *deteriorated quite dramatically* – how – what – I mean how – how is that stopped? You know, reversed? What has to happen?'

He jumped up from his desk, went over to a floor-to-ceiling bookshelf, then came back holding a brown, wedge-shaped object, cleared a space on his desk and set it down.

'This is what an adult human liver looks like. Caitlin's would be just a little smaller.'

Lynn looked at it, the way she had looked at it a thousand

times before. On a plain pad he started drawing what looked like a lot of broccoli. She listened as he explained, patiently, how the bile ducts worked, but when he had finished the diagram she knew no more than she already knew about the way the bile ducts worked. And besides, there was only one question that mattered to her now.

'Surely there must be some way to reverse the failure?' she asked. But her voice carried no conviction. As if she knew – as if they both knew – that after six years of hoping against hope, they were finally arriving at the inevitable.

'I'm afraid that what's going on here is not reversible. In Dr Granger's view we are in danger of running out of time.'

'What do you mean?'

'She hasn't responded to any medication and there aren't any other drugs out there that we can give her.'

'There must be something you can do? Dialysis?'

'For kidney failure, yes, but not for liver failure. There's no equivalent.'

He fell silent for some moments.

'Why not, Ross?' she probed.

'Because the liver's functions are too complex. I'll draw you a cross-section and show—'

'I don't want another fucking diagram!' she shouted at him. Then she started crying. 'I just want you to make my darling angel better. There must be something you can do.' She sniffed. 'So what will happen, Ross?'

He bit his lip. 'She's going to have to have a transplant.'

'A transplant? Shit, she's only fifteen years old! FIFTEEN!'

He nodded, but said nothing.

'I'm not shouting at you – I'm sorry – I . . .' She fumbled in her bag for a handkerchief, then dabbed her eyes. 'She's

just been through a lot in her life, poor angel. A transplant?'
she said again. 'That is really the only option?'

'Yes, I'm afraid it is.'

'Or?'

'To put it bluntly, she won't survive.'

'How long do we have?'

He raised his hands helplessly. 'I can't tell you that.'

'Weeks? Months?'

'A few months, at most. But it could be a lot less if her
liver continues to fail at this rate.'

There was a long silence. Lynn stared down at her lap.
Finally, and very quietly, she asked, 'Ross, are there risks
with a transplant?'

'I'd be lying if I said there weren't. The biggest problem
is going to be finding a liver. There is a shortage because
there is a lack of donors.'

'She's a rare blood group too, isn't she?' Lynn said.

Checking his notes, he said, 'AB negative. Yes, that is
rare – about 2 per cent of the population.'

'Is the blood group important?'

'It's important, but I'm not sure of the exact criteria. I
think there can be some cross-matching.'

'What about me – could I give my liver to her?'

'It's possible to give a partial liver transplant – using one
of the lobes, yes. But you'd have to have a compatible blood
type – and I don't think you are big enough.'

He searched through a few index cards, then read for a
moment. 'You're A positive,' he said. 'I don't know.' The
doctor gave a bleak, wintry smile of sympathy but near
helplessness. 'That is something Dr Granger will be better
able to tell you. Also whether your diabetes would be a
factor.'

It scared her that his man she trusted so much suddenly seemed lost and out of his depth.

'Great,' she said bitterly. Diabetes was another of the unwelcome souvenirs of her marriage break-up. Late-onset Type-2, which Dr Hunter told her might have been triggered by stress. So she hadn't even been able to go on comfort-food binges to console herself. 'Caitlin's going to have to wait for someone who is the right blood group match to die? Is that what you're saying?'

'Probably, yes. Unless you have a family member or a close friend who is a match, who would be willing to donate part of their liver.'

Lynn's hopes rose a little. 'That's a possibility?'

'Size is a factor – it would need to be a large person.'

The only large person she could immediately think of who would be approachable was Mal. But then she dismissed that, remembering that he'd contracted Hepatitis B in the past, which ruled him out as a donor – they had found that out some years ago, during a period of trying to be responsible citizens.

Lynn did a quick mental calculation. There were 65 million people in the UK. Maybe 45 million of them teenagers or older. So two per cent would be about 900,000 people. That was a lot of people. There must be people with AB negative blood dying every day.

'We're going to be in a queue, right? Like vultures? Waiting for someone to die? What if Caitlin freaks out at the thought?' she said. 'You know what she's like. She doesn't believe in killing *anything*. She gets upset when I kill flies!'

'I think you should bring her in to see me – if you want to I could have a chat with her later on today. A lot of families find that donating the organs of someone who's died can give some purpose and value to their death. Do you want me to try to explain this to her?'

Lynn gripped the sides of her chair, trying to put aside her own inner terror. 'I can't believe I'm thinking this, Ross. I'm not a violent person – even before Caitlin's influence, I never *liked* killing flies in my kitchen. Now I'm sitting here actually *willing* some stranger to die.'

6

The morning rush-hour traffic on Coldean Lane that had
been halted by the accident was already backed up almost
to the bottom of the hill. To the left was part of the
sprawling post-war council housing estate of Coldean, to
the right, beyond a flint wall, were the trees marking the
eastern boundary of Stanmer Park, one of the city's biggest
open spaces.

PC Ian Upperton cautiously edged the nose of the Road
Policing Unit's BMW out past the rear of the stationary,
chuntering bus that was at the end of the queue until he
could see the road ahead, then, with the siren flailing the
still air, he launched the car up the wrong side of the road.

PC Tony Omotoso sat next to him in silence, scanning
the vehicles ahead in case any of them in their impatience
tried to do something stupid like pulling out or turning
round. Half the drivers on the road were either blind or
drove with their music too loud to hear sirens, only looking
in their mirrors to do their hair. He felt tight, clenched up
with anxiety, the way he always felt on the way to a road
traffic collision, as accidents were now officially called in
the ever-changing police lexicon. You never knew what you
were going to find.

In a bad accident, for many people their car turned
from friend to deadly foe, spiking them, slicing them, crushing them and, in some horrific cases, cooking them. One
moment they would be cruising along, listening to their
music or chatting happily, the next – just a fraction of a

second later – they were lying in agony in a tangle of metal with edges as sharp as razors, bewildered and helpless. He loathed idiots on the roads, people who drove badly or recklessly, and the twats who didn't put their belts on.

They were reaching the crest of the hill now, where there was a nasty dogleg junction, with Ditchling Road joining Coldean Lane from the west and east, and he saw a blue Range Rover at the front of the queue with its hazard flashers blinking. A short distance on was an old-model white 3-Series BMW cabriolet slewed across the road with its driver's door open and no one inside. There was a massive V-shaped dent behind the door and the rear wheel was stoved in. The rear window was shattered. Just beyond it, a knot of people were standing in the road. Several turned their heads as the police car pulled up and some moved aside.

Through the gap they opened up, Omotoso saw, facing them on the far side of the crest of the hill, a stationary small white Ford van. Spread-eagled, motionless on the ground close to it, was a motorcyclist, a trail of dark crimson blood running from inside his black helmet and pooling on the road. Two men and a woman were kneeling beside him. One of the men appeared to be talking to him. A short distance away lay a red motorcycle.

'Another Fireblade,' Upperton said grimly, almost under his breath as he brought the car to a halt.

The Honda Fireblade was a classic born-again-biker machine, one of the motorcycles *de choix* for blokes in their forties who had ridden in their teens, had now made some money and wanted a bike again. And naturally they wanted the fastest machine on the road, though they had no real understanding of just how much faster – and harder to handle – modern bikes had become during the intervening years. It was a grim statistic, evidenced by what Omotoso and Upperton – and dozens of other Road Policing Officers like them – saw daily, that the highest risk age group were not tearaway teenagers but middle-aged businessmen.

Omotoso radioed in that they were at the scene, and was told that an ambulance and fire crew were on their way. 'We'd better have the RPU inspector up here, Hotel Tango Three-Nine-Nine,' he told the controller, giving him the call sign for the duty Road Policing Unit inspector. This looked bad. Even from here he could see that the blood wasn't the light, bright red of a superficial head wound, but the ominous colour of internal bleeding.

Both men got out of the car, assessing the scene as quickly and as well as they could. One thing Tony Omotoso had learned in this job was never to jump to rapid conclusions about how any accident had happened. But from the skid marks and the positions of the car and the bike, it looked as if the car had pulled out into the path of the motorcycle – which must have been travelling at speed to have caused that kind of damage and spun the car around.

The first priority on his mental checklist was danger from other road users. But all the traffic seemed securely halted in both directions. He heard the wail of a siren approaching in the distance.

'She pulled out, fucking stupid woman. Just pulled straight out!' a male voice shouted to them. 'He didn't stand a chance!'

Ignoring the voice, they ran up to the motorcyclist. Omotoso edged between the people already beside him and knelt down.

'He's unconscious,' the woman said.

The victim's dark, tinted visor was down. The police officer knew it was important not to move him if at all possible. As gently as he could, he lifted up the visor, then touched the man's face, opened his lips, felt inside his mouth for his tongue.

'Can you hear me, sir? Can you hear me?'

Behind him, Ian Upperton asked, 'Who is the driver of the BMW?'

A woman walked up to him, clutching a mobile phone, her face sheet white. In her forties, she was brassy-looking, with bleached blonde hair, and was wearing a fur-trimmed denim jacket, jeans and suede boots.

Subdued, she spoke in the gravelly voice of a heavy smoker. 'Me,' she said. 'Shit, oh shit, oh shit. I didn't see him. He came up like the wind. I didn't see him. The road was clear.' She was shaking, in shock.

The officer, long practised, put his face up close to hers, much closer than he needed just to hear her. He wanted to smell her, or, more particularly, smell her breath. He had a keen nose and he could frequently detect last night's alcohol on someone who had been on a bender. There might be just the faintest trace now, but it was hard to tell, as it was so heavily masked by minty chewing gum and the reek of cigarette tobacco.

'Would you step into my car, front passenger seat? I'll be with you in a few minutes,' Upperton said.

'She pulled straight out!' a man in an anorak said to him, almost incredulously. 'I was right behind him.'

'I'd appreciate your name and address, sir,' the PC said.

'Of course. She just pulled straight out. Mind you, he was travelling,' the man admitted. 'I was in my Range Rover.' He jerked a thumb. 'He absolutely flew past me.'

Upperton could see the ambulance arriving. 'I'll be right back, sir,' he said, and hurried down to meet the paramedics.

How they handled the scene from here would very much depend on their initial assessment. If in their view it looked likely to be a fatality, then they would have to close the road until the Crash Scene Investigators had carried out their survey. In the meantime he radioed the controller and asked for two more units.

7

Festive parties had started early this year. At just after quarter to nine on Wednesday morning Detective Superintendent Roy Grace was sitting in his office nursing a hangover. He never used to suffer from hangovers, or at least very rarely, but recently they seemed to have become a regular occurrence. Maybe it was an age thing – he would be forty next August. Or maybe it was . . .

What exactly?

He should be feeling more settled in himself, he knew. For the first time in coming up to ten years since his wife, Sandy, had vanished, he was in a steady relationship, with a woman he really adored. He had recently been promoted to head up Major Crime, and the biggest obstacle to his career, Assistant Chief Constable Alison Vosper, who had never liked him, was moving to the other end of the country to take up a Deputy Chief Constable position.

So why, he kept wondering, did he so often wake up feeling like shit? Why was he drinking so recklessly suddenly?

Was it the knowledge that Cleo, who was about to turn thirty, was subtly – and sometimes not so subtly – angling for commitment? He had already effectively moved in with her and Humphrey, her mongrel rescue puppy – at least on a semi-permanent basis. The reason was in part that he really did want to be with her, but also because his mate and colleague Detective Sergeant Glenn Branson, whose marriage was on the rocks, had become an increasingly permanent lodger in his house. Much though he loved this man, they were too much of an odd couple to live together, and it was easier to leave Glenn to his own devices, although it pained Roy to see the mess he kept the place in – and in particular the mess he had made of Roy's prized vinyl and CD music collection.

He drained his second coffee of the morning, then unscrewed the cap of a bottle of sparkling water. Last night he had attended the Christmas dinner of the staff of Brighton and Hove City Mortuary, in a Chinese restaurant on the Marina, and then, instead of doing the sensible thing and going home afterwards, he had gone on with a crowd to the Rendezvous Casino, where he had drunk several brandies – which always gave him the worst hangovers – lost a rapid £50 on roulette and a further £100 at a blackjack table, before Cleo had – fortunately for him – dragged him away.

Normally at his desk by seven in the morning, he had just arrived in the office ten minutes ago, and so far the only task he had been able to perform, other than making himself coffee, was logging on to his computer. And tonight he had to go out again, to the retirement party of a chief superintendent called Jim Wilkinson.

He stared out of the window, at the car park and the ASDA supermarket across the road, then at the urban landscape of his beloved city beyond. It was a fine, crisp morning, the air so clear he could see the distant tall white chimney of the power station at Shoreham Harbour, with the blue-grey ribbon of the English Channel beyond, before it blended into the sky on the distant horizon. He'd only been in this office for a short while, after moving across from the other side of the building, where his view had been of the grey slab of the custody block, so this fine view was still something of a novelty and a joy. But not today.

Gripping his coffee mug in both hands, he saw to his dismay it was shaking. Shit, how drunk had he got last night? And from his hazy memory, Cleo had not drunk anything, which was just as well, as she'd been able to drive him back to her place. And – bloody hell – he could not even remember if they'd made love.

He shouldn't have driven here this morning, he knew. He was probably still way over the limit. His stomach felt like a revolving cement mixer and he wasn't sure whether the two fried eggs Cleo had forced down him had been a good idea or not. He was cold. He unhooked his suit jacket from the back of his chair and pulled it back on, then peered at his computer screen, glancing through the over-night serials – the list of every logged incident in the city of Brighton and Hove. New items got added by the minute and older ones that were still current got updated.

Among the more significant were a homophobic attack in Kemp Town and a serious assault in King's Road. One, which had just been updated, was an RTC on Coldean Lane, a collision between a car and a motorcycle. It had first been logged at 08.32 and had just been updated with the infor-mation that H900, the police helicopter with a paramedic on board, had been requested.

Not good, he thought, with a slight shiver. He liked bikes and used to have them in his teens, when he first joined the police force and was dating Sandy, but he hadn't ridden one since. A former colleague, Dave Gaylor, had bought himself a cool black Harley with red wheels when he retired, and, now that he had free use of a car as part of his promotion, Grace was tempted to replace his Alfa Romeo, which had recently been written off in a chase, with a bike – when the bastards at the insurance company finally coughed up – or rather, *if*. But when he'd mentioned it to

Cleo, she had gone ballistic, despite being a little reckless behind the wheel herself.

Cleo, who was the Senior Anatomical Pathology Technician (as chief morticians were now known, in the new politically correct jargon which pervaded every aspect of police life, and which Roy privately detested with a vengeance) at Brighton and Hove City Mortuary, launched into a litany of the fatal injuries she witnessed regularly on her hapless overnight motorcyclist guests at the mortuary every time he raised the subject. And he knew that in some medical circles, particularly those working in trauma, where black humour was prevalent, bikers were nicknamed Donors on Wheels.

Which explained the presence of a pile of motoring magazines, featuring road tests and listings of used cars – but no bikes – that occupied some of the few remaining square inches of space on his absurdly cluttered desk.

In addition to all the files relating to his new role, and the mountains of Criminal Justice Department files on impending trials, he had inherited back the command of all the Sussex Police Force's cold-case murder files, following the recent sudden departure of a colleague. Some sat in green plastic crates, occupying most of the floor space that was not already taken up by his desk, the small, round conference table and four chairs, and his black leather go-bag, which contained all the equipment and protective clothing he needed to have with him at a crime scene.

His work on the cold-case files progressed painfully slowly – partly because neither he nor anyone else here at HQ CID had enough time to devote to them, and partly because there was little more that could be done on them proactively. The police had to wait for advances in forensics, such as new developments in DNA analysis, to reveal a suspect, or for family loyalties to change – perhaps a wife who had once lied to protect her spouse becoming aggrieved and deciding to shop him. The situation was about to change, however, because a new team had been approved to work under him, reviewing all the outstanding cold cases.

Grace felt bad about unsolved murders, and the sight of the crates was a constant reminder to him that he was the last chance the victims had of justice being done, the last chance the families had of closure.

He knew most of the files' contents by heart. One case concerned a gay vet called Richard Ventnor, found battered to death in his surgery twelve years ago. Another, which moved him deeply, concerned Tommy Lytle, his oldest cold case. At the age of eleven, twenty-seven years ago, Tommy had set out from school, on a February afternoon, to walk home. He'd never been seen again.

He looked back at the Criminal Justice Department files again. The bureaucracy demanded by the system was almost beyond belief. He swigged some water, wondering where to start. Then decided to look at his Christmas present list instead. But he only got as far as the first item, a request from the parents of his nine-year-old goddaughter, Jaye Somers. They knew he liked to give her gifts that made her think he was cool and not a boring old fart. They were suggesting a pair of black suede Ugg boots, size three.

Where did you buy Ugg boots from?

One person would definitely know the answer. He stared down at a green crate, the fourth in a stack to the right of his desk. The Shoe Man. A cold case that had long intrigued him. Over a period of time, several years back, the Shoe Man had raped six women in Sussex, killing one of them, probably by accident, in panic, it had been concluded. Then he had inexplicably stopped. It might have been that his last victim had put up a spirited fight, and had managed to partially remove his mask, enabling an Identikit drawing of the man to be made, and that had scared him off. Or perhaps he was now dead. Or had moved away.

Three years back, a forty-nine-year-old businessman in Yorkshire who had raped a string of women in the mid-1980s, and had always taken their shoes afterwards, had been arrested. For a time Sussex Police had hoped he might be their man too, but DNA testing ruled that out. Besides, the rapists' methods were similar but not identical. James Lloyd, the Yorkshireman, took both shoes from his victims. The Sussex Shoe Man took just one, always from the left foot, together with his victims' panties. Of course, there could have been more than six. One of the problems with tracking down rapists was that victims were often too embarrassed to come forward.

Of all criminals, Grace hated paedophiles and rapists the most. These men destroyed their victims' lives forever. There was no real recovering from a kiddie fiddler or a rapist. The victims could try to put their lives back together, but they could never forget what had happened to them.

He had entered the police force not just because his father had been a police officer, but because he had genuinely wanted a career in which he could make a difference – however small – to the world. In recent years, excited by all the technological developments, he now had one overriding ambition. That the perpetrators behind the victims whose files filled all these crates would one day be brought to justice. Every damn one of them. And at the very top of his current list was the creepy Shoe Man.

One day.

One day the Shoe Man would wish he had never been born.

8

Lynn left the doctor's surgery in a daze. She walked up the
street to her clapped-out little orange Peugeot, which had
one odd wheel with a missing hubcap, opened the door and
climbed inside. She usually left it unlocked in the – as yet
unrequited – hope that someone might steal it and she
could collect on the insurance.

Last year, the man at the garage had told her that it
would never get through its next MOT safety and emissions
test without major work, and that it would cost more to put
right than the car was worth. Now that test was due in just
over a week's time and she was dreading it.

Mal would have been able to fix the car himself – he
could mend anything. God, how she missed that. And
someone to talk to now. Someone who could have supported her in the conversation she was about to have – and
was utterly dreading – with her daughter.

She pulled her mobile phone from her bag and dialled
her best friend, Sue Shackleton, blinking hard, crushing
tears from her eyes. Like herself, Sue was a divorcee and
now a single mother with four kids. What's more, she always
seemed to be irrepressibly cheerful.

As Lynn spoke, she watched a traffic warden swagger-
ing down the pavement, but she did not need to worry as
there was over an hour yet to run on her pay-and-display
sticker on the window. Sue was, as ever, sympathetic but
realistic.

'Sometimes in life these things happen, darling. I know

someone who had a kidney transplant, what, must be seven years ago now, and he's fine.'

Lynn nodded at the mention of Sue's friend, whom she had met. 'Yes, but this is a bit different. You can survive on dialysis for years without a kidney transplant, but not with a failing liver. There is no other option. I'm frightened for her, Sue. This is a massive operation. So much could go wrong. And Dr Hunter said he couldn't guarantee it would be successful. I mean, shit, she's only *fifteen*, for Christ's sake!'

'So what's the alternative?'

'That's the point, there isn't one.'

'Your choice is simple, then. Do you want her to live or to die?'

'Of course I want her to live.'

'So accept what has to happen and be strong and confident for her. The last thing she needs right now is you throwing a wobbly.'

Those words were still ringing in her ears five minutes later as she ended the call, promising to meet Sue later in the day for a coffee, if she was able to leave Caitlin.

Be strong and confident for her.

Easy to say.

She dialled Mal's mobile, unsure where he was at the moment. His ship moved around from time to time and recently he had been working out of Wales in the Bristol Channel. Their relationship was amicable, if a little stilted and formal.

He answered on the third ring, on a very crackly line.

'Hi,' she said. 'Where are you?'

'Off Shoreham. We're ten miles out of the harbour mouth, heading to the dredge area. Be out of range in a few minutes – what's up?'

'I need to talk to you. Caitlin's deteriorated – she's very ill. Desperately ill.'

'Shit,' he said, his voice already sounding fainter as the crackling got worse. 'Tell me.'

She blurted out the gist of the diagnosis, knowing from past experience how quickly the signal could fade. She was just about able to make out his reply – the ship would be back in Shoreham in about seven hours, he would call her then, he told her.

Next, she phoned her mother, who was at a coffee morning at her bridge club. Her mother was strong, and seemed to have become even stronger in the four years since Lynn's father had died, once admitting to Lynn that they really had not liked each other very much for years. She was a practical woman and nothing ever seemed to fluster her.

'You need to get a second opinion,' she said right away. 'Tell Dr Hunter you want a second opinion.'

'I don't think there's much doubt,' Lynn said. 'This is not just Dr Hunter – it's the specialist too. What's happening is what we've feared all along.'

'You absolutely must have a second opinion. Doctors get things wrong. They are not infallible.'

Lynn, with some reluctance, promised her mother she would ask for a second opinion. Then, after she had finished and was driving back home, she churned it over in her mind. How many more second opinions could she get? During these past years she had tried everything. She'd scoured the Internet, looking at each of the big US teaching hospitals. The German hospitals. The Swiss ones. She'd tried all the alternative options she could find. Healers of every kind – faith, vibration, distant, hands-on. Priests. Boluses of coloidal silver. Homeopaths. Herbalists. Acupuncturists.

Sure, maybe her mother had a point. Maybe the diagnosis could be wrong. Perhaps another specialist might know something Dr Granger did not and could recommend something less drastic. Perhaps there was some new medication that could treat this. But how long did you keep looking while your daughter continued to go downhill? How long before you had to accept that surgery was perhaps, in this case, the only option?

As she turned right at the mini-roundabout off the London Road, into Carden Avenue, the car heeled over, making a horrible scraping sound. She changed gear and heard the usual metallic knocking underneath her from the exhaust pipe, which had a broken bracket. Caitlin said it was the Grim Reaper knocking, because the car was dying.

Her daughter had a macabre sense of humour.

She drove on up the hill into Patcham, her eyes watering as the immensity of the situation started to overwhelm her. *Oh shit.* She shook her head in bewilderment. Nothing, nothing, *nothing* had prepared her for this. How the hell did you tell your daughter that she was going to have to have a new liver? And probably one taken from a dead body?

She turned up the hill into their street, then made a left into her driveway, pulled on the handbrake and switched off the engine. As usual it juddered on for some moments, spluttering and shaking the car, and banging the exhaust pipe beneath her again, before falling silent.

The house was a semi in a quiet residential avenue and, like many homes in this city, on a steep hill. It had views, across trees that masked the London Road and the railway line, of some of the swanky, dreamy houses and massive gardens of Withdean Road on the far side of the valley. All the houses in her avenue were of the same basic design:

three-bedroomed, 1930s, with a rounded, metalled Art Deco influence which she had always liked. They had small front gardens with a short driveway in front of the attached garage and good-sized plots at the rear.

The previous owners had been an elderly couple and when Lynn moved in she'd had all kinds of plans to transform it. But after seven years here, she had not even been able to afford to rip out the manky old carpets and replace them, let alone carry out her grander schemes of knocking through walls and re-landscaping the garden. Fresh paint and some new wallpaper were all she had managed so far. The dreary kitchen still had a fusty old-people smell to it, despite all her efforts with pot pourri and plug-in air fresheners.

One day, she used to promise herself. *One day*.

The same *one day* that she promised herself she would build a little studio in the garden. She loved to paint scenes of Brighton in watercolours and had had some modest success in selling them.

She unlocked the front door and went inside, into the narrow hallway. She peered up the stairs, wondering if Caitlin was out of bed yet, but could hear no sound.

Heavy-hearted, she climbed the stairs. At the top, taped to Caitlin's door, was a large handwritten sign, red letters on a white background, saying: *KNOCK, PURLEASE*. It had been there for as long as she could remember. She knocked.

There was no answer, as normal. Caitlin would be either asleep or blasting her eardrums with music. She went in. The contents of the room looked as if they had been scooped up wholesale from somewhere else by a bulldozer's shovel, brought here and tipped in through the window.

Just visible beyond the tangle of clothes, soft toys, CDs, DVDs, shoes, make-up containers, overflowing pink waste bin, upended pink stool, dolls, mobile of blue perspex butterflies, shopping bags from Top Shop, River Island, Monsoon, Abercrombie and Fitch, Gap and Zara, and dartboard with a purple boa hanging from it, was the bed. Caitlin was lying on her side, in one of the many extraordinary positions in which she slept, arms and legs akimbo, with a pillow over her head, bare bottom and thighs protruding from the duvet, iPod earpieces plugged into her ears, the television on, playing a repeat of a show Lynn recognized as *The Hills*.

She looked like she was dead.

And for one terrifying moment Lynn thought she was. She rushed over, her feet tangling in her daughter's mobile phone charger wire, and touched her long, slender arm.

'I'm asleep,' Caitlin said grumpily.

Relief surged through Lynn. The illness had made her daughter's sleep patterns erratic. She smiled, sat down on the edge of the bed and stroked her back. With her mop of short, gelled black hair, Caitlin looked like a bendy doll sometimes, she thought. Tall, thin to the point of emaciation, and gangly, she seemed to have flexible wire inside her skin rather than bones.

'How are you feeling?'

'Itchy.'

'Want some breakfast?' she asked hopefully.

Caitlin wasn't a full-blown anorexic, but close. She was obsessed with her weight, hated any food like cheese or pasta, which she called *eating fats*, and weighed herself constantly.

Caitlin shook her head.

'I need to talk to you, darling.' She looked at her watch. It was 10.05. She had told them yesterday at work that she would be in late, and she was going to have to phone again in a minute and tell them she would not be in at all today. The doctor only had a short window of time, mid-afternoon, to see Caitlin.

'I'm busy,' her daughter grunted.

In a sudden fit of irritation, Lynn pulled out the ear-pieces. 'This is important.'

'Chill, woman!' Caitlin replied.

Lynn bit her lip and was silent for some moments. Then she said, 'I've made an appointment with Dr Hunter for this afternoon. At half past four.'

'You're doing my head in. I'm seeing Luke this afternoon.'

Luke was her boyfriend. He was enrolled in some course in IT at the University of Brighton which he had never been able to explain to her in a manner she could understand. Among the total wasters Lynn had encountered in her life, Luke was up there in a class of his own. Caitlin had been dating him for over a year. And in that year Lynn had managed to extract about five words from him, and those with some difficulty. *Yep, yeah, like, you know* seemed to be the absolute limits of his vocabulary. She was beginning to think that the attraction between the two of them must be because they both came from the same planet – somewhere at the far end of the universe. Some sodding galactic cul-de-sac.

She kissed her daughter's cheek, then tenderly stroked her stiff hair. 'How are you feeling today, my angel? Other than itching?'

'Yeah, OK. I'm tired.'

'I've just been to see Dr Hunter. We have to talk about this.'

'Not right now. I'm like cotchin. OK?'

Lynn sat very still and took a deep breath, trying to

control her temper. 'Darling, that appointment with Dr Hunter is very important. He wants to make you better. It seems the only way we may be able to do this is by giving you a liver transplant. He wants to talk to you about it.'

Caitlin nodded. 'Can I have my earpieces back? This is one of my favourite tracks.'

'What are you listening to?'

'Rihanna.'

'Did you hear what I said, darling? About a liver transplant?'

Caitlin shrugged, then grunted. 'Whatever.'

9

It took just under an hour and a half for the *Arco Dee*, making a plodding twelve knots, to reach the dredge area. Malcolm Beckett spent most of this time carrying out his daily routine tests of all forty-two of the ship's audible alerts and warning lights. He had just completed some mainten-ance on three, the engine room alarm, the bilge alarm and the bow-thruster failure alarm, and was now on the bridge, testing each of the related warning lights on the panel.

Despite the biting, freshening wind, it was a gloriously sunny day, with a gentle swell making the ship's motion comfortable for all on board. It was the kind of day, ordi-narily, that he loved best at sea. But today there was a dark cloud in his heart: Caitlin.

When he finished the lights, he checked the weather report screen for any updates, and was pleased to see the forecast for the rest of the day remained good. The outlook for tomorrow, he read, was south-west five to seven, veering west five or six, with a moderate or rough sea state and occasional rain. Less pleasant but nothing to worry about. The *Arco Dee* could dredge in a constant Force Seven, but beyond that working conditions became too dangerous on board and they risked damage to dredging gear, especially the drag head pounding on the seabed.

She had originally been built for sheltered estuary work and her flat bottom allowed her a draught of just thirteen feet fully loaded. That was useful for working in ports with sandbars, such as Shoreham, where at low tide the harbour entrance became too shallow for shipping to pass through. The *Arco Dee* was able to come and go up to an hour either side of low water; but the downside was that she was uncomfortable in a heavy sea.

In the cosy warmth of the spacious, high-tech bridge there was an air of quiet concentration. Ten nautical miles south-east of Brighton, they were almost over the dredge area now. Yellow, green and blue lines on a black screen, forming a lopsided rectangle, marked out the 100 square miles of seabed leased from the government by the Hanson Group, the conglomerate which owned this particular dredging fleet. The land was as precisely marked out as any farm onshore, and if they strayed out of this exact area, they risked heavy fines and losing their dredging rights.

Commercial dredging was, in a sense, underwater quarrying. The sand and gravel that the ship sucked up would be graded and sold into the construction and landscaping industries. The best-grade pebbles would end up on smart driveways, the sand would be used in the cement industry, and the rest would be either crushed up into concrete and tarmac mixes, or used for rubble ballast in the foundations of buildings, roads and tunnels.

The captain, Danny Marshall, a lean, wiry, good-natured man of forty-five, stood at the helm, steering with the two toggle levers that controlled the propellers, giving the ship more manoeuvrability than a traditional wheel and rudder. Sporting a few days' growth of stubble, he wore a black bobble hat, a chunky blue sweater over a blue shirt, jeans and heavy-duty sea boots. The first mate, similarly attired, stood watch over the computer screen on which the dredge area was plotted.

Marshall clicked on the ship-to-shore radio and leaned forward to the mike. 'This is *Arco Dee*, Mike Mike Whiskey

Echo,' he said. When the coastguard responded, he radioed in his position. Working out on one of the busiest shipping lanes in the world, where visibility could fall to just a few yards in the frequent mists and fogs that came down over the English Channel, it was important for all positions to be noted and updated regularly.

Like his other seven crewmates, most of whom had worked together for the past decade, the sea was in Malcolm Beckett's blood. A bit of a rebel as a child, he had left home as soon as he could to join the Royal Navy as a trainee engineer, and had spent his first years at sea travelling the world. But, like the others on this ship who had begun their careers on ocean-going vessels, when his first child, Caitlin, was born, he wanted to find work that kept him at sea but enabled him to have some kind of family life.

Dredging had been the perfect solution. They were never at sea for longer than three weeks and returned to harbour twice a day. On the periods when the ship was based here in Shoreham, or in Newhaven, he was even able to nip home on occasions for an hour or so.

The captain reduced speed. Malcolm checked the engine revs and temperature gauges, then glanced at his watch. They would be back in phone range of the shore in about five hours. Five o'clock this evening. The phone call from Lynn had left him deeply disturbed. While he had always found Caitlin a difficult child, he was immensely fond of her and saw a lot of himself in her. On the days that he took her out, he was always amused by her complaints about her mother. They seemed to be exactly the same issues that he had had with Lynn too. In particular, her obsessive worrying – although, to be fair, Caitlin had given them both plenty to worry about over the years.

But this time it had sounded even worse than anything before and he felt frustrated that the call had been cut short. And very worried.

He pulled on his hard hat and high-visibility jacket, left the bridge and clambered down the steep metal steps to the gridded companionway, then down on to the main deck. He could feel the sharpness of the winter breeze rippling his clothes as he walked across to get into position to supervise the lowering of the dredge pipe into the sea.

A couple of his former navy colleagues, whom he met up with from time to time for a drink, joked that dredgers were nothing more than floating vacuum cleaners. In a sense they were right. The *Arco Dee* was a 2,000-ton Hoover. Which meant 3,500 tons when the dust bag was full.

Mounted along the starboard side of the ship was the dredge pipe itself, a 100-foot-long steel tube. For Malcolm, one of the highlights of each voyage was watching the dredge pipe sink out of sight into the murky depths. It was the moment when the ship truly seemed to come alive. The sudden clanking din of the pumping and chute machinery starting up, the sea all around them churning, and in a few moments water, sand and gravel would be thundering into the hold, turning the whole centre of the vessel, which was the cargo hold, into a ferocious cauldron of muddy water.

Occasionally, something unexpected, like a cannonball or part of a Second World War aircraft or, on one nerve-racking occasion, an unexploded bomb, got sucked up and jammed in the drag head – the mouth of the pipe. Over the years, so many historical artefacts had been dredged up from the ocean floor that official procedures had been established for dealing with them. But no guideline existed for what the *Arco Dee* was about to haul up on this occasion.

When the hold was full, all the water would drain off

through openings in the spillways, leaving what was, effectively, a sand and pebble beach in the middle of the ship.
Malcolm liked to walk along it as they headed back to
harbour, crunching through some of the hundreds of shells
that got scooped up, or occasionally coming across a hapless fish or crab. Some years ago he had found what was
later identified as a human leg bone, a tibia. Even after all
these years, the mysteries of the sea, especially what lay
beneath it, filled him with a childish excitement.

*

In about twenty minutes or so it would be time to raise the
dredge pipe. Malcolm, taking a quick break in the empty
mess room, sat on a battered sofa, cradling a mug of tea
and eating a tabnab – as scones were called in navy slang.
The television was on, but the picture was too blurry to
make anything out. His attention wandered distractedly to
the evening meal menu, which was scrawled in red marker
pen on a whiteboard: *Cream of leek soup, Bread roll, Scotch
egg, Chips, Fresh salad, Steamed sponge and custard.* Once
they returned to port, there were several hours of hard work
unloading the cargo before dinner, and by then normally
he would be ravenous. But at the moment, his thoughts on
Caitlin, he lost interest in the scone after a couple of bites
and dropped it in the bin. As he did so, he heard a voice
behind him.

'Mal . . .'

He turned to see the second mate, a burly Scouser in
overalls, hard hat and thick protective gloves.

'We've got a blockage in the drag head, Chief. I think we
need to raise the pipe.'

Mal grabbed his hard hat, following the second mate
out on to the deck. Looking upwards, he immediately saw

only a trickle of water coming down the chute. Blockages were unusual because normally the heavy steel pincers of the drag head pushed obstacles clear of the nozzle, but just occasionally a fishing net was sucked up.

Shouting out instructions to his crew of two, Mal waited till the suction pumps and the chute were switched off, then activated the winding gear to raise the pipe. He stood, peering over the side, watching the churning water as it slowly came into view. And when he saw the object that rose to the surface, firmly wedged between the massive steel claws, he felt a sudden tightening in his gullet.

'What the fuck's that?' the Scouser said.

For a moment, they all fell silent.

10

Roy Grace felt increasingly that his life was a constant challenge against the clock. As if he was a contestant in a game show that did not actually offer any prize for winning, because it had no end. For every email he succeeded in answering, another fifty came in. For every file on his desk that he managed to clear, another ten were brought in by his Management Support Assistant, Eleanor Hodgson, or by someone else – most recently by Emily Gaylor, from the Criminal Justice Department, who was there to assist him in preparing his cases for trial, but who seemed to take a malevolent delight in dumping more and more bundles of documents on his desk.

This week he was the duty Senior Investigating Officer, which meant that if any major crime happened in the Sussex area, he would have to take charge. He silently prayed to whichever god protected police officers that it would be a quiet week.

But that particular god was having a day off.

His phone rang. It was an operator called Ron King he knew from the Force Control Department. 'Roy,' he said. 'I've just had a call from the coastguard. A dredger out of Shoreham has pulled up a body, ten miles out in the Channel.'

Oh great! Grace thought. *All I bloody need.* Being a coastal city, Brighton received a quantity of dead bodies from the sea every year. Some were floaters, usually suicide victims or unfortunate yacht crew who had gone overboard.

Some were people who had been buried at sea, hooked in nets by fishermen who hadn't read their charts and had trawled over one of the areas marked out for funerals. Mostly, they could be dealt with by a uniformed PC, but the fact that he was being called indicated something was not right.

'What information do you have about it?' he asked dutifully, making a mental note not to say anything to King about his cats. Last time the controller had gone on about them for ten minutes.

'Male, looks young, early to mid-teens. Not been down long. Preserved in plastic sheeting and weighted.'

'Not a burial at sea?'

'Doesn't sound like it. Not the usual kind of floater either. The coastguard said the captain is concerned it looks like it might be some kind of ritual killing – apparently. There is a strange incision on the body. Do you want me to ask the coastguard to send a boat out to bring it in?'

Grace sat still for a moment, his brain churning, switching his thoughts into investigation mode. Everything on his desk and in his computer was now going to have to wait, at least until he had seen the body.

'Is it on the deck or in the cargo hold?' he asked.

'It's wedged in the drag head. Beyond slitting open the plastic sheeting to see what it was, they haven't moved it.'

'They're operating out of Shoreham?'

'Yes.'

Grace had been on a dredger which had hauled up a severely decomposed body some years ago and remembered a little about the machinery.

'I don't want the body moved, Ron,' he said. There could be key forensic evidence lodged around the body or in the nozzle of the dredge pipe. 'Tell them to secure and preserve it as best they can, and get them to make an exact note on the chart where the body came up.'

As soon as he had terminated his call with Ron, he made a further series of calls, assembling the immediate team he needed. One was to the Coroner, informing her of the incident and requesting a Home Office pathologist to attend. Most bodies taken or washed up from the sea would be collected by the mortuary team straight away, after a cursory examination by a police surgeon or paramedic at the scene to certify death, no matter how obvious it was that the person was dead, and then assessed back at the mortuary for a suspicious or natural death. But here, Grace felt from the sound of it, there was little doubt this was suspicious.

Thirty minutes later he was at the wheel of a pool Hyundai, heading towards the harbour, with Detective Inspector Lizzie Mantle, with whom he had worked on a number of previous inquiries, beside him. She was a highly competent detective, and the fact that she was nice to look at was another bonus. She had shoulder-length fair hair, a pretty face, and was dressed, as she always seemed to be, in a man's style of suit, today in a blue chalk-stripe over a crisp white blouse. On some women it would have looked quite butch, but on her it was businesslike while still feminine.

They drove around the end of the harbour, passing the private driveway leading to the cul-de-sac where Heather Mills's house was.

Seeing Grace turn his head, as if perhaps to get a glimpse of the Beatle's former wife, she asked, 'Did you ever meet Paul McCartney?'

'No.'

'You're quite into music, aren't you?'

He nodded. 'Some.'

'Would you have liked to be a rock star? You know, like one of the Beatles?'

Grace thought about it for a moment. It was not something he had ever considered. 'I don't think so,' he said. 'No.'

'Why not?'

'Because,' he said. Then he hesitated, slowing down, looking out for the right part of the quay. 'Because I have a crap voice!'

She grinned.

'But even if I was able to sing, I always wanted to do something that would make a difference.' He shrugged. 'You know? A difference to the world. That's why I joined the police force. It may sound clichéd – but it's why I do what I do.'

'You think a police officer can make more difference than a rock megastar?'

He smiled. 'I think we corrupt fewer people.'

'But do we make a *difference*?'

They were passing a lumber yard. Then Grace saw the dark green van bearing the gold crest of the city of Brighton and Hove Coroner, parked close to the edge of the quay, and pulled up a short distance from it. None of the rest of the team had arrived so far.

'I thought the ship was supposed to be here already,' he said a little irritably, mindful of the time, and of the retirement party he had to be at tonight. Several of the top brass of the Sussex Police Force would be there, which meant it would be a good opportunity to do a spot of brown-nosing, so he had been anxious to be there punctually. But there was no chance now.

'Probably delayed in the lock.'

Grace nodded, and climbed out of the car, walking to the very edge, still limping and tender from rolling his beloved Alfa Romeo during a pursuit a while back. He stood beside an iron bollard, the wind feeling icy on his face. The light was fading fast, and if it wasn't such a cloudless sky, it would already be almost dark. A mile or so in the distance he could see the closed lock gates and an orange super-structure, probably that of the dredger, beyond. He pulled his overcoat tightly around himself, shivering against the cold, dug his hands into his pockets and pulled on his leather gloves. Then he glanced at his watch.

Ten to five. Jim Wilkinson's retirement party started at seven, over on the far side of Worthing. He had planned to go home and change, then collect Cleo. Now, by the time he finished here, depending on what he found, and on how much examination the pathologist would want to do in situ, he would be lucky to make the party at all. The one blessing was that they had been allocated Nadiuska De Sancha, the quicker – and more fun – of the two specialist Home Office pathologists they worked with most regularly.

On the far side of the harbour he saw a large fishing boat, its navigation lights on, chug away from its berth. The water was almost black.

He heard doors open and slam behind him, then a chirpy voice said, 'Cor, you're going to cop it from the missus if you're late. Wouldn't want to be in your shoes, Roy!'

He turned to see Walter Hordern, a tall, dapper man, who was always smartly and discreetly attired in a dark suit, white shirt and black tie. His official role was Chief of Brighton and Hove Cemeteries, but his duties also included spending a part of his time helping in the process of collecting bodies from the scene of their death and dealing with the considerable paperwork that was required for each one. Despite the gravitas of his job, Walter had a mischievous sense of humour and loved nothing better than to wind Roy up.

'Why's that, Walter?'

'She's gone and spent a bleedin' fortune at the hairdresser's today – for the party tonight. She'll be well miffed if you blow it out.'

'I'm not blowing it out.'

Walter pointedly looked at his own watch. Then raised his eyes dubiously.

'If necessary I'll put you in charge of the sodding investigation, Walter.'

The man shook his head. 'Na, I only like dealing with stiffs. You never get any lip from a stiff. Good as gold, they are.'

Grace grinned. 'Darren here?'

Darren was Cleo's assistant in the mortuary.

Walter jerked a thumb at the van. 'He's in there, on the dog-and-bone, having a barney with his girlfriend.' He shrugged, then rolled his eyes. 'That's wimmin for you.'

Grace nodded, texting his:

> *Ship not here yet. Going to be late. Better meet u there. XXX*

Just as he stuck his phone back in his pocket, it beeped twice sharply. He pulled it back out and looked at the display. It was a reply from Cleo:

> *Don't be 2 late. I have something to tell you.*

He frowned, unsettled by the tone of the message, and by the fact that there was no '*X*' on the end. Stepping out of earshot of Walter and DI Mantle, who had just climbed out of the car, he called Cleo's number. She answered immediately.

'Can't talk,' she said curtly. 'Got a family just arrived for an identification.'

'What is it you have to tell me?' he said, aware his voice sounded anxious.

'I want to tell you face to face, not over the phone. Later, OK?' She hung up.

Shit. He stared at the phone for a moment, even more worried now, then put it back in his pocket.

He did not like the way she had sounded at all.

11

Simona learned to inhale Aurolac vapour from a plastic bag. A small bottle of the metallic paint, which she was able to steal easily from any paint store, would last for several days. It was Romeo who had taught her how to steal, and how to blow into the bag to get the paint to mix with air, then suck it in, blow it back into the bag again and inhale it again.

When she inhaled, the hunger pangs went.

When she inhaled, life in her home became tolerable. The home she had lived in for as far back as she could, or rather *wanted* to remember. The home she entered by scrambling through a gap in the broken concrete pavement and clambering down a metal ladder beneath the busy, unmade road, into the underground cavity that had been bored out for inspection and maintenance of the steam pipe. The pipe, thirteen feet in diameter, was part of the communal central-heating network that fed most of the buildings in the city. It made the space down here snug and dry in winter, but intolerably hot during the spring months until it was turned off.

And in a tiny part of this space, a tight recess between the pipe and the wall, she had made her home. It was marked out by an old duvet she had found, discarded, on a rubbish tip, and Gogu, who had been with her as far back as she could remember. Gogu was a beige, shapeless, mangy strip of fake fur that she slept with, pressed to her face, every night. Beyond the clothes she wore and Gogu, she had no possessions at all.

There were five of them, six including the baby, who lived here permanently. From time to time others came and stayed for a while, then moved on. The place was lit with candles, and music played throughout the days and nights when they had batteries. Western pop music that some-times brought Simona joy and sometimes demented her, because it was always loud and rarely stopped. They argued about it constantly, but always it played. Beyoncé was singing at the moment and she liked Beyoncé. Liked the way she looked. One day, she dreamed, she would look like Beyoncé, sing like Beyoncé. One day she would live in a house.

Romeo told her she was beautiful, that one day she would be rich and famous.

The baby was crying again and there was a faint stink of shit. Valeria's eight-month-old son, Antonio. Valeria, with all their help, had managed to keep him hidden from the authorities, who would have taken him from her.

Valeria, who was much older than the rest of them, had been pretty once, but her face at twenty-eight, haggard and heavily lined from this life, was now the face of an old woman. She had long, straight brown hair and eyes that had once been sultry but were now dead, and was dressed brightly, an emerald puffa over a ragged, turquoise, yellow and pink jogging suit, and red plastic sandals – scavenged, like most of their clothes, from bins in the better parts of the city, or accepted eagerly from hand-out centres.

She rocked her baby, who was wrapped up in an old, fur-lined suede coat, in her arms. The damn child's crying was worse than the constant music. Simona knew that the baby cried because he was hungry. They were all hungry, almost all of the time. They ate what they stole, or what they bought with the money they begged, or got from the old newspapers they occasionally sold, or from the wallets and purses they sometimes pickpocketed from tourists, or from selling the mobile phones and cameras they just grabbed from them.

Romeo, with his big blue eyes like saucers, his cute, innocent face, his short black hair brushed forward and his withered hand, was a fast runner. Fast as hell! He did not know how old he was. Maybe fourteen, he thought. Or perhaps thirteen. Simona did not know how old she was either. The stuff had not started to happen yet, the stuff that Valeria told her about. So Simona reckoned she was twelve or thirteen.

She did not really care. All she wanted was for these people, her *family*, to be pleased with her. And they were pleased every time she and Romeo returned with food or money or, best of all, both. And, sometimes, batteries. Returned to the rank smells of sulphur and dry dust and unwashed bodies and baby shit, which were the smells she knew best in the world.

Somewhere in a confused haze that was her past, she remembered bells. Bells hanging from a coat, or perhaps a jacket, worn by a tall man with a big stick. She had to approach this man and remove his wallet without making the bells ring. If just one bell tinkled, he whacked her on the back with the stick. Not just one whack, but five, sometimes ten; sometimes she lost count. Usually she passed out before he had finished.

But now she was good. She and Romeo made a good team. She and Romeo and the dog. The brown dog that had become their friend and lived under a collapsed fence on the edge of the street above them. Herself in her blue sleeveless puffa over a ragged, multicoloured jogging suit, woollen hat and trainers, Romeo in his hooded top, jeans and trainers too, and the dog, which they had named Artur.

Romeo had taught her what kind of tourists were best. Elderly couples. They would approach them as a trio, she, Romeo and the dog on a length of rope. Romeo would hold out his withered hand. If the tourists recoiled in revulsion and waved them away, by the time they were gone, she would have the man's wallet in her puffa pocket. If the man dug in his pockets to find them some change, by the time Romeo accepted it, she would have the woman's purse safely out her handbag and in her own pocket. Or if the people were sitting in a café, they might just grab their phone or camera from the table and run.

The music changed. Rihanna was singing now.

She liked Rihanna.

The baby fell silent.

Today had been a bad day. No tourists. No money. Just a small amount of bread to share around.

Simona curled her lips around the neck of the plastic bag, exhaled, then inhaled, hard.

Relief. The relief always came.

But never any hope.

12

A quarter to six, and for the third time today, Lynn was sitting in a doctor's waiting room, this time the consultant gastroenterologist's. A bay window looked out on to the quiet Hove street. It was dark outside, the street lights on. She felt dark inside too. Dark and cold and afraid. The waiting room with its tired old furniture, similar to Dr Hunter's, did nothing to lift her gloom, and the lighting was too dim. A tinny sound of music leaked from the headset plugged into Caitlin's ears.

Then Caitlin stood up suddenly and began staggering around, as if she had been drinking, scratching her hands furiously. Lynn had spent all afternoon with her and knew she had drunk nothing. It was a symptom of her disease.

'Sit down, darling,' she said, alarmed.

'I'm kind of tired,' Caitlin said. 'Do we have to wait?'

'It's very important that we see the specialist today.'

'Yeah, well, look, right, I'm quite important too, OK?' She gave a wry smile.

Lynn smiled. 'You are the most important thing in the world,' she said. 'How are you feeling, apart from tired?'

Caitlin stopped and looked down at one of the magazines on the table, *Sussex Life*. She breathed deeply in silence for some moments, then she said, 'I'm scared, Mummy.'

Lynn stood up and put an arm around her, and unusually Caitlin did not shrink and pull away. Instead she nestled against her mother's body, took her hand and gripped it hard.

Caitlin had grown several inches in the last year and Lynn still had not got used to having to look upwards at her face. She had clearly inherited her father's height genes, and her thin, gangly frame looked more like some kind of bendy doll than ever today, albeit a very beautiful one.

She was dressed in the careless style she always favoured, a grungy grey and rust-coloured knitted top over a T-shirt, with a necklace of small stones on a thin leather loop, jeans with frayed bottoms and old trainers, unlaced. Additionally, in deference to the cold, and perhaps to conceal her swollen, pregnant-looking belly, Lynn guessed, her camel-coloured duffel coat that looked like it had come from a charity shop.

Caitlin's short, spiky, jet-black hair protruded above the Aztec patterned band that covered much of her head and her piercings gave her a vaguely Gothic look. She had a stud in the centre of her chin, a tongue stud and one ring through her left eyebrow. Out of sight at the moment, but which the specialist would no doubt expose when he examined her, were the ring on her right nipple, the one through her belly button and the one in the front of her vagina, the insertion of which she had coyly confessed to her mother, in one of their rare moments of closeness, had been *rather embarrassing*.

This truly had turned into the day from hell, Lynn thought. Since leaving Dr Hunter's surgery this morning, then returning with Caitlin this afternoon, her whole life seemed to have been upended, as if it had gone through a seismic shift.

And now her phone was ringing. She pulled it out of her handbag and looked at the display. It was Mal.

'Hi,' she said. 'Where are you?'

'Just coming through the lock at Shoreham. We've had

a shitty day – dredged up a corpse. But tell me about Caitlin.'

She filled him in on her consultations with Dr Hunter, all the time eyeing Caitlin, who was still pacing around the waiting room, which was about a third of the size of Dr Hunter's. She was now picking up and putting down one magazine after the other with great urgency, as if she needed to read all of them but could not decide where to begin.

'I'll actually know more in about an hour. We've just come from Dr Hunter straight to the specialist. Are you going to be in range for a while?'

'At least four hours,' he said. 'Might be longer.'

'OK.'

Dr Granger's secretary appeared. A matronly woman in her fifties, with her hair in a tight bun, she had a distancing smile on her face. 'Dr Granger will see you both now.'

'I'll call you back,' Lynn said.

Unlike Ross Hunter's spacious surgery, Dr Granger's consulting room was a cramped space, on the first floor, with barely enough room for the two chairs in front of his small desk. Angled so that they could be clearly seen by all his patients were framed photographs of a perfect, smiling consultant's wife and three equally perfect, smiling children.

Dr Granger was a tall man in his forties, with a big nose and a thinning thatch of hair, dressed in a pinstriped suit, with a crisp shirt and a neat tie. There was a slight aloofness about him, which made Lynn think he could as easily have passed for a barrister as a doctor.

'Please sit down,' he said, opening a brown folder, inside which Lynn could see a letter from Ross Hunter. He then sat down himself, reading it.

Lynn took and gently squeezed Caitlin's hand, and her

daughter made no effort to remove it. Dr Granger was making her feel uncomfortable. She didn't like his coldness, or the over-the-top display of family photos. They seemed to give out a message that read, *I am OK and you are not. What I have to say will make no difference to my life. I will go home tonight and have dinner and watch TV and then perhaps tell my wife I want sex with her, and you – well, tough ... you will wake up tomorrow in your private hell, and I will wake up as I do every morning, full of the joys of spring and with my happy children.*

Having finished reading, he leaned forward with the faintest thaw in his expression. 'How are you feeling, Caitlin?'

She shrugged, then was silent for some moments. Lynn waited for her to speak. Caitlin extracted her hand from her mother's and began scratching the back of each hand in rotation.

'I itch,' she said. 'I itch everywhere. Even my lips itch.'

'Anything else?'

'I'm tired.' She looked sulky suddenly. Her normal look. 'I want to feel better,' she said.

'Do you feel a little unsteady?'

She bit her lip, then nodded.

'I think Dr Hunter has told you the results of the tests.'

Caitlin nodded again, without making eye contact, then rummaged in her soft, zebra-striped handbag and pulled out her mobile phone.

The consultant's eyes widened as Caitlin stabbed some buttons, reading the display. 'Yes,' she said distantly, as if to herself. 'Yup, he told me.'

'Yes,' Lynn stepped in hastily. 'He has, he's – he's told us the news – you know – what you have told him. Thank you for seeing us so quickly.'

Somewhere outside, along the street, a car alarm was shrieking.

The consultant looked at Caitlin again for a moment, watching her send a text and then put the phone back in her bag.

'We have to act quickly,' he said.

'I don't really understand exactly what has changed,' Caitlin said. 'Can you sort of explain it to me in simple terms? Sort of, like, *idiot* language?'

He smiled. 'I'll do my best. As you know, for the past six years you've been suffering from primary sclerosing cholangitis, Caitlin. Originally you had the milder – if you can call it that – juvenile form, but recently and very swiftly it has turned into the advanced adult form. We've tried to keep it under control with a mixture of drugs and surgery for the past six years, in the hope that your liver might cure itself – but that only happens very rarely, and I'm afraid in your case it has not. Your liver has now deteriorated to a point where your life would be in danger if we did not take action.'

Her voice very small suddenly, Caitlin said, 'So I'm going to die, right?'

Lynn grabbed her hand and squeezed hard. 'No, darling, you are not. Absolutely not. You are going to be fine.' She looked at the doctor for reassurance.

The doctor replied impassively, 'I've been in touch with the Royal South London Hospital and arranged for you to be admitted there tonight for assessment for transplantation.'

'I hate that fucking place,' Caitlin said.

'It is the best unit in the country,' he replied. 'There are other hospitals, but this is the one we work with normally from down here.'

Caitlin rummaged in her bag again. 'The thing is, I'm busy tonight. Me and Luke are going to a club. Digital. There's a band I need to see.'

There was a brief silence. Then the consultant said, with far more tenderness than Lynn had imagined he was capable of, 'Caitlin, you are not at all well. It would be very unwise to go out. I need to get you into hospital right away. I want to find you a new liver as quickly as possible.'

Caitlin looked at him for a moment through her jaundiced yellow eyes. 'How do you *define* well?' she asked.

The consultant, his face thawing into a smile, said, 'Would you really like my definition?'

'Yes. How do you define *well*?'

'Being alive and not feeling sick might be a good place to start,' he said. 'How does that sound to you?'

Caitlin shrugged. 'Yup, that's probably quite good.' She nodded, absorbing the words, clearly thinking about them.

'If you have a liver transplant, Caitlin,' he said, 'the chances are good that you will start to feel well again and get back to normal.'

'And if I don't? Like – don't have a transplant?'

Lynn wanted to butt in and say something, tell her daughter just exactly what would happen. But she knew she had to keep silent and play this out as an onlooker.

'Then,' he said baldly, 'I'm afraid you will die. I think you have only a short time to live. A few months at the most. It could be much less.'

There was a long silence. Lynn felt the grip of her daughter's hand suddenly and she squeezed back, as hard as she could.

'Die?' Caitlin said.

It came out as a trembling whisper. Caitlin turned to her mother in shock, stared at her face. Lynn smiled at her, unable to think for a moment of anything she could say to her child.

Nervously, Caitlin asked, 'Is this true? Mum? Is this what they already told you?'

'You are very seriously ill, darling. But if you have a transplant it will be fine. You'll be well again. You'll be able to live a completely normal life.'

Caitlin was silent. She withdrew her hand and put a finger in her mouth, something Lynn had not seen her do in years. There was a beep, then a fax machine on a shelf near the doctor printed out a sheet of paper.

'I've been on the Net,' Caitlin said abruptly. 'I Googled liver transplants. They come from dead people, right?'

'Mostly, yes.'

'So I'd be getting a dead person's liver?'

'There is no absolute guarantee we'll be lucky in getting you a liver at all.'

Lynn stared at him in stunned silence. 'What do you mean, *no guarantee*?'

'You both have to understand,' he said in a matter-of-fact way that made Lynn want to rise up and slap him, 'that there is a shortage of livers and that you have a rare blood group, which makes it harder than for some people. It depends if I can get you in as a priority – which I am hoping I can. But your condition is technically "chronic" and patients with "acute" liver failure tend to get priority. I'll have to fight that corner for you. At least you tick some of the right boxes, being young and otherwise healthy.'

'So, if I get one at all, it's likely I'm going to spend the rest of my life with a dead woman's liver in me?'

'Or a man's,' he said.

'How great is that?'

'Isn't that a lot better than the alternative, darling?'

Lynn asked, and tried to take her hand again, but was brushed away.

'So this is going to be from some organ donor?'

'Yes,' Neil Granger said.

'So I would be carrying around for the rest of my life the knowledge that someone died and I've got a bit of them inside me?'

'I can give you some literature to read, Caitlin,' he said. 'And when you go up to the Royal, you will meet a lot of people, including social workers and psychologists, who will talk to you all about what it means. But there is one important thing to remember. The loved ones and families of people who have died often take great comfort from knowing that the death wasn't completely in vain. That that person's death has enabled someone else to live.'

Caitlin was pensive for some moments, then she said, 'Great, you want me to have a liver transplant so that someone else can feel good about their daughter's, or husband's, or son's death?'

'No, that's not the reason. I want you to have it so I can save your life.'

'Life sucks, doesn't it?' Caitlin said. 'Life really sucks.'

'Death sucks even more,' the consultant replied.

13

Susan Cooper had discovered that there was a fine view from this particular window, just past the lifts on the seventh floor of the Royal Sussex County Hospital, across the rooftops of Kemp Town to the English Channel. All today, the sea had been a brilliant, sparkling blue, but now, at six o'clock on this late November evening, the falling darkness had turned it into an inky void, stretching to infinity beyond the lights of the city.

She was staring out at that vast blackness now. Her hands rested on the radiator, not for the warmth it gave off but merely to support her drained body. She stared silently, bleakly, through the reflection of her face in the window, feeling the draught of cold air through the thin glass. But feeling little else.

She was numb with shock. She could not believe this was happening.

She made a mental list of the people she still needed to call. She'd dreaded breaking the news to Nat's brother, to his sister in Australia, to his friends. Both his parents had died in their fifties, his father from a heart attack, his mother from cancer, and Nat used to joke that he would never make old bones. Some joke.

She turned, padded back to the Intensive Care Unit and rang the bell. A nurse let her in. It was warmer in here than out in the corridor. The temperature was maintained high enough for the patients to lie in hospital pyjamas, or naked, without any risk of catching cold. It was an irony, she thought, although she did not dwell on it, that she had once worked as a nurse here, in this very unit. It was in this hospital that she and Nat had met – shortly after he had started as a junior registrar.

She felt movement inside her. The baby was kicking. *Their* baby. Thirty weeks old. A boy.

As she turned right, walking past the central nursing station, where a prosthetic leg had been abandoned on a chair, she heard the swishing of a curtain being pulled. She looked across at the far corner of the ward and her heart lurched inside her. A nurse was drawing the blue privacy curtain around Bed 14, Nat's bed. Sealing it from prying eyes. They were about to start some new tests and she wasn't sure she had the courage to be with him while they did. But she had sat by his side almost all day and she knew she had to be there now. Had to keep talking to him. Had to keep hoping.

He had compound and depressed skull fractures, a lesion to the cervical region of his spinal cord that was likely to leave him a quadriplegic if he survived, as well as an almost irrelevant – at this stage – fractured right clavicle and fractured pelvis.

She hadn't prayed in years, but she found herself praying repeatedly today, in silence, always the same words: *Please, God, don't let Nat die. Please, God, don't let him.*

She felt so damn useless. All her nursing skills and she could not do a thing. Except talk to him. Talk and talk and talk, waiting for a response that did not come. But maybe now would be different . . .

She walked back across the shiny floor, passing a hugely fat woman in the bed to her right, the rolls of flesh on her face and body looking like the contours of a 3-D map. One of the nurses told her the woman weighed thirty-nine stone. A sign on the end of the bed said DO NOT FEED.

To her left was a man in his forties, his face the colour of alabaster, intubated, a forest of wires taped to his chest and head. He looked, to her experienced eye, as if he had recently come out of heart-bypass surgery. There was a large, cheery get-well card propped on an instrument table beside him. At least he was on the mend, she thought, with a good chance of walking out of this hospital, rather than being carried out.

Unlike Nat.

Nat had been in steady decline throughout the day and, although she was still clinging to a desperate, increasingly irrational hope, she was starting to sense a terrible inevitability.

Every few minutes her phone, turned to silent, vibrated with yet another message. She had stepped out to reply to some. To her mother. To Nat's brother, who had been here this morning, wanting an update. To his sister in Sydney. To her best friend, Jane, whom she had called tearfully this morning, an hour after arriving here, telling her that the doctors weren't sure whether he would live. Others she ignored. She did not want to be distracted, just wanted to be here for Nat, willing him to pull through.

Every few moments she heard the *beep-beep-bong* of a monitor alarm. She breathed in the smell of sterilizing chemicals, catching the occasional tang of cologne and a faint, background note of warm electrical equipment.

Inside the curtained space, propped up in a bed that had been cranked to a thirty-degree angle, Nat looked like an alien, bandaged and wired, with endotracheal and naso-gastric tubes in his mouth and nostrils. He had a probe in his skull to measure intracranial pressure, and another on one finger, and a forest of IV lines and drains from bags suspended from drip stands running into his arms and abdomen. Eyes shut, he lay motionless, surrounded by racks of monitoring and life-support apparatus. Two computer display screens were mounted to his right, and there was a laptop on the trolley at the end of the bed with all his notes and readings on it.

'Hello, darling,' she said. 'I'm back with you.' She stared at the screens as she spoke.

There was no reaction.

The exit tube from his mouth ended in a small bag, with a tap at the bottom, half filled with a dark fluid. Susan read the labels on the drip lines: Mannitol, Pentastarch, Morphine, Midazolam, Noradrenaline. Keeping him stable. Life support. Preventing him from slipping away, that was all.

The only signs that he was alive were the steady rising and falling of his chest and the blips of light on the monitor screens.

She looked at the drip lines into the back of her husband's hands, and the blue plastic tag bearing his name, then at the equipment again, seeing some machinery and displays that were unfamiliar. Even in the five years since she had left nursing for a commercial job in the pharmaceutical industry, new technology that she did not recognize had come in.

Nat's face, a mess of bruises and lacerations, was a ghostly shade of white she had never seen before – he was a fit guy who played a regular game of squash, and normally always had colour in his face despite the long – crazily long – hours of his job. He was strong, tall, with long, fair hair, almost rebelliously long for a doctor, not long past thirty and handsome. So handsome.

She closed her eyes for an instant to stop the tears

coming. *So damn sodding handsome. Come on, darling. Come on, Nat, you are going to be OK. You are going to get through this. I love you. I love you so much. I need you.* Feeling her stomach, she added, *We both need you.*

She opened her eyes and read the dials on the monitors, the digital displays, the levels, looking for some small sign that could give her hope, and not finding it. His pulse was weak and erratic, his blood oxygen levels way too low, brainwaves scarcely registering on the scale. But surely he was just asleep and would wake up in a moment.

She had been in the hospital since ten this morning, arriving after the phone call from the police. It was another irony that she had been due to come to this same hospital for a scan today. That was why she had still been at home when the phone rang, instead of at Harcourt Pharmaceuticals, where she worked on the team monitoring clinical trials of new drugs.

It had helped that she knew her way around the labyrinth of the hospital's buildings and also that plenty of people who worked here knew her and Nat, so she wasn't given the usual platitudes and kept out of the way, but instead got straight talking from the medical team, however unpalatable it was.

By the time she had arrived here, half an hour behind Nat, he was already in the CT unit, having a brain scan. If it had shown a blood clot he would have been transferred to the neurological unit at Hurstwood Park for surgery. But the scan had shown there was massive internal haemorrhaging, which meant there was nothing surgical that could be done. It was a wait and see situation, but it appeared more than likely that he had irreversible brain damage.

The medical team had stabilized him for four hours in

A&E, during which time there had been no change in his condition and his total lack of responsiveness persisted.

On the Glasgow Coma Score tests, before he had been sedated, Nat had produced a result of 3 out of a possible 15. He had no eye response to any verbal commands, or to pain, or to pressure applied directly to either eye, giving him the minimal score of 1. He gave no verbal response to any questions or comments or commands, giving him a score of 1 on this verbal part of the test. And he had no response to pain, giving him a score of only 1 in the motor response section. The maximum a person could score was 15. The minimum was 3.

Susan knew what that result meant. A score of 3 was a grim, though not 100 per cent reliable, indicator that Nat was brain dead.

But miracles happened. In her nursing years in this unit, she had known patients with a score of 3 go on to make full recoveries. OK, it was a tiny percentage, but Nat was strong. He could make it.

He would!

The short, friendly Malaysian nurse, Saleha, who had been with Nat one-on-one for the whole afternoon, smiled at Susan. 'You should go home and get some rest.'

Susan shook her head. 'I want to keep talking to him. People respond sometimes. I remember seeing it happen.'

'Does he have favourite music?' the nurse asked.

'Snow Patrol,' she said, and thought for a moment. 'And the Eagles. He likes those bands.'

'You could try getting some of their CDs and playing them to him. Have you got an iPod?'

'At home.'

'Why don't you get it? You could get his wash stuff at

the same time. Some soap, a facecloth, toothbrush, his shaving stuff, deodorant.'

'I don't want to leave him,' Susan said. 'In case . . .' She shrugged.

'He's stable,' Saleha said. 'I can call you if I think you should get back here quickly.'

'He'll be stable all the time you keep the machines on, won't he? But what happens when you switch them off?'

There was an awkward silence, during which both women knew the answer. The nurse broke it. She said cheerily, 'What we have to hope is that there will be some improvement overnight.'

'Yes,' Susan said, her voice choking as she tried to hold back the tears.

She stared at Nat's face, at his motionless eyelids, willing him to move, willing those eyes to open and his lips to smile.

But there was no change.

14

David Browne, the Crime Scene Manager, and James Gartrell, a police forensic photographer, had arrived a short while ago in separate vehicles. Browne, a lean, muscular man in his early forties, with close-cropped ginger hair and a cheery, freckled face, dressed in a heavy padded anorak, jeans and trainers, and Gartrell, burly and intense, with short dark hair, were busy on the main deck of the *Arco Dee*, photographing and videoing the scene.

Browne had agreed with Roy Grace that there was no useful purpose to be served in treating the ship as a crime scene, and none of the three men, or Lizzie Mantle, had bothered changing into protective clothing. Grace had merely secured the immediate area around the drag head with crime-scene tape.

The Detective Superintendent stood by the cordon now, gratefully cradling a mug of hot coffee, informally interviewing the captain and the chief engineer, whose comments were being noted down by DI Mantle, who was standing next to him. He glanced at his watch. It was ten past six.

The captain, Danny Marshall, wearing a high-visibility jacket over his thick pullover, was looking worried, and repeatedly checking his watch too. The chief engineer, Malcolm Beckett, dressed in a grimy white boiler suit and hard hat, was a tad less edgy, but Grace could sense both men were tense. Clearly they were upset about the body, but equally clearly they were worried about the commercial implications of the disruption to their schedule.

Another crew member came over to them, holding a sheet of graph paper on which was printed a set of coordinates, giving the precise position on the seabed where the body had been dredged up from.

Lizzie Mantle copied the information into her notebook, then slipped the square of paper into a plastic evidence bag and pocketed it. The body had been heavily weighted down, but even so, as Grace knew from previous experience, there were strong currents in the English Channel and bodies could get moved considerable distances. He would need to get the underwater team to calculate the probable dump site.

He was suddenly aware of the burble of a motorcycle, then his radio crackled and he heard the voice of the young female Police Community Support Officer he had posted at the bottom of the gangway to ensure that no unauthorized person came on board.

'The paramedic's just arrived, sir,' she said.

'I'll come down.'

Roy walked across the deck and heard the motorcycle engine more loudly. A single headlight swept the quay. Moments later, under the glare of the ship's spotlights, he saw a BMW motorbike, in paramedic livery, halt and the driver dismount and kick down the stand. Graham Lewis balanced the bike carefully, then pulled off his helmet and leather gloves and began removing his medical bag from the pannier.

However obvious it might be to an attending police officer that someone was dead, under the requirements of the Coroner, unless the remains were little more than bones, or the head was detached or missing, formal certifying of death had to be done at the scene by a qualified medic. In the past, a police surgeon would have been required to turn up, but in a recent change of practice it was now paramedics who performed this role.

Grace descended the perilous rope gangway to greet him, passing the PCSO at the bottom, and was glad to see that none of the local journalists, who usually got to murder scenes quicker than blowflies, had yet materialized.

The paramedic, a short, wiry man with curly grey hair, had the sort of kind, caring face that would give instant reassurance to any accident victim he attended. And he was irrepressibly cheery, despite all he saw daily in his career.

'How are you doing, Roy?' he greeted the Detective Superintendent breezily.

'Better than the poor chap on the ship,' Grace replied. *Although not that much better if I don't make it to the party before it ends*, he nearly added. 'I don't think you're going to be needing that bag. He's about as dead as they get.'

He led Graham Lewis back up the wobbly gangway on to the deck, then along, under the glare of the ship's lights, past the cable reels and orange rails of the conveyor belt, which would normally have been busily and noisily clanking away, shifting the cargo from the hold on to the chute, which would then discharge it on to the quay. But now it was silent. The paramedic followed Roy Grace to the far side of the ship.

The claws of the steel drag head, suspended a couple of feet above the deck, looked like a pair of gigantic, parallel crab pincers. Jammed between them was a parcel of black plastic tarpaulin, with several ropes wound around it. Several more lengths of rope, looped through eyeholes sewn into the tarp, were tied around a cluster of concrete breeze blocks, which now lay on the grimy, orange-painted metal of the deck.

'He's in the bag,' Grace said. 'They've cut it open but they haven't touched him.'

Graham Lewis walked up and peered in through the long slit which had been opened up along part of the length. Roy Grace watched alongside him, horrified but deeply curious.

The paramedic pulled on a pair of latex gloves, then tugged the sheeting open wider, revealing the full length of the motionless, almost translucent, greyish-white body inside. It was a young man, in his late teens, Grace estimated, and from his condition he did not look as if he had been in the water for very long.

There was a strong smell of plastic, and a fainter reek of decay, but not the terrible, cloying, rotting-meat reek of death that Grace had long come to associate with a body that had been dead for a while. This person had been dead for only a few days, he guessed, but the post-mortem would hopefully give them a better steer on this.

The youth was thin, but from under-nourishment rather than exercise, Grace judged, noting the lack of muscle. He was about five foot seven or eight, with an angular, rather awkward-looking face and short black hair, some of which lay in a peak across his forehead.

The paramedic rotated his head slightly. 'No immediate sign of any head trauma,' he said.

Grace nodded, but his eyes – and his thoughts – were on a different part of the body. He was staring at the abdomen. In particular, at the neat vertical incision down the centre, from the base of the neck to below the belly button, stopping at the edge of the thick triangle of pubic hair, and the large sutures closing it up.

His eyes met the paramedic's, then he looked down again. Stared at the incision. At the penis, almost black in colour, lying on top of the hairs, limp and wrinkled, like the cast-off skin of a snake. He could not help continuing to stare at it for a moment. The penises of dead men always seemed so profoundly sad, as if the ultimate symbol of manhood, through its motionlessness, became the ultimate symbol of death. Then his eyes returned to the incision.

'What the hell is that?' Graham Lewis asked. 'There's no scar tissue, so it has been made post-mortem – or close to it.'

'It looks very neat,' Grace said. 'Surgical?'

Danny Marshall, who was standing a short distance away, next to DI Mantle, asked her anxiously how much longer it would be before the body was off-loaded and they could sail again – they had already lost over an hour of valuable discharging time. The *Arco Dee* needed to operate round the clock to earn its keep. Which meant never missing a tide. Another hour's delay and they would not unload in time to make tonight's tide.

She told him the decision would be Roy Grace's.

For the first time in his career Marshall could understand the behaviour of a couple of skippers of fishing vessels he had met who had pulled up bodies from the deep in their nets, and confessed they had chucked them straight back rather than endure the delays that police procedures would inflict on them.

'Definitely. That is not a wound,' Lewis said. 'This poor bastard's had surgery. But . . .' He hesitated.

'But what?' Grace prompted.

'That incision definitely looks like a post-mortem one to me.'

'Any idea how long you are going to be, Detective Superintendent?' the captain asked.

'It depends on the pathologist,' Grace told him apologetically.

'We have to wait?'

At that moment, Grace's phone rang. 'Speak of the devil,' he said. It was the Home Office pathologist, Nadiuska De Sancha.

'Roy,' she said, 'I'm so sorry. I've been called to an emergency. I don't know what time I'll be able to get to you. Four or five hours at least, maybe longer.'

'OK, I'll call you back,' he said.

The paramedic was taking the man's pulse. Just going through the motions. A formality.

Grace made a decision. It was partly influenced by his desire to get to the party, but more so by the reality of the situation. There was a crew of eight on this dredger, all of whom he had already spoken to. Each person could testify that the body had been hauled up out of the sea. The photographer, James Gartrell, had taken all the photographs and the footage he needed. The body was contained within the plastic sheeting, hauled up from the seabed, which made it extremely unlikely there was any forensic evidence on the ship itself – anything there might have been would have washed off in the water on the way to the surface.

He would be totally within his rights to impound the ship as a crime scene, but in his judgement that would serve no purpose. All the *Arco Dee* had done was haul the body up from the ocean floor. The vessel was no more a crime scene than a helicopter that hauled up a floater from the surface. The cause of death would be determined in the mortuary.

'Good news for you!' Grace said to Danny Marshall. 'Let me have the names and addresses of all your crew members and you are free to go.' Then he turned to the paramedic.

'Let's get the body ashore – keep him wrapped in the plastic.'

'OK if I drop you off a statement later?' Graham Lewis said. 'I have to coach a young rugby team tonight.'

'Coach?'

'Yup!'

'You're a rugby coach?'

'Yes.'

'I didn't know that. I run the CID rugby team. We need a new coach.'

'Give me a call.'

'I will. Tomorrow's fine for the statement,' Grace said.

Then he looked down at the bony, mutilated body again. *Who are you?* he wondered. *Where are you from? Who made that incision on your body? And why?*

Always the *why*.

It was the first question Roy Grace asked, privately, at every murder scene he attended. And for a man still young for his rank, he had attended far too many.

Too many to feel shocked any more.

But not too many not to care.

15

Lynn hated this drive at the best of times, the long slow crawl up the A23 through suburban south London. They were heading for the Royal South London Hospital, in Crystal Hill, where Caitlin was going to spend the next four days being assessed by the pre-transplant team there.

The last time Lynn had come up this way was back in April, when she had taken Caitlin to IKEA to choose some new furnishings for her bedroom. At least that had been fun – inasmuch as battling through the Sunday afternoon crush at IKEA could be any sane person's idea of fun.

But they did have a treat at the end of the ordeal – in fact, a double treat so far as Lynn was concerned, because Caitlin did something she very rarely did. She had not just eaten something she would normally have turned her nose up at for being *unhealthy*, but had totally pigged out on it.

It was after they had finally got through the checkout queue, with their purchases of a bedside table, lamp, bed-cover, wallpaper and curtains. They had gone to the restaurant area and eaten meatballs and new potatoes, followed by ice cream. Even naughtier, they'd bought two hotdogs as well, swamped in mustard and ketchup, as a treat for their supper, but had eaten them in the car long before they had reached home. Lynn had half expected Caitlin to want to stop and throw them up at any moment, but instead her daughter had sat there with a grin on her face, licking her lips from time to time and proclaiming, 'That was wicked! Totally wicked!'

It was one of the few occasions in her life that Lynn could ever remember seeing Caitlin actually enjoy her food, and she had hoped at the time – a hope that was later dashed – that it might herald the start of a new and more positive phase of her daughter's life.

They were passing IKEA now, the tall, floodlit smoke-stacks with the blue and yellow bands near the top, on their left. She glanced at Caitlin in the passenger seat beside her, hunched over her mobile phone, engrossed in texting. She had been texting non-stop for the past hour since they had left Brighton. The glare of oncoming headlights lit up her face, a ghostly, yellow-tinged white.

'Fancy some meatballs, darling?'

'Yeah, right,' Caitlin said sleepily, without looking up, as if her mother was offering her poison.

'We're just passing IKEA – we could stop.'

She worked the keypad for some moments, then said, 'They wouldn't be open now.'

'It's only quarter to eight. I think they're open until ten.'

'Meatballs? Yuck. Do you want to poison me or something?'

'Remember when we came here in April, to get the stuff for your room? We had some then and you really enjoyed them.'

'I read about meatballs on the Net,' Caitlin said, suddenly becoming animated. 'They're full of fat and crap. You know, some meatballs – they've even got bits of bone and hooves in. It's like some burgers – they literally put the whole cow in a crushing machine. Like, everything, right? The head, skin, intestines. That way they can say it is pure beef.'

'Not IKEA's.'

'Yeah, I forgot, you worship at the altar of IKEA. Like their stuff is blessed by some Nordic god.'

Lynn smiled, reached out a hand and touched her daughter's wrist. 'It would be better than the hospital food.'

'Yeah, well, don't worry. I'm not going to eat *anything* while I'm in that fucking place.' She tapped her keypad again. 'Anyhow, we just ate supper.'

'I ate, darling. You didn't touch your food.'

'Whatever.' She texted some more. Then she said, 'Actually, that's not true. I had some yoghurt.' She yawned.

Lynn halted the Peugeot at traffic lights, removed her hand for a moment to put the gear lever into neutral, then put it back again on Caitlin's wrist. 'You must eat something tonight.'

'What's the point?'

'To keep up your strength.'

'I'm being strong.'

She squeezed her daughter's wrist, but there was no response. Then she dug the map out of the door pocket and briefly checked it. The exhaust pipe banged on the underside of the car as the engine idled. The lights turned green. She jammed the map back into the pocket, wrenched the sticky gear lever into first and let out the clutch.

'How are you feeling?'

'I'm scared. And I'm so tired.'

Following the traffic, she changed gear again, then up into third, and squeezed Caitlin's wrist once more.

'You're going to be fine, darling. You are in the best possible hands.'

'Luke's been on the Internet. He just texted me. He said that nine out of ten people on the liver transplant waiting list in the USA die before they get one. That three people die every day in the UK waiting for a transplant. And there's 140,000 people in the USA and Europe waiting for transplants.'

In her fury, Lynn did not notice the brake lights on the vehicles ahead were glowing and she had to stamp on the brakes, locking up the front wheel to avoid rear-ending a van. *The Internet!* she thought. *Sod the fucking Internet. Sod that jerk, Luke. Has that brainless twerp not got anything better to do than spook my daughter?*

'Luke's wrong,' she said. 'I discussed it with Dr Hunter earlier. It's just not true. What happens is that some very sick people get put on the waiting list far too late. But that's not your situation.'

She tried to think of something else to say that would not sound patronizing. But her mind was suddenly a blank. The consultant, Dr Granger, had said they would *try* to get her a priority position on the waiting list. But, equally candidly, he'd said that he could not guarantee it. And there was the added problem of Caitlin's blood group.

She drove on in silence, to the sound of the steady *click-click-click* of Caitlin's phone keys and the occasional *ping-ping* of an incoming text.

'Do you want some music on, darling?' she said finally.

'Not the crap stuff that you have in this car,' Caitlin retorted, but at least she said it good-humouredly.

'Why don't you try to find something on the radio?'

'Whatever.' Caitlin leaned forward and switched the radio on. An old Scissor Sisters song was playing: 'I don't feel like dancin''.

'That's me,' Caitlin said. 'No dancing today.'

Lynn gave her a wry smile. In the sudden flare of a street light, a thin, scared ghost in the passenger seat smiled wistfully back.

16

'Well, well, guess who's here! And you've even beaten the blowflies to this one!' Roy Grace said, as, followed by DI Mantle, he walked past the scene guard at the bottom of the gangway and reluctantly acknowledged the reporter from the local Brighton newspaper, the *Argus*.

It did not seem to matter what time of the day or night, Kevin Spinella always turned up ahead of all other reporters, particularly when there was a whiff of a suspicious death.

Or perhaps it was the whiff of death itself. Perhaps the young reporter's razor-sharp nose could smell death from the same four-mile distance as blowflies.

Either that or he had found some way of cracking the latest secure police radio network. Grace always suspected he had an insider in the police and was determined, one day, to find out, but at this moment his thoughts were on something else entirely. He needed to get to the party for Chief Superintendent Jim Wilkinson as quickly as possible and find out just what Cleo had meant when she'd said coldly, *I want to tell you face to face, not over the phone.*

Just what did this woman he loved so much want to tell him? And why had she sounded so off? Was she going to dump him? Tell him she had found someone else? Or that she was going back to her previous boyfriend, her born-again Christian barrister jerk?

OK, her ex was an Old Etonian, and Grace knew he

could never compete with that. Cleo came from a different background from his own, a wholly different class league. Her family were rich, she had been educated at a private boarding school and she was ferociously intelligent.

By comparison, he was just a dumb, middle-class copper, the son of a middle-class copper. And he had no aspirations beyond that; that was all he wanted to be and all he would ever be. He loved his work and he loved his colleagues. He would happily admit that if he could just freeze time, he would like to remain in his job forever.

Had Cleo now realized that?

Despite all his attempts to keep pace with her Open University degree studies in philosophy, he was falling way behind. Had she decided he was simply not bright enough for her?

'Nice to see you, Detective Superintendent Grace, Detective Inspector Mantle.'

The reporter flashed a big smile and stepped right into their path. For a moment, their faces were so close he could smell Spinella's spearmint chewing gum.

'So what brings two senior detectives to the harbour on a chilly night like this?'

The reporter had a thin, keen-eyed face and a short, modern haircut. He was wearing a beige, gumshoe mackintosh with the collar turned up, over a thin, summer-weight suit and a carefully knotted tie. His tasselled black shoes looked cheap and loud.

'You don't look like you're dressed for fishing,' Lizzie Mantle quipped.

'Fishing for facts,' he retorted, with a quizzical raise of his eyebrows. 'Or perhaps *dredging* them up?'

Behind him, the mortuary van began driving off. Spinella turned to glance at it for a second, then he looked back at the two detectives.

'Could either of you give me a comment?'

'Not at this stage,' Grace said. 'I may hold a press conference after the post-mortem tomorrow.'

Spinella pulled out his notepad, flipping it open. 'Might be just another floater, then. Can I quote you on that, Detective Superintendent?'

'I'm sorry, I've no comment,' Grace said.

'A burial at sea, perhaps?'

Grace walked on past him towards his car. Spinella padded along beside him, keeping pace.

'Bit odd, isn't it, that it was weighted down with concrete breeze blocks?'

'You've got my mobile number. Call me tomorrow around midday,' Grace said. 'I might know something by then.'

'Such as what that incision on the body is?'

Grace stopped in his tracks. Then, restraining himself with great difficulty, he remained silent. *Where the hell had he got that from?* It had to be one of the crew members. Spinella was a past master at wheedling information from strangers.

Spinella grinned, knowing he had wrong-footed the detective. 'Some kind of ritual killing, perhaps? A black magic rite?'

Grace thought quickly, not wanting some sensational headline appearing in the morning edition that would frighten people. But the truth was Spinella might be right. That incision was very strange. It was, as Graham Lewis said, very much like the kind of incision made during a post-mortem. During a ritual too?

'OK, here's the deal. If you hold back writing anything

other than just the basic facts, that a dredger pulled up an unidentified body, I'll give you clear water on the story tomorrow as soon as the PM is done. Fair enough?'

'Clear water!' Spinella nodded approvingly. 'Very appropriate, considering where we are. I like it! Nice one, Detective Superintendent! Nice one indeed!'

17

Simona was hungry and she was wet. She had been walking for hours through the dark city streets in the pelting rain. This was always a bad time of year, the cold weather keeping people indoors, the lack of tourists. Hopefully there would be richer pickings in the weeks to come, as Christmas got nearer and the shopping crowds started.

She trudged past a bank that was closed, its windows dark, and wondered what people did inside banks. Important people. Rich people. Then a hotel: a doorman eyed her warily, as if signalling he was guarding the important people inside from her. Next she passed a closed mini-mart, glancing ravenously through its windows at the cans of food and jars of pickles.

She didn't even have any metallic paint to inhale to take away the hunger pangs. Earlier in the evening she'd had an argument with Romeo and they'd fought over the last bottle and dropped it, and the paint had poured down a gutter. He'd stomped off with the dog and the remnants of the bottle, saying he was going home to get out of the rain. But she was hungry and hadn't wanted to go back to the underground hole until she had found some food. Besides, the crying of the baby had been worse than ever.

The only thing she had eaten since yesterday was a couple of French fries, thin as matchsticks, which she had scavenged from a discarded carton on the pavement near a McDonald's. For a while she stood, begging, outside an expensive-looking restaurant, tantalized by the smells of sizzling garlic and roasting meats, but all the dry, satisfied-looking people who had come out and climbed into their cars had ignored her, as if she was invisible.

Cars and taxis and vans sluiced past her now. She walked on, her trainers sodden, splashing through one puddle after another and not caring. Ahead of her was the Gara de Nord railway station – it would be dry inside. Some of her friends would probably be there, until the police threw them out at midnight, and they might have some food. Or she might be able to steal a chocolate bar from the station shop, which would still be open.

She climbed up the steps and went inside Bucharest's vast, dimly lit main railway terminus. Puddles lay on the floor, glinting eerie reflections of the white, overhead sodium bulbs that stretched away, in pairs, to the far end of the building. Directly ahead, above her, was a large electronic noticeboard that read: PLECARI DEPARTURES. The round clock set into the board said 23.36.

There destinations were listed, with departure times for later that night and the next morning. Some were cities and towns she knew by name, but there were plenty she had never heard of. People talked about other places sometimes. Jobs you could get in other countries where you could earn good money and live in a nice house, and where it was always warm. She heard the clanking, rolling sound of railway carriage wheels. Maybe she could just get on a train and go to wherever it went, and maybe it would be warm there, with lots of food and no babies crying.

She passed a closed café on her right, with the sign, white on a blue background, METROPOL. Sitting on the ground in front of it was an old, bearded man in a woollen hat, ragged clothes and gumboots, swigging from a bottle of spirits of some kind. There was a filthy sleeping bag beside him, and everything else he owned seemed to be crammed into a tartan carrier. He nodded in recognition at Simona and she nodded back. Like most of the street people, they knew people by their faces, not by their names.

She walked on. Two cops in bright yellow jackets stood over to her left, young, mean-looking guys smoking cigarettes and looking bored. They were waiting for closer to midnight, when they would pull out their truncheons and clear out all the homeless people.

To her right was the brightly lit confectionery stall. A coffee-vending machine stood outside it with the name NESCAFE along the top. The blue-coloured counter was flanked by cabinets containing soft drinks and bottles of beer. A smart-looking man of about fifty appeared to be buying up the shop. He was dressed in a brown sports jacket, blue trousers and polished black shoes, and was filling bag after bag with packets of biscuits, sweets, chocolates, nuts and cans of soft drinks.

She stood for a moment, wondering if there was an opportunity to grab something, but the man who ran the place had already clocked her and was watching her like a hawk from the other side of the counter. If he did not catch her, the two policemen would, and she did not want a beating. Although, she considered, at least in prison she would be dry and get some food. But then they would take her back to the home, the institution.

In the institution they had sent her to school and she had liked that. She liked learning, knew she had to learn if she was ever to change her life. But she hated the institution, the other bitchy girls, the vile head who made her touch him, who beat her when she refused to take his thing in her mouth and locked her in a room, in darkness, with rats scratching, for days on end.

No, she did not want to go back there.

She passed a platform and stood still, watching the tail lights of a train pulling away, picking up speed. A solitary cleaner, in a fluorescent yellow jacket like the ones the cops were wearing, pushed a broom along the glistening wet surface of the platform.

Then she saw them, huddled in a corner, half hidden from view by a concrete pillar, and she felt a sudden surge of joy. Six familiar faces – seven if you counted the baby. She walked towards them.

Tavian, who was tall and thin, with a touch of Romany in his skin colouring, saw her first and smiled at her. He was always smiling. Not many people smiled all the time in her world, and Simona liked that he did. She liked his lean, handsome face, his warm, brown eyes, his thick, manly eyebrows. He was wearing a blue woollen hat with ear flaps, a military camouflage jacket over a grey, nylon windcheater and several layers beneath, and holding the sleeping baby, dressed in a corduroy jumpsuit and wrapped in a blanket. He was nineteen and this was his third child. The first two had been taken into care.

Beside him stood Cici, the baby's mother. Cici, who she thought was about seventeen, was always smiling too, as if this whole life was a big joke that made you laugh all the time. Tiny, and still plump from her pregnancy, she wore baggy green jogging trousers and white trainers that looked so new they must have been freshly stolen today. Her face was round and pudgy, with a couple of front teeth missing, and was encased in her blue and white striped hoodie. She reminded Simona of pictures of Eskimos she had once seen, in a geography lesson at school.

She did not know the names of the others in the group. One was a sour-looking boy of about thirteen, dressed in a knitted ski hat, a bulky black jacket, jeans and trainers, who always had his hands in his pockets, like he did tonight, and who said nothing. Next to him stood another boy, who could have been his elder brother, with a weaselly face, a thin moustache, and spikes of fair hair matted to his forehead by the rain, smoking a hand-rolled cigarette.

There were two other girls. One, the eldest of this group, was in her mid-twenties and looked Romany too. She had long, lank dark hair and her skin was wizened by years of outdoors life. The other, who was twenty, but looked twice her age, was parcelled up in a fleece-lined jacket over bulky thermal trousers, holding a lit cigarette in one hand. In the other hand was a plastic bag containing a bottle of paint, the neck of which she held to her nose, inhaling and exhaling with her eyes closed.

'Simona! Hey!' Tavian raised his hand in greeting.

Simona slapped him a high five.

'How are you? Where's Romeo?' Tavian greeted her.

She shrugged. 'I saw him earlier. How are you all? How's the baby?'

Cici beamed at her, but said nothing. She rarely spoke. It was Tavian who responded.

'They tried to take the baby, two nights ago, but we ran!'

Simona nodded. The authorities did that: they would take the baby from you, but leave you. They would put the baby into some kind of state home. Like the ones she had run away from, repeatedly, from the time she was about eight years old until, four or five years ago now, she had managed to stay away permanently.

There was a silence. They were all looking at her. Tavian and Cici smiling, the others vacantly, as if they expected her to have brought something – food, or perhaps news – but she had brought nothing out of the dark, wet night.

'Have you found anywhere new to sleep?' she asked.

Tavian's smile momentarily faded and he shook his head forlornly. 'No, and the police are worse recently. They are hitting us all the time, moving us on. Sometimes, if they have nothing else to do, they follow us through the night.'

'The ones who tried to take the baby?'

He shook his head, extracted a bent cigarette stub from a box and lit it, rocking the baby gently with his free arm. 'Not them, no. They called someone, some special unit.'

'I heard of a good place, where there is space – along by the heating pipe,' Simona said.

He shrugged indifferently. 'We're OK. We are managing.'

She never really understood this group. They were no different from herself and they had no more than she had. In some ways she was better off, because she at least had a place to go to that was her home. These people were completely nomadic. They slept wherever they could – in alleys, in the shelter of shop-front porches, or out in the open, huddled together for warmth. They knew about the heating pipes, but they never went to them. She did not understand that, but there was a lot about the people she met that she did not understand.

Like the man approaching them now, laden with carrier bags. The man she had seen at the confectionery stall. He was middle-aged, with a slightly smug smile that made Simona instantly wary of him.

'You look hungry, so I bought you some food,' he said, and beamed enthusiastically, holding the bags out.

Suddenly they were all pushing past her, jostling, grabbing at the bags. The man stood there releasing them contentedly. He was of stocky build, with a pleasant, cultured-looking face and well-groomed hair. His open-neck white shirt, his brown jacket, his dark blue trousers and his shiny shoes all looked expensive, but she wondered why, on a night like this, he was not wearing a coat – he could clearly afford one.

Just one bag he held back, waiting until the rush had subsided and people had retreated, each inspecting their sudden windfall, and then he handed it to Simona. She peered inside at a treasure trove of sweets and biscuits.

'Please,' he said, 'help yourself. Take everything. It's yours!' He was looking at her intently.

She dug her hand in, took out a Mars bar, unwrapped and bit into it greedily. It tasted so good. Incredible! She bit some more, then more still, as if afraid someone would snatch it from her, cramming the last of it into her mouth until it was packed so full she could barely chew. Then she dug her hand into the bag again and took out a chocolate-coated biscuit, which she began to unwrap.

Suddenly there was a commotion. She felt a painful thud on her shoulder and cried out in shock, turning round, her bag falling to the floor. A cop was standing behind her, black truncheon raised, a leer of hatred on his face, about to strike her again. She put her hands up and felt a blow on her wrist so hard and painful she was sure he had broken it. He was raising his arm to strike again.

There were police all around them. Seven or eight of them, maybe more.

She heard a loud crack and saw Tavian fall over.

Cici screamed, 'My baby, my baby!'

Simona saw a truncheon strike Cici full in the mouth, busting her gums open and splintering her teeth.

Truncheon blows were hailing down on them all.

Suddenly she felt her hand being gripped and was jerked backwards, clear of the police. As she turned, she saw it was the man who had bought the sweets. A tall, bony cop with a small, rat-like mouth, brandishing his truncheon as if it was going to hit them both, shouted out something. The man dug his hand into his jacket pocket and produced a cluster of banknotes.

The cop took the money and waved them away, then turned his attention back to the mob, raising his truncheon and bringing it down with a sickening thud on someone's back – Simona could not see whose.

Bewildered, she stared at the man, who was pulling her hand once more.

'Quick! Come, I'll get you away.'

She looked at him, unsure whether she could trust him, then back at the mêlée. She saw Cici on her knees, screaming hysterically, blood pouring from her mouth, no longer holding the baby. All of the street people were on the ground now, a shapeless, increasingly bloody mound, sinking further and further beneath the hail of batons. The police were laughing. They were having fun.

This was sport to them.

Moments later, still being pulled by her rescuer's iron grip, she tripped down the stairs of the station's front entrance, out into the pelting rain and towards the open rear door of a large black Mercedes.

18

The problem with buffets, Roy Grace always found, was that you tended to pile your plate high with food before you had actually studied everything that was on the table. Then, just when you were already looking terminally greedy, you noticed the king prawns, or the asparagus spears, or something else that you really liked, for the first time.

But there was no danger of his doing that now, at Jim Wilkinson's retirement party. Although he had not eaten much all day, he had little appetite. He was anxious to get Cleo into a quiet corner and ask her what she had meant by the text she had sent him earlier, at the quayside.

But from the moment he arrived at the Wilkinsons' packed bungalow, Cleo had been engaged in conversation with a group of detectives from the Divisional Intelligence Unit and had given him no more than the briefest smile of acknowledgement.

What the hell was up with her? he fretted. She was looking more beautiful than ever this evening, and was dressed perfectly for the occasion in a demure blue satin dress.

'How are you doing, Roy?' Julie Coll, the wife of a chief superintendent in the Criminal Justice Department, asked, joining him at the buffet table.

'Fine, thanks,' he said. 'You?' He remembered suddenly that she'd had a mid-life change of career and had recently qualified as an air stewardess. 'How's the flying?'

'Great!' she said. 'Loving it.'

'With Virgin, right?'

'Yes!' She pointed at a bowl of pickled onions. 'Have one of those. Josie makes them herself – they're fab.'

'I'll go back to my seat – perhaps you could put some on my tray when you bring it over.'

She grinned at him. 'Cheeky sod! I'm not on duty now!' Then she speared a couple of onions and piled them on the heap on her plate. 'So, still no news?'

He frowned, wondering what she was referring to for a moment. Then realized. It never went away, however much he tried to forget. There were reminders of Sandy all the time.

'No,' he said.

'Is that your new lady over there? The tall blonde?'

He nodded, wondering how much longer she would be his lady.

'She looks lovely.'

'Thanks.' He gave a thin smile.

'I remember that conversation we had a while back, at Dave Gaylor's party – about mediums?'

He racked his brains, trying to think. He remembered Julie had lost a close relative and had picked his brains about a good medium to go to. He did vaguely remember they'd had a conversation, but could not recall any details.

'Yes.'

'I've just found a new one – she's really brilliant, Roy. Amazingly accurate.'

'What's her name?'

'Janet Porter.'

'Janet Porter?' The name did not ring a bell.

'I haven't got her number on me, but it's in the book. She's on the seafront, just near the Grand. Call me tomorrow and I'll give it to you. I think you'll be astonished.'

During the past nine years since Sandy's disappearance, Grace had lost count of the number of mediums he had been to. Most of them had been recommended highly, just like this one now. None of them had come up with anything positive. One had said that Sandy was working in spirit for a healer and that she was happy to be back with her mother. A slight problem with that one, Grace had decided, since her mother was still very much alive.

A small handful of the mediums, the ones he had found most credible, had been adamant that Sandy was not in the spirit world. Which meant, they explained, that she was not dead. He was left as baffled today as he had been on the night of her disappearance.

'I'll think about it, Julie,' he said. 'Thanks, but I'm sort of trying to move on.'

'Absolutely, Roy. I understand.'

She moved on too and for a few moments Grace had the buffet to himself. He eyed the new Chief Constable, Tom Martinson, who had only been in Sussex for a few weeks, wanting to ensure he got to chat to him. Martinson, who was forty-eight, was slightly shorter than himself, a strong, fit-looking man with short dark hair and a pleasant, no-nonsense air about him. At the moment he was busily tucking into his food, while engaging energetically in conversation with a group of brown-nosing officers who were surrounding him.

Grace forked a small slice of ham and some potato salad on to his plate, ate them on the spot and put the plate down, to avoid the hassle of walking around with it.

Then, as he turned around, Cleo was standing right behind him, a glass of what looked like sparkling water in her hand. In total contrast to how cold she had sounded over the phone, she was smiling warmly. Beaming.

'Hi, darling,' she said. 'Well done, you're not that late! How did it go?'

'Fine. Nadiuska's happy to wait until the morning to start the PM. How are you?'

Still smiling, she jerked her head, signalling him to follow. At that moment, he saw the Chief Constable break away from the group and head, alone, to the buffet table. This would be the perfect moment to introduce himself!

But he saw Cleo beckoning and did not want to risk her getting caught in another conversation with someone else. He was desperate to know what was going on.

He followed her, weaving through a packed conservatory, acknowledging greetings from colleagues with just a cursory nod. Moments later they stepped outside into the back garden. The night air felt even colder than at the harbour and was thick with the smell of cigarette smoke, wafting over from a mixed group of men and women who were standing in a huddle. The smoke smelled good and, if he'd had his cigarettes with him, he would have lit up. He could have done with one, badly.

Cleo pushed open a gate and walked a short distance down the side of the house, past the dustbins and into the carport at the front. She stopped by Wilkinson's Ford Focus estate. They were private here.

'Well,' she said, 'I've got some news for you.' She shrugged, twisting her hands, and he realized it wasn't for warmth but because she was nervous.

'Tell me?'

She twisted her hands some more and smiled awkwardly. 'Roy, I don't know how you are going to take this.' She gave him an almost childlike smile of bewilderment, then a kind of hopeful shrug. 'I'm pregnant.'

19

The tall man walked up the spiral staircase, then stopped at the top for a moment, checking that his valet-parking stub and his coat-check ticket were securely slotted inside his crocodile-skin wallet. Then he surveyed the Rendezvous Casino's high-value floor unhurriedly and thoroughly, taking it in the way a policeman might take in a room.

In his late forties, he had the lean physique of a man who works out. His face was craggy and his thinning jet-black hair was slicked back. He looked handsome under tonight's dimmed bulbs, but coarser in broad daylight. He was dressed in a black cashmere blouson jacket over an open-neck plaid shirt, with a heavy gold chain around his exposed neck, expensive jeans, Cuban-heeled snake-skin boots and, even though they were indoors and it was nearly ten o'clock at night, aviator sunglasses. On one wrist he wore a chunky gold chain-link bracelet and on the other a large Panerai Luminor watch. Although he looked, like he always did, as if he did not belong here but in some more flash establishment, he was one of the casino's regular high-rollers.

Chewing a piece of gum, he observed the four roulette tables, the blackjack tables, the three-card poker tables, the craps tables and the slots, his eyes behind those glasses scanning every face, then the restaurant at the far end, again scanning every diner, until he was satisfied. Finally he strode unhurriedly towards the table he liked, his regular table, his *lucky* table.

Four people were already playing and looked as if they had been there a while. One was a middle-aged Chinese woman who was another regular here; with her were a young couple who were dressed for a party they had either been to or were on their way to, and a stocky bearded man in a thick jumper who looked as though he would have been more at home in a geology lecture.

The wheel was spinning slowly, the ball rolling around the rim. The tall man laid £10,000 in bundles of £50 notes on the green baize roulette table, his eyes fixed on the male croupier, who gave him a nod, then said, 'No more bets.'

The ball tumbled off the rim, rattled and clacked, bouncing across the trivets, then was silent, settled in. Everyone, except for the tall man, craned to look as the wheel slowed further. Deadpan, the croupier said, 'Seventeen. Black.'

The number popped up on the electronic display screen behind the wheel. The Chinese woman, who had covered most of the table with chips, except for 17 and its immediate neighbours, swore. The young, slightly drunk girl, who was almost falling out of her black dress, gave a small whoop of joy. The croupier cleared away the losing chips, then prepared the payouts for the winning ones, paying the biggest first, while the tall man kept his eye on his bundle of notes.

Then the croupier took the bundle and counted the cash with practised hands. He almost did not need to, as he had done it countless times before and knew exactly how much it would be. 'Ten thousand pounds,' he said clearly, for the benefit of the punter and for the voice-recording equipment. The Chinese woman, who was in her fifties, gave the tall man a respectful glance. This was big money by this casino's standards. The croupier stacked up his chips.

He took them and began to play immediately, rapidly covering the twelve numbers of the Tier, as well as placing some on the outside of the layout on Odd, but the majority he put down on the previous six winning numbers as displayed on the electronic board by the wheel. He covered the numbers straight up as well as all splits and corners. In moments his chips covered large areas of the board, like pins marking conquered territory on a map. As the croupier moved to spin the wheel – he was under a direction to spin it every ninety seconds – the others scrambled to place their bets too, stretching across the table, stacking up their chips on top of those of other players.

The croupier gave the wheel a gentle spin and flicked the ball into play.

Down on the floor below, the report from the CCTV room operator was brief and clear in Campbell Macaulay's earpiece.

'Clint is here.'

'Usual place?' the casino director murmured, his lips barely moving.

'Table Four.'

Casinos had been Campbell Macaulay's world all his working life. He had risen up through the ranks, from croupier to pit boss to manager, eventually running them. He loved the hours, the atmosphere, the calm and the energy that coexisted inside all casinos, and he also liked the whole business side of it. Punters might have the occasional big win, just as they had the occasional big loss, but in the long term the business model was remarkably steady.

There were really only two things he disliked about his job. The first was having to deal with the compulsive gamblers who financially ruined themselves in his – and other – casinos. Ultimately, they did the industry no good. And equally he disliked the phone calls waking him in the middle of the night in his time off to tell him that a regular small-time player, or a complete stranger, had just put a huge bet – maybe £60,000 – on a table, because that was the kind of thing that occurred when you were becoming the victim of a gaming scam. Which was why anyone suspicious was carefully watched.

If you were a good gambler, and you understood everything about the game you were playing, you could greatly reduce the amounts you lost. In blackjack and in craps, gamblers who knew what they were doing could make it close to a level playing field between themselves and the casino. But most people did not have the knowledge, or the patience, which had the result of pushing the casino's profit margin from just the few percentage points of its advantage on most of the gaming tables, to an average 20 per cent of the amount a punter played with.

Immaculately coiffed, and dressed as he was every day and night in a quiet, dark suit, perfectly laundered shirt, elegant silk tie and gleaming black Oxfords, Macaulay glided almost unseen through the downstairs poker room of the Rendezvous Casino. This space was busy tonight, with one of the regular tournaments they held. Five tables, occupied by ten players each, just off the main room. The players were a shabby, slovenly bunch, wearing everything from jumpers and jeans to baseball caps and trainers. But they were all local people of substance and paid good entrance money.

When he had started his career, twenty-seven years earlier, most casinos had a smart dress code and he regretted the lack of elegance he saw today. But, in order to attract the punters, he understood the necessity of moving with the times. If the Rendezvous did not want these high-rollers, plenty of other casinos in the city would welcome them.

He took a brief walk through the busy, gleaming kitchen, nodding at the head chef and some of his underlings, watching a tray of prawn cocktail and smoked salmon platters heading out to the dining room, then went through into the main downstairs gambling room.

It was filling up. He cast his eye across the slots and it looked as if about two-thirds of them were busy. All the blackjack tables, the three-card poker tables, the roulette wheels and the craps table were in use. Good. There was often a lull in this pre-Christmas period, but business was building up nicely, with yesterday's takings up almost 10 per cent on the previous week.

He walked across the room, passing all the tables in turn, making sure that each croupier and pit boss saw him, then took the escalator up to the high-value room. As he alighted at the top, he saw Clint straight away, standing like a sentinel at his regular table.

Clint was here at least three nights a week, arriving around ten and leaving somewhere between two and four in the morning. They had given him that sobriquet because Macaulay's assistant, Jacqueline, once said he reminded her of the actor Clint Eastwood.

In the days before the smoking ban, like the actor in his early Westerns, Clint always had a slim cigar wedged between his lips. Now he chewed gum. Sometimes he came alone, sometimes he was accompanied by a woman – rarely the same woman, but they all seemed from the same mould. He was alone tonight. There had been one with him two nights ago, a tall, young, raven-haired beauty in a miniskirt and thigh-high leather boots, dripping with bling.

She looked, as they all did, as if she was being rented by the hour.

Clint always drove himself here in a black Mercedes SL55 AMG sports car, gave the valet-parking attendant a £10 tip when he arrived and the same when he left, regardless of whether he had won or lost. And he gave the same amount to the coat-check girl on arrival and on departure.

He never uttered more than a grunt or a monosyllabic word to anyone, and he always turned up with exactly the same amount of money, in cash. He bought his chips at the table, then at the end of the night handed them in at the downstairs cashier.

Although he bought £10,000 worth of chips, he bet only with £2,000 worth of them – but that was still ten times the amount of the average punter here. He understood the game and always bet big, but cautiously, on permutations that would give him small gains, but, equally, only small losses. Some nights he walked away up, some nights down. According to the casino's computer, he lost an average each month of 10 per cent of his initial stake. So, £600 a week, £30,000 a year.

Which made him a very good customer indeed.

But Campbell Macaulay was curious. When time permitted, he liked to watch Clint from the CCTV room. The man was up to something and he could not figure it out. He did not seem out to scam the casino – if that was his intention, Macaulay reckoned, he would have done it a long time ago. And most scamming tended to be at the blackjack tables, which, throughout his career, had been most vulnerable to fraud from card counters and bent croupiers. Money laundering was Macaulay's best guess about Clint. And if that was his game, it was not Macaulay's problem. Nor did he want to risk losing a good customer.

Traditionally, casinos had long been about cash. And casino operators did not like to grill their customers about the provenance of their money.

All the same, he did once, dutifully, mention his name to the head of the local police licensing team, Sergeant Wauchope. It was more to protect his own back, in case Clint was up to something illicit that he had failed to spot, than out of civic duty. His first loyalty was, and always had been, to the casino company, Harrahs, the Las Vegas giant, which had always looked after him.

The name that Clint used on the guest register here was Joe Baker, so it had come as a surprise when the Licensing Officer, returning the favour, had given him the privileged information that the Mercedes was registered to Joseph Richard Baker, an alias used by one Vlad Cosmescu.

That name meant nothing to Campbell Macaulay. But it had, for some considerable time, been on Interpol's radar. There was no warrant out for his arrest at this stage. He was merely listed on the files of several police forces as a *person of interest*.

20

Outside Bucharest's Gara de Nord, the chauffeur closed the door of the Mercedes with a solid *thud*. And for a moment, cocooned in the sudden silence of the interior of the car, on the big, soft seat, breathing in the rich smells of leather, Simona felt safe. The man who had rescued her entered on the far side and closed his door with the same *thud*.

Her heart thudded too.

The chauffeur climbed in the front and started the engine. The interior lights dimmed, then went off completely. As the car rolled forward, there was a sharp *clunk* beside her, like a door lock clicking, and she wondered what it was. Then she felt a sudden panic. Who was this man?

Seated on the other side of the big armrest, he smiled at her and, in a gentle, reassuring voice, asked, 'Are you OK?'

She nodded, bewildered by the events of the past few minutes.

'Are you hungry?' he asked.

She was still a little wary of him, and there was that smug expression she continued to dislike, but he did not look a bad person. There were strangers, rich strangers, who occasionally came up to you and gave you money or food. Not often, but it happened, the way it seemed to be happening now. She nodded.

'What is your name?'

'Simona,' she replied.

'What is your favourite food?'

She shrugged. She didn't know what her favourite food was. No one had ever asked her before.

'Do you like meat? Pork?'

She hesitated. 'Yes.'

'Potatoes?'

She nodded.

'Fried sausage?'

Again she nodded.

The man leaned forward, took a glass from a cabinet in front of him, poured whisky into it and gave it to her. She cupped the glass in her hand and took a long gulp. She stiffened in surprise at the deep, fiery sensation as it went down her throat. Then, moments later, she felt a pleasant, warm feeling ripple inside her. Stretching her legs out in front of her, she swallowed some more, draining the glass.

She had only drunk whisky once before, a bottle Romeo had stolen from a shop, but this tasted much better, much smoother.

The man's mobile phone rang. He answered it, at the same time pouring more whisky into her glass, then began talking business to someone in America. She knew it was America because he asked how the weather was in New York. He was negotiating some kind of a deal and it sounded important. But occasionally he turned and smiled at her, and each time, with each gulp of whisky she took, she trusted him more.

The driver, who had said nothing, piloted the car in silence. His hair was cropped to a light fuzz and she suddenly saw, in the flare of oncoming headlights, the top of a tattoo. It was a snake, its tongue forked as if striking, rising out of the right side of his shirt collar, curling around his neck and up towards his chin. Outside, the lights of

Bucharest glided past and rain pattered softly on the windows.

Simona had never been in a plane, but she wondered if this was what it felt like to fly. Music came from a speaker somewhere behind her head, a man singing. It sounded English or American, she could not tell which, a soft, rich voice. 'I've got you under my skin' was playing but she did not speak enough English to understand the meaning.

She looked out of the window, trying to get her bearings. They were passing the big place that Romeo told her the former president had built. He said it was called the People's Palace, but she had never been inside it. It belonged to another world, another kind of people, just the way this car, the man in the back seat and the music all belonged to another world that was beyond her reach, and beyond her comprehension.

But the whisky made it all fine. She liked the man more and more, liked this car, liked the city that she had traipsed through, cold and hungry, just a short while ago, that was now gliding past. Maybe, just maybe, this man could help her to change her life.

After a short while, the car turned down a street she did not recognize, then slowed. In front of her, electric gates slid open and they drove through them, stopping in front of a tall house with a floodlit entrance.

The driver opened Simona's door and took the empty glass from her hand. Feeling drunk and unsteady, she tottered out into the wind and rain. The man stepped out too, put an arm around her shoulder and gently encouraged her up stone steps to a front door, which was opened by a middle-aged woman dressed in a uniform, a maid, perhaps.

The house smelled of polish, like a museum.

'Her name is Simona,' the man said. 'She needs food and then a hot bath.'

The woman smiled at her. A kind smile. 'Follow me,' she said. 'Are you very hungry?'

Simona nodded.

They walked across a marble floor, along a hallway lined with fine paintings, statues and grand furniture, and into a huge, modern kitchen. A widescreen television on the wall was switched off. Simona stared around in wonder. She had never in her life been in a place so grand. It was like pictures she had seen in magazines and on the television in the homes she had once been in.

The woman told her to sit at a table, then moments later produced the finest plate of food Simona had ever seen. It was piled with roast pork, sausage, lard, cheese, pickled watermelon, tomatoes and potatoes, and accompanied by another plate with large, crusty bread rolls and a tumbler of Coca-Cola.

Simona ate with both hands, cramming the food into her mouth as fast as she could, scared that it would be taken away again before she had finished. The woman sat opposite her, watching her in silence, nodding encouragement occasionally.

'You live on the streets?' the woman asked at one point.

Simona nodded.

'How is it?'

Speaking while chewing, she said, 'We have a place under the heating pipe. It's OK.'

'But not enough food?'

Simona shook her head.

'When did you last have a bath?'

Simona shrugged, chewing a thick piece of crackling. A bath? She could not remember. Not since the last time she had run away from the hostel. Not for years. She washed from bottles of water from the street pipes, when it was not too cold.

'I have a beautiful bath waiting for you,' the woman said.

When Simona finished the plateful, the woman brought her another, this time a huge bowl-shaped doughnut covered in melting vanilla ice cream. Simona gulped it down, ignoring the spoon on the dish beside it. She tore it apart with her fingers and crammed it into her mouth, eating it faster and faster, then scooped every last drop of the ice cream from the plate with her hand and licked it off. Her stomach ached, she was so full, and her head was swimming with the whisky. She started to feel a little queasy.

The woman stood up and beckoned. Wiping her hands on her jogging suit, Simona followed her up a grand, curved marble staircase, then along a wide corridor, lined with more fine paintings, and into a bathroom that simply stopped her in her tracks. She stared around in awe.

It was almost impossibly beautiful and magnificent – and vast. And equally almost impossible to believe she was here, standing in it.

On the ceiling were paintings of clouds and angels. The walls and the floor were all in black and white marble tiling, and in the centre was a huge, sunken tub, big enough for several people, overflowing with bubbles, and surrounded by nude male and female marble statues on plinths.

'So beautiful,' she whispered.

The woman smiled. 'You are a lucky girl,' she said. 'Mr Lazarovici is a good man. He likes to help people. He is a very good man.'

She began helping Simona out of her clothes, until she

was naked. Then she took her hand, steadying her as she stepped into the hot – deliciously hot, almost too hot – water and sank down. The woman eased her head back, until her hair was under the water, then up a little and rubbed in a deliciously scented shampoo. She rinsed it off, then put more shampoo on and rinsed that off too.

Simona lay there, luxuriating in it, staring at the angels above her, wondering if this was what it was like to be an angel, the whisky and the food making her relaxed and drowsy despite her queasiness. She was close to drifting away as the woman soaped her, every inch of her body, then rinsed her off. Then she helped her out of the bath, wrapping her in a vast soft white towel, drying her carefully and thoroughly, before leading her through into an en-suite bedroom that was even more magnificent.

The centrepiece was a huge, canopied two-poster bed. Simona stared at erotic paintings of nudes in gilt frames all around the walls. Some were single females or males, some were couples. She took in a man and a woman making love. Two women entwined in oral sex. A man sodomizing another. There were tall windows, up to the ceiling, with rich, swagged drapes. A chaise longue and other fine furnishings.

'The room is OK for you?' the woman asked.

Simona smiled and nodded.

The woman removed the towel and helped Simona, who was becoming increasingly sleepy, into the silky white sheets of the bed. Then she left the room.

Simona lay there, bathed in soft light from two huge table lamps, and began drifting into sleep. After some minutes, she was not sure how long, the door opened. She opened her eyes instantly.

The man who had brought her here, Mr Lazarovici,

came in. He was naked beneath a black silk dressing gown that was open at the front and he had a massive erection below a large paunch.

As he walked towards the bed he said, 'How are you, my beautiful angel of the Gara de Nord?'

She felt a prickle of anxiety through her haze of wooziness.

'I'm great,' she murmured. 'Thank you so much for everything. I'm so tired.'

Then his erection was touching her left cheek. 'Suck him,' he said. His voice was cold and hard.

She looked at him, suddenly more awake and alert. There were dark rings around his eyes and menace in the inky blackness of his pupils.

'Suck him,' he repeated. 'Aren't you grateful to me? Don't you want to show me your gratitude?'

He climbed on to the bed and manoeuvred himself so that his erection and his balls were right over her face. Afraid, she put up her right hand and held the shaft, then took him in her mouth tentatively. It tasted of stale sweat.

Then she felt a stinging blow on her cheek. 'Suck him, bitch!'

She took him in deeper, closing her mouth around it, moving up and down the shaft.

'Owww! You fucking stupid woman, you want me to take your teeth out or something?'

She stared at him, wild-eyed, sobering fast.

Suddenly he pushed her chin away, pulling himself free. 'God, you ungrateful bitch!' Then, wrenching her shoulders harshly, causing her to cry out in pain, he turned her over, right over, until her face was buried in the pillow, and for a moment she thought he intended to suffocate her.

Then she felt his fingers probing her vagina and thought

she was going to throw up. She struggled to swallow the bile that rose in her throat. Then they moved from her vagina to her anus. Moments later she felt his erection trying to enter it.

Then, shrieking with pain, she felt him entering her. Further. Further.

'No! Gogu!' she screamed, almost choking on more bile. Further.

She felt as if she was splitting in two.

Further.

She shook her head, her whole body, in desperation, trying to break free. He grabbed a clump of her wet hair and banged her face hard into the pillow, so hard she could not breathe. Then entered her further. Further still.

She was whimpering. Crying. Calling, 'Gogu, Gogu, Gogu!' Struggling. Struggling against the pain. Struggling for breath.

'Fuck you, ungrateful little bitch,' he whispered into her ear.

She turned her face sideways, gulping down air, crying in agony.

'Fuck you, bitch!' he hissed.

His erection was getting even bigger. Busting her in half.

'Fuck you, fuck you, fuck you, bitch!' He smashed his fist into the side of her face. 'Fuck you, ungrateful little bitch from the gutters!'

He pushed even deeper inside her.

She screamed out again and he rammed her face hard against the pillow, holding her there, jamming her airways. She struggled, tried to lift her head, but he kept it down, hard. Panic seized her, through the pain. She shook, trying to move, but she was pinned, as if a spike had been rammed through her. She began shaking in the final throes of suffocation, her chest hurting so much she thought it would collapse. Then he jerked her head back and kissed her deeply on the lips, as she gulped in air, his air, from his lungs.

Then he broke his mouth away. 'Tell me you like this. Tell me you are grateful to me.' He held his face hard against her cheek. 'Tell me you are grateful to me for saving you. Say it. Say you are grateful! Say thank you!'

'I hate you!' she gasped.

He slammed the ball of his thumb against her cheek. Then he smashed his fist into her eye socket. He paused for a second before gripping her hair with both hands, so hard she was sure he was going to rip it from her scalp. He continued holding her hair as she felt him ejaculating inside her. Then she vomited.

*

Some time later, Simona did not know when – she had lost all track of time – she was in the back of the big black car once more. The same music she recognized from before was playing, that same rich voice singing those words of a song that had no meaning for her: 'I've got you under my skin'.

The same Bucharest night was gliding past the window. She hurt all over. The most terrible pains. Her face felt puffy. Her head hurt. When she had arrived at the Gara de Nord she had felt dirty all over. Now she felt clean all over, but dirty inside. Filthy.

She wanted to cry but she hurt too much. And she did not want this man with the snake tattoo, who was driving, who had not spoken one word, but kept looking at her in the mirror and smiling at her, a filthy, dirty lecherous smile, to have any encouragement from her.

She just wanted to go home. Home. Home to Romeo, to the dog, to the screaming baby. To the people who cared about her. To her family.

He was stopping the car. The street was dark, and she had no idea where she was. He was opening the rear door and climbing in. Pushing himself next to her. He had banknotes in his hand. 'Good money!' he said, grinning. He pressed them into her hand, then unzipped himself.

She stared at him as he wiggled his erection out of his trousers. Stared at the tattoo of the striking snake that rose from his shirt collar.

'Good money!' he said.

Then he grabbed her hair, just like the man had done, and pulled her face down on to his erection.

She closed her lips over the head, then bit, as hard as she could, until she could taste blood in her mouth, until her ears were ringing with his screams. Then she grabbed the door handle, pulled it down, pushed with all her strength, stumbled out and ran into the night.

She ran without stopping, lost and disoriented, through an endless maze of dark streets and closed shops, knowing that if she kept running, kept running, kept running, she would eventually find somewhere she recognized, some-where that would give her bearings and take her back to her home under the road.

In the blindness of her panic as she ran, she did not see that the black car, driven erratically but keeping a safe distance, was following her.

21

After driving for several minutes through the labyrinth of the Royal South London Hospital grounds, Lynn halted the Peugeot in frustration in the driveway outside the Emer-·gency entrance, as the way ahead was barred by a metal barrier. It was just after half past nine in the evening.

'Jesus!' she said, exasperated. 'How the hell is anyone supposed to find their way around here?'

It was the same every time; they always got lost here. Construction work was going on constantly and the liver unit was never in the same building twice – at least, that was how it seemed to her. And since the last time, a good two years ago, the whole traffic layout appeared to have changed.

She stared around in frustration at the institutional-looking buildings surrounding them. Tall monoliths, a mish-mash of architectural styles. Close to the car was a barrage of red, yellow and pale green signs and she had to strain to read them in the glow from the street lighting. None contained the name of the wing she was looking for, the Rosslyn Wing, which she had been told to access via the Bannerman Wing.

'Must be in the wrong place,' Caitlin said, without looking up from her texting.

'Is that what you think?' Lynn asked, more good-humouredly than she felt.

'Uh huh. Like, if we were in the right place, we'd be

there, wouldn't we?' She tapped her keys in furious concentration.

Despite her tiredness and her fear and her frustration, Lynn found herself grinning at her daughter's curious logic. 'Yes,' she said. 'Quite right.'

'I'm always right. Just have to ask me. I'm like the Oracle.'

'Perhaps the Oracle could tell me which way to go now.'

'I think you'll have to start by reversing.'

Lynn backed a short distance, then stopped alongside more signs. *Hopgood Wing*, she read. *Golden Jubilee Wing. Main Hospital Entrance. Variety Club Children's Outpatients.* 'Where the hell is Bannerman?'

Caitlin looked up from her texting. 'Chill, woman. It's like a television game, you know?'

'I hate it when you say that!'

'What, *television game*?' Caitlin teased.

'*Chill, woman!* OK? I don't like it when you say that.'

'Yep, well, you are so stressed. You're stressing me.'

Lynn looked behind her and began reversing again.

'Life's a game,' Caitlin said.

'A game? What do you mean?'

'It's a game. You win – you live, you lose – you die.'

Lynn brought the car to a sudden halt and turned to face Caitlin. 'Is that what you really think, darling?'

'Yep! They've hidden my new liver somewhere in this complex. We have to find it! If I find it in time, I live. If I don't, tough shit!'

Lynn giggled. She put an arm around Caitlin's shoulders and pulled her close, kissing her head, breathing in the scents of her hair shampoo and gel. 'God, I love you so much, darling.'

Caitlin shrugged, then in a deadpan voice said, 'Yep, well, I'm quite worth loving really.'

'Sometimes!' Lynn retorted. 'Only sometimes!'

Caitlin nodded, a resigned look on her face, and resumed her texting.

Lynn reversed out on to Crystal Hill, drove a short distance forwards and finally found the main entrance for vehicles. She turned left into it, passed a cluster of yellow ambulances parked outside the curved glass façade of an almost incongruously modern block, then finally saw the *Bannerman Wing* sign and turned right into the car park opposite a Victorian building that looked as if it might recently have had a facelift.

A couple of minutes later, carrying Caitlin's overnight holdall, she walked past a man wearing a coat over his hospital pyjamas who was sitting on a bench beside a floodlit statue, smoking a cigarette, and entered the columned entrance porch of Bannerman Wing. Caitlin, dressed in a lime-green hoodie, ripped jeans with frayed bottoms and untied trainers, trailed behind her.

There were twin vertical perspex signs in front of them, printed with the words ROYAL SOUTH LONDON, and a row of white columns stretching ahead down the hallway. To the right was a visitors' information desk, where a large black woman was on the phone. Lynn waited for her to finish the call, glancing around.

A bewildered-looking grey-haired man with a red holdall in one arm and a black handbag in the other was shuffling forwards in slippers. To her left, a cluster of people sat around in a waiting area. One, an old man, was in a motorized wheelchair. Another old man, in a beanie and tracksuit, sat slumped on a green stool, with a wooden walking stick out in front of him. A youth in a grey hoodie and jeans was plugged into an iPod. A young man, with despair on his face, wearing a blue T-shirt, jeans and trainers, was seated, bent forward, his hands clasped between his thighs, as if waiting for someone or some*thing*.

The whole place seemed filled with a late-night air of tired, silent desperation. Further along she saw a shop, like a small supermarket, selling sweets and flowers. A shell-suited elderly woman with blue-rinsed hair emerged, opening a chocolate bar.

The woman behind the desk ended her call and looked up pleasantly. 'Can I help you?'

'Yes, thank you. Shirley Linsell in the Rosslyn Wing is expecting us.'

'Can you give me your names?'

'Caitlin Beckett,' Lynn said. 'And her mother.'

'I'll tell her. Take the lift to the third floor and she'll meet you there.' She pointed down the corridor.

They walked along, past the shop, past signs reading, BUTT OUT, SMOKING BAN IN ALL NHS HOSPITALS and DON'T INFECT. PROTECT and past weary-looking, disoriented people coming in the opposite direction. Lynn had always been spooked by hospitals, remembering the countless visits to Southlands Hospital in Shoreham when her father had had a stroke. Other than maternity wards, hospitals were not happy places. Hospitals were where you went when bad things happened to you or to people you loved.

At the end of the corridor they reached an area, in front of the steel doors of the lift, that was bathed in an iridescent purple light. It was more like the light she would expect to find in a disco, or on the set of a science fiction film, Lynn thought.

Caitlin paused from her texting to look up. 'Cool,' she said with an approving nod. Then, in a breathless rush of excitement, 'Hey! You know what, Mum? This is a clue!'

'A clue?' Lynn questioned.

Caitlin nodded. 'Like *beam me up* from *Star Trek*, right?' Then she grinned mysteriously. 'They put this on for us.'

Lynn gave her daughter a quizzical look. 'OK. So why did they do that?'

'We find out on the third floor. That's our next clue!'

As they rode the slow lift, Lynn was pleased that Caitlin seemed to have perked up. All her life she had had strong mood swings and recently the disease had made them worse. But at least she was coming in here with a positive attitude, for the moment.

They stepped out on the third floor, to be greeted by a smiling woman in her mid-thirties. She was pleasant-looking, a classic English rose face framed with long, brown hair, and she was dressed in a white blouse, with a knitted pink top and black trousers. She gave Caitlin a warm smile first, then Lynn, then turned back to Caitlin. Lynn noticed she had a tiny burst blood vessel in her left eye.

'Caitlin? Hi, I'm Shirley, your transplant coordinator. I'm going to be looking after you while you are here.'

Caitlin eyeballed her levelly for some moments and said nothing. Then she looked down at her phone and resumed her endless texting.

'Shirley Linsell?' Lynn asked.

'Yes. And you must be Caitlin's mum, Lynn.'

Lynn smiled. 'Nice to meet you.'

'I'll take you along to your room. We've got a nice single room for you, Caitlin, for the next few days. And we've arranged an overnight room nearby for you, Mrs Beckett.' Addressing them both, she added, 'I'm here to answer any questions that you have, so please ask anything you like, anything at all that you want to know.'

Still looking down at her phone, Caitlin said, 'Am I going to die?'

'No, of course not, darling!' Lynn said.

'I wasn't asking you,' Caitlin said. 'I was asking Shirley.'

There was a brief, uncomfortable silence. Then the transplant coordinator said, 'What makes you think that, Caitlin?'

'I'd have to be pretty fucking stupid not to, wouldn't I?'

22

Roy Grace followed the tail lights of the black Audi TT, which was some distance ahead of him and drawing further away all the time. Cleo didn't seem to fully understand what speed limits were. Nor, as she approached the junction with Sackville and Nevill roads, what traffic lights were for.

Shit. He felt a stab of fear for her.

The light turned amber. But her brake lights did not come on.

His heart was suddenly in his mouth. Being T-boned by a car running a stop light produced some of the worst injuries you could have. And it was not only Cleo in that speeding car now. It was their child too.

The lights went red. A good two seconds later, the Audi hurtled through them. Roy gripped his steering wheel hard, fearing for her.

Then she was safely over and continuing along Old Shoreham Road, approaching Hove Park on her left.

He halted his unmarked Ford Focus estate at the lights, his heart hammering, tempted to call her, to tell her to slow down. But it was no use, this was how she always drove. She was worse, he had come to realize in the five months they had been dating, than his friend and colleague Glenn Branson, who had only recently passed his Police High Speed Pursuit test and liked to demonstrate his skills behind the wheel – or rather, lack of them – to Roy at every opportunity.

Why did Cleo drive so recklessly when she was so

meticulous in everything else she did? Surely, he reasoned, someone who worked in a mortuary and handled, almost every day, the torn and broken bodies of people killed on the roads would take extra care when driving. And yet one of the consultant pathologists for Brighton and Hove, Dr Nigel Churchman, who had recently transferred up north, raced cars at weekends. Perhaps, he sometimes thought, if you worked in such close proximity to death, it made you want to challenge and defy it.

The lights changed. He checked there was no one doing a Cleo coming across, then drove over the junction, accelerating, but mindful that there were two cameras on the next stretch of road. Cleo totally denied that she drove fast, as if she was blind to it. And that scared him. He loved her so much, and even more so tonight than ever. The thought of anything happening to her was more than he could bear.

For nearly ten years after Sandy vanished, he had been unable to form any relationship with another woman. Until Cleo. During all that time he had constantly been searching for Sandy, waiting for news, hoping for a call, or for her to walk in through the front door of their home one day. But that had begun to change now. He loved Cleo as much as, and maybe even more than, he had ever loved Sandy, and if she did suddenly reappear, no matter how good her explanation, he strongly doubted he would leave Cleo for her. In his mind and in his heart he had moved on.

And now this most incredible thing of all. Cleo was pregnant! Six weeks. Confirmed this morning, she had told him. She was carrying his child. Their child.

It was so ironic, he thought. In their life together before her disappearance, Sandy had been unable to conceive. The first few years they hadn't worried about it, having made a decision to wait a while before starting a family. But then, when they had begun trying, nothing had happened. During that last year before she had disappeared, they had both had fertility tests. The problem turned out to be with Sandy, some biochemistry to do with the viscosity of the mucus in her fallopian tubes that the specialist had explained in detail, and Roy had done his best to understand.

The specialist had put Sandy on a course of medication, although he had told her there was less than a 50 per cent chance of it working, and that had depressed her, making her feel inadequate. Sandy always liked to be in charge. Probably one of the reasons why she too had liked to drive fast, commanding the road, he thought. She was the one who created the Zen minimalist look inside their house and who designed the garden. She always made the arrangements when they went away. Sometimes he wondered if she had been more depressed than he had realized about her infertility problem. And whether that might have been the reason behind her disappearance.

So many unanswered questions.

But now the vacuum in his life was filled. Dating Cleo had brought him a sense of happiness he had never believed would be possible again. And now this news, this incredible news!

He saw her car ahead, this time stopped at the lights at the junction with Shirley Drive, where there was a safety camera.

Please, darling, please drive a little less crazily! Don't go and wipe yourself out in a wreck, just when I have found you. Just when life is beginning for us.

When life is growing inside you.

He saw her brake lights come on before the next camera and finally caught up with her car at the next lights. Then he followed her, right into Dyke Road and along to the

Seven Dials roundabout. Half past eleven on a Wednesday night and there were still quite a few people on the streets, in this densely populated area.

Instinctively checking out every face, he soon saw someone he recognized, a ragged, small-time drug dealer and police informant, Miles Penney, shambling along, head bowed, cigarette dangling from his lips. From his slow pace it did not look as if he was on his way either to score or to sell tonight, and besides Grace didn't care what he did. So long as Penney didn't rape or murder anyone, he was part of another division's set of problems.

He followed Cleo on down past the railway station, then through the network of narrow streets of the North Laine district, filled with its mix of terraced houses, individual shops, cafés and restaurants, and antiques dealers, until she found a resident's parking space near her home. Grace pulled up on a single yellow line in sight of her car and got out, casting a wary eye around for any moving shadows, feeling doubly protective of Cleo all of a sudden.

He followed her through the gates of the converted warehouse building where she had her town house, and put an arm around her as she pressed the entrance keypad.

She wore a long black cape over her dress, and he slipped his hand inside it and pressed the palm against her stomach.

'This is amazing,' he said.

She stared at him with wide-open, trusting eyes. 'Are you sure you're OK with this?'

He slipped his hand out of her cape, then cupped her face in both his hands. 'With all my heart. I'm not just OK with this, I'm incredibly happy. But – I don't know how to express it. This is one of the most incredible things ever.

And I think you will be a wonderful mother. You will be amazing.'

'I think you will be a wonderful father,' she said.

They kissed. Then warily, because it was late and dark, he glanced around again, checking the shadows. 'Just one thing,' he said.

'What?'

'Your driving is something else. I mean, Lewis Hamilton, eat your heart out!'

'That's a bit rich coming from a man who drove his car over Beachy Head!' she said.

'Yep, well, I had a good reason for that. I was in a pursuit situation. You just did eighty in a forty limit and shot a red light for no reason at all.'

'So? Book me!'

They stared into each other's eyes. 'You can be such a bitch at times,' he said, grinning.

'And you can be such an anal plod!'

'I love you,' he said.

'Do you, Grace?'

'Yes. I adore you and I love you.'

'How much?'

He grinned, then held her close and whispered into her ear. 'I want you inside, naked, then I'll show you!'

'That's the best offer I've had all night,' she whispered back.

She tapped out the numbers. The gate lock clicked and she pushed it open.

They walked through, across the cobbled yard and up to her front door. She unlocked it and they went inside, straight into a scene of utter devastation.

A black tornado hurtled through the mess and launched

itself into the air, hitting Cleo in her midriff and almost knocking her over.

'Down!' she yelled. 'Humphrey, down!'

Before Grace had a chance to prepare himself, the dog head-butted him in the balls.

He staggered back, winded.

'HUMPHREY!' Cleo yelled at the labrador and border collie-cross.

Humphrey ran back into the devastation that had been the living room and returned with a length of knotted pink rope in his mouth.

Grace, getting his breath back and wincing from the stabbing pain in his groin, stared around the normally immaculate, open-plan room. Potted plants were lying on their sides. Cushions had been dragged off the two red sofas and several were ripped open, spilling foam and feathers everywhere across the polished oak floor. Partially chewed candles lay on their sides. Pages of newspaper were strewn all around, and a copy of *Sussex Life* magazine lay with its front cover half torn off.

'BAD BOY!' Cleo scolded. 'BAD, BAD BOY!'

The dog wagged his tail.

'I AM NOT HAPPY WITH YOU! I AM VERY, VERY ANGRY. DO YOU UNDERSTAND?'

The dog continued to wag his tail. Then he jumped up at Cleo once more.

She gripped his face in her hands, knelt and bellowed at him. 'BAD BOY!'

Grace laughed. He couldn't help it.

'Fuck!' Cleo said. She shook her head. 'BAD BOY!'

The dog wriggled himself free and launched himself at Grace again. This time the Detective Superintendent was prepared and grabbed his paws. 'Not pleased with you!' he said.

The dog wagged his tail, looking as pleased as hell with himself.

'Oh fuck!' Cleo said again. 'Clear this up later. Whisky?'

'Good plan,' Grace said, pushing the dog away. It came straight back at him, trying to lick him to death.

Cleo dragged Humphrey out into the backyard by the scruff of his neck and shut the door on him. Then they went into the kitchen. Out in the yard, Humphrey began howling.

'They need two hours' exercise a day,' Cleo said. 'But not until they are a year old. Otherwise it's bad for their hips.'

'And your furniture.'

'Very funny.' She chinked ice cubes into two glass tumblers from the dispenser in the front of her fridge, then poured several fingers of Glenfiddich into one and tonic water into the other. 'I don't think I should be drinking anything,' she said. 'How virtuous is that?'

Grace felt badly in need of a cigarette and checked his pockets, but he remembered he had deliberately not brought any with him. 'I'm sure the baby won't mind a wee dram or two. Might as well get him or her used to the stuff at an early age!'

Cleo handed him a tumbler. 'Cheers, big ears,' she said.

Grace raised his glass. 'Here goes, nose.'

'Up your bum, chum!' she completed the toast.

He drained his glass. Then they stared at each other. Outside, Humphrey was still howling. *Him or her.* He hadn't thought about that. Was it a boy or a girl? He didn't mind. He would worship that child. Cleo would be a wonderful mother, he knew that, unquestionably. But would he be a good father? Then he followed Cleo's gaze across at the mess.

'Want me to clear up?' he asked.

'No,' she said. Then she kissed him very slowly and very sensually on the lips. 'I'm badly in need of an orgasm. Do you think you might be up for that?'

'Just one? Could do that with my eyes shut.'

'Bastard.'

23

Vlad Cosmescu chewed his gum, his eyes following the ivory ball skittering across the trivets of the roulette wheel. It made a steady rattling sound at first, then clack-clack-clacked as the wheel slowed, followed by sudden silence as it dropped into a slot.

24. Black.

Adjusting his aviator glasses on the bridge of his nose, he stared with a satisfied smile at his stack of £5 chips straddling the line between 23 and 24, then watched the croupier scoop away the losing chips from other numbers and combinations, including several of his own. Shooting his cuff, he glanced at his watch and observed that it was ten past twelve. So far it was not going well; he was down £1,800, close to his self-imposed limit for a night's outlay. But maybe, with this win on his Tier strategy, his second in two consecutive spins, his luck was turning.

Cosmescu stacked half his winnings with the rest of his remaining chips, then joined in with the other players at the table – the reckless Chinese woman who had been playing all the time he had been there, and several others who had recently arrived – in laying out their new bets. By the time the wheel had been spinning for several seconds and the croupier had called out 'No more bets', almost every number was covered in chips.

Cosmescu always used the same two systems. For safety he played the Tier, betting on the numbers which made up a one-third arc of the wheel opposite zero. You would not win a lot with this system, but normally you didn't lose a lot either. It was a strategy that enabled him to stay at the table for hours, while he worked on refining his own system, which he had been developing patiently over some years. Cosmescu was a very patient man. And he always planned everything with extreme care, which was why the phone call he was about to get would upset him so much.

His system was based on a combination of mathematics and probability. On a European roulette table there were thirty-seven numbers. But Cosmescu knew that the odds against all thirty-seven of those numbers coming up on thirty-seven consecutive spins of the wheel were millions to one against. Some numbers would come up twice, or three, or even four times within a few spins, and sometimes even more than that, while others would not come up at all. His strategy, therefore, was only to bet on numbers, and com-binations of numbers, that had already come up, as some of those, for sure, would be coming up again.

Looking at the number 24 again, he pressed his big toe down twice on the pressure pad inside his right boot, then he pressed six times inside his left boot. Later, when he got home, he would download the data from the memory chip in his pocket into his computer.

The system was still a long way from perfect and he continued to lose on plenty of occasions, but the losses were getting smaller, in general, and less frequent. He was sure he was close to cracking it. Then, if he did, he would make his fortune. And then . . . well, he would not need to be anyone's hired lackey. Besides, hey, if he didn't, it all helped to pass the time. He had plenty of that on his hands. Too much.

He lived a lonely life in this city. He worked from his apartment, a big glass and steel place, high up, central, and he kept himself to himself, deliberately not mixing with others. He waited for his orders from his overlord, then, when he carried them out, he would wash some of the cash here in the casino, as instructed. It was a good arrangement. His *sef*, or boss, needed someone he could trust, someone who was tough enough to do the jobs but would not try to rip him off. And they both spoke the same language.

Two languages, in fact. *Romanian* and *Money*.

Vlad Cosmescu had few interests outside money. He never read books or magazines. Occasionally he'd watch an action film on television. He thought the Bourne films were OK, and he liked *The Transporter* series too, because he identified with Jason Statham's loner character in those. He watched the occasional sex film too, if he was with one of his girls. And he worked out, two hours a day, in a large gym. But everything else bored him, even eating. Food was simply fuel, so he ate when he needed to, and just sufficient, never more. He had no interest in the taste of food and did not understand the British obsession with cookery shows on television.

He liked casinos because of the money. You could see it in casinos, you could breathe it, smell it, hear it, touch it, and you could even taste it in the air. That taste was more delicious than any food he had ever eaten. Money brought you freedom, power. The ability to do something about your life and your family's life.

It had given Cosmescu the ability to take his handicapped sister, Lenuta, out of a *camin spital*, a state home-hospital tucked away in the village of Plataresti, twenty-five miles north-east of Bucharest, and into a beautiful home in hills above Montreux in Switzerland, overlooking Lake Geneva.

When he had first seen her, ten years ago, after a lot of

enquiries and a lot of bribes to find her, she was classed as an *irrecupable*. She was lying in an old, caged cot, eleven years old, eating only milk and crushed grain. With her skeletal figure and pot belly from starvation, and ragged strip of cloth as a nappy, she looked like a victim in a concentration camp.

There were thirty cots in that cramped room, with vertical bars, side by side and jammed next to each other, like animal cages in a laboratory. The stench of vomit and diarrhoea was overpowering. He watched stronger children, all retarded in some way, all still on the same bottled milk with crushed grain, despite the fact that some were in their mid-teens, if not older, swigging their liquid food then sticking their arms through the bars of their cages and taking the bottles from the younger, weaker ones – and being ignored by the solitary carer, who sat in her office, unqualified and unable to cope.

As the ball rattled over the metal slots of the wheel again, Cosmescu's mobile phone, on silent, vibrated. He slipped it out of his pocket, at the same time clocking the winning number, 19. *Shit.* That was a bad number for him, a total loss on that one. He moved a short distance from the table, entering the number with his toes, and looked at the display. It was a text from the *sef*.

> *Want to speak right now.*

Cosmescu slipped out of the casino and crossed the car park, making his way towards the Wetherspoon's pub, where he knew there was a payphone downstairs. When he reached it, he texted its number on his mobile phone, then waited. Less than a minute later, it rang. It was noisy in the packed pub and he had to hold the phone close to his ear.

'Yes?' he said.

'You've screwed up,' the voice at the other end said. 'Big time.'

Cosmescu talked for several minutes before returning to his table at the casino. When he did so, his concentration was gone. His losses increased, passing his limit, growing to £2,300 and then £2,500. But instead of stopping, anger drove him. Anger and gambler's folly.

By twenty past three in the morning, when he finally decided to call it quits, he was just over £5,000 down. His worst loss ever on a single night.

Despite that, he still tipped the coat-check girl and the valet-parking guy their regular, crisp, fresh £10 note each.

24

Roy Grace, dressed in his tracksuit, baseball cap and jogging shoes, let himself out of Cleo's front door just before half past five. In the glow of the street lights, the pre-dawn darkness was an amber mist and a cold wind blew salty drizzle on to his face.

He was burning with excitement and had barely slept, thinking about Cleo and the baby growing inside her. It was an incredible feeling. If he had been asked to put it into words he could not, at this moment, have done so. He felt a strange sense of empowerment, or responsibility, and, for the first time in his career, a shift in his priorities.

He walked across the yard and let himself out of the gate, glancing up and down the street, checking for anything that might look wrong. Every police officer he had ever met was the same. After a few years of being in the force you automatically clocked everything around you, constantly, whether you were in a street, a shop or a restaurant. Grace jokingly called it a *healthy culture of suspicion*, and there were plenty of times in his career when that had served him well.

As he set off on this late November Thursday morning, feeling more protective of Cleo than ever, nothing he saw on the deserted streets of Brighton aroused any suspicion in him. Ignoring the pain in his back and ribs from his car roll-over, he ran along the narrow pedestrianized cobbles of Kensington Gardens, past its cafés and boutiques, a second-hand furniture store and an antiques and bric-à-brac market, then along Gardner Street, past Luigi's, one of the shops where Glenn Branson, his self-appointed style guru, insisted on taking him from time to time to spruce up his wardrobe.

As he reached deserted North Street, he saw headlights and heard the roar of a powerful engine. Moments later a black Mercedes SL sports coupé flashed past, its driver barely visible through the darkened windows. A tall, lean male figure was the sense of him that Grace got, but that was all. He wondered what the man was doing out at this hour. Returning from a party? Rushing to a ferry port or airport? You didn't see many expensive cars this early in the morning. Mostly it was the cheaper cars and vans of manual workers. There were, of course, any number of legitimate reasons why the Mercedes would be on the road, but all the same he memorized the number: GX57 CKL.

Crossing over, he ran on through the narrow streets and alleys of the Lanes and then finally reached the seafront promenade. It was deserted except for a solitary man walking an elderly, plump dachshund. Limping less as he warmed up, he ran down the ramp, past the front of a large nightclub, the Honey Club, which was dark and silent, then stopped for some moments and touched his toes several times. Then he stood still, breathing in the tangs of the beach, of salt, oil, putrid fish, boat varnish and rotting weed, listening to the roar and sucking of the sea. The drizzle felt like cooling spray against his face.

This was one of the places he loved most in the city, down at sea level. Especially now, early morning, when it was deserted. The sea had a hold on him. He loved all of its sounds, smells, colours and changing moods; and especially the mysteries it contained, the secrets it sometimes yielded, such as the body last night. He could never imagine living somewhere landlocked, miles away from the sea.

The Palace Pier, one of the great landmarks of the city, was still lit up. New owners had changed its name to Brighton Pier a few years back, but to him and to thousands in the city it would always be the *Palace* Pier. Tens of thousands of bulbs burned along its length, along the roof-tops of its structures, making the helter-skelter look like a beacon rising into the sky, and he wondered, suddenly, how long it would be before the pier was obliged to switch everything off at night to save energy.

He turned left and ran towards it, and then into the shadows beneath its dark, girdered mass – the place where, twenty years ago, he and Sandy had had their first kiss. Would his child one day kiss his – or her – first date here too, he wondered, as he emerged on the far side. He covered a further half-mile, then headed back to Cleo's house. A short circuit today, just over twenty minutes, but it left him feeling refreshed and energized.

Cleo and Humphrey were still asleep. He had a quick shower, microwaved the bowl of porridge Cleo had left out for him, gulped it down while flicking through the pages of yesterday's *Argus*, then headed off to the office, pulling into his parking space at the front of Sussex House, the CID headquarters, at a quarter to seven.

If he didn't get interrupted, he would have a clear hour and a half to deal with his overnight emails and the most urgent of the paperwork before heading to the mortuary for the post-mortem on the Unknown Male, as the body hauled up by the dredger was named at this moment.

First he logged on to the computer and ran his eye over the overnight serials. It had been a quiet night. Among the highlights were a street robbery on a male in Eastern Road, an office break-in, a drunken brawl at a wake at a council estate in Moulescoomb, a trailer overturned on the A27, and six cars broken into in Tidy Street. He paused to read that item thoroughly, as it was just around the corner from Cleo's home, but the report did not say much. He moved on to a fight at a bus stop on the London Road in the early hours, then the reported theft of a moped.

All minor stuff, he noted as he continued, scanning the entire list. Moments later he heard his door open, followed by an all-too-familiar voice.

'Yo, old-timer! You come in early, or are you just leaving for the night?'

'Very funny,' Grace said, looking up at his friend – and now permanent lodger – Glenn Branson, who looked, like he always did, as if he was all suited and booted to go partying. Tall, black, his shaved head shiny as a snooker ball, the Detective Sergeant was a sharp dresser. Today he wore a shiny grey three-piece suit, a grey and white striped shirt, black loafers and a crimson silk tie. He was holding a mug of coffee in his hand.

'Heard you were bigging it up with the new CC last night,' Branson said. 'Or should I say brown-nosing?'

Grace smiled. He'd been so excited by Cleo's news that he had struggled to think of anything intelligent to say to the Chief Constable when he'd finally had a few moments with him at the party, and he knew he had failed to make the impression on him that he had hoped for. But that didn't matter. Cleo was pregnant! Carrying *their* child. Did anything else really matter? He would have loved to tell Glenn the news, but he and Cleo had agreed last night to keep it quiet. Six weeks was too soon; a lot could happen. So instead he said, 'Yep, and he's very concerned about you.'

'Me?' Glenn said, looking worried suddenly. 'Why? What did he say?'

'It was something about your music. He said that any-one with your taste in music would make a crap police officer.'

For a moment, the DS frowned again. Then he jabbed a finger towards Grace. 'You bastard!' he said. 'You're winding me up, right?'

Grace grinned. 'So, what news? When do I get my house back?'

Branson's face fell. 'You throwing me out?'

'I could murder a coffee. You could make me a coffee in lieu of the next month's rent. Deal?'

'Bargain. Could have this one but it's got sugar in it.'

Grace wrinkled his face in disapproval. 'Kills you, that stuff.'

'Yeah, well, sooner the better,' Branson said bleakly, and disappeared.

Five minutes later Branson was sitting on one of the chairs in front of the Detective Superintendent's desk, cra-dling his mug of coffee. Grace peered dubiously at his. 'Did you put sugar in this?'

'Oh shit! I'll make you another.'

'No, it's OK. I won't stir it.' Grace stared at his friend, who looked terrible. 'Did you remember to feed Marlon?'

'Yeah.' He nodded pensively. 'Me and Marlon, we've bonded. We're like soulmates.'

'Really? Well, don't get too close to him.'

Marlon was the goldfish Grace had won at a fairground nine years ago and the fish was still going strong. It was a surly, antisocial creature that had eaten every companion he'd bought for it. Although the six-foot two-inch detective sergeant was probably beyond even that greedy creature's appetite, he decided. Then he quickly glanced back at the screen, noting a sudden update on the cars broken into in

Tidy Street. Two youths had been arrested breaking into a car directly beneath a CCTV camera around the corner, in Trafalgar Street.

Good, he thought with some relief. Except they would probably be released on bail and be back on the streets again tonight.

'Any developments in the Branson household?'

A few months ago, in an attempt to salvage his marriage, Branson had bought his wife, Ari, an expensive horse for eventing, using compensation he had received for an injury. But that turned out to have resulted in little more than a brief truce in a terminally hostile relationship.

'Any more horses?'

'I went over last night to see the kids. She told me I'll be getting a letter from her solicitor.' Branson shrugged.

'A divorce lawyer?'

He nodded glumly.

Grace's sadness for his friend was only slightly tempered by the realization that this meant Branson would be lodging at his house for a considerable time to come – and he did not have the heart to throw him out.

'Maybe we could have a drink tonight and chat?' Branson asked.

Much though he loved this man, Grace responded with a less than enthusiastic, 'Yup, sure.' His chats with Glenn about Ari had become interminable, always going over and over the same ground. The reality was that Glenn's wife not only no longer loved him, but didn't even *like* him. Privately, Grace thought she was the kind of woman who would never be satisfied with what she had in any relationship, but each time he tried to tell his friend that, Glenn responded defensively, as if he still believed there was a solution, however elusive.

'Actually, tell you what, mate,' Grace said, 'are you busy this morning?'

'Yeah – but nothing that can't wait a few hours. Why?'

'Got a body hauled up by a dredger yesterday. I put DI Mantle in charge, but she's on a course up in Bramshill Police College today and tomorrow. Thought you might like to come to the post-mortem.'

Branson's eyes widened as he shook his head in mock disbelief. 'Boy, you really know how to treat someone when they're down, don't you! You're going to cheer me up by taking me to see a floater having a post-mortem, on a wet November morning. Man, that's guaranteed to be a laugh a minute.'

'Yep, well, it might do you good to see someone worse off than yourself.'

'Thanks a lot.'

'Besides, Nadiuska's performing it.'

Quite apart from her professional skills and her cheery personality, Nadiuska De Sancha, the forty-eight-year-old Home Office pathologist, was a striking-looking woman. A statuesque redhead with Russian aristocratic blood, she looked a good decade younger than her years and, despite being happily married to an eminent plastic surgeon, enjoyed flirting and had a wicked sense of humour. Grace had never encountered any officer in the Sussex Police Force who did not fancy her.

'Ah!' Branson said, perking up suddenly. 'You didn't tell me that bit!'

'Not that you are so shallow it would have made any difference to your decision.'

'You're my boss. I do whatever you tell me.'

'Really? I've never noticed.'

25

Sergeant Tania Whitlock shivered as a cold draught blew steadily in through the window beside her desk. The right side of her face felt as if it was turning to ice. She sipped some hot coffee and glanced at her watch. Ten past eleven. The day was already almost half gone and the piles of reports and forms on her desk that she had to fill in were still alarmingly high. Outside a steady drizzle fell from grey skies.

The window gave her a view across the grass runway and parking area of Shoreham Airport, the oldest civil airport in the world. Built in 1910, on the western extremity of Brighton and Hove, it was now mostly used by private aircraft and flying schools. Some years ago an industrial estate had been developed on land at the edge of the airport, and it was in one of these buildings, a converted warehouse, that the Specialist Search Unit of Sussex Police was based.

Tania had barely heard the drone of an aero engine all morning. Hardly any planes or helicopters had taken off or landed. It seemed that this weather didn't inspire anyone to go anywhere, and the low cloud ceiling discouraged inexperienced pilots with only visual flight rating.

Please let it continue to be a quiet day, she thought, then turned her attention back to her current task. It was a standard statement form for the Coroner, with space for diagrams, detailing how members of her team had dived last Friday, in Brighton Marina, to recover the body of a yachtsman who had missed his footing, apparently drunk, according to witnesses, and fallen off his gangplank with an outboard motor strapped to his back.

Twenty-nine years old, the sergeant was short and slim, with an alert, attractive face and long dark hair. Wrapped up at this moment in a blue fleece jacket for warmth, over her uniform blue T-shirt, baggy blue trousers and work boots, she looked fragile and delicate. No one meeting her for the first time would have guessed that for the previous five years before her posting here, she had been a member of Brighton and Hove Police's elite Local Support Team, the front-line police officers who carried out raids and arrests, dealt with public disorder and any other situation where violence was anticipated.

The Specialist Search Unit comprised nine police officers. One, Steve Hargrave, had been a professional deep-sea diver before joining the force. The others had trained at the Police Dive School in Newcastle. One member of the team was an ex-Marine, another a former traffic cop – and a legend in the force because he had once booked his own father for not wearing a seat belt. Tania, the only female, headed the unit, which had, by anyone's definition, the grimmest task in the entire Sussex Police Force.

Their role was to recover dead bodies and human remains, and to search for evidence in locations which were considered beyond the abilities or too hazardous or too grim for regular police officers. Most of their work involved finding victims underwater – in canals, rivers, lakes, wells, the sea – but their remit had no limits. Among the previous twelve months' highlights – or lowlights, depending on perspective – her team had recovered forty-seven separate body parts from a particularly horrific car smash, in which six people had died, and the incinerated remains of four people from a light air-craft crash. Partially obscuring the view of parked private planes from her window was a trailer, in police livery, containing sufficient body bags to cope with a wide-bodied-airliner disaster.

Humour helped to keep the unit sane, and every member had a nickname. Hers was Smurf, because she was small and turned blue underwater. Of all the people she had worked with since joining the police, ten years ago, this team was just the greatest. She liked and respected each of her colleagues, and the feeling was mutual.

The building in which they operated housed their diving equipment, including a large Zeppelin inflatable capable of carrying the entire team, a drying room and their lorry, which was equipped with everything from climbing to tunnelling apparatus. They were on permanent standby, 24/7.

Most of the space in Tania's small, cluttered office was filled with filing cabinets, on the front of one of which was a massive yellow radiation-warning sticker. A whiteboard above her desk listed in blue and turquoise marker pen all immediate priorities. Beside it hung a calendar and a photograph of her four-year-old niece, Maddie. Her laptop, plastic lunch box, lamp, phone and piles of files and forms took up most of the space on her desk.

During the winter months it was permanently freezing cold in here, which was why she had her fleece jacket on. Despite the asthmatic wheezing of the blower heater at her feet, her fingers were so cold she was finding it hard to grip her ballpoint pen. It would feel warmer at the bottom of the English Channel, she thought.

She turned the page of the dive log, then made more notes on the form. Suddenly her phone rang, distracting her, and she answered it a little absently.

'Sergeant Whitlock.'

Almost instantly she switched to full attention. It was Detective Superintendent Roy Grace, from HQ CID, and it was unlikely that he would be calling for a chat about the weather.

'Hi,' he said. 'How's things?'

'Fine, Roy,' she said, transmitting more enthusiasm than she actually felt today.

'Did I hear a rumour that you got married not long ago?'

'In the summer,' she said.

'He's a lucky guy!'

'Thank you, Roy! I hope someone tells him! So – what can I do for you?'

'I'm at Brighton mortuary – we're doing a Home Office PM on a young male hauled up yesterday by the dredger, *Arco Dee*, about ten miles south of Shoreham Harbour.'

'I know the *Arco Dee* – it operates mostly out of Shoreham and Newhaven.'

'Yes. I think I'm going to need you guys to take a look and see if there's anything else down there.'

'What information can you give me?'

'We have a pretty good fix on the position where they found it. The body was wrapped in plastic and weighted down. It could be a burial at sea, but I'm not sure about that.'

'Presumably the *Arco Dee* hauled it up from a designated dredge area?' she said, starting to make notes on her pad.

'Yes.'

'There's a specific charted area for burials at sea. It's possible a body could drift from there in the currents, but unlikely if it was a professional burial. Want me to come over?'

'If you wouldn't mind?'

'I'll be there in half an hour.'

'Thanks.'

As she hung up, she grimaced. She'd been planning to leave early today to get home to cook her husband, Rob, a special meal tonight. He loved Thai food and she'd stopped and bought everything she needed on the way in – including some fresh prawns and a very plump sea bass. Rob, a pilot with British Airways long haul, was home tonight before going away again for nine days. By the sound of it, her plans had just headed out the window.

Her door opened and Steve Hargrave, nicknamed Gonzo, peered in. 'Just wondered if you were busy, chief, or if you had a couple of minutes for a chat.'

She gave him an acidic smile that could have dissolved a steel girder in less time than it took for him to register her displeasure.

Raising a finger as he started retreating, he said, 'Not a good moment, right?'

She continued smiling.

26

Who are you? Roy Grace wondered, staring down at the naked body of Unknown Male, who was laid out on his back on the stainless-steel table in the centre of the post-mortem room, beneath the cold glare of the overhead lights. Someone's child. Maybe someone's brother too. Who loves you? Who will be devastated by your death?

It was strange, he thought. This place used to give him the creeps every time he came here. But that had all changed when Cleo Morey arrived as the new Senior Anatomical Pathology Technician. Now he came here eagerly, at any opportunity. Even in her blue gown, green plastic apron and white rubber boots, Cleo still looked incredibly sexy.

Maybe he was just perverse, or perhaps it was true what they said about love blinding you.

It struck him that mortuaries shared something in common with lawyers' offices. Not many people, other than their staff, came to mortuaries because they were happy. If you were an overnight guest here, it meant you were pretty seriously dead. If you were a visitor, it meant that someone you knew and loved had just died, suddenly, unexpectedly and quite often brutally.

Housed in a long, low, grey pebbledash-rendered bungalow, just off the Lewes Road gyratory system and adjoining the beautiful, hillside setting of Woodvale Cemetery, Brighton and Hove City Mortuary consisted of a covered receiving bay, an office, a multi-faith chapel, a glass-sided viewing room, two storage areas, recently refurbished with wider fridges to accommodate the increasing trend of obese cadavers, an isolation room for suspected deaths from AIDS and other contagious diseases, and the main post-mortem room, where they were now.

On the far side of the wall he heard the whine of an angle-grinder. Building work was going on to extend the mortuary.

The greyness of the day outside was grimly matched by the atmosphere in here. Grey light diffused through the opaque windows. Grey tiled walls. Brown and grey speckled tiles on the floor that were a close match to the colour of a dead human brain. Apart from the blue surgical gowns worn by everyone in here, and the green plastic aprons of the mortuary staff and the pathologist, the only colour in the whole room was the bright pink disinfectant in the upended plastic dispenser by the washbasin.

The post-mortem room reeked, permanently and unpleasantly, of Jeyes Fluid and Trigene disinfectant – sometimes compounded by the stomach-churning, freshly unblocked-drain stench that came from opened-up cadavers.

As always with a Home Office post-mortem, the room was crowded. In addition to himself, Nadiuska and Cleo, there were Darren Wallace, the Assistant Mortuary Technician, a young man of twenty-one who had started life as a butcher's apprentice; Michael Forman, a serious, intense man in his mid-thirties, who was the Coroner's Officer; James Gartrell, the burly forensic photographer; and a queasy-looking Glenn Branson, who was standing some distance back. Grace had observed several times in the past that, despite the Detective Sergeant's big, tough frame, he always had a problem at post-mortems.

Unknown Male's flesh was a waxy off-white. It was the colour Roy Grace had long associated with bodies in which the life forces had ceased, but on which decomposition had not yet begun to present, to the naked eye at least, its hideous processes. The winter weather and the cold of the seawater would have helped to delay the onset, but it was clear that Unknown Male had not been dead for long.

Nadiuska De Sancha, her red hair clipped up, tortoise-shell glasses perched on her finely sculpted nose, estimated that death had probably occurred four or five days ago – but she was not able to get closer than that. Nor was she able to establish, for the moment at any rate, the precise cause of death, largely on account of the fact that Unknown Male was short of most of his vital organs.

He was a good-looking young man, with close-cropped, downy black hair, a Roman nose and brown eyes that were fixed open. His body was lean and bony – but from under-nourishment rather than exercise, Grace judged from the lack of muscle tone. His genitals were modestly covered by the fleshy triangle of skin from his sternum, which had been removed and placed there by Nadiuska, as if to afford him some dignity in death. The flesh of his chest and stomach, either side of the massive incision running down his midriff, was clamped back, revealing a startlingly hollow ribcage, with the intestines, like shiny, translucent rope, coiled beneath.

On the wall to their left was a chart for listing the weight of the brain, lungs, heart, liver, kidneys and spleen of each cadaver examined in here. There was a dash against each item, except for the brain, the only vital organ the cadaver still possessed, and very likely to be the only one that would go to his grave with him.

The pathologist removed his bladder, laid it on the metal dissecting tray, which was on raised legs above the cadaver's thighs, then made one sharp incision to open it. She carefully bottled and sealed samples of the fluid that poured out, for tests.

'What's your assessment so far?' Grace asked her.

'Well,' she said, in her exquisite broken English, 'the cause of death is not absolute at this moment, Roy. There's no petechial haemorrhaging to indicate suffocation or drowning, and with the absence of his lungs I can't say for sure at this point if he was dead prior to immersion. But I think we can surmise, from the fact that his organs were removed, that was pretty likely.'

'Not many surgeons operate underwater,' Michael Forman quipped.

'I don't have much to go on from the stomach contents,' she continued. 'Most of it has been dissolved by the digestion process, although that slows post-mortem. But there are some particles of what looks like chicken, potato and broccoli – so that indicates he was capable of eating a proper meal in the hours preceding death. That is not really consistent with his absence of organs.'

'In what way?' Grace asked, conscious of the inquisitive eyes of the Coroner's Officer and Glenn Branson.

'Well,' she said, and waved her scalpel down his opened midriff. 'This is the kind of incision a surgeon would make if he was harvesting organs from a donor. All the internal organs have been surgically excised, by someone experienced. Consistent with this is the fact that the blood vessels have all been tied off with sutures before being cut through to remove the organs.' She pointed. 'The perinephric fat that would have been around the kidneys – the *suet*, if you are a cook – has been opened with a blade.'

Grace reminded himself not to eat suet for a long time to come.

'So,' Nadiuska continued, 'all this would indicate that he was an organ donor. Now, what directs me even more towards this possibility is the presence of these external indications of medical intervention.' She pointed again. 'A needle mark in the back of the hand.' She gestured at the neck. 'A puncture mark.' Then she pointed at the right elbow. 'Another puncture mark in the antecubital fosse. These are consistent with the insertion of cannulae for drips and drugs.'

Then, taking a small torch, she gently levered open the dead man's mouth with her gloved fingers and shone the beam in. 'If you look closely you can see reddening and ulceration to the inside of the windpipe, just below the voice box, which would have been caused by the balloon inflated on the end of the endotracheal ventilator tube.'

Grace nodded. 'But he ate a meal of solids – he couldn't have done that with an endotracheal tube, right?'

'Absolutely right, Roy,' she said. 'I don't understand this.'

'Perhaps he was an organ donor who was subsequently buried at sea, and then carried by currents away from the burial zone?' Glenn Branson suggested.

The pathologist pursed her lips. 'It's a possibility. Yes,' she concurred. 'But the majority of organ donors tend to be on life support for a period of time, during which they would be intubated and on intravenous drip feeds. It is odd to me that there is undigested food in his stomach. When I do the tox screen, that may show up muscle relaxants and other drugs that would be used for the removal of organs for transplant.'

'Can you give me an approximation of how many hours from when he had eaten until he died?

'From the state of the food, four to six at maximum.'

'Couldn't he have died suddenly?' Grace asked. 'A heart attack, or a car – or maybe motorbike – accident?'

'He doesn't have injuries consistent with a serious accident, Roy. He has no head or brain trauma. A heart attack or an asthma attack is a possibility, but considering his age – late teens – both, I would say, are a little improbable. I think we could be looking for some other cause.'

'Such as?' Grace scribbled a sudden note on his pad, thinking of something that would need following up.

'I can't speculate at this stage. Hopefully lab tests will tell us something. If we could get his identity, that might help us also.'

'We're working on that,' he said.

'I'm sure it is the lab tests that will provide the key. I think it is very unlikely that the tapings are going to produce anything, as he wasn't in waterproof wrapping,' the pathologist went on. Then she paused briefly, before adding, 'There is one other thought. This food in the stomach. In the UK, because there is no automatic organ harvesting without consent, it does often take many hours from brain death for consent to be obtained from next of kin. But in countries where there is just an opt-out, like Austria and Spain, then the process can be much quicker. So it is possible that this man is from one of those countries.'

Grace thought about this. 'OK, but if he died in Spain or Austria, what is he doing ten miles off the coast of England?'

There was a shrill ring on the doorbell. Darren, the Assistant Mortuary Technician, hurried out of the room. A couple of minutes later he returned with Sergeant Tania

Whitlock, from the Specialist Search Unit, gowned and in protective boots.

Roy Grace brought her up to speed. She asked to see the plastic sheeting and weights in which the body had been found, and Cleo took her out into the storage area to show her. Then they returned to the post-mortem room. The Home Office pathologist was busy dictating notes into her machine. Grace, Glenn Branson and Michael Forman were standing near the cadaver. The photographer walked out to the storage area to start working on close-ups of the wrapping and binding.

'Do you think he could have drifted in the currents from a designated burial-at-sea area?' Grace asked Tania.

'It's possible,' she said, breathing in through her mouth, trying to ignore the stench. 'But those weights are pretty heavy, and we've had mild weather conditions recently. I can get you a plot done, showing where it might have come from with lesser weights on, if that would be helpful.'

'It might be. Could it be a burial at sea where they got the position wrong?'

'A possibility,' she said. 'But I've checked with the *Arco Dee*. They found him fifteen nautical miles east of the designated Brighton and Hove burial-at-sea site. It would be a pretty big error.'

'That's what I'm thinking too,' he said. 'We have a fairly precise position where he was brought up from, right?'

'Very accurate,' the Sergeant said. 'To within a couple of hundred yards or so.'

'I think we should take a look at what else might be down there, as quickly as possible,' Grace said. 'Do you have time to start today?'

Tania looked at the clock on the wall and then, as if

mistrusting it, at her chunky diver's watch. Next she glanced at the window. 'Sunset is about four o'clock today,' she said. 'Ten miles out in the Channel, the sea's going to be quite choppy – we'd need to rent a bigger dive boat than our inflatable for working out there. We have about three hours of daylight left. What I suggest is we get a dive boat sorted for first light in the morning – this time of year there are a few deep-sea fishing charter boats that don't have many customers. We can start at dawn. But in the mean-time, we can get out to the area in the inflatable and buoy it off, to make sure the dredgers don't disturb anything else down there.'

'Brilliant!' he said.

'That's what we're here for!' she said, feeling a lot more cheerful than when she had arrived. She could get all that organized and still make it home in time to prepare the meal.

Turning to Glenn Branson, Grace said, 'You look a bit peaky.'

He nodded. 'Yeah. Does it to me every time, this place.'

'You know what you need?'

'What?'

'A spot of sea air! A nice cruise.'

'Yeah. A cruise would be very nice.'

'Good!' Grace gave him a pat on the back. 'You're going on one tomorrow morning with Tania.'

Branson screwed up his face and pointed at the window. 'Shit, man, the forecast's crap! I thought you meant the Caribbean or something!'

'Start with the Channel. It's a good place to get your sea legs.'

'I haven't even got any yachting gear!' he moaned.

'You won't need any, you'll be larging it on the first-class deck!'

Tania eyed Glenn dubiously. 'The forecast's not great. Are you a good sailor?'

'No, I'm not,' he said. 'Believe me!'

27

There had been no deterioration in Nat's condition over-night, which was one blessing, Susan thought, trying to find positive things as she sat on her long vigil beside his bed. But there had been no improvement either. He continued to be a silent stranger, propped up at his thirty-degree angle, wired and plumbed into the almost bewildering array of life-support and monitoring apparatus.

The round institutional clock on the wall said ten to one. Nearly lunchtime, which would not mean much to Nat, or to most of his fellow patients here in the ITU. The nutrients entered his body all day and night through a constant trickle down the nasogastric tube. And suddenly, despite her tiredness, Susan smiled at a thought. She was always chiding Nat for being late for meals. His hours as a medic at the hospital were utterly erratic and often, with no prior warning, he had to stay on late into the night. But even when he was at home, he always had *just one more email to check, darling!* whenever she called out to him that lunch or dinner was on the table.

Well, at least you are not late for your meals in here, she thought, and smiled again wistfully. Then she sniffed, pulled a tissue from the pocket of her jacket and dabbed away tears that were rolling down her cheeks.

Shit. This cannot be how it ends. Surely not?

As if in agreement, or to give her reassurance, the baby kicked inside her.

'Thank you, Bump,' she whispered.

Since the consultant, dressed in an open-necked shirt and grey trousers, accompanied by a group of gowned medics, had finished his round half an hour or so ago, the ITU seemed eerily quiet. Almost the only sounds were the alarms going off every few minutes, sounds that were increasingly getting on Susan's nerves. There were alarms on the vital-signs monitors of each of the patients.

Despite the fact that there was one nurse on duty for every patient in here, the place seemed deserted. There was some activity going on behind the drawn blue curtains of the bed opposite, and Susan could see a woman polishing the floor, a yellow warning sign saying CLEANING IN PRO-GRESS set out near her. A couple of beds along, a physiotherapist was massaging the legs of an elderly, wired and intubated man. All the patients were silent, some sleeping, some staring vacantly. Susan had seen several visitors come and go, but at the moment she was the only one on the ward itself.

She heard again the almost musical *beep-beep-bong* of an alarm, like the chimes on an aircraft from an irritated passenger trying to summon a stewardess. It was coming from somewhere out of sight, over on the far side of the ward.

Nat was in Bed 14. The beds in here were numbered from 1 to 17. But, in fact, there were only sixteen beds in this unit. Because of superstition, there was no Bed 13. So Bed 14 was actually Bed 13.

Nat was a good doctor. He thought about everything, analysed everything, rationalized everything. He had no truck with superstition of any kind. Whereas Susan had always been very superstitious. She didn't like to see a single magpie without spotting a second one, or to stare at a new moon through glass, and she would never, ever, knowingly walk under a ladder. She was not at all happy that he was in this particular bed. But the ward was full, so she could hardly ask for him to be swapped with someone else.

She stood up, stifling a yawn, and walked a couple of paces to the end of the bed, where the nurse's laptop sat on a trolley. Yesterday had been a long day. She'd stayed here until close on midnight, then had driven home and tried to sleep, but after a few fitful hours, she'd given up. Instead she had showered, made herself a strong coffee, collected some of Nat's Eagles and Snow Patrol CDs and his wash things, as the nurse had suggested, and driven back.

The iPod headset had been plugged into his ears for several hours now, but so far he had shown no response. Usually, even seated in his den, he swayed, nodded his head, rolled his shoulders, waved his arms around in slow motion whenever he played his music. He was a great dancer on the occasions when he let his hair down. She remembered being mesmerized by his timing when he'd rock 'n' rolled with her the first time they'd danced together, at a nurse's birthday party.

Now she stared at him. At the ribbed, see-through endotracheal tube in his mouth. At the tiny probe in his skull, taped in place, that measured his intracranial pressure. At all the other stuff taped to him and cannulated into him. At the hump from the cage raising the weight of his bedclothes off his broken legs. She looked at the main monitoring screen, at the spikes and waveforms indicating the state of his vital signs.

Nat's heart rate was currently 77, which was OK. His blood pressure, 160 over 90, was OK too. His oxygen saturation levels were fine. The ICP moved between 15 and 20. In a normal person it should be below 10. Above 25 would be a concern.

'Hello, Nat, darling,' she said, and touched his right arm, above the identity tag and the plasters holding the drip lines in place. Then she gently removed the iPod earpieces and put her mouth close to his right ear, trying to sound as cheerful and positive as she could. 'I'm here with you, my darling. I love you. Bump's been kicking quite a bit. Can you hear me? How are you feeling? You're doing OK, you know! You are hanging in there. You are doing fine! You are going to be absolutely fine!'

She waited some moments, then replaced the earpieces again and walked around the white swivel hoist which held several pieces of apparatus, including the syringe pumps that supplied the drugs keeping him stable and sedated, and his blood pressure up. She continued along the blue linoleum floor, past the blue curtains on the rail behind the bed and up to the window, with its blue venetian blinds. Then she stared down to her left, at a long line of traffic queuing for the car park. Directly below her was a modern, paved courtyard, with benches and picnic tables, and a tall, smooth sculpture that she found creepy, because it looked like a ghost.

She was crying again. Then, as she dabbed her eyes, she heard that damn alarm again. But much louder than before. *BEEP-BEEP-BONG.*

She turned. Stared at the waveforms on the monitor, feeling a sudden, terrible panic. 'Nurse!' she called, looking around, bewildered, then running towards the nursing station. 'Nurse! Nurse!'

The volume of the alarm was increasing every second, deafening her.

Then she saw the big, cheery, bald male nurse, who had come on duty at half past seven that morning, sprinting past her towards Nat, his face a mask of anxiety.

28

The baby had been quiet for several hours and now it was Simona who was crying. She lay, holding Gogu tight to her face, curled up beside the heating pipe. She sobbed, slept a little, then woke and sobbed again.

All the others, except for Valeria and the baby, were out. On the crackly music system, Tracy Chapman was singing 'Fast Car'. Valeria often played Tracy Chapman; the baby seemed to like her music and went quiet, as if the songs were lullabies. Outside, up on the road above them, it was a cold, wet day, rain on the verge of sleet, and an icy draught blew in down here. The flames of the candles, jammed on to stalagmites of melted wax on the concrete floor, guttered, making the shadows jump.

They had no electricity, so candles provided the only light and they used them sparingly. Sometimes they bought them with money they got from selling stuff they stole, or with the cash from picking pockets and snatching hand-bags, but mostly they shoplifted them from mini-markets.

On occasions when they were desperate – although Simona really did not like doing this – they stole candles from Orthodox churches. Working with Romeo, distracting onlookers, they would cram their pockets full of the thin, brown candles, the ones bereaved people paid for and lit for their loved ones, placing them in large three-sided metal boxes; one box for the living and the other for the dead.

But she was always scared that God would punish them

for this. And as she lay sobbing now, she wondered if that had been God's punishment last night.

She had never been to church, and no one had ever taught her how to pray, but the carer at the home she had been in had told her about God, that he watched her all the time and would punish her for every bad thing that she did.

Beyond the yellow glow of the flames, where the shadows never moved, darkness stretched away into the distance, until the tunnel housing the pipe ended at the point where the pipe surfaced and then ran overground across the suburb of Crângaşi. There were whole communities of street people there, she had seen, who lived in shanty villages, in makeshift huts built against the pipe. Simona had lived in one for a while herself, but inside it was small and cramped, and the roof let the rain in.

She preferred to be here. There was more space and it was dry. Although she never liked to be here entirely alone – she had always been afraid of that darkness beyond the candles, and the mice and rats and spiders it contained. And something else, far worse.

Romeo used to explore the darkness, but he never found anything, other than skeletons of rodents and, once, a broken supermarket basket. Then, one day, Valeria had brought a man back here. She regularly had men here, screwing noisily and openly, not caring who saw. But this particular man spooked them all. He had a ponytail, a silver cross hanging from his neck, and he carried a Bible. He did not want to sleep with her, he told her. He wanted to talk to them all about God and the devil. He told them that the devil lived in the darkness beyond the candles, because, like them, the devil needed the warmth of the pipes.

And he told them that the devil was watching them all, and they were damned because of their sins, and they should be careful when they slept, in case he crawled out of that darkness and snatched one of them.

Simona called out suddenly, 'Valeria, is God punishing me?'

Valeria left the baby asleep, on a bed made from a quilted jacket, and walked across to Simona, crouching to avoid hitting her head on the rivets that protruded from the cross-girders supporting the road above them. She was dressed in the same clothes as always, emerald puffa over her gaudy-coloured jogging suit, her lank brown hair hanging as straight as laces either side of her haunted face. Then she put an arm around Simona.

'No, that was not God punishing you. It was a bad person, just a bad person, that's all.'

'I don't want this life any more. I want to go away from here.'

'Where do you want to go?' she asked.

Simona shrugged helplessly, then began sobbing again.

'I want to go to England,' Valeria said. She smiled wistfully, and her face suddenly came alive. She nodded. 'England. We are in the EU now. We can go.'

Simona continued to sob for some minutes, then she stopped. 'What is the EU?'

'It's a thing. It means Romanian people can go to England.'

'Would it be better in England?'

'I met some people a while ago who were going. They had jobs as erotic dancers. Big money. Maybe you and I could be erotic dancers.'

Simona sniffed. 'I don't know how to dance.'

'I think there are other jobs. You know, in bars, restaurants. Maybe in a bakery even.'

'I'd like to go,' Simona said. 'I'd like to go now.' She

sniffed. 'Will you come with me? Maybe you and me and Romeo – and the baby, of course.'

'There are people who know. I have to find someone who can help. Do you think Romeo will want to come too?'

She shrugged. Then behind them, they heard Romeo's voice.

'Hi! I'm back and I have something!'

He jumped down from several rungs up the ladder and walked over to them, dripping wet and panting, his hood up over his head. 'I ran,' he said. 'Long way. Several places, you know, watched me, they got to know us. I had to go a long way. But I got it!' His huge, saucer-like eyes were smiling brightly as he dug his hand inside his jacket and pulled out the pink plastic bag.

He stopped and coughed violently for some moments, then removed a squat, plastic bottle of metallic paint and twisted the lid to snap the seal.

Simona watched him, everything else suddenly gone from her mind.

He poured a small amount of the paint into the bag, then, holding it by the neck, passed it to her, making sure she had a good grip on it before letting go.

She brought the neck to her mouth, blew into it, as if inflating a balloon, then inhaled deeply through her mouth. She exhaled, then inhaled deeply again. And a third time. Now, suddenly, her face relaxed. She gave a distant smile. Her eyes rolled up, then down, glazing over.

For a short while, her pain was gone.

*

The black Mercedes drove slowly along the road, tyres sluicing through the rain, windscreen wipers *clop-copping*. It passed a small, run-down mini-market, a café, a butcher's, an Orthodox church covered in scaffolding, a car wash, with three men hosing down a white van, and a cluster of dogs, their fur ruffled by the wind.

Two people sat in the back of the car, a neat-looking man in his late forties, wearing a black coat over a grey, roll-neck jumper, and a woman, a little younger, with an attractive, open face beneath a tangle of fair hair, who wore a fleece-collared leather jacket over a baggy jumper, tight jeans and black suede boots, and big costume jewellery. She looked as if she might once have been a minor rock star, or an equally minor actress.

The driver pulled over in front of a decrepit high-rise building, with laundry hanging from half the windows and a dozen satellite television dishes fixed to the bare walls, and turned off the engine. Then he pointed through the windscreen at a jagged hole where the road met the pavement.

'There,' he said. 'That's where she lives.'

'So there's likely to be several of them down there,' the man in the back said.

'Yes, but careful of the one I told you about,' the driver said. 'She's feisty.'

With the wipers off, the steady droplets of rain were fast turning the screen opaque. Passers-by became blurred shapes. That was good. On top of the blacked-out windows, that would make it even harder for anyone to see in. The cars in this neighbourhood were beat-up wrecks. Every person walking past was going to notice the gleaming S-Class Mercedes, and wonder what it was doing here and who was inside.

'OK,' the woman said. 'Good. Let's go.'

The car pulled away.

Beneath the tarmac under its tyres, the baby slept.

Valeria read a newspaper that was several days old. Tracy Chapman was singing 'Fast Car' again. Romeo held the neck of the plastic bag in his mouth, exhaling and inhaling.

Simona lay on her mattress, serene now, her head full of dreams of England. She saw a tall clock tower called Big Ben. She dropped cubes of ice into a glass, then poured in whisky. Lights glided past her. The lights of a city. People in that city smiled. She heard laughter. She was in a huge room with paintings and statues. It was dry in this room. She felt no pain in her body or her heart.

When, a long time later, she woke, her mind was set.

29

Lynn Beckett woke with a start. For some moments she had no idea where she was. Her right leg felt numb and her back ached. She stared, bewildered, at a cartoon on a television set that was mounted on a wall high up above her, suspended on a metal arm. On the screen, a man was being strapped to a catapult and aimed at a brick wall. Moments later he flew through it, leaving the wall intact but with an imprint of himself, like a stencil.

Then she remembered, and began gently pummelling her thigh, trying to get the circulation going. She was in Caitlin's private room, off a small ward in the liver unit of the Royal South London Hospital. She must have drifted off. There was a faint smell of food. Mashed potatoes. As well as disinfectant and polish. Then she saw Caitlin beside her, lying in bed in her nightdress, her hair tousled, staring as ever at her mobile phone, reading something on the display. Beyond her, through the window of the small room, Lynn saw part of a crane, and the breeze blocks and spikes of a building under construction.

Despite having been allocated a bedroom, she had slept here last night, beside Caitlin. At one point, in agony from the cramped position of the chair, she had climbed into the bed and slept, curled up against her daughter, like spoons.

They had been woken at some horribly early hour and Caitlin had been wheeled off for a scan. Then, a while later, she had been wheeled back. Different nurses had come in and taken blood samples. At nine Lynn, feeling grungy and unwashed, had phoned work, telling her tough but kind team manager, Liv Thomas, that she did not know when she would be back. Liv was understanding about it, but suggested Lynn might want to work some extra hours in the following week to keep on target. Lynn said she would do her best.

And she sure as hell needed the money. It was costing her a fortune to be up here: £3 a day for Caitlin's access to the TV and phone service; £15 per day to park; the cost of eating in the hospital canteen. And all the time running the risk of her employers deciding enough was enough and sacking her. She had used the entire, modest divorce settlement with Mal for the down payment on the house she now lived in with Caitlin, wanting to give her a proper home, to raise her with as much normality and security as possible. But it had been, and continued to be, a worrying financial stretch for her. As an additional worry, she was faced with having to come up with the money to fix her car, to get it through the imminent MOT.

Her job paid well, but her pay was performance-related, like a salesman's. She needed to put in the hours to reach her targets and there was always the lure of a weekly bonus to the best performer. She took home, in a normal week, a lot more than a secretary/receptionist or a PA could earn in Brighton and Hove, and as she had no formal qualifications she considered herself lucky. But by the time she had paid the household bills and for petrol, Caitlin's guitar lessons and all the stuff Caitlin had to have, like her mobile to keep in contact with her friends, and laptop and her clothes, as well as a few luxuries, like their bargain package holiday this summer to Sharm el Sheikh, she was left with very little. In addition, she was forever having to top up Caitlin's empty current account. Her eight years at the debt collection agency had given her a morbid fear of owing money and for that reason she hated having to use credit cards herself.

Mal had at least been fair on the divorce settlement, and he did help out a little with his daughter, but Lynn was too proud to consider asking him for more. Her mother did what she could as well, but money was tight for her too. At the moment, Lynn had just over £1,000 put aside, which she had been saving all year, determined to give Caitlin a good Christmas – not that she was ever sure whether her daughter really connected to Christmas. Or to birthdays. Or to anything, really, that she had always considered *normal life*.

She wasn't sure she could risk leaving Caitlin today and driving back to Brighton for work. Caitlin was not happy about being here and was in one of her strange moods, more angry than afraid. If she left her, she was scared her daughter might check herself out. She glanced at her watch. It was ten to one. On the screen, the man was in a house, making angry faces and puffing himself up. He ran out, straight through the front door, taking the whole front of the house with him. Despite herself, Lynn grinned. She'd been a sucker for cartoons all her life.

Caitlin was now tapping keys on her phone.

'I'm sorry, darling,' her mother said. 'I drifted off.'

'Don't worry about it,' Caitlin said, grinning suddenly, without taking her eyes from her phone. 'Old people need their sleep.'

Despite her woes, Lynn laughed. 'Thanks a lot!'

'No, really,' Caitlin said with a cheeky grin. 'I just saw a programme about it on television. I thought about waking

171

you, cos you ought to see it. But, you know, as it was about old people needing their sleep, I thought it was better not to!'

'You cheeky monkey!' Lynn tried to move, but both her legs had stiffened up.

There was a grinding roar of construction machinery outside. Then the door opened and the transplant coordinator they had met last night came in.

Today, rested and in daylight looking even more the English rose, Shirley Linsell was wearing a blue sleeveless cardigan over a white blouse and dark brown slacks.

'Hi,' she said. 'How are we today?'

Caitlin ignored her, continuing to text.

'Fine!' Lynn said, resolutely rising to her feet and pounding her dead thighs with both fists. 'Cramp!' she said, by way of explanation.

The transplant coordinator gave her a brief, sympathetic smile, then said, 'The next test we are going to do is a liver biopsy.' Walking across to Caitlin, she went on, 'You are busy – got a lot of messages?'

'I'm sending out instructions,' Caitlin said. 'You know, like what to do with my body and stuff.'

Lynn saw the shock on the coordinator's face and the quizzical look on her daughter's, that expression she so often had where it was impossible to tell if she was joking or being serious.

'I think we have plenty of options for making you better, Caitlin,' Shirley Linsell said in pleasant tone that did not patronize Lynn's daughter.

Caitlin pressed her lips together and looked up with a wistful expression. 'Yeah, well. Whatever.' She shrugged. 'Best to be prepared, right?'

Shirley Linsell smiled. 'I think it's best to be positive!'

Caitlin rocked her head sideways a few times, as if weighing this up. Then she nodded. 'OK.'

'What we'd like to do now, Caitlin, is to give you a small local anaesthetic, then we will take a tiny amount of your liver out with a needle. You won't feel any pain at all. Dr Suddle will be here in a minute to tell you more about it.'

Abid Suddle was Caitlin's consultant. A youthful, handsome thirty-seven-year-old of Afghan descent, he was the one person who, in Lynn's view, Caitlin always seemed comfortable with. But he wasn't always around, as the medical team were constantly being rotated.

'You won't take too much, will you?' Caitlin asked.

'Just the tiniest amount.'

'You know, like, I know it's fucked. So I sort of need whatever I've got left.'

The coordinator gave her a strange look, again uncertain whether Caitlin was joking.

'We'll take the absolute minimum we need. Don't worry. It's a minute amount.'

'Yep, well, I'll be pretty pissed off if you take too much.'

'We don't have to take any,' the coordinator assured her gently. 'Not if you don't want us to.'

'Right, cool,' Caitlin said. 'That would mean Plan B, right?'

'Plan B?' the transplant coordinator queried.

Caitlin spoke, still staring at her phone. 'Yep, if I decide I don't want your tests.' Her expression was blank, unreadable. 'That would be Plan B, wouldn't it?'

'What do you mean exactly, Caitlin?' Shirley Linsell asked gently.

'Plan B means I die. But, personally, I think Plan B is a pretty crap plan.'

30

After the post-mortem on Unknown Male, Roy Grace drove back to CID headquarters. He spent the entire journey talking on his hands-free to Christine Morgan, the Donor Liaison Sister at the Royal Sussex County Hospital, learning as much as he could about the human organ transplant process, in particular the administration of the supply of organs and donation procedures.

He finished the call as he drove into the car park at the front of Sussex House, manoeuvred around a parking cone marking off a space reserved for a visitor and pulled into his parking slot. Then he switched off the engine and sat, deep in thought, puzzling over who this dead young man was and what might have happened to him. Rain rattled on the roof and pattered on the windscreen, steadily covering it, turning the white wall in front of him into a shimmering, blurry mosaic.

The pathologist was convinced the organs had been professionally, surgically removed. The young man's heart, lungs, kidneys and liver were gone, but not his stomach, intestines or bladder. From her own experience with organ donor bodies she had processed through the mortuary, Cleo had confirmed that families of donors often gave consent for those items, but wanted the eyes and skin retained.

The big inconsistency remained that Unknown Male had eaten a meal only hours before. A maximum of six hours before, the pathologist had estimated. Christine Morgan had just told him that even in the event of the sudden death of a victim who was on the National Organ Donor Register and carrying a donor card, it was extremely unlikely, to the point of pretty much an impossibility, that the organs would be harvested so quickly. There was paperwork to be signed by the next of kin. Matching recipients to be found on the databases. Specialist surgical organ recovery teams to be dispatched from the different hospitals where the organs would be taken for transplant. Normally the body, even if brain-stem dead, would be kept on life-support systems, to keep the organs perfused with blood, oxygen and nutrients until removed, for many hours, and sometimes days.

The timing was not absolutely impossible, she told Roy. But she had never experienced a situation where things had happened so quickly, and the young man had definitely not been in her hospital.

He picked up his blue, A4 notebook from the passenger seat, rested it against the steering wheel and wrote *AUSTRIA? SPAIN? OPT-OUT COUNTRIES?* Was it really a possibility that Unknown Male was an Austrian or Spanish organ donor buried at sea? Austria was a landlocked country. And if he was from Spain could he have drifted over 100 miles in just a few days?

Improbable enough to be discounted at this stage.

He felt hungry suddenly and glanced at the car clock. It was quarter past two. He never normally had much of an appetite after a post-mortem, but it had been a long time since his early-morning bowl of porridge.

Turning up the collar of his raincoat, he sprinted across the road, climbed over a low but awkward brick wall, ran up the short, muddy track and through the gap in the hedge, the standard shortcut to the ASDA superstore which served as Sussex House's unofficial canteen.

*

Ten minutes later he was seated at his desk and unwrapping a dismally healthy-looking salmon and cucumber sandwich. Some while back Cleo had started quizzing him on what he ate when he wasn't with her, knowing his tendency for junk food while at work and that for the past nine years he had survived on microwaved instant meals at home.

So at least he could look her in the face tonight and tell her he had eaten a Healthy Option sandwich. He would just conveniently omit the Coke, the KitKat and the caramel doughnut.

He quickly glanced through the post his MSA, Eleanor, had piled on his desk. On the top was a typed note in response to the Police National Computer registration plate check he had requested on the Mercedes he had seen earlier this morning, GX57 CKL. It was registered to a Joseph Richard Baker at an address he recognized as a high-rise block close to the seafront, behind the Metropole Hotel. The name was vaguely familiar but nothing that ran up any flags. There was no marker on the vehicle. There was a Joe Baker who had long been around the seedier side of Brighton, running saunas and massage parlours. It figured he would be out late and in a flash set of wheels.

He turned his attention to his emails, noting a few that needed urgent replies, then logged on to the serials. As he glanced through them, noting the usual domestics, muggings, break-ins, moped thefts and RTCs, but not major incidents, he took a bite of the sandwich, wishing he had gone for the All Day Breakfast option of a triple-decker egg, bacon and sausage wedge instead. Then, unscrewing the cap of the Coke, he remembered his promise yesterday to the *Argus* reporter. Reaching for his Rolodex, he spun it to find the man's card and dialled his mobile number.

It sounded as if Kevin Spinella, who answered instantly, was also eating his lunch.

'I don't have much for you,' Grace told him. 'I'm not holding a press conference. Instead I'm just going to send out a press release, so I'll give you the exclusive I promised. OK?'

'Very good of you, Detective Superintendent. I appreciate it.'

'Well, I think most of it you already know. The dredger, *Arco Dee*, pulled up the body of an unidentified male, believed to be in his mid-teens, yesterday afternoon, ten miles south of Shoreham Harbour, in its designated dredge area. A Home Office post-mortem was carried out this morning and the cause of death is as yet undetermined.'

'Would that be on account of all the vital organs being missing, Detective Superintendent?'

How the hell do you know that? This was a real, ongoing problem, Grace realized. Where did Spinella get his information from? Some day soon he was going to find the leak. Was it someone here, within HQ CID, or at the Coroner's Office, or in one of the uniform divisions or even at the mortuary? He thought carefully before answering, listening to the somewhat unpleasant sound of the reporter chewing.

'I can confirm that the body has been subject to recent surgery.'

'An organ donor, right?'

'I'd rather you didn't print that for the moment.'

There was a long silence. 'But I'm correct?'

'You would be correct to print that the body has been subject to recent surgery.'

Another silence. Then a reluctant, 'OK.' More chewing, followed by, 'What can you tell me about the body?'

'We estimate it has only been in the water for a few days at most.'

'Nationality?'

'Unknown. Our priority is to track down his identity. It would be helpful to me if you printed something along the lines that Sussex Police would like to hear from anyone with a missing teenage boy who has been subject to recent surgery.'

'Foul play is suspected presumably?'

'It is possible that the victim died lawfully and was buried at sea – and then drifted.'

'But you are not ruling out foul play?'

Again Grace hesitated before replying. Every conversation he had with this reporter was like a game of chess. If he was able to get Spinella to word the story the way he wanted, it could be very helpful in generating public response. But if it was printed sensationally, all it would do was frighten the citizens of Brighton and Hove.

'Look,' he said. 'If I tell you, you'll promise not mention anything about organs at this stage?'

More chewing down the earpiece. Followed by the sound of a paper or cellophane wrapping being torn off. Then, 'OK, deal.'

'Sussex Police are treating this as a suspicious death.'

'Top man! Thank you.'

'Here's something else for you, but not to be printed. I'm having the area scanned and police divers are going down tomorrow.'

'You'll let me know what they find?'

Grace assured him he would and ended the call. Then he finished his lunch and, almost instantly, his stomach feeling uncomfortably bloated, began to regret the doughnut.

Checking his electronic diary, he saw a reminder that he needed to send a request to Cellmark Forensic Services, the private laboratory at Abingdon which now handled Sussex CID's DNA testing, for the six-monthly check on the DNA profiles of his cold cases.

While the perpetrators had so far eluded justice, there was always the chance that a relative would have their DNA taken by the police after committing an offence – even for something as comparatively minor as a drunk-driving charge. Parents, children and siblings could provide enough of a match, so although this was a considerable expense out of the force's annual forensic budget, it did occasionally produce results to justify the outlay. He emailed his MSA, instructing her to put in a request.

As he had reflected many times, being a detective was a bit like fishing. Endless casting, endless patience. He glanced at the seven-pound six-ounce brown trout, stuffed and mounted in a glass case fixed to a wall in his office, and alongside it, a huge stuffed carp which Cleo had recently given him, with the terrible pun, *Carpe diem*, embossed on the brass plaque at its base. He referred to the trout, occasionally, when briefing young, fresh-faced detectives, making an increasingly tired joke about patience and big fish.

Then he focused his mind back on Unknown Male and made a series of phone calls to assemble his initial inquiry team. All the while, he kept staring at the damn fish, his eyes moving back and forth between them. Water. Fish lived in water. In the sea and in rivers. Then he realized why he kept staring at them.

A few years back, the headless and limbless torso of an

unidentified African boy had been found in the Thames. Grace was sure he remembered, from all the publicity at the time, that this boy had had his internal organs removed too. It had turned out to be an occult ritual killing.

Feeling a sudden surge of adrenalin, Grace tapped out a search command for details of the file he knew he had saved somewhere on his computer.

31

Sometimes, Roy Grace wondered whether computers had souls. Or at least a sense of humour. He had not yet elevated Unknown Male to Major Incident status, but because the investigation was now a formal operation the protocols required that it be allocated a name. The Sussex Police Computer had a program for this purpose, and the name it allocated the Detective Superintendent was bizarrely apt. Operation Neptune.

Shoulder to shoulder around the small, round table in his office were five detectives whom he had come to regard as his most trusted team.

Detective Constable Nick Nicholl was in his late twenties, short-haired and tall as a beanpole, a zealous detective and a handy centre forward, whom Grace had encouraged to take up rugby, thinking he would be perfect to play in the police team, of which he was now president. But the poor man was permanently bleary-eyed and zapped of energy, thanks to the joys of recent fatherhood.

Rookie Detective Constable Emma-Jane Boutwood, a slim girl with an alert face and long fair hair scooped up in a bun, had nearly been killed in a recent operation, when she had been crushed against a wall by a stolen van. She was still officially convalescing and entitled to more leave, but she had begged to come back, determined to get on with her career, and had already proved her worth to him in an earlier operation.

Shabbily dressed, with a bad comb-over and reeking of

tobacco, Detective Sergeant Norman Potting was an old-school policeman, politically incorrect, blunt and with no interest in promotion – he had never wanted the responsibility, but nor had he wanted to retire when he reached fifty-five, the normal police pension age for a sergeant, and would probably extend his service. He liked to do what he was best at doing, which he called *plodding and drilling*. Plodding, methodical police work, drilling down deep beneath the surface of any crime, drilling for as long and as deep as he needed until he hit a seam that would lead him somewhere. A veteran of three failed marriages, he was currently on his fourth, with a young Thai woman who, he boasted proudly at every opportunity, he had found via the Internet.

Detective Sergeant Bella Moy, an attractive woman in her mid-thirties, with a tangle of hennaed hair, was something of a lost soul. Unmarried – although, like many, married to the police force – she was stuck living with, and looking after, her elderly mother.

The fifth was Glenn Branson.

Also attending were the Crime Scene Manager, David Browne, and the HOLMES analyst, Juliet Jones.

A phone rang, to the tune of 'Greensleeves'. Everyone looked around. Embarrassed, Nick Nicholl plucked the offending machine out of his pocket and silenced it.

Moments later, another phone rang. The *Indiana Jones* theme. Potting yanked his phone out, checked the display and silenced it.

In front of Grace lay his A4 notebook, his red case-file folder, his policy book and the notes Eleanor Hodgson had typed up for him. He opened the proceedings.

'The time is 4.30 p.m., Thursday 27 November. This is the first briefing of Operation Neptune, the investigation into the death of Unknown Male, retrieved yesterday, 26 November, from the English Channel, approximately ten nautical miles south of Shoreham Harbour, by the dredger *Arco Dee*. Our next briefing will be at 8.30 a.m. tomorrow, and we will then hold briefings here in my office at 8.30 a.m. and 6.30 p.m. until further notice.'

He then read out a summary of the post-mortem report from Nadiuska De Sancha. Another phone began ringing. This time David Browne dived into his pocket to retrieve it, checked the display, then silenced it.

When Grace had finished the report, he continued, 'Our first priority is to establish the young man's identity. All we know at this stage is that he was in his mid-teens, and his internal organs appear to have been professionally removed. A fingerprint check on the UK database has proved negative. DNA has been sent to the lab on a three-day turnaround, but as that takes us into the weekend, we won't get their report until Monday, but I doubt whether we'll get a hit.'

He paused for a moment. Then he addressed DS Moy.

'Bella, I need you to get the dental photographs out. It's a massive task, but we'll start local and see what we get.'

'There is a designated charted area for burials at sea, right, chief?' Norman Potting said.

'Yes, fifteen nautical miles east of Brighton and Hove – it's a burial ground for everyone from Sussex,' Roy Grace replied.

'Don't the prevailing winds and currents run west to east?' the DS continued. 'I remember that from geography lessons when I was at school.'

'Around the time they built the ark?' quizzed Bella, who was not a Norman Potting fan.

Grace gave her a stern, cautioning look.

'Norman's right,' Nick Nicholl said. 'I used to do a bit of sailing.'

'It would take some storm to move a body that far in a few days,' Potting said, 'if it was weighted down. I just spoke to the coastguard. He'd need to see the weights, then he could try to plot a movement path.'

'Tania Whitlock's on that already,' Grace said. 'But we need to speak to all the organ transplant coordinators in the UK and see if we can find a connection with our teenager. Norman, I'd like to task you with that. We already have one negative, from the Royal Sussex County Hospital.'

Potting nodded and made a note on his pad. 'Leave it with me, chief.'

'We can't rule out the possibility that the body came from another county, can we?' Bella Moy asked.

'No,' Grace said. 'Or from another country. I would like you to speak to our counterparts in the ports of France bordering the English Channel. Also, Spain should be checked out as a priority.' He explained his reasons.

'I'll get on to it straight away.'

'We don't yet know the cause of death, right?' Nick Nicholl asked.

'No. I want you to do a trawl with Crime Intelligence Bureaux around the country and see if you can find any other cases of a similar nature. And I want you to check the Mispers list for Sussex, Kent and Hampshire for any possible match to our Unknown Male.'

That was a big task, he knew. Five thousand people were reported missing in Sussex alone each year – although the majority were missing for only a short time.

Then he handed Emma-Jane Boutwood a folder. 'These are the briefing notes we were given in September in Las Vegas, at the International Homicide Investigators' Association Symposium, on the headless and limbless torso of a boy, believed to be Nigerian, pulled from the Thames in 2001 missing his vital organs. The case is unsolved, but it's almost certainly a ritual killing of some kind. Take a look through and see if there are any comparisons with our young man.'

'Has anyone checked the dredge area to see if there is any evidence down there?' Potting asked.

'The SSU are going out at first light. Glenn will be with them.' He looked at his colleague.

Branson grimaced back at him. 'Shit, chief, I did tell you this morning, I don't really do boats very well. They're, like, way out of my comfort zone. I threw up the last time I went on a Channel ferry. And that was dead calm. The forecast's crap for tomorrow.'

'I'm sure our budget will stretch to seasickness pills,' Grace said breezily.

32

Forget seasickness, Glenn Branson thought. The speed humps along the southern perimeter road of Shoreham Harbour were really doing it for his stomach. Those, combined with a bad hangover and an early-morning row with his wife, kicked him off on this Friday morning in a mood that was a long way south of sunny. It was as dark as the grim, grey, early-morning sky through his windscreen.

To his left he drove past a long, deserted pebble beach, to his right were the big, ugly, industrial structures, the warehouses, gantries, stacks of containers, conveyor belts, barbed-wire fences, power station, bunkering station and storage yards of a commercial seaport.

'I'm working, for fuck's sake, aren't I?' he said into the hands-free.

'I have to be at a tutorial this afternoon at three,' his wife said. 'Could you pick the kids up and be with them until I get home?'

'Ari, I'm on an operation.'

'One minute you're complaining I don't let you see the kids, then, when I ask you to look after them for just a few hours, you give me crap about being busy. You need to make your mind up. Do you want to be a father or a policeman?'

'Shit, that's not fair.'

'It's perfectly fair, Glenn. This is what our marriage has been like for the past five years. Every time I ask you to help me to have a life of my own, you pull the *I can't, I've got a job on* number, or, *I've got an urgent operation on,* or, *I've got to see Detective Superintendent Roy Sodding Grace.*'

'Ari,' he said. 'Please, love, be reasonable. You're the one who encouraged me to join the force. I don't get why you're so fucking angry about it all the time.'

'Because I married you,' she said. 'I married you because I wanted a life with you. I don't have a life with you.'

'So what do you want me to do? Go back to being a bouncer? Is that what you want?'

'We were happy then.'

The turn-off was ahead of him. He indicated, then waited for a cement truck that was racing down from the opposite direction, thinking how simple it would be to pull out in front of it and end it all.

He heard a click. The bitch had hung up on him.

'Shit,' he said. 'Fuck you!'

He drove in through a timber yard, past massive planks piled high on either side of him, and saw the quay of Aldrington Basin directly ahead. Slowing to a crawl, he dialled his home number. It went straight to the answering machine.

'Oh, come on, Ari!' he muttered to himself, hanging up.

Parked to his right was a familiar vehicle, a massive yellow truck, emblazoned with the Sussex Police logo and the wording SPECIALIST SEARCH UNIT in large blue letters along the side.

He parked just behind it, tried Ari once more and again got the answering machine. Then he sat for a moment, pressing his fingers against his temples, trying to ease the pain that was like a vice crushing his skull.

He was stupid, he knew. He should have had an early night, but he hadn't been able to sleep, not for ages now, since he had left home. He'd sat up late on the floor of Roy Grace's living room, alone and tearful, going through his friend's music collection, drinking his way through a bottle of whisky that he'd found – and needed to remember to replace – playing songs that brought back memories of times with Ari. Shit, such good times. They had been so much in love with each other. He was missing his kids, Sammy and Remi. Desperately missing them. Feeling totally lost without them.

His eyes misty with sadness, he climbed out of the car into the cold, wet, salty wind, knowing he needed to put on a brave face and get through today, the way he had to get through every day. He took a deep breath, sucking in air that was thick with the smells of the sea, and fuel oil, and freshly sawn timber. A gull cried overhead, flapping its wings, stationary against the headwind. Tania Whitlock and her team, all wearing black baseball caps marked POLICE in bold lettering, red waterproof windcheaters, black trousers and black rubber boots, were loading gear into a tired-looking deep-sea fishing boat, the *Scoob-Eee*, that was moored alongside the quay.

Even here in the shelter of the harbour basin, the *Scoob-Eee* was rocking from the choppy waves. On the far side of the harbour was a cluster of white petroleum storage tanks. Beyond them, steep grass banking rose up to the main road and a row of houses.

The DS, dressed in a cream raincoat over his beige suit and tan, rubber-soled yachting shoes, strode over to the team. He knew them all. The unit worked closely with the CID on major crimes, as they were trained in search techniques, especially in difficult or inaccessible places, such as sewers, cellars, river banks and even burnt-out cars.

'Hi, guys!' he said.

Nine heads turned towards him.

'Lord Branson!' said a voice. 'Dear fellow, welcome aboard! How many pillows will you be requiring on your bed?'

'Hello, Glenn!' Tania said pleasantly, ignoring her colleague as she lugged a large coil of striped yellow breathing and communication lines over to the edge of the quay, and handed them down to another of her colleagues on the boat.

'Where do you think you're going dressed like that?' said Jon Lelliott. 'A cruise on the *Queen Mary*?'

Lean and muscular, with a shorn head, Lelliott was known as WAFI, which stood for Wind Assisted Fucking Idiot. He passed a folded body bag that reeked of Jeyes Fluid down to Arf, a man in his mid-forties, with a boyish face and prematurely white hair, who took it and tidily stowed it.

'Yeah, got a first-class cabin booked, with my own butler,' Glenn Branson said with a grin. He nodded at the fishing boat. 'Presumably this is the tender that's going to take me to it?'

'In your dreams.'

'Anything I can do to help?'

Arf held a heavy red anorak up to Glenn. 'You'll need this. Going to be lumpy and wet out there.'

'I'll be fine, thanks.'

Arf, the oldest and most experienced member of the team, gave him a bemused look. 'You sure about that? I think you'll need some boots.'

Glenn lifted a leg, showing his dainty yellow sock. 'These are boat shoes,' he said. 'Like, non-slip.'

'Slipping's going to be the least of your problems,' said Lelliott.

Glenn grinned and pushed back his coat sleeve, baring part of his wrist. 'See that, Arf, the colour, right? Black, yeah? My ancestors rowed the Atlantic in slave ships, yeah? I got the sea in my blood!'

*

When they had finished loading the gear, they assembled on the quay for the pre-dive briefing, given by Tania Whit-lock, who was reading her notes from a clipboard.

'We are proceeding to an area ten nautical miles south-east of Shoreham Harbour, and the coastguard will be informed that we will be diving in that area,' she said. 'In terms of risk assessment on board, we will be out in the main shipping lanes, so everyone needs to keep a careful watch – and to inform the coastguard if any vessel is heading too close. Some of the larger tanker and container ships using the Channel have a clearance of only a few feet above the seabed in places, so they present a real danger to divers.'

She paused and everyone nodded their understanding.

'Other than shipping, the risk assessment for the divers is low,' she continued.

Yep, thought Steve Hargrave. *Apart from drowning, decompression illness and risk of entanglement.*

'We will be diving in approximately sixty-five feet of water in poor visibility, but this is a dredge area and there will be an undulating seabed, with no underwater obstruc-tions. The *Arco Dee* is dredging in a different area this morning. Yesterday we surveyed the area using sonar, where we identified, and buoyed, two anomalies. We will commence our dive on these today. Because of the tidal current we will wear boots for standing on the seabed rather than fins. Any questions?'

'Do you think these *anomalies* are bodies?' Glenn asked.

'Nah, just a couple of first-class passengers enjoying the pool facilities,' quipped Rod Walker, who was known as Jonah.

Ignoring the titter of laughter, Tania Whitlock said, 'I will dive first, and then WAFI. I will be attended by Gonzo, and WAFI will be attended by Arf. When we have investigated and videoed the anomalies, and brought them to the surface, if appropriate, we will consider whether any further diving will serve any purpose, or whether to spend the time scanning a broader area. Any questions at this stage?'

A couple of minutes later, Lee Simms, a burly former Marine, gripped Glenn Branson's hand as he stepped off the quay and jumped down on to the slippery, rain-sodden deck.

Instantly Glenn felt the rocking motion of the boat. It reeked of putrid fish and varnish. He saw some netting, a couple of lobster pots and a bucket. The engine rattled into life and the deck vibrated. He breathed in a lungful of diesel exhaust.

As they cast off, in the falling rain and the gloomy light, no one, other than Glenn, noticed the dull glint of glass from the binoculars that were trained on them, from the far side of one of the petroleum storage tanks, across the harbour. But when he peered again into the gloom, he couldn't see anything. Had he imagined it?

*

Vlad Cosmescu was dressed in a black bobble-hat and the dark blue overalls and heavy boots of a workman. Next to his skin he wore the latest in thermal underwear, which was doing a good job of keeping out the biting cold. But he wished he had linings inside his thin leather gloves; his fingers were going numb.

He had been at the harbour since four o'clock this morning. From a distance, in the darkness, he had watched Jim Towers, the wiry, heavily bearded old sea dog from whom the police had chartered the boat. He had observed him prepare her, filling up her fuel and water tanks, then motoring her eastwards from her moorings at the Sussex Motor Yacht Club to further up the harbour, to the agreed departure point in Aldrington Basin. Towers tied the boat up, then left her, as instructed. The Specialist Search Unit had already been given a spare set of ignition and locker keys the night before.

It was ironic, Cosmescu thought, considering the number of fishing boats readily available for charter at this time of the year, that the police had chosen the same boat that he had. Always assuming, of course, that it *was* coincidence. And he was not a man who was comfortable with assumptions. He preferred hard facts and mathematical probabilities.

He had only discovered when he got talking to Jim Towers, when they were out at sea, that before he had retired to run his fishing trips, Towers had been a private investigator. PIs were themselves often ex-cops – or at least had plenty of friends in the police. Cosmescu had paid Towers big money. More money for that single trip than he would have earned in a year of charters. Yet now, just a few days later, he was letting ten cops go out on that boat!

Cosmescu didn't like the way that smelled.

He had long believed in the old adage: *Keep your friends close, but your enemies closer.*

And at this moment Jim Towers could hardly be closer. He was bound up so tightly with duct tape that he looked like an Egyptian mummy, lying securely in the rear of Cosmescu's small white van. The van was registered in the name of a building firm that existed but never traded, and he normally kept it parked out of sight, inside a secure lock-up.

For the moment, it was parked in a side street, just off the main road behind him. Just a couple of hundred yards away.

Quite close enough.

*

Twenty minutes later, after a slow journey through the lock, the boat headed out of the shelter of the harbour moles into the open sea. Almost instantly the water became rougher, the small boat pitch-poling through the waves in the rising offshore wind.

Glenn was seated on a hard stool, under the shelter of the open cabin that was little more than an awning, next to Jonah, who was at the helm. The DS held on to the compass binnacle in front of him, checking his phone every few minutes as the harbour and shoreline receded, in case there was a text from Ari. But the screen remained blank. After half an hour he was starting to feel increasingly queasy.

The crew took the piss out of him relentlessly.

'That what you always wear on a boat, Glenn?' Chris Dicks, nicknamed Clyde, asked him.

'Yeah. Cos, like, usually I have a private cabin with a balcony.'

'Get well paid in CID, do you?'

The boat was vibrating and rolling horribly. Glenn was taking deep breaths, each one containing exhaust fumes and varnish and rotted fish, and occasional snatches of Jeyes Fluid – the smell that every police officer associates with death. He was feeling giddy. The sea was becoming a blur.

'Hope you brought your dinner jacket,' WAFI said. 'You're going to need it if you are planning on dining at the captain's table tonight.'

'Yeah, course I did,' Glenn replied. It was becoming an effort to speak. And he was freezing cold.

'Keep looking at the horizon, Glenn,' Tania said kindly, 'if you feel queasy.'

Glenn tried to look at the horizon. But it was almost impossible to tell where the grey sky met the grey roiling sea. His stomach was playing hoopla. His brain was trying to follow it, with limited success.

Between himself and the skipper, Jonah, who sat on a padded seat, holding the large, round wheel, was the Humminbird sidescan imaging sonar screen.

'These are the anomalies we picked up yesterday, Glenn,' Tania Whitlock said.

She ran a replay on the small blue screen. There was a line down the middle, made by the Towfish sonar device which had been trawled behind the boat. She pointed out two small, barely visible black shadows.

'Those could be bodies,' she said.

Glenn was not sure exactly what he was meant to be looking at. The shadows looked tiny, the size of ants.

'Those there?' he asked.

'Yes. We're about one hour away. Coffee?'

Glenn Branson shook his head. *One hour*, he thought. *Shit. A whole hour more of this.* He wasn't sure he could swallow anything. He tried staring at the horizon, but that made him feel even worse.

'No, thanks,' he said. 'I'm fine.'

'Are you sure? You look a little peaky,' Tania said.

'Never felt better in my life!' Glenn said.

Ten seconds later he leapt off his stool, lurched to the side of the boat and threw up violently. Last night's microwaved lasagne and a lot of whisky. As well as this morning's single piece of toast.

Fortunately for him, and even more so for those near him, he was on the leeward side.

33

Some while later, Glenn was woken by the rattle of the anchor chain. The engine died and suddenly the deck was no longer vibrating. He could feel the motion of the boat. The deck pushing him up, then sinking down beneath him again, rolling him left and right in the process. He heard the creak of a rope. The whine of a winch. The pop-hiss of a canned drink being opened. The crackle of radio static. Then Tania's voice.

'Hotel Uniform Oscar Oscar. This is Suspol Suspol on board MV *Scoob-Eee*, calling Solent Coastguard.' *Suspol* was the nautical call sign for Sussex Police.

He heard a crackled response. 'Solent Coastguard. Solent Coastguard. Channel sixty-seven. Over.'

Then Tania again. 'This is Suspol. We have ten souls on board. Our position is ten nautical miles south-east of Shoreham Harbour.' She gave the coordinates. 'We are over our dive area and about to commence.'

Again the crackly voice. 'How many divers with you, Suspol, and how many in the water?'

'Nine divers on board. Two going in.'

Glenn was dimly aware that he had a blanket or a tarpaulin over him and he was no longer so cold. His head was swirling. He wanted to be anywhere, absolutely anywhere, but here. He saw Arf peering down at him.

'How are you feeling, Glenn?'

'Not great,' a disembodied voice that sounded like his own responded.

The stink of Jeyes Fluid was even stronger suddenly.

Arf had a kindly, avuncular face, shaded by the peak of his black baseball cap. Wisps of white hair blew loose on either side, like threads of cotton.

'There are two kinds of seasickness,' Arf said. 'Did you know that?'

Glenn shook his head feebly.

'The first kind is when you are afraid that you are going to die.'

Glenn stared back at him.

'The second,' Arf said, 'is when you are afraid that you are *not* going to die.'

Around him, Glenn heard laughter.

There was a third kind, Glenn reckoned, which was the one he was experiencing now. It was when you had actually died, but you weren't able to leave your body.

*

Tania, in her drysuit, was snipping the corners off the white body bag she was taking down with her, to allow the water to flow out in the event of a recovery. Like a lot of police equipment, these bags were not suitable for underwater work, so they had to be adapted.

With her umbilical plumbed into the surface supply panel and comms system, attended by Gonzo, she tested her suit and mask for leaks, and then the breathing and comms lines of her three-core umbilical. When they were both satisfied, she checked her watch.

For all trained divers, awareness of the risk of the bends, or decompression sickness, was a vital part of their operating procedure. The bends was caused by nitrogen particles building up in the blood. It could be excruciatingly painful, sometimes fatal, and the way to avoid it was by taking frequent stops on the way up from the seabed, some of them for long periods, depending on the length and depth of the dive. Dive time began the moment the diver left the surface.

She looked once more at her umbilical, checked the position of the pink marker buoy a few yards from the boat, then launched herself backwards, jumping clear of the boat, and plunged into the turbulent sea.

For a moment, as she went under the surface in a maelstrom of bubbles, she experienced the beautiful calm that lay beneath. Total silence, except for the hollow, echoing roar of her breathing. Then she bobbed up and, instantly, waves broke over her. She gave Gonzo the thumbs-up.

Although she had dived countless times, both for her work and at every opportunity on holiday, entering the water gave her a fresh adrenalin rush each time. No two dives were ever the same. You didn't know what you were going to find or experience. And she still could not quite believe her luck that she had landed this job, with this unit, which gave her the opportunity to dive somewhere almost weekly.

Although, admittedly, diving for bodies in filthy canals full of discarded fridges, garden tools, coiled chicken wire, supermarket trolleys and stolen cars was a poor substitute for the tropical fish and marine fauna of the Maldives.

She looked around for the pink buoy, which had momentarily disappeared behind a wave, swam a few clumsy strokes over to it, then gripped the heavily weighted shot line with her rubber gloves and sank a short distance below the surface.

It was instantly calm again here. This was always a moment she loved, descending from the waves and the wind into a completely different world. She continued steadily down, swallowing to equalize the pressure in her ears, keeping an arm looped around the rope, the visibility rapidly fading, until she was in total darkness.

When she reached the bottom, her feet sinking into the sand, she could see nothing at all. On fine days there was reasonable visibility underwater in the Channel. But today the currents had churned up the sand and silt on the bottom into cloud that was as dark as a coal cellar. There was no point in switching on her camera and her torch, she would have to do it all by feel.

She checked the luminous depth gauge on her wrist, struggling to read the dial. It indicated sixty-seven feet. Her lapsed time since she had entered the sea was two minutes. She signalled to the surface by speaking on her voice comms: 'Diver made bottom. Starting work.' Then she felt for the underwater jackstay line.

Yesterday, when the scanner had picked up the two anomalies on the seabed, they had gridded them with anchored marker buoys and jackstay lines – ropes on the seabed held down by leaded weights.

What she now had to do, with the body bag tucked under her left arm, was swim across the seabed, skimming the surface, holding the jackstay line with her left hand and sweeping with her right. She would move her right hand away from her body, then back to it, in a continual arc, until she struck the object she was looking for. If she reached the weight at the far end, she would shift it a couple of feet to the right and then work her way back along it. When she arrived at her starting point, she would move that weight a couple of feet to the right and repeat the process.

The scanner was not sophisticated enough to tell her

what the anomalies on the seabed were, giving only shape and approximate size. Each one was approximately six feet long and a couple of feet wide. Consistent with a human body. But not necessarily bodies. They could have been pieces of equipment or discarded rubbish from a ship, or unexploded torpedoes from the war or the wreckage of a crashed plane, or plenty of other things. The worst thing, when underwater in darkness, was striking a sharp object.

Something bumped into her mask, then was gone. A bottom-feeder fish, a sole or a plaice or a flounder, or maybe an eel, she assumed.

Slowly, holding the jackstay line with her left hand, she started swimming through the inky blackness. She swept her right arm backwards and forwards, in a continual arc, like a windscreen wiper.

Every time she searched like this, her mind wanted to play games with her. It wanted to remind her of every horror film she had ever seen. Of every kind of monster or demon that might be lurking on the seabed, waiting for her.

But she had dived in plenty worse places than open sea. She had dived to recover the body of a ten-year-old boy in a canal. She had dived in reservoirs, in ditches and in potholes. In her view, there was nothing that would hurt her here. There was just an *anomaly*.

Suddenly her hand struck something.

It felt like a human face inside plastic.

And, despite herself, her heart burst clean out of her chest. And she damn nearly spat her face mask off in shock.

A bolus of iced water exploded through her veins.

Shit-shit-shit.

Her husband, the BA pilot, didn't dive. She had tried to explain the excitement, the rush, to him many times. He got all the excitement he needed in the cockpit of a 747, he told her. It was dry and warm there, with plenty of hot drinks and food from the first-class galley. And now, for a moment, she understood his point.

She ran her hand over the face. The head. Feeling through the heavy-duty plastic sheeting. Shoulders. Back. Buttocks. Thighs. Legs. Feet.

34

'Nice dog!' the woman said. 'What breed is he?' She spoke with a foreign accent.

It was a dumb question. Only a visitor to Bucharest would ever ask such a question. Romeo, kneeling in the weeds beside the dirt road, was giving the dog its daily meal. He had no idea what breed it was. Like most of the thousands of stray dogs that roamed the outer districts of Bucharest, it was a mongrel. Twenty-nine years before Romeo had been born, one of Ceaușescu's early acts as president was to throw the Romanian bourgeoisie out of their homes. Most were forced to leave behind their dogs, which ran wild and had been living and breeding on the streets ever since.

But the dogs were smart, figuring out that if they were mean, people would kick them and throw stones at them, but if they were friendly, they got fed. Over the years the stray dogs and the street people of the city had bonded. The dogs guarded the street people and, in turn, the street people fed the dogs.

'I'd say he's got some schnauzer in him,' the woman said.

She looked at the boy's cute, grubby face, and his round blue eyes, and his jet-black hair, messily cut, and his withered left hand. She observed his clothes, his worn-out jeans, his ragged, hooded top and his threadbare trainers, studying him carefully, as if inspecting him. Although she already knew for sure the kind of person he was and the world he inhabited. And, crucially, how to get through to him.

The boy thought the woman had a kind face. She was pretty, with a tangle of fair hair that was being blown about by the wind, casually dressed, but in the kind of expensive clothes that did not belong here in this district. An elegant, shiny, tight-fitting leather jacket, with the collar turned up, over a dark roll-neck jumper of fine wool, studded jeans tucked into black suede boots, big jewellery and beautiful black leather gloves. The kind of woman he would see emerging from a limousine outside one of the big hotels, laden with shopping bags, or being disgorged, in her finery, at a smart restaurant. People like her inhabited a different world from his own.

'His name's Artur,' he said.

'That's a nice name.' She smiled and said it out aloud. '*Artur. Artur.* Yes, a very nice name. It suits him!'

The boy pulled some out-of-date kidneys from a plastic bag and put them in Artur's mouth. The dog ate them greedily, in one gulp. Then he dug his hand into the bag again. There was a butcher around the corner who was always kind to him, giving him strips of meat, pieces of offal and bones every day.

'What's your name?' she asked.

'Romeo.'

The boy was sizing her up. A wealthy visitor. Rich pickings! He pulled out a rank pig's trotter and the dog clamped its jaws on to it.

The woman smiled. 'Do you live around here?' she asked, although she already knew full well that he did, and where.

He nodded, eyeing her. Eyeing her handbag. It was ruched leather, with chains and buckles, and a huge brass clasp on it. In his mind, he was sizing it up, thinking of all the things it might contain. A purse with cash, a mobile phone. Maybe some other stuff too, like an iPod, that he could sell. He glanced around, but so far as he could see she was unaccompanied. There were no smart cars parked nearby that she could have come from.

He could grab the bag and run!

But at the moment, she had the strap over her shoulder and her left arm was looped through the chain, gripping the top of the bag with her gloved hand, as if streetwise herself. He would need to distract her.

'Where are you from?' he asked.

'I'm from Germany,' she said. 'München. Munich. Have you been to Germany?'

'No.'

'Would you like to go there?'

He shrugged.

'What country would you like to go to, if you could?'

He shrugged again. 'Maybe England.'

Her eyes widened. 'Why England?'

The dog had almost finished the huge trotter and was looking at him expectantly.

'They have jobs there. You can be rich in England. You can get a nice apartment.'

'Really?' She feigned surprise.

'I heard that.' Romeo checked inside the plastic bag, to ensure he had missed nothing, then dropped it. The wind sent it skittering away. Immediately, another dog, a mis-shapen brown and white creature, ran after it, pounced and began pawing at it.

The woman still had a tight grip on her leather bag.

'Would you like an air ticket to England? I might be able

to arrange it for you, if you would really like to go. I could get you a job.'

Their eyes met. Hers were beautiful, the colour of blue steel. She was smiling, looking sincere. He looked back at the handbag. Almost as if she knew what he was thinking, she kept her grip on it.

'What kind of job?'

'What do you want to do? What are your skills?'

A truck rumbled slowly by, close to the verge. Romeo looked up at its large, dirty wheels, its black, rusting under-belly, its billowing exhaust. If he was going to do it, this would be a good moment. Push her, grab the bag, run!

But suddenly he was more interested in what she was saying. Skills? There was a boy who had stayed with them recently, who talked about his brother who worked as a cock-tail waiter in London and was earning over 400 lei a day. That was a fortune! Not that he knew anything about making cocktails. Someone else had said recently you could make that sort of money cleaning hotel rooms in London too.

'Making cocktails,' he replied. 'Also, I'm a good cleaner.'

'Do you have friends in London, Romeo?' she asked.

Artur whined, as if wanting more food.

The woman opened her handbag and took out a fat purse. From it she removed a banknote. It was a 100 lei note. She handed it to Romeo. 'I want you to buy some food for Artur, OK?'

He looked at her, then nodded solemnly.

Then she handed him another banknote. This was a 500 lei banknote. 'That's for you to buy anything you want, OK?'

He stared at the money and back at the woman. Then, as if afraid she was suddenly going to snatch them back, he stuffed the money into his trouser pocket.

'You are kind,' he said.

'I want to help you,' she replied.

'What's your name?'

'Marlene,' she said.

Despite her smile and her generosity, something about the woman was making Romeo very wary. He knew, from others he had talked to, that there were organizations that helped people who were living on the streets, but he had never tried to find one. He had been warned that sometimes, if you went to see them, you could end up getting taken into a government institution. But perhaps this woman really would help him get to England.

'Charity?' he asked. 'You are with a charity?'

She hesitated for an instant. Then, smiling and nodding her head vigorously, she replied, 'Yes, charity. Absolutely. Charity!'

35

Despite the arrival of two black, heavy-duty plastic body bags at the Brighton and Hove City Mortuary, containing the bodies that had been recovered from the Channel this morning, Roy Grace was in the sunniest mood he had been in for years.

He didn't mind that it was quarter to three on a Friday afternoon and that the post-mortems, depending on how soon Nadiuska De Sancha arrived, were likely to wipe out his plans for the evening. He was floating on air.

He was going to be a father! That thought now dominated everything else. And at last night's poker game he had won £550, his biggest win in as long as he could remember!

What he loved most about poker, apart from the camaraderie of an evening relaxing with a bunch of male friends and colleagues, was the psychology of the game. You were very unlikely to win if you came to the table in a downer of a mood. But if you were upbeat, your enthusiasm could be infectious and you could, even with modest cards, dominate the game. But he hadn't just had modest cards last night, he'd been on a complete roll. He'd had one hand of four tens, countless trips – three cards of a kind – full house after full house, and a bunch of high flushes.

Alone with Cleo for a few moments, in the small mortuary office, with the sound of the kettle coming slowly to the boil, he put his arms around her and kissed her.

'I love you,' he said.

'Do you?' she said, grinning. 'Do you really?' All gowned up, she raised her arms. 'Even like this?'

'To the ends of the earth and back.'

He truly did. After the poker game he had gone back to her house and showered the cash over the bed. Then he had lain awake beside her, too wired to sleep, thinking about his life. About Sandy. About Cleo. He wanted to marry Cleo, he was sure of that. More sure of that than of anything. He had made his mind up that in the morning he would start the process, long overdue, of having Sandy declared legally dead.

And first thing this morning he had contacted a Brighton solicitor he had been recommended to, Susan Ansell, and done just that. He had made an appointment with her.

Cleo kissed him. 'Only to the ends of the earth?'

He smiled, checked the door to make sure no one was coming in, then kissed her again. 'How about to the ends of the universe?'

'Better,' she said. Then she raised her palms upwards and wiggled her fingers, indicating more was required.

'And to the ends of any other universe that we might discover.'

'Better still!' She kissed him again.

Then he stopped, feeling a sudden chill, wishing he had not started on that analogy. Sandy had been a fan of the *Hitchhiker's Guide to the Galaxy*. He remembered her favourite being the second book in the series, called *The Restaurant at the End of the Universe*. Why the hell did her shadow have to keep falling over everything, darkening his happiest moments? It sometimes felt as if he was being stalked by a ghost.

'You OK?' Cleo said.

'Very OK!'

'You sort of disappeared for a second.'

'I was overwhelmed by your beauty.'

She grinned again. 'You're such a good liar, aren't you, Grace?'

Grinning back, he said, 'I wasn't lying!'

'You spend half your time interviewing criminals who are lying convincingly. Don't tell me that hasn't rubbed off on you!'

He held her shoulders, firmly but gently, and stared into her eyes. 'I would never lie to you,' he said. 'I would never want to lie to you.'

'I feel the same way about you,' she replied.

They stood in comfortable silence for some moments. The kettle rumbled to the boil, then clicked off. Distracted for an instant, Roy looked past her, at an L-shaped row of chairs beside the cluttered desk. At the table in the corner, on which sat a small Christmas tree, covered in glitter and shiny balls. At the walls, which were even more cluttered than the desk, with framed certificates, a calendar, a photograph of Brighton Pier at sunset and a row of clipboards on hooks, containing details of all their current, hapless residents in the fridges. And at the *Argus* newspaper lying on a chair.

Kevin Spinella's piece on the finding of Unknown Male appeared on page five. It was a small column, pretty much reporting the facts as Grace had relayed them, with Grace's appeal to the public. To his relief, Spinella had kept to his agreement not to mention anything about organs.

There was a shrill ring at the door.

Cleo glanced up at the CCTV monitor on the wall and said, 'Your chum's just arrived.'

Grace turned to the screen and saw Glenn Branson's face. He was not looking a particularly happy bunny.

'I'll go,' he said.

He walked down the short corridor, past the changing room, and pulled open the door. He was shocked by the sight that greeted him. He'd rarely seen Glenn looking anything other than immaculate. Now the Detective Sergeant stood in front of him, in the rain, looking a complete wreck. His tan shoes were sodden, his white shirt was spotted with dark marks, his silk tie was covered in blotches, and awry, and his cream mac was a patchwork of brown stains the colour of rust and oil, and what looked like shiny fish scales.

'Where the hell have you been?' Grace asked. 'Kick-boxing in an abattoir? Or mud-wrestling in a fish market?'

'Very funny, old-timer. Next time you send me on a cruise, I'll book the tickets myself.'

Grace stepped back to let him in.

'Nadiuska here yet?' Branson asked.

'She just phoned. She's ten minutes away. I thought you said you were going home to change.'

'Yeah, well, I did, didn't I? Got back to your place and there were two sodding letters waiting for me.'

'Feel free about redirecting your post there.'

Branson looked at his friend, unsure for a moment whether he was being sarcastic or genuine. He could not tell and decided not to push his luck. 'One was from Ari's solicitor, all pompous, right? Telling me that she's been instructed by Ari, who is commencing divorce proceedings, and that I should get myself a solicitor, like I just rode into town in the back of a lorry and don't know anything about the law.'

Grace shut the door behind him. 'Sounds to me like you need to get one, PDQ.'

'I'm ahead of you. I got one already.'

'Act for a lot of tramps, does he?'

'Actually, it's a she.'

'Very wise. They can be a lot more brutal than men.'

Glenn swayed suddenly and put his arm out on the wall to steady himself. For a moment Grace wondered if he was drunk.

'The ground's still swaying. I've been back on dry land for more than two hours and it's still moving under me!'

'So, your ancestors on the slave ship? Nautical life didn't rub off on you? Not in your genes, then?'

'Who told you about that slave ship stuff?'

'Your fame as a seafarer goes before you.'

'Did you ever see that film, *Master and Commander*?'

Grace frowned.

'Russell Crowe.'

He nodded. 'Yep. Saw it.'

'That's how I feel. Like I'm one of his crew who took a cannonball in the stomach.'

'Listen, mate. Ari may be hacked off with you, but that doesn't give her automatic rights to screw your life up.'

'You're wrong. Shit, do you remember *Kramer versus Kramer*?'

'Meryl Streep?'

Glenn Branson smiled for a fleeting instant. 'Fuck, I'm impressed. Two films in a row I've mentioned that you've actually seen! Yeah, Meryl Streep and Dustin Hoffman. Well, that's about my situation.'

'Except you're not as good-looking as Dustin Hoffman.'

'You know how to kick a man when he's down, don't you?'

'In the nuts. It's the only place.'

Branson peeled off his mac. 'So, right, the other letter is the divorce petition from the court. You can't believe this, man, you can't fucking believe what she is saying!'

The Detective Sergeant slung his mac over his arm, held out his fingers and began counting them off. 'She says there is an irretrievable breakdown, OK? She's alleging unreasonable behaviour by me. That I'm not interested in sex any more. That I'm drinking excessively – yeah, well, that's true, she's driving me to fucking drink, right? She's citing *lack of affection*.'

He dug his hand inside his mackintosh and pulled out several sheets of folded paper, clipped together. Reading from the top one, he said, 'Apparently I refuse to join in with the family. I shout at her when we are in a car together. I keep her short of money – shit, I bought her a fucking horse! And get this – apparently I don't appreciate how Ari looks after our children.' He shook his head. 'That's rich, that is! What am I supposed to do? Tell everyone, *Sorry, I know this is a murder inquiry, but I have to get home and bath Remi*?'

The words gave Roy Grace a sudden chill. He suddenly realized that's exactly where he was going to be when his child was born. It was normal for him to be in his office by seven in the morning, if not even earlier. And not to get home until eight, or even later. When his child was born, could he change those hours?

Not without harming his career.

He looked at Glenn, stared into his questioning eyes. And he knew the answer was one that the DS was not going to like. To be a good police officer was to be married to the force. For those thirty years until you collected your pension – and longer now, if you wanted – your work would come first. You were a lucky person if your spouse or partner accepted that. A tragically large number, like Glenn's wife, Ari, did not.

'You know the problem?' Grace said.

Branson shook his head.

'She's probably right. A little insensitive, sure, but fundamentally right. You have to decide if you want a successful career or a successful marriage. It is possible to combine both, but you need a very tolerant and understanding partner.'

'Yeah, well, the irony is I joined the police so that my kids could be proud of their dad.'

'So they should be.'

'So how proud of me would they be if I quit?'

'And went back to being a bouncer? Or a security guard at Gatwick? It's not what job you do,' Grace said, 'it's the person you are. You can be a good, very human bouncer. You can be a vigilant security guard. You can be a crap cop. It's what you are inside, not what it says on your badge or your ID card.'

'Yeah, yeah. Sure. But you know what I mean.'

'Look, I've told you before, with the mess I've made of my life, I'm not the right person to give marital advice. But you know what I really think? If Ari loved you, really loved you, she'd stick with it. I'm not sure she does really love you at all – all this legal process and stuff she's throwing at you. I think if you did quit the force to appease her, at some point she'd want something else. Whatever you do is ultimately going to be wrong for her. I think she's that kind of restless person. Appeasing her will never be more than a short-term solution. So, if I were you, I'd stay with your career.'

Branson nodded gloomily.

'Know what Winston Churchill said about appease-ment?' said Roy.

'Tell me?'

'An appeaser is one who feeds a crocodile, hoping it will eat him last.'

36

The two bodies had been dumped in the sea in an identical way to Unknown Male, trussed up in plastic sheeting tied with blue cord and weighed down with breeze blocks.

They arrived at the mortuary parcelled in two further layers, the white plastic forensic bags in which they had been brought to the surface by the police divers, and the heavier-duty black plastic body bags in which they had been hauled up on to the dive boat, and in which they had remained until arriving at the mortuary.

The first to be unwrapped, in a tediously slow process, was a young teenage boy, perhaps a year or two older than the previous body, Nadiuska estimated. Less good-looking, with a beaky nose and a face badly pockmarked from acne, Unknown Male 2 was also missing his heart, lungs, kidneys and liver. They had been surgically removed in the same meticulous way.

Nadiuska was now working on the layers around the body of a young girl, also in her mid-teens, she estimated. Death took away the personality from a face, Grace always thought, leaving it a blank, which made it difficult to tell what people had *really* looked like when they were alive. But even with her pale, waxy skin and her long brown hair, tangled and matted, he could see she had been quite beautiful, if far too thin.

The pathologist was of the opinion that these two bodies had been in the water for the same length of time as Unknown Male. It wouldn't take a rocket scientist, Grace figured, to work out the probability that all three of them had gone into the sea together.

Which raised the stakes from the initial discovery of a single body considerably. In his mind, he had now dismissed any possibility that these were formal burials at sea that had drifted from the official seabed grave area. So who were these three teenagers? Where had they come from? Who were their parents? Who was missing them? Had they been dumped overboard from one of the dozens of foreign-registered merchant ships that travelled down the English Channel around the clock, from just about every country in the world?

There were no marks on Unknown Male 2's body to suggest death from an accident or a blow to the head. There were puncture marks on his skin, just like the earlier body, consistent, as Nadiuska had just repeated, with organ removal for transplant.

A dark shadow was moving across Grace's mind. For most of the time, he stood in the corridor that led into the now very crowded post-mortem room, mobile phone to his ear, making one call after another. His first had been to his MSA, Eleanor Hodgson, getting her to clear his diary for the immediate days ahead. There were just two dates he hoped to be able to keep. One, tonight, was his promise to a colleague to visit a football game at the Crew Club in Whitehawk. He might be able to make that if DI Mantle took the 6.30 briefing meeting instead of him.

The second, was the CID dinner dance tomorrow night, which, with over 450 attending, was going to be quite a bash. It had been a tough year and he was looking forward to taking Cleo, now that their relationship was out in the open, and relaxing with his colleagues. And maybe getting an opportunity to improve on the poor impression he reckoned he had made with the new Chief Constable on Wednesday night.

Cleo, who had spent weeks fretting about what she was going to wear, and an amount equal to the GDP of an emerging African nation buying a dress, would be deeply disappointed if they now did not make it.

After going through his diary, Grace had then made a series of calls expanding his Outside Inquiry Team from the original six, to twenty-two. Now, as he stood talking to Tony Case, the Senior Support Officer at Sussex House, organizing space for his new team in one of the building's two Major Incident Rooms, he watched Nadiuska at work, carefully taping the high-tensile cords around the breeze blocks, in the hope of finding a tell-tale skin cell or glove fibre from whoever had tied them. When each strip lost its tackiness, she bagged it for microscopic inspection later.

Michael Forman, the Coroner's Officer, stood beside her, observing carefully and occasionally making notes, or checking his BlackBerry. David Browne, the Crime Scene Manager, was in attendance, along with two of his SOCOs. One of them, the forensic photographer, James Gartrell, was once more taking photographs of every stage of the post-mortem, while the other was dealing with the packaging in which the two corpses had arrived. At the next table along, Cleo and Darren were tidying up Unknown Male 2, suturing the incision once more.

Every time you thought you had seen it all, Roy Grace mused, some new horror would surprise you. He had read about people in Turkey and South America who got talking to beautiful women in bars and then woke up hours later in bathtubs full of ice, with sutured incisions down one side of their body and missing a kidney. But until now he had dismissed such stories as urban myths. And he knew the importance of never jumping to conclusions.

But three young people at the bottom of the sea with their vital organs professionally removed . . .

The press would have a field day. The citizens of Brighton and Hove would be worried when this news came out, and he already had two – as yet unreturned – urgent messages on his mobile phone to call the *Argus* reporter, Kevin Spinella. He would need to orchestrate the press carefully, to maximize public response in helping to identify the bodies, without causing any undue distress. But equally, he knew that the best way to grab the public's attention was with a sensational headline.

Press conferences were not popular at weekends, so he could buy himself some time until Monday. But he was going to have to throw a few titbits to Spinella – and as a starting point the *Argus*, with its wide local circulation, could be the most helpful in the short term.

So what was he going to tell him? And, equally importantly, what was he going to conceal? He had long learned that in any murder inquiry you always tried to hold back some information that would be known only to the killer. That helped you eliminate time-waster phone calls.

For the moment, he put the press out of his mind, concentrating on what he could learn from the three bodies recovered so far. In his notebook, he jotted down *Ritual killings?* and ringed the words.

Yes, a very definite possibility.

Could they possibly have been organ donors who had all wanted to be buried at sea? Too unlikely to be considered seriously at this stage.

A serial killer? But why would he – or she – bother with

the careful suturing after removal of the organs? To put the police off the scent? Possible. Not to be dismissed at this stage.

Organ trafficking?

Occam's razor he wrote next, as the thought suddenly came into his mind. Occam was a fourteenth-century philosopher monk who used the analogy of taking a razor-sharp knife to cut away everything but the most obvious explanation. That, Brother Occam believed, was where the truth usually lay. Grace was inclined to agree with him.

Grace's favourite fictional detective, Sherlock Holmes, held to the dictum: *When you have eliminated the impossible, whatever remains, however improbable, must be the truth.*

He looked at Glenn Branson, who was standing in a corner of the room with a worried expression on his face, talking on his mobile phone. It would do him good to have a challenge, Grace thought. Something to get his teeth into and distract him from all his nightmarish legal problems with Ari, who, privately, Grace had never liked.

Walking over to him, and waiting for him to finish a call, Grace said, 'I need you to do something. I need you to find out everything you can about the world of trafficking in human organs.'

'Need a new liver, do you, old-timer? I'm not surprised.'

'Yeah, yeah, very funny. Get Norman Potting to help you. He's good at researching obscure stuff.'

'*Dirty Pretty Things!*' Branson said. 'See that movie?'

Grace shook his head.

'That was about illegal immigrants selling kidneys in a seedy hotel in London.'

Suddenly he had the Detective Superintendent's attention. 'Really? Tell me more.'

'Roy!' Nadiuska called out. 'Look, this is interesting!'

Grace, followed by Glenn Branson, walked over to the corpse and stared down at the tiny tattoo she was pointing to. He frowned.

'What's that?'

'I don't know,' she said.

He turned to Glenn Branson. The DS shrugged and then, stating the obvious, said, 'It's not English.'

37

Romeo clambered down the steel ladder, holding a huge grocery bag under one arm. Valeria was sitting on her old mattress, leaning against the concrete wall, rocking her sleeping baby. Tracy Chapman was singing 'Fast Car' yet again. Again. Again. The fucking song was starting to drive him crazy.

He noticed three strangers, in their mid-teens, on the floor, slouched against the wall opposite Valeria. They were just sitting there, looking strung out on Aurolac. The telltale squat plastic bottle with its broken white seal and the yellow and red label bearing the words *LAC Bronze Argintiu* lay on the floor in front of them. The rank smell of this place hit him, as it did each time, and with particular force now in contrast to the fresh, windy, rainy air outside. The mustiness, the fetid body smells, dirty clothes and the soiled-nappy stench of the baby.

'Food!' he announced breezily. 'I got some money and I bought amazing food!'

Only Valeria reacted. Her big, sad eyes rolled towards him, like two marbles that had run out of momentum. 'Who gave you money?'

'It was a charity. They give money to street people like us!'

She shrugged her shoulders, uninterested. 'People who give you money always want something back.'

He shook his head vigorously. 'No, not this person. She was beautiful, you know? Beautiful inside!' Then he walked over to her and opened up the bag for her to inspect the contents. 'Look, I bought you stuff for the baby!'

Valeria dug her hand in and pulled out a tin of condensed milk. 'I'm worried about Simona,' she said, turning it around and reading the label. 'She hasn't moved all day. She just cries.'

Romeo walked over and squatted down beside Simona, putting an arm around her. 'I bought you chocolate,' he said. 'Your favourite. Dark chocolate!'

She was silent for some moments and then she sniffed. 'Why?'

'Why?'

She said nothing.

He pulled out a bar and put it under her nose. 'Why? Because I want you to have something nice, that's why.'

'I want to die. That would be nice.'

'You said yesterday you wanted to go to England. Wouldn't that be nicer?'

'That's a dream,' she said, staring bleakly ahead. 'Dreams don't come true, not for people like us.'

'I met someone today. She can take us to England. Would you like to meet her?'

'Why? Why would she take us to England?'

'Charity!' he replied brightly. 'She has a charity to help street people. I told her about us. She can get us jobs in England!'

'Yeah, sure, as erotic dancers?'

'Any kind of jobs we want. Bars. Cleaning rooms in hotels. Anything.'

'Is she like the man I met at the station?'

'No, she is a nice lady. She is kind.'

Simona said nothing. More tears trickled down her cheeks.

'We can't stay like this. Is that what you want, to stay like this for all our lives?'

'I don't want to be hurt any more.'

'Can't you trust me, Simona? Can't you?'

'What is trust?'

'We've seen England on television. In the papers. It's a good country. We could have an apartment in England! We could have a new life there!'

She started crying. 'I don't want a new life any more. I want to die. Finish. It would be easier.'

'She's coming by tomorrow. Will you at least meet her, talk to her?'

'Why would anybody want to help us, Romeo?' she asked. 'We're nothing.'

'Because there are some good people in the world.'

'Is that what you believe?' she asked bleakly.

'Yes.'

He unwrapped the chocolate bar and broke off a section, holding it in front of her. 'Look. She gave me money for food, for treats. She's a good person.'

'I thought the man at the railway station was a good person.'

'Can you imagine being in England? In London? We could live in an apartment in London. Making good money! Away from all this shit! Maybe we'll see rock stars there. I've heard that a lot of them live in London!'

'The whole world is shit,' she replied.

'Please, Simona, at least come and meet her tomorrow.'

She raised a hand and took the chocolate.

'Do you really want to spend another winter down here?' he asked.

'At least we are warm here.'

'You don't want to go to London because it is warm

here? Right? How great is that? Maybe it's warm in London too.'

'Go fuck yourself!'

He grinned. She was perking up. 'Valeria wants to come too.'

'With the baby?'

'Sure, why not?'

'She's coming tomorrow, this woman?'

'Yes.'

Simona bit one square off the chocolate strip. It tasted good. So good she ate the whole bar.

38

Roy Grace stood on the touchline of the football pitch, beneath the glare of the floodlights, and jammed his glove-less hands deep into his raincoat pockets, shivering in the biting wind high up here in Whitehawk. At least the rain had stopped and there was a clear, starry sky. It felt cold enough for a frost.

It was the Friday night football league and tonight the Crew Club's teenagers were playing against a team from the police. He had just made the last ten minutes of the game, in time to see the police being hammered 3–0.

The city of Brighton and Hove straddled several low hills and Whitehawk sprawled over one of the highest. A council development of terraced and semi-detached houses, and low- and high-rise blocks of flats, built in the 1920s to replace the slums occupying the land before, Whitehawk had long – and somewhat unjustly – held a dark reputation for violence and crime. A few of its warrens of streets, many with fabulous views across the city and the sea, were inhabited and dominated by some of the city's roughest crime families, and their reputation infected everyone's on the estate.

But during the past few years a carefully run community initiative supported by Sussex Police had radically changed that. At its heart was the Crew Club, sponsored by local industry to the tune of £2 million. The club boasted a smart, ultra-modern and funky-looking centre that could have been designed by Le Corbusier, which housed a range of facilities for local youngsters, including a well-equipped computer room, a music recording studio, a video studio, a spacious party room, meeting rooms and, in the grounds surrounding it, numerous sports facilities.

The club was a success because it had been created by passion, not by bureaucrats. It was a place where local kids did actually want to go and hang out. It was cool. And at its heart were a couple of Whitehawk residents, Darren and Lorraine Snow, whose vision it had been and whose energy drove it.

Both wrapped up in coats, scarves and hats so that their faces were almost invisible, they flanked Roy Grace now, along with a handful of parents and a few police colleagues. It was the first time Grace had visited, and, in his capacity as president of the Police Rugby Team, he was mentally sizing up the opportunities for a rugby challenge here. They were tough and plucky, the youngsters on that pitch, and he was quite amused to see them giving the force players a hard time.

A group thundered past, jostling, grunting and cussing, and the ball rolled over the line. Instantly the ref's whistle blew.

But Grace's focus was distracted by the post-mortems he had attended today, and yesterday, and the task that lay in front of him. Pulling out his pocket memo pad, he jotted down some thoughts, gripping his pen with almost numb fingers.

Suddenly there was a ragged cheer and he looked up, momentarily confused. A goal had been scored. But by which side?

From the cheers and the comments, he worked out it was the Crew Club team. The score was now 4–0.

Privately he smiled again. The Sussex Police team were

being coached by retired Detective Chief Superintendent Dave Gaylor, who was an accredited football referee. As well as being a personal friend. He looked forward to ribbing him after the game.

He looked up at the stars for a moment and his thoughts suddenly flashed back to his childhood. His father had had a small telescope on a tripod and spent many hours studying the sky, often encouraging Roy to look as well. Grace's favourite had been the rings of Saturn, and at one time he could have distinguished all the constellations, but the Plough was the only one he recognized easily now. He needed to re-educate himself, he decided, so that one day he could pass on that same knowledge – and passion – to his child. Although, he wondered wryly, would it again be mostly forgotten in time?

Then his focus went back to the inquiry. Unknown Males 1 and 2 and Unknown Female.

Three bodies. Each short of the same vital organs. Each of them teenagers. Just one possible clue to their identity: a badly executed tattoo on the upper left forearm of the dead young woman. A name perhaps . . .

One that meant nothing to him. But one that, he sensed, held the clue to all their identities.

Had they come from Brighton? If not, from where? He wrote down on his pad: *Coastguard report. Drifting?*

They could not have drifted far with those weights attached. In his own mind he was sure their proximity to Brighton made it likely that the three teenagers had died in England.

What was happening? Was there a monster at large in Brighton who killed people and stole their organs?

Experienced surgeon, he wrote down, echoing Nadiuska De Sancha's assessment.

He looked up for a moment again at the stars in the night sky, then back at the floodlit pitch. Tania Whitlock's Specialist Search Unit had scanned the area and not found any more bodies. So far.

But the English Channel was a big place.

39

'You know, Jim,' Vlad Cosmescu said, 'it's a very big place, the English Channel, no?'

Jim Towers, bound head to foot in duct tape once again, including his mouth, was only able to communicate with his captor via his eyes. He lay on the hard fibreglass deck of the prow cabin of the *Scoob-Eee* and was further concealed from anyone who might have looked down into the boat from the quay by a tarpaulin which smelled faintly of someone's vomit.

Cosmescu, his feet in tall gumboots, steered the boat out of the mouth of Shoreham Harbour and into the open sea, a little concerned at the size of the swell. The northerly wind was stronger out here than he had realized and the sea much choppier. He sat on the plastic seat, his navigation lights on, making sure he appeared to the coastguard, and to anyone else who might be watching, just like any other fishing boat heading out for a night's sport.

Wrinkling his nose at the smell of diesel exhaust being blown forward by the wind, he watched the illuminated compass swinging in its binnacle, steering a 160-degree course that he reckoned should take him out into mid-Channel, well away from the dredge area which he had carefully memorized from the chart.

A mobile phone rang, a very muted warbling sound. For an instant the Romanian thought it was from somewhere under the decking; then he realized it must be in one of the retired PI's pockets. After several rings it stopped.

Towers just looked up at him, with the inert eyes of a beached fish.

'It's probably OK to speak now. Not too many people around to hear you,' Cosmescu said.

He cut the throttle, stepped down into the cabin and tore the duct tape from the other man's mouth.

Towers gasped in agony. It felt as if half his face had been ripped away.

'Look,' he said, 'it's my wedding anniversary today.'

'You should have told me that sooner. I'd have got you a card,' Cosmescu said, with only the faintest trace of humour. He stepped back quickly to the wheel.

'You didn't give me a chance to warn you. My wife's going to be worried. She was expecting me back. She'll have contacted the coastguard and the police by now. That would have been her ringing.'

As if on cue, the phone beeped twice, indicating a message.

'Is that so?' Cosmescu said breezily, not giving away his concern at this unexpected news. He kept an eye on the riding lights of a fishing boat some way off, and on the lights of a big ship out in the distance heading east. 'In that case we will have to be quick! So, tell me what you have to say!'

'I made a mistake,' Towers said. 'A mistake, OK? I screwed up.'

'A mistake?'

Cosmescu dug in his pockets and pulled out a Silk Cut. Cupping his hands over his gold lighter, he lit it, inhaled deeply and then exhaled the smoke down at the man.

The sweet smell tantalized the former PI. 'Could I cadge one, please?'

Cosmescu shook his head. 'Smoking is very bad for your

health.' He took another deep drag. 'And you have a law in England now, don't you? Smoking is banned in the work-place. This is your workplace.'

He blew more smoke down at the other man.

'Mr Baker, I'm sure we can sort this out – you know – your grievance with me.'

'Oh yes, we can,' Cosmescu said, gripping the wheel tightly, as the boat ploughed through a big wave. 'I agree with you.'

He glanced at the depth gauge. Sixty feet of water beneath them. Not deep enough. They motored on in silence for some moments.

'I paid you twenty thousand pounds, Mr Towers. I thought that was very generous. I thought it might be the start of a nice business arrangement between us.'

'Yeah, it was extremely generous.'

'But not enough?'

'Plenty. It was plenty.'

'I don't think so. You are an experienced sailor, so you know these waters. Do you know what I think, Mr Towers? You took me to the dredge area deliberately. You reckoned there was a good chance the bodies would be found there.'

'No, you are wrong!'

Ignoring him, Cosmescu went on, 'I'm a gambling man. I like to play percentages. Now, the dimensions of the English Channel are twenty-nine thousand square miles. I paid you to take me to a place where those bodies would never be found. You took me to a dredge area that is just a hundred square miles. Do the maths, Mr Towers.'

'You have to believe me, please!'

Cosmescu nodded. 'Oh yes. I've done the maths. A hundred feet is the maximum depth for a dredger. In just a hundred and thirty feet of water, no one would have found them, Mr Towers. Are you going to tell me that an experienced boatman like yourself did not know this? That in all the years you have been operating your business from Shoreham, you never saw the dredge area marked on the chart?'

'I made a navigation error, I swear it!'

Cosmescu smoked in silence for a short while, then continued, 'You see, I'm a gambler, Mr Towers, and I think that you are too. You took a punt on this dredge area and you got lucky. You figured that if the bodies were discovered, you could blackmail me for a lot of money to keep quiet.'

'That's really not true,' Towers said.

'If you had had the opportunity to get to know me better, Mr Towers, you would know that I am a man who always plays the percentages. You might not win so much that way, but you stay in the game longer.'

Cosmescu finished his cigarette and tossed it overboard, watching the hot red tip sail through the air, before disappearing into the black water.

'I'm sure we can work this out – find something that you will be happy with.'

Cosmescu watched the compass. The boat was very skittish and he had to correct the wheel sharply to bring her back on course.

'You see, Mr Towers, I have to take a gamble now. If I kill you, there is a chance I will get caught. But if I let you live, there is also a chance I will get caught. In my view, that is a much bigger chance, I'm sorry to inform you.'

Cosmescu pulled a roll of duct tape from his windcheater pocket, together with the bone-handle knife that he always carried. It was one he had learned to trust over the years. A button in the side released the blade, which with a flick of his wrist, would swing out and lock into place. And, as past experience showed, it was tough enough not to break when it struck human bone. He kept it as sharp as a razor and indeed on one occasion on his travels, when he did not have his razor with him, it had given him a very satisfactory shave.

'I think now we have said everything we have to say to each other, no?'

'Please – look – I could—'

But that was as far as he got before the Romanian sealed his lips again.

*

Forty minutes later the lights of the Brighton and Hove coastline were still visible, but disappearing every few moments behind the inky blackness of waves. Cosmescu, finishing another cigarette, killed the engine and switched off the navigation lights. There was a comfortable 150 feet of water beneath them. This was a good place.

He was still smarting from the phone call he had received two nights ago in the casino, when he was told in no uncertain terms by his paymaster that he had fucked up. The man was right, he had fucked up. He had broken the rule that you never involve others unless you absolutely had to. He should have just hired a boat and taken the bodies out himself in the first place. There was nothing at all to driving it and navigating – a child of four could do it.

But he'd had a good reason; or at least it had seemed good at the time. A guy repeatedly hiring a boat in the cold winter months and going out on his own would soon arouse suspicion. All boats heading in and out of the harbour were noticed, and suspicious ones watched. But the coastguard would not bat an eyelid at a local fisherman taking his charter boat in and out, however often he went.

Now, watched only by the stars and the silent eyes of the boat's owner, he unclipped and pulled up some of the decking, then, with the aid of a torch, identified the sea cocks. He tested one and instantly icy seawater flooded in. Good. At least Towers kept his boat well maintained.

He walked to the stern, unrolled the grey, inflatable Zodiac dinghy he had bought the previous day, and lifted clear the oxygen cylinder, petrol tank and Yamaha outboard motor, which were parcelled up inside it, along with a paddle.

Ten minutes later, perspiring from exertion, the Romanian had the Zodiac in the water, tied up alongside, with its engine running at tick-over speed. It bobbed up and down alarmingly, but it would be more stable, he reckoned, when he added his body weight to it.

The deck was now awash and water was bubbling up steadily from the two opened sea cocks. It was already almost up to Jim Towers's chin. Cosmescu, glad of his rubber boots, shone the beam on his face, watching the man's eyes, which were frantically trying to communicate with him.

Now the water was over Towers's chin. Cosmescu switched off the torch and scanned the horizon. Except for the lights of Brighton and the occasional sparkle of phosphorescence on a cresting wave, there was just darkness. He listened to the slap of the sea on the hull. He could feel the *Scoob-Eee* settling down deeper into the water, rocking progressively less under the water ballast it was now sinking at a fast rate.

He switched the torch back on and saw Jim Towers

frantically trying to raise his head above the water, which now completely covered his mouth.

'My advice, Mr Towers, is, just before the water reaches your nostrils, take a very deep breath. That will buy you a good extra minute or so of life. There are a lot of things that a human being can do in sixty seconds. You may even have an extra ninety seconds, if you are a fit man.'

But by this time he wasn't sure if the other man could still hear him. It seemed unlikely, as the water was immersing his face.

And the dinghy was parallel with the deck rail.

Textbook stuff! Never leave a sinking boat until you can step *up* into the life raft. Ninety seconds later, he did just that and cast it free, then motored away into the darkness. Then he waited, circling slowly, until the black silhouette disappeared beneath the surface, sending up large bubbles, some of which he could hear above the burble of the outboard.

Then he twisted the throttle grip and felt the surge of acceleration as the prow of the Zodiac rose, then thumped over a wave. Spray lashed his face. The prow surged down the far side of a wave, then thumped over another. Freezing, salty water sloshed over him. The little craft pulled sharply left, then right. For a moment he felt a twinge of panic that he was not going to make it, that he was going to get flipped over. But then they crested a wave and the lights of Brighton, blurry through his salty eyes, seemed just that little bit brighter. That little bit closer.

Gradually, the sea quietened as he neared the coast. He aimed for the lights of the pier and the Marina to the east of it. Beyond the Marina was the under-cliff walk. Few people, if anyone at all, would be there on this blustery, freezing November night. Or on any of the beaches.

That it was Jim Towers's wedding anniversary tonight was a problem. Another potential fuck-up. Unless he had been lying. What if the man's wife had called the police? The coastguard? Perhaps his disappearance would be reported in the local paper. He would have to watch carefully and see what was printed, then work around it.

Twenty minutes later, the silhouette of the cliffs in front of him, the Marina a safe distance to his left, he twisted the throttle up to maximum for several seconds, then cut the engine. He unscrewed the two wing nuts holding the five-horsepower engine to the transom and jettisoned the outboard into the sea.

The Zodiac continued travelling forward under its own momentum. In the lee of the cliffs, there was barely any wind to impede his progress. Gripping the paddle, he kept the prow of the craft pointing inshore, listening to the increasingly loud sound of breaking waves on shingle, until they jerked to an abrupt halt.

A wave broke over the stern, drenching him.

Cursing, he jumped out, and into water far deeper and far colder than he had estimated. Right up to his shoulders. A wave sucked him back and for an instant he panicked. Shingle gave way beneath his boots. He leaned forward, determinedly, dragging the craft by the line attached to its bow. Then he tumbled on to the hard pebbles of the beach.

Another wave broke and this time the prow of the Zodiac bashed him on the back of his head. He cursed again. Stumbling to his feet, he fell forward again. Then he clambered up, struggling to get a purchase on all the mad loose stuff beneath him. He took several more steps forward, until the dinghy became a dead weight behind him.

He dragged it on up the beach, then listened carefully in the darkness, watching all around him. Nothing. No one.

Just the crashing of waves and the sucking of water on shingle.

He pulled the rubber stops out of each side of the dinghy, and slowly rolled it up, expelling the air. Then, using his knife, he cut the deflated craft, which was like a giant bladder, into several strips and scooped them into a bundle.

Struggling under its wet weight, he made his way along the walk beneath the cliffs to where he had left his van earlier today, in the ASDA superstore car park in the Marina, depositing strips into each of the rubbish bins he came to on his route.

It was a few minutes to midnight. He could have used a drink and a couple of hours at the roulette table in the Rendezvous Casino to calm down. But in his bedraggled state that was not a smart option.

40

Including Roy Grace, there were twenty-two detectives and support staff assembled around two of the three communal work stations in Major Incident Room One, on the top floor of Sussex House.

The Major Incident Suite, reached through a warren of cream-painted corridors, occupied about a third of this floor. It comprised two Major Incident Rooms, of which MIR One was the larger, two witness interview rooms, a conference room for police and press briefings, the Crime Scene labs, and several offices for SIOs based elsewhere to move into during major investigations here.

MIR One was bright and modern-looking. It had small windows set high up with vertical blinds, as well as one frosted-glass ceiling panel, on which rain was pattering. There were no decorations to distract from the purpose of this place, which was absolute focus on the solving of serious violent crimes.

On the walls were whiteboards, to which had been pinned photographs of the three victims of Operation Neptune. The first young man was shown in plastic sheeting in the slipper of the drag head of the *Arco Dee* dredger, then during various stages of his post-mortem. There were photographs of the second and third victims in their body bags on the deck of the *Scoob-Eee* deep-sea fishing boat, then also during their post-mortems. One, blown up larger than the others, was a close-up of the upper arm of the female, showing the tattoo with a ruler across it to give a sense of scale.

Also pinned to the whiteboard, providing light relief, was a picture of the Yellow Submarine from the Beatles album, beneath the words Operation Neptune. It had become traditional to illustrate the names of all operations with an image. This one had been devised by some wag on the inquiry team – probably Guy Batchelor, Grace guessed.

The morning's copy of the *Argus* lay beside Grace's open policy book and his notes, typed up by his MSA, which were in front of him on the imitation light-oak surface. The headline read: TWO MORE BODIES FOUND IN CHANNEL.

It could have been a lot worse. Kevin Spinella had done an uncharacteristically restrained job, writing up the story pretty much as Grace had spun it to him, saying that the police suspected the bodies had been dumped from a vessel passing through the Channel. It was enough to give the local community the information they were entitled to, enough to get them thinking about any teenagers they knew who had recently had surgery and had subsequently disappeared, but not enough to cause panic.

For Grace, this had become a potentially very important case. A triple homicide on the home turf of the new Chief Constable, within weeks of his commencing in the post. No doubt the poisonous ACC Vosper had already told Tom Martinson exactly what she thought of Grace, whose clumsy attempt to strike up conversation with him at Jim Wilkinson's retirement party would have added credibility to her opinion. He intended to get a few minutes with Martinson at the dinner dance tonight, and an opportunity to assure him that this case was in good hands.

Dressed casually, in a black leather jacket over a navy sweatshirt and a white T-shirt, jeans and trainers, Roy Grace opened proceedings. 'The time is 8.30 a.m., Saturday 29 November. This is the fourth briefing of Operation Neptune, the investigation into the deaths of three unknown persons, identified as Unknown Male 1, Unknown Male 2, and Unknown Female. This operation is commanded by myself, and by DI Mantle in my absence.'

He gestured to the Detective Inspector opposite him for the benefit of those who did not know her. Unlike many of the team in here, who were also dressed in casual weekend gear, Lizzie Mantle still wore one of her trademark masculine suits, today's a brown and white chalk-stripe, her only concession to the weekend being to wear a brown roll-neck sweater instead of a more formal blouse.

'I know several of you are going to the CID dinner dance tonight,' Grace continued, 'and because it is the weekend, a lot of people we need to speak to won't be around, so I'm going to give some of you Sunday off. For those working over the weekend, we'll have just one briefing tomorrow, at midday, by which time some of those at the ball will have slept off their hangovers.' He grinned. 'Then we return to our routine at 8.30 a.m. on Monday.'

At least Cleo understood the long and frequently antisocial hours his work demanded of him, and was supportive, he thought with some relief. That was in marked contrast to his years with Sandy, for whom his weekend working was a big issue.

He glanced at his notes. 'We are waiting on the pathologist's toxicology results, which may help us with the cause of death, but they won't come through until Monday. Meantime, I'm going to start with reports for Unknown Male 1.'

He looked at Bella Moy, who had her habitual box of Maltesers open in front of her. She plucked one out, as if it was her drug, and popped it into her mouth.

'Bella, anything on dental records?'

Rolling the chocolate around inside her mouth, she said, 'No match so far, Roy, for Unknown Male 1, but something that may be significant. Two of the dentists I went to see commented that the condition of the young man's teeth was poor for his age – indicative of bad nutrition and healthcare, and perhaps drug abuse. So it is likely he came from a deprived background.'

'There was nothing about dental work on his teeth that gave the dentists any clue to his nationality?' Lizzie Mantle quizzed.

'No,' Bella said. 'There is no indication of any dental work, so it is quite possible he has never been to a dentist. In which case we are not going to find a match.'

'You'll have the three sets to take around on Monday,' Grace said. 'That should broaden your chances.'

'I could do with a couple of other officers with me to cover all the dental practices quickly.'

'OK. I'll check our manpower resources after the meeting.' Grace made a quick note, then turned to Norman Potting. 'You were going to speak to organ transplant coordinators, Norman. Anything?'

'I'm working my way through all the ones at every hospital within a hundred-mile radius of here, Roy,' Potting said. 'So far nothing, but I've discovered something of interest!' He fell tantalizingly silent, with a smug grin.

'Do you want to share it with us?' Grace asked.

The DS was wearing the same jacket he always seemed to wear at weekends, whether winter or summer. A crumpled tweed affair with shoulder epaulettes and poacher's pockets. He dug his hand into one, with slow deliberation, as if about to pull out something of great significance, but instead just left it there, irritatingly jingling some loose coins or keys as he spoke.

'There's a world shortage of human organs,' he announced. Then he pursed his lips and nodded his head sagely. 'Particularly kidneys and livers. Do you know why?'

'No, but I'm sure we are about to find out,' Bella Moy said irritably, and popped another Malteser into her mouth.

'Car seat belts!' Potting said triumphantly. 'The best donors are those who die from head injuries, with the rest of their bodies left intact. Now that more people wear seat belts in cars, they only tend to die if they are totally mangled, or incinerated. How's that for irony? In the old days, people would hit the windscreen head-first and die from that. It's mostly motorcyclists today.'

'Thank you, Norman,' said Grace.

'Something else that might be of interest,' Potting said. 'Manila in the Philippines is now actually nicknamed *One Kidney Island*.'

Bella shook her head cynically and said, 'Oh, come on. That's an urban myth!'

Grace cautioned her with a raised hand. 'What's the significance, Norman?'

'It's where wealthy Westerners go to buy kidneys from poor locals. The locals get a grand – a substantial sum of money by their standards. By the time you've bought it and had it transplanted, you're looking at forty to sixty grand.'

'Forty to sixty thousand pounds?' Grace repeated, astonished.

'A liver can fetch five or six times that amount,' Potting replied. 'People who've been on a waiting list for years get desperate.'

'The people here aren't Filipinos,' Bella said.

'I spoke to the coastguard again,' Potting said, ignoring her. 'Gave him the weight of the breeze blocks holding down our first poor sod. He doesn't think the weather conditions of the past week would have been strong enough to have moved him. Most of the current is on or near the surface. Maybe if there had been a tsunami, but not otherwise.'

'Thank you. That's good information,' Grace said, noting it down. 'Nick?'

Glenn Branson, still looking ragged, raised a hand. 'Sorry to interrupt. Just a quick point, Roy. All three of these persons could have been killed in another country, or even on a ship, and just dumped into the Channel, right? The story that you told the *Argus*?'

'Yes. A few more miles further off the coast and they would not have been our problem. But they were found inside UK territorial waters, so they are. I've already got two of our researchers compiling a list of every known vessel that has passed through the Channel in the last seven days. But I don't know yet how we are going to find the resources to follow up that information, or even if it's worth trying.'

'Well,' Branson went on, 'the bodies were found in about sixty-five feet of water – so if they hadn't drifted they were dropped there, from a boat or a plane or a chopper. Some of the bigger container ships and supertankers using the English Channel need more draught than that, so we should be able to eliminate quite a bit of shipping. Also, I would have thought that any boat skipper would know from the Admiralty charts that it was a dredge area, and keep clear of it as a dump site if he didn't want these to be discovered. A chopper or private plane pilot might not have looked at the Admiralty charts – or noticed. So I think we ought to check out the local airports, particularly Shoreham, find out what aircraft have been up during the past week and check them out.'

'I agree,' DI Mantle said. 'Glenn's making a good point.

The problem is we don't know what might have taken off from a private airfield without filing a flight plan. If it was a light aircraft on a mission to dump bodies, it's quite possible the pilot wouldn't have done.'

'Or it could have been a plane from overseas somewhere,' Nick Nicholl said.

'I doubt that, Nick,' Grace said. 'Any foreign aircraft, say from France, would just go out a few miles into the Channel. They wouldn't fly into British airspace.'

Branson shook his head. 'No, sorry, chief, I disagree. They might have done it deliberately.'

'How do you mean *deliberately*?' DI Mantle asked.

'Like, a double-bluff kind of thing,' the DS replied. 'Knowing we might find them and assume they were from England.'

Grace smiled. 'Glenn, I think you've watched too many films. If someone from overseas was dumping bodies in the sea, they'd be doing it because they didn't want them to be found – and they wouldn't fly that close to the English coastline.' He jotted down a note. 'But we need to check every local airport and flying club – and air traffic controllers. And that can be done over the weekend, as they'll be open.'

David Browne raised a hand. The Crime Scene Manager, in his early forties, could easily have passed for the actor Daniel Craig's freckled, ginger-haired brother. It had long been a standing joke among his colleagues that a few years back, when the film company was casting the new James Bond, it had sent the contract to the wrong man. Dressed in a zippered fleece jacket, over an open-neck shirt, jeans and trainers, with his powerful shoulders and close-cropped hair, he appeared every inch an action man. But Browne's looks belied his thorough approach to crime scenes, and his tireless attention to detail, which had taken him almost as high up the SOCO ladder as it was possible to rise.

'All three bodies were wrapped in similar industrial-strength PVC, which can be purchased from any hardware or DIY store. They were bound with high-tensile cord that's again widely available. My view is whoever did this wasn't intending them to come back up. So far as the perp was concerned, it was *job done.*'

'What are the chances of finding out where these items were purchased?' Grace asked.

'It wasn't a big quantity,' Browne said. 'Not enough to stick in anyone's mind. There are hundreds of places that sell them. But it would be worth doing a trawl of all the local suppliers. Most of them will be open over the weekend.'

Grace made another note on his *Resourcing* list. Then he turned to DC Nicholl again.

'Nick?'

'I've checked the Mispers lists. They have quite a number of missing teenagers who could be matches. They want me to let them have photographs of the victims.'

'Chris Heaver's been given photographs of all three of them. He's preparing sanitized versions to release to the press on Monday. You can send them to the Missing People office at the same time.'

Chris Heaver was the Facial Identification Officer.

'We'll also get them circulated to every police station in the south-east, and see if we can get them on *Crimewatch* if we've no joy by the time the next show screens. Anyone know when that is?'

'Tuesday week,' Bella said. 'I checked.'

Grace screwed up his face in disappointment. It was a long time to wait. Then he addressed the young DC, Emma-Jane Boutwood.

'E-J?'

'Well,' she said, in her plummy, public-school voice, 'I've looked into the case of the headless and limbless torso of the small boy that was recovered from the Thames in 2001. The police gave the poor little chap, who has never been identified, the name Adam. It was eventually established that he had come from Nigeria by the examination of microscopic granules of plants found in his intestines. The expert used was a Dr Hazel Wilkinson of the Jodrell Laboratory at Kew Gardens.'

David Browne, the Crime Scene Manager, raised his hand again. 'Roy, we know Hazel – we've worked with her on a number of cases.'

'OK,' Grace said. 'E-J, will you arrange to get her what she needs from Nadiuska?'

'Yes, and there's something else. I read about this in hospital.' She gave a wan smile and a shrug. 'Thought I might as well try to make use of my time there! One of the forensic labs we use for DNA, Cellmark Forensics, has a US parent, Orchid Cellmark. I've been in touch with a helpful guy over there called Matt Greenhalgh – he's the Director of Forensics. He told me their labs in the US have been making progress analysing the isotopes in enzymes in DNA. Matt said they have established that food – in particular its constituent minerals – is sufficiently localized to get a region of origin, if not an actual country. Lab samples from Unknown Male 1 have been expressed out there and we should hear back early in the week.'

'Good. Thanks, E-J,' he said. He pondered the value of this for a moment, when foodstuffs were now regularly shipped all over the world. But it might help. Then he stood up and walked over to one of the whiteboards and pointed at the close-up photograph of the female's upper arm. 'Do you all see this?'

Everyone in the room nodded. It was a crude tattoo, one inch long, spelling RARES.

'Rares?' Norman Potting said. 'Could be a bad spelling of *rash*! Which might mean it's a nasty rash!' He chuckled at his own joke.

'My guess is it's a name,' Roy Grace said, ignoring him. 'The most likely thing a teenage girl would have tattooed on her arm is the name of a boyfriend. This one looks as if she might have done it herself. Anyone ever heard of this name?'

No one had.

'Norman and E-J, I'm tasking you with finding out if this is a real name – and in which country. Or what it means if it isn't a name.'

Then he looked at DI Mantle. 'I know you've been out of the loop for a couple of days on your course, Lizzie. Anything you need to know at this stage?'

'No, I'm up to speed, Roy,' she said.

'Good.'

Still on his feet, he glanced around the room and looked at the HOLMES analyst, Juliet Jones, a dark-haired woman in a brown-striped shirt.

'Over the weekend we need a scoping operation – check with every county force in the UK to see if they have anything remotely similar. We can't assume this is about transplants. It's the most obvious line of enquiry, but we mustn't rule out having a lone nutter on our hands. Nadiuska reckons that whoever did this has surgical skills. We need to find out from the Home Office about every surgeon, and doctor with surgical skills, who has been released from prison or from a mental home in the last couple of years as another starting point.' He thought for a moment. 'And all surgeons who have been struck off who might have a grievance.' He noted this down as an action for the researchers.

'What about the Internet, Roy?' asked David Browne. 'I recall that someone advertised a kidney for sale on eBay a few years ago. It would be worth a trawl.'

'Yes, that's a very good point.' He turned to Lizzie Mantle. 'Can you get the High-Tech Crime Unit on to that? See if anyone is advertising organs for sale.'

'Do you *really* think anyone would do that, Roy?' Bella asked. 'Kill victims and *sell* their organs?'

Grace had long passed the period when he questioned human potential for evil. You could take the most horrific thing your brain was capable of imagining, then multiply it by a factor of ten and it still would not bring you close to the levels of depravity that people were capable of.

'Yes,' he said. 'Unfortunately, I do.'

41

Half past three and it was already growing dark outside. Lynn stood at her kitchen table, staring out of the window, waiting for the microwave, which was making a sound like a chainsaw inside a metal dustbin, to finish its cycle. Rain was pelting down and the back garden, which she tended proudly for most of the year, now looked badly neglected.

The autumn roses needed dead-heading, and the grass, beneath a carpet of fallen leaves, needed cutting again now, even though it was the end of November – *thank you, global warming*, she thought. Maybe next weekend she would have the energy and enthusiasm. If . . .

A big *if*.

If she could get through the terrible fear for Caitlin that was gripping her, almost paralysing her mind, making it impossible to concentrate on anything, even the newspaper.

There was something about Sunday afternoons that she had never liked, for as far back as she could remember. A feeling of gloom that the weekend was ending and it was back to the real world the next day. But it wasn't just gloom this afternoon. She felt sick with fear for Caitlin and helpless – and angry at her helplessness. Seeing her daughter's frightened face these past days in the hospital and being unable to offer her anything but words of reassurance, a few teenage magazines and some CDs was eating away at her soul.

Helping people was one of the things she had always done best in life. For two years during her mid-teens she had helped her younger sister, Lorraine, crippled and bed-ridden after being knocked off her bike by a lorry, slowly get back to health and start walking again. Five years ago, she had again helped Lorraine through her divorce and then through the battle she had finally lost against breast cancer.

After her own divorce, her mother had been her rock, but she was growing old and, although still strong, at some point in the coming years Lynn knew that she would lose her too. If she lost Caitlin as well, she would be utterly alone in the world, and that selfish thought scared her almost as much as the pain of seeing Caitlin suffering now.

The last few days in the Royal South London had been a living hell. They had organized a room for her for the past three nights, in a Salvation Army training centre across the street from Caitlin's ward, but she had barely spent any time in it, not wanting to miss out on any of the examinations and tests for transplant suitability that Caitlin had been put through, almost around the clock. She'd chosen instead to sleep in a chair next to her daughter's bed.

She had lost count of the people her daughter had seen. All the different members of the transplant team, the social workers, the nurses, the registrar, the consultant hepatologist, the consultant surgeon, the anaesthetist. All the scans, the blood tests, the base line measurements, the imaging, lung function, cardiac assessments and seemingly endless and repetitive clinical reviews.

'I'm just an exhibit, right?' Caitlin had said, despairingly, at one point.

The one person to whom Caitlin responded, the consultant, Dr Abid Suddle, had assured them both, this morning, that hopefully a match would be found very quickly, despite Caitlin's rare blood group. It was possible within just a few days, he said.

Lynn always felt reassured by him. She liked the man's energy, his warmth and his genuine concern. She saw he was someone who worked incredibly long hours and she believed he truly would go the extra mile for Caitlin, but the fact remained that there was a world shortage of livers and Caitlin had a rare blood group. And there was another problem. As had already been explained to them, Caitlin had chronic liver disease. Priority was given to those with acute liver disease.

Dr Suddle had explained that there were other, not so rare blood groups that could be a match in liver transplants, so that needn't be a cause for worry. Caitlin was going to be fine, he told her. And Lynn knew that Dr Abid Suddle did want her to be fine.

But she also knew he was part of a system. He was just one exhausted member of a very big, very overworked and permanently exhausted but caring team. And Luke, who had frightened her, had made her go to the Internet herself. It was hard to find an accurate figure for the number of people in the UK waiting for a liver transplant. Dr Suddle had admitted privately that 19 per cent at the Royal died before one became available. And she felt sure he was not telling her the whole truth. Priorities got shifted at every week's Wednesday meeting. In all the down-time she had, she talked to patients who found themselves endlessly bumped down the list by others in worse condition than themselves.

It was a lottery.

She felt so damn helpless.

The thick wodge of the *Observer* newspaper and all its supplements lay on the table and she glanced at one of the front-page headlines, forecasting more economic gloom, falling property prices, rises in bankruptcies. And tomorrow, going back to work again, she would have to deal with the human fallout from all of that stuff.

She felt sorry for almost everyone she spoke to on the phone when she was at work. Decent, ordinary folk who had got themselves into a financial mess. There was one woman, Anne Florence, almost the same age as herself, and with a sick teenage daughter. Her problems had begun a few years back when she bought a car on hire purchase for £15,000, but failed to keep up the insurance payments and then the car was stolen. It left her still owing the hire purchase company, but without a car.

Unable to afford another car, she had gone ahead and bought one using plastic. And had then taken out new cards, using the cash limits of each new one to pay off the previous ones.

For over a year now, Lynn had almost weekly renegotiated her monthly repayments on a £5,000 debt to one card company, a client of her firm, allowing her smaller and smaller repayments. But to make matters worse, she had fallen badly into arrears with her mortgage. She knew it was only a matter of time before the poor woman lost her house – and everything else.

She wished she had a magic wand that could make everything OK for Anne Florence, and the dozens like her she dealt with daily, but all she could do was be sympathetic but firm. And she was a damn sight better at being *sympathetic* than at being *firm*.

Max, their tabby cat, rubbed himself against her legs. She knelt and stroked him, feeling the reassurance of his soft, warm fur.

'You're lucky, Max,' she said. 'You don't know all the shit that happens in human lives, do you?'

If Max did, he wasn't letting on. He just purred.

She picked up the phone and dialled her best friend, Sue Shackleton, on whom she could always rely for cheery support. But the phone went to Sue's voicemail. She remembered, vaguely, something about Sue's new boy-friend taking her away to Rome for the weekend. She left a message, then hung up forlornly.

As she did so, the microwave pinged. She waited for another minute, then opened the door and took out the pizza. She then cut it into sections, put it on a tray and carried it through into the lounge.

As she opened the door, the television was blaring. On the screen she recognized two of the characters of *Laguna Beach*, one of the soaps her daughter was addicted to. Caitlin was lying on the sofa, her head on Luke's chest, barefoot, her toes curled, two cans of Coke open on the glass-topped coffee table. She looked at her daughter's face for a moment, saw her totally absorbed in the programme, smiling at something, and for an instant she felt over-whelmed by a rush of emotion. She had a strong desire to cradle Caitlin in her arms.

God, the girl needed reassurance – *deserved* reassur-ance. And she deserved someone a lot better than that dickhead, with his stupid, lopsided hairstyle, on the sofa with her.

She was still furious at him for spooking Caitlin – and herself – with the statistics about the numbers of people on transplant waiting lists – and their mortality rate.

'Pizza!' she said, a lot more cheerfully than she felt.

Luke, in a hoodie, ripped jeans and untied trainers,

peered at her from under his slanted fringe, then raised a hand as if he was directing traffic.

'Yeah! Cool! I'm cool with pizza.'

You'd look even cooler wearing it as a hat, Lynn thought. She could have happily dumped it all on his head. Instead, she kept calm, put the tray down, exited the room and returned to the kitchen. Ignoring the Sunday newspaper, she picked up the Val McDermid crime novel she had been reading for the past few days, in the hope of immersing herself in a different world for an hour or so.

In the novel a man was putting a victim into a replica of a medieval torture machine and Lynn suddenly thought how pleasant it would be to put Luke into such a machine.

Then she put the book down and cried.

42

Susan Cooper was utterly exhausted. She had lost track of the days since Nat's accident. Apart from brief trips home for a shower and change of clothing, she had lived here, in this ITU ward, since last Wednesday. It was now, according to the *Daily Mail* newspaper on her lap, Monday.

The paper was full of advertisements bordered with holly, and cheery, festive articles and tips. How to avoid a Christmas hangover! How to avoid putting on those extra pounds during the festive season! How to decorate your tree using recycled household rubbish! A hundred great Christmas gift ideas! How to buy your man a gift he will never forget!

How about, *How to help your man live until Christmas*, she thought bleakly, or, *How to help your man live long enough to see his unborn child*?

In the last five days there had been no change. The five longest days of her life. Five days of living in a chair at Nat's bedside in the blue ITU ward. She was sick of the sight of blue. Sick of the pale blue of the walls, the blue of the curtains that at the moment were drawn around his bed, the blue of the venetian blinds, the blue tops and trousers of the nursing staff and the doctors. The only different colour came from all the cards he had been sent. She'd given the flowers to another ward, as there was no room in here.

She toyed with going into the curtained area, but it was crowded with medics at the moment. An alarm suddenly chimed. *BEEP-BEEP-BONG.* Then stopped almost instantly. She hated that alarm more and more. Every damn time it spooked her. Then another one chimed on the far side of the ward. She put the paper down and stood up, needing a break.

There was another alarm chime from Nat's bed and she wondered again whether to check inside the curtain. But she had been checking constantly, quizzing every member of the medical staff day in and day out, and knew she must be close to driving them demented. She decided to go out of the ward for a few minutes to get a change of scenery.

She walked past several beds, the occupants mostly intubated and silent, either asleep or staring vacantly, and stopped by the hygienic hand-rub dispenser on the wall by the door. Dutifully giving her hands a squirt and massaging the gunk into her skin, she then pressed the green button to unlock the door, pushed it open and stepped out of the ward. She walked, like a zombie, along the corridor, past the door on her left to the quiet room and the one on her right to the larger, but no more cheerful, waiting room, past an abstract painting that looked like a collision between two trucks filled with multicoloured cuttlefish, and further along the corridor to the window on the far side of the lift.

This had become her window on the outside world.

It was the window she stared through on to an alternative reality. Rooftops and soaring gulls, and the Channel beyond. A world of tranquil normality. A world in which Nat was fine. A world in which the grey hulls of ships passed along the grey horizon, and in which, yesterday, she had watched the distant white sails of yachts out of the Marina racing around marker buoys. The winter racing series, the Frostbite Series. She knew all about it, because for a couple of years, on Sunday mornings that he had off, Nat had crewed on one of those yachts, grinding winches. He had enjoyed the fresh air and, like squash, found it a good escape from the pressures of the hospital.

Then he had bought the motorbike and instead had spent his free Sunday mornings racing around the country-side with a group of other born-again bikers. The bike she hated so much.

Oh shit, she thought. *Oh shit, oh shit, oh shit.*

As if sensing her mood, her baby moved inside her.

'Hi, Bump,' she said. Then she pulled out her mobile phone. Eight missed calls. New message after new message after new message. Nat's brother. His sailing friends. His squash partner. His sister. Jane, her best friend, and two other girlfriends, as well.

She heard footfalls behind her. Soft and squeaky on the linoleum. Then a female voice she did not recognize.

'Mrs Cooper?'

She turned and saw a pleasant-looking woman who was holding a clipboard loaded with forms. In her late thirties, the woman had long, light brown hair pulled back into a bun, a brown and cream striped top, black trousers and soft black shoes. On her chest was pinned a badge which read, *Specialist Nurse.*

'I'm Chris Jackson,' she said, then smiled sympatheti-cally. 'How are you?'

Susan shrugged and gave a wan smile. 'Not great, if you want to know the truth.'

There was a brief moment of hesitation and Susan felt awkward, sensing something bad was coming.

'Could we have a chat for a few minutes, Mrs Cooper?' the nurse asked. 'If I'm not interrupting anything, that is.'

'Yes, fine.'

'Perhaps we could go into the quiet room. Can I get you a cup of tea?'

'Thank you.'

'How do you take it?'

'Milk, no sugar.'

A few minutes later Susan was seated on a green chair with wooden arms in the windowless quiet room. There was a corner table with what looked like a bedside table lamp with a fringed shade on it. A small mirror was mounted on one wall, a print of a dreary landscape on another, and there was a tiny fan, switched off. The atmosphere was oppressive.

Chris Jackson returned with two cups of tea and sat opposite her. She smiled, pleasantly but awkwardly.

'May I call you Susan?'

She nodded.

'I'm afraid, Susan, it's not looking good.' She stirred her tea. 'We've done everything we can for your husband. Because of who he is, and the affection the staff have for him, everyone has put in even more effort than normal. But in five days he has not responded, and I'm afraid there has been a development this morning.'

'What's that?'

'The frequent check of his pupils reveals that there's been a change in the brain consistent with raised pressure.'

'His pupils have blown, right?' Susan said.

Chris Jackson gave a grim smile. 'Yes, of course. With your background, you'd understand.'

'And I understand the severity of his brain damage. How much longer do you – do you think – you know . . .' She started choking on the words. 'That he'll be with us?'

'There are more repeat tests to be done, but it's looking

conclusive. Is there anyone you would like to call? Any other family members you would like to be here, to say goodbye to him, and to give you support?'

Susan put her cup and saucer down, dug in her handbag for a tissue, then dabbed her eyes and nodded.

'His brother – he's on his way down from London anyway – he should be here soon. I – I—' She shook her head, sniffed and took a deep breath, trying to calm herself while fighting back tears. 'How sure are you?'

'There was a rise in his blood pressure to 220 over 110. Then it plunged to 90 over 40. Do you understand the significance of that?'

'Yes.' Susan nodded, her eyes becoming a damburst of tears. 'Nat has effectively died. Right?'

'I'm afraid so,' said Chris Jackson very quietly.

Susan nodded, pressing the tissue hard against each eye in turn. The other woman waited patiently. After a few minutes, Susan sipped some tea.

'Look,' Chris Jackson said. 'There is something I'm going to talk to you about now. Because your husband is in here, and his body is intact, to a large extent, you have the option of donating his vital organs to help save the lives of others.'

She paused, waiting for a reaction.

Susan stared silently down into her cup.

'A lot of people get comfort from this. It means that the death of their loved one can at least help to save the lives of others. It would mean that something positive comes out of Nat's death.'

'I'm pregnant,' she said. 'I'm carrying his child. He's not going to see it now, is he?'

'But at least something of him will live on in this child.'

Susan stared at her tea again. It felt as if there was a band of steel tightening around her gullet.

'How – I mean, if I – he – donated organs, would he be – you know – disfigured?'

'He would receive the same medical care as if he was a living patient. He wouldn't be disfigured, no. There would be just one incision down his chest.'

After a long silence, Susan said, 'I know Nat always supported the concept of organ donation.'

'But he didn't carry a donor card? Or join the register?'

'I think he would have done, in time.' She shrugged and dabbed her eyes again. 'I don't think he expected to – to . . .'

The nurse nodded, sparing her from finishing the sentence. 'Not many people do,' she said.

Susan laughed bitterly. 'That fucking motorbike. I didn't want him to have it. Right? If only I'd put my foot down.'

'It's very hard to stop strong-minded people from doing things, Susan. You cannot blame yourself, now or ever.'

There was another long silence. Then she said, 'If I gave consent, would you give him an anaesthetic?'

'If that's what you want, yes. But it isn't necessary. He can't feel anything at all.'

'How much of him would you take?'

'Whatever you wanted.'

'I don't want you to take his eyes.'

'That's fine, I understand.' Her pager bleeped suddenly. She glanced at it, then put it back in its holster. 'Would you like another cup?'

Susan shrugged.

'I'll make you another cup and I'll get the consent forms. I will need to go through his medical history with you.'

'Do you know who his organs will go to?' Susan asked.

'No, not at this stage. There's a national database for organs – kidneys, heart, liver, lungs, pancreas and the small bowel – with over eight thousand people waiting. Your husband's would be allocated on a match and priority basis – finding recipients who would have the best chance of success. We would write to you and tell you who has benefited from his donation.'

Susan closed her eyes to stop the tears.

'Get the forms,' she said. 'Just get the sodding forms before I change my mind.'

43

The Denarii Collection Agency, for whom Lynn Beckett worked, was located on two floors of one of Brighton and Hove's newest office blocks, close to the railway station in the trendy New England Quarter.

The agency, named after the ancient Roman coins, had customers from the full range of companies providing consumer credit – banks, building societies, mail-order catalogues, stores which supplied their own credit cards, hire purchase companies – and in the worsening economic climate, business was booming. Some of their business came from simply chasing bad debts for specific clients. But a big part was bad debt portfolios that they purchased in bulk, taking a gamble on how much they would be able to recover.

At a quarter past five on Monday afternoon, Lynn was seated at her ten-person work station. Her team was called the Harrier Hornets. Each team was identified by its name, which hung above it on a board suspended from the ceiling. The other, fiercely competitive teams in the huge open-plan office were called Silver Sharks, Leaping Leopards and Denarii Demons. Over on the far side of the office was the litigation department, beneath a sign which said Legal Eagles, and beyond them was the dialler management team, which monitored the calls the collection agents made.

Normally she liked being here. She liked the camaraderie and the friendly rivalry. This was fuelled by huge flat screens around the walls constantly showing bonuses to be won, which ranged from a box of chocolates to outings, such as dinner in a posh restaurant or a night at the dogs. The screen in her line of view currently depicted an animated cooking pot filled with gold coins, together with the words THE COLLECTED BONUS POT £673. Often, she felt, the atmosphere was akin to being in a casino.

By the end of the week that would have grown even larger, and either one of the collection agents in her team or one in a rival team would be taking it home as a bonus. She could do with that right now, she thought, and it was still possible. So far she was having a good start to the week, despite the interruptions.

God, I want to win that! she thought. It would pay for the car, and a treat for Caitlin – and help with her mounting monthly credit card payments.

There was a fine view across Brighton, now in winter darkness, from the office, but when she was at work she concentrated so hard she rarely had time to appreciate it. Right now, she had her phone headset on, a mug of tea cooling in front of her, and was focusing as best she could on working through her call list.

She stopped, as she did every few minutes, and looked with a heavy heart up at the photograph of Caitlin that was pinned to the red partition wall, directly above her computer screen. She was leaning against a whitewashed house in Sharm el Sheikh, looking tanned, in a T-shirt and shorts and a cool pair of sunglasses, and giving the photographer – Lynn – a jokey supermodel pout.

Then, returning to her call sheet, she dialled a number and a gruff male voice answered in a Geordie accent.

'Yeah?'

'Good afternoon,' she said, politely. 'Is that Mr Ernest Moorhouse?'

'Um, who's speaking?' He sounded evasive suddenly.

'My name is Lynn Beckett. Is that Mr Moorhouse?'

'Well, yeah, it might be,' he said.

'I'm phoning from Denarii Collection Agency, following up a letter we sent you recently, regarding eight hundred and seventy-two pounds that you owe on your HomeFixIt store card. Could I just check your identity?'

There was a moment's silence. 'Ah,' he said, 'sorry, I misunderstood you. I'm not Mr Moorhouse. You must have a wrong number.'

The line went dead.

Lynn redialled and the same voice answered. 'Mr Moorhouse? It's Lynn Beckett from Denarii. I think we got disconnected.'

'I just told you, I'm not Mr Moorhouse. Now eff off and stop bothering me or I'll come round to New England Quarter and ram this phone up your blooming arse.'

'So you did get my letter?' she went on, unperturbed.

His voice rose several octaves and decibels. 'What part of *I'm not Mr Fucking Moorhouse* don't you understand, you stupid cow?'

'How did you know I am in New England Quarter, unless you got my letter, Mr Moorhouse?' she asked, still keeping calm and polite.

Then she lifted the headset away from her ears as a torrent of abuse came back. Suddenly the mobile phone in her handbag began ringing. She pulled it out and glanced at the display. It showed *Private Number*. She pressed the kill button.

When the abuse had ended, she said, 'I should warn you, Mr Moorhouse, that all our calls are recorded for training and monitoring purposes.'

'Yeah? Well, I'm going to warn you something, Miss

Barnett. Don't you ever call me again at this time of day and start talking to me about money. Do you understand?'

'What time of day would be better for you?'

'NO FUCKING TIME OF DAY. OR NIGHT. DO YOU UNDERSTAND?'

'I'd like to see if we could make a plan for you to start paying this off on a weekly basis. Something you can afford.'

Again she had to hold the headset away from her ears.

'I can't fucking afford nothing. I lost my fucking job, didn't I? I got fucking Gordon Brown in my fucking pocket. I got fucking bailiffs knocking at my door for bigger fucking debts than this. Now go away and don't ever fucking call me again. DO YOU FUCKING UNDERSTAND ME?'

Lynn took a deep breath. 'How about if you started off by paying us just ten pounds a week? We'd like to make it easy for you. A repayment plan that you would be comfortable with.'

'ARE YOU FUCKING DEAF?'

The phone went dead again. Almost instantly, her mobile beeped, with a message.

She made a note on Ernest Moorhouse's file. She'd arrange for him to be sent another letter, then follow it up with another call next week. If that did not work, and it rather sounded as if it wouldn't, then she would have to hand it over to litigation.

Surreptitiously, because private calls were frowned upon, she brought her phone to her ear and checked her message.

It was from the transplant coordinator at the Royal South London Hospital, asking her to call back urgently.

44

There had been another suspicious death in the city over the weekend, a forty-year-old known drug dealer called Niall Foster, who had fallen seven floors from his seafront flat. It had the hallmarks of a suicide, but neither the Coroner nor the police were comfortable about coming to an early conclusion. The small inquiry team that had been set up to investigate had been allocated the third work station in MIR One, so to avoid interrupting them when they were there, and to more comfortably accomodate his growing team, Grace was now holding some of his twice-daily briefings in the conference room, across the corridor.

His team, which had expanded even further, were seated at the large rectangular table, with twenty-four occupied red chairs pulled up around it. At one end of the room, directly behind the Detective Superintendent, was a curved two-tone blue display board bearing the words www.sussex.police.uk and an artistic display of five police badges on a blue background, with the Crimestoppers name and number prominently displayed beneath each of them. On the wall at the opposite end was a plasma screen.

Grace felt under even more pressure than usual on this investigation now. At the dinner dance on Saturday night he had managed to have another chat with the new Chief Constable and had been surprised by how well briefed on the inquiry Tom Martinson was. He realized it wasn't just going to be the ACC, Alison Vosper, watching his every step but Martinson himself. The three bodies were bringing the city of Brighton and Hove under increasing national media scrutiny, which meant, in particular, a focus on the competence of Sussex CID. The only thing keeping the discovery of the three bodies from attracting wider news coverage at the moment was that two small girls had been missing from their home in a village near Hull, for over a week, which meant most media attention was focused on them and their immediate family.

'The time is 6.30 p.m., Monday 1 December,' Grace announced. 'This is the eighth briefing of Operation Neptune, the investigation into the deaths of three unknown persons.' He sipped some coffee, then went on. 'I held a very uncomfortable press conference this morning. Someone's leaked about the missing organs.'

He stared at his most trusted colleagues in turn: Lizzie Mantle, Glenn Branson, who was dressed in an electric-blue suit as if ready for a night out, Bella Moy, Emma-Jane Boutwood, Norman Potting and Nick Nicholl, certain it was none of them, nor another face in the room, DS Guy Batchelor. In fact, he was pretty sure it wasn't anyone here. Nor did he think it was the mortuary team. Or the press office. Perhaps someone in the Force Control Room . . . One day, when he had the time, he would find out, he promised himself that.

Bella held up a copy of the London *Evening Standard* and a late edition of the *Argus*. The *Standard* headline read: ORGAN THEFT RIDDLE OF BODIES IN CHANNEL. The *Argus*: CHANNEL BODIES MISSING VITAL ORGANS.

'You can be sure there will be more tomorrow in the morning papers,' he said. 'There are a couple of TV news crews crawling all over Shoreham Harbour and our PRO's been fielding calls from radio stations all afternoon.' He nodded at Dennis Ponds, whom he had asked to attend this briefing.

A former journalist, the public relations officer looked more like a City trader than a newspaper man. In his early forties, with slicked-back black hair, mutantly large eyebrows and a penchant for slick suits, he had the tough task of brokering the ever-fragile relations between the police and the public. It was often a no-win situation, and he had been given the sobriquet Pond Life by those officers who remained suspicious of anyone with anything to do with the press.

'I'm hoping the coverage will help bring members of the public forward,' Ponds said. 'I've circulated touched-up photographs of all three to every paper and television news station and to the Internet news feeds.'

'Is Absolute Brighton TV on your list?' Nick Nicholl asked, referring to the city's relatively new Internet channel.

'Absolutely!' Ponds replied, then beamed, as if pleased with his wit.

Grace glanced down at his notes.

'Before we have your individual reports, there's been one interesting serial today,' he said. 'Might be nothing, but we should follow it up.' He looked at Glenn Branson. 'You'd be the man, as you're our nautical expert.'

There was a titter of laughter.

'Projectile-vomiting expert, more likely,' Norman Potting chuckled.

Ignoring him, Grace went on, 'A fishing boat, called the *Scoob-Eee*, based at Shoreham, has been reported missing since Friday night. Probably nothing, but we need to monitor anything out of the usual anywhere along the coast.'

'Did you say *Scoob-Eee*, Roy?' Branson asked.

'Yes.'

'That – that's the boat I went out on, on Friday, with the SSU.'

'You didn't tell us you bloody sank it, Glenn!' quipped Guy Batchelor.

Glenn ignored him, thinking hard and very shocked. Missing as in *stolen* or *sunk*? Turning to Grace, he asked, 'Do you have any more information?'

'No – see what you can find.'

Branson nodded, then sat in silence, only half concentrating on the rest of the briefing.

'Sounds like racketeers to me,' Norman Potting said all of a sudden.

Grace looked at him quizzically.

Potting nodded. 'It was Noël Coward, wasn't it? What he said about Brighton. *Piers, queers and racketeers*. Sums it up, doesn't it?'

Bella gave him a huffy stare. 'So which one are you?'

'Norman,' Grace said, 'there are people who would find that offensive. All right?'

For a moment the DS looked as if he was going to argue back, but then he appeared to think better of it. 'Yes, chief. Understood. Just trying to make the point that with three bodies missing their organs, we could be looking at racketeering – in human organs.'

'Anything you want to expand on that?'

'I've given a brief to Phil Taylor and Ray Packham down in the High-Tech Crime Unit to see what they can find on the Internet. I've had a trawl myself, and yes, it's widespread.'

'Any UK connections?'

'Not so far. I'm widening the search as far as I can, with Interpol – in particular Europol. But I don't think we're going to get any quick answers from them.'

Grace concurred with that. Having had many previous experiences with Interpol, he knew that the organization could be infuriatingly slow – and at times arrogant.

'But I have come up with something that may be of interest,' Potting said. He heaved himself up from his chair and walked over to the whiteboard, on which was fixed the blow-up photograph of the tattoo on the teenage girl's arm. Pointing at it, he said the name aloud: 'Rares.'

Bella rattled the Maltesers in her box and took out one.

'I did some checking, mostly on the Internet,' Potting went on. 'It's a Romanian name. A man's first name.'

'Definitely Romanian – and nowhere else?' Grace asked him.

'Unique to Romania,' Potting responded. 'Of course, that doesn't necessary mean this Rares, whoever he might be, is Romanian. But it's an indicator.'

Grace made a note. 'Good, that's very helpful, Norman.'

Potting belched and Bella shot him daggers. 'Oops, pardon me.' He patted his belly. 'Something else, Roy, that I think might be relevant,' he ploughed on. 'The United Nations publishes a list of rogue countries involved in human trafficking for organ transplants. I checked it out.' He smiled grimly. 'Romania features on it – prominently.'

45

The hospital offered to send an ambulance, but Lynn didn't want that, and she was sure Caitlin wouldn't either. She decided to take her chances with the Peugeot.

Mal's phone went straight to voicemail, which indicated he was at sea, so she sent him an email, knowing he could pick those up:

> Matching liver donor found. She is having the transplant tomorrow at 6 a.m. Call me when you can. Lynn

For once in the car Caitlin did not send any texts. She just gripped her mother's hand all the time that Lynn did not need it for changing gear, a weak, clammy, frightened grip, her jaundiced face flashing in the street lights and in the stark glare of oncoming headlights, like a yellow ghost.

A record on Southern Counties radio ended and the news came on. The third item was speculation that there was a human organ theft ring operating in Sussex. A policeman came on the radio, someone called Detective Superintendent Roy Grace, speaking with a strong, blunt voice: 'It is far too early in our investigation to speculate, and one of our main lines of enquiry at this stage is to find out if these bodies were dumped by a passing ship in the Channel. I want to reassure the public that we consider this an isolated incident, and—'

Lynn punched the CD button, hastily silencing the radio.

Caitlin squeezed her mother's hand again. 'You know where I'd really like to be right now, Mum?'

'Where, darling?'

'Home.'

'You want me to turn the car round?' Lynn said, shocked.

Caitlin shook her head. 'No, not our house. I'd like to be *home*.'

Lynn blinked away the tears that were forming. Caitlin was talking about Winter Cottage, where she and Mal had lived when they had got married, and where Caitlin had grown up, until the divorce.

'It was nice there, wasn't it, angel?'

'It was bliss. I was happy then.'

Winter Cottage. Even its name was evocative. Lynn could remember that summer day when she and Mal had first gone to see it. She was six months pregnant with Caitlin at the time. There had been a long drive down a cart track, past a working farm, to the small, ramshackle cottage, ivy-clad, with its cluster of falling-down outbuildings and bro-ken-paned greenhouse, but a beautifully tended lawn and a collapsed little Wendy house that Mal had lovingly rebuilt for Caitlin.

She could remember that first day so well. The musty smells, the cobwebs, the rotting timbers, the ancient range in the kitchen. The view to die for out across the softly rolling South Downs. Mal putting his strong arm around her shoulders and squeezing her, discussing all the things he could do himself to fix it up, with her help. A big project, but their project. Their *home*. Their piece of paradise.

And she could imagine, standing there then, what it would be like in winter, the sharp cold smells, the burning firewood, rotting leaves, wet grass. The place felt so safe, so secure.

Yes. Yes. Yes.

Every time Caitlin brought it up, it made her sad. And it made her even sadder that still, over seven years after they had moved out, when Caitlin was just eight, she referred to Winter Cottage – and in particular its little Wendy house – as her *home*. And not the house they lived in now. That hurt.

But she could understand. Those eight years at Winter Cottage were Caitlin's healthy years. The time in her life that she had been carefree. Her illness had begun a year later, and at the time Lynn had wondered whether the stress of seeing her parents' marriage break up had been a contributing factor. She always would.

They were passing the IKEA chimneys again. Lynn was starting to feel they were becoming a symbol in her life. Or some kind of new marker posts. Old, normal life south of those chimney stacks. New, strange, unknown, reborn life north of them.

On the CD, Justin Timberlake began singing 'What Goes Around Comes Around'.

'Hey, Mum,' Caitlin said, suddenly sounding as if she was perking up. 'Do you think that's the case, you know, what he's singing, right?'

'How do you mean?'

'What goes around, comes around. Do you believe in that?'

'You mean do I believe in karma?'

Caitlin thought for some moments. 'I'm saying, like, I'm taking advantage of someone who's died. Is that right?'

Someone who had died in a motorcycle accident, Lynn

had been told by the hospital, but she had not given that detail to Caitlin, and did not want to, fearing it would distress her. 'Maybe you need to take a different perspective. Perhaps that person has loved ones who will get comfort from knowing that some good will come out of their loss.'

'It's just so weird, isn't it? That we don't, like, even know who it is. Do you think I could ever – meet – the family?'

'Would you want to?'

Caitlin was silent for a while, then she said, 'Maybe. I don't know.'

They drove on in silence again for a couple of minutes.

'You know what Luke said?'

Lynn had to take a deep breath to restrain herself from retorting, *No, and I don't want to know what that sodding moron said.* Through gritted teeth, sounding a lot more cheery and interested than she felt, she replied, 'Tell me.'

'Well, he said that some people who have transplants inherit stuff from the donors. Characteristics – or changes in their tastes. So, if the donor had a craving for Mars Bars, you might get that. Or liked a particular kind of music. Or was good at football. Sort of from their genes.'

'Where did Luke get that gem from?'

'The Internet. There's loads of sites. We looked at some of them. You can inherit their dislikes too!'

'Really?' Suddenly Lynn perked up. Maybe this liver would come from someone who disliked dickheads with stupid hair.

'There are verified case histories,' Caitlin said, brightening up even more. 'There are, really! OK, right, you know I'm frightened of heights?'

'Uh huh.'

'Well, there's this woman I read about in America who

was terrified of heights, and she had a transplant and got the lungs of a mountain climber, and now she's a fanatical climber!'

'You don't think that was simply because she felt better, having lungs that worked properly?'

'No.'

'It sounds amazing,' Lynn said, not wanting to appear sceptical, and keen to keep her daughter's enthusiasm up.

'And there's this one, right, Mum? There was a man in Los Angeles who received a woman's heart, and before he hated shopping – and now he wants to go shopping all the time!'

Lynn grinned. 'So, what characteristic would you most like to inherit?'

'Well, I've been thinking about this! I'm rubbish at drawing. Maybe I'll get the liver from someone who was a brilliant artist!'

Lynn laughed. 'Yep, there's all kinds of possible bonuses! See, you're going to be fine!'

Caitlin nodded. 'With a cadaverous liver inside me. Yeah. I'll be fine, just a bit *liverish*.'

Lynn laughed again, and was pleased to see her daughter break into a smile. She squeezed her hand tightly and they drove on companionably for some minutes, listening to the music, and the knocking rattle of the exhaust pipe beneath them.

Then, as her laughter faded, she felt a tightening band, like cold steel, inside her. There were risks with this operation which had been spelled out to both of them. Things could and did go wrong. There was a realistic possibility that Caitlin could die on the operating table.

But without the transplant, there was no realistic possibility that Caitlin would live longer than a few months.

Lynn had never been a churchgoer, but since earliest childhood, for much of her life, she had said her prayers every night. Five years ago, in the week immediately after her sister had died, she had stopped praying. Just recently, since Caitlin became seriously ill, she had started again, but only half-heartedly. She wished, sometimes, that she could trust God, and surrender all her concerns to Him. How much simpler that would make everything.

She squeezed her daughter's hand again. Her living, beautiful hand that she and Mal had created, maybe in God's image, maybe not. But certainly in her image. God could strut his stuff, but it was she who was going to be there for Caitlin in the coming hours, and if the Lord wanted to play Mr Nice Guy then she would welcome that with open arms. But if he wanted to screw around with her mind and her emotions and her daughter's life, he could go take a hike.

Even so, at the next traffic lights she briefly closed her eyes and said a silent prayer.

46

Roy Grace was gripped with panic. He was running across grass, running at the edge of the cliff, with its sheer drop of a thousand feet, with a howling wind blowing in his face, almost pushing him to a standstill, so that he was just running on the spot.

Meanwhile a man was running towards the edge of the cliff, holding the baby in his arms. His baby.

Grace threw himself forward, grabbing the man's waist in a rugby tackle, bringing him down. The man broke free and rolled, determinedly, cradling the baby like a ball he was not going to lose, rolling over and over towards the cliff edge.

Grace gripped his ankles, jerking him back. Then suddenly the earth beneath him gave way, with a crack like thunder, a huge chunk of the cliff breaking off like a crumbling piece of stale cake, and he was plunging, plunging with this man and his child, plunging down towards the jagged rocks and the boiling sea.

'Roy! Darling! Roy! Darling!'

Cleo.

Cleo's voice.

'Roy, it's OK, darling. It's OK!'

He opened his eyes. Saw the light on. Felt his heart hammering. He was drenched in sweat, as if he was lying in a stream.

'Shit,' he whispered. 'I'm sorry.'

'Falling again?' Cleo said tenderly, looking at him with concerned eyes.

'Beachy Head.'

It was a recurring dream he had been having for weeks. But it wasn't just about an incident he'd been involved with there. It was also about a human monster he'd arrested a few months ago.

A sick monster who had murdered two women in the city, and had tried to kill Cleo as well. The man was behind bars, with bail refused, but even so, Grace felt suddenly nervous. Above the thudding of his heart and the roar of the blood coursing in his ears, he listened to the silence of the city at night.

The clock radio panel showed 3.10 a.m.

Nothing stirred in the house. Rain was falling outside.

Pregnant with his child, Cleo seemed more vulnerable than ever to him now. It had been a while since he had checked on the man, although he had recently dealt with some of the pre-trial paperwork. He made a mental note to make a call to ensure that he was still safely in custody and had not been released by some woolly-minded judge doing his bit to ease the overcrowding in England's prisons.

Cleo stroked his brow. He felt her warm breath on his face. It smelled sweet, faintly minted, as if she had just brushed her teeth.

'I'm sorry,' he said, his voice low, barely above a whisper, as if that would be less intrusive.

'You poor darling. You have so many nightmares, don't you?'

He lay there, the sheet below him sodden and cold with his perspiration. She was right. A couple of times a week, at least.

'Why was it you stopped going to therapy?' she asked him, then kissed each of his eyes, softly, in turn.

'Because . . .' He shrugged. 'It wasn't helping me to

move on.' He eased himself up in bed a little, staring around.

He liked this room, which Cleo had decorated mostly in white – with a thick white rug on the bare oak floor, white linen curtains, white walls, and a few pieces of elegant black furniture, including a black lacquered dressing table – still damaged from the attack on her.

'You're the only thing that's helped me to move on. You know that?'

She smiled at him. 'Time is the best healer,' she said.

'No, you are. I love you. I love you so much. I love you in a way I never thought it would be possible to love anyone again.'

She stared at him, smiling, blinking slowly, for some moments.

'I love you too. Even more than you love me.'

'Impossible!'

She pulled a face at him. 'Calling me a liar?'

He kissed her.

47

Glenn Branson lay wide awake in the spare room of Roy Grace's house, which had now become his second home – or, more accurately at the moment, his main residence.

It was the same every night. He drank heavily, trying to knock himself out, but neither the booze nor the pills the doctor had prescribed seemed to have any effect. And his body, which he normally kept in shape by working out relentlessly at home or in the gym, was starting to lose muscle tone.

I'm bloody falling apart, he reflected gloomily.

The room had been decorated by Sandy in the same Zen minimalistic style as the rest of this house. The bed was a low, futon-style affair, with an uncomfortable slatted headboard that, because of his tall frame, he constantly bashed his skull on as he tried to stop his feet sticking out the other end. The mattress was as hard as concrete and the frame of the bed felt loose, wobbling precariously and creaking every time he moved. He kept meaning to sort it out with a spanner, tightening the nuts, but away from work he was so despondent he didn't feel like doing anything. Half his clothes, still in their zipped plastic covers, lay across the armchair in the small room – some of them had been there for weeks and he still had not got round to hanging them up in the almost empty wardrobe.

Roy was quite right when he told him he was turning the house into a tip.

It was 3.50 a.m. His mobile phone lay beside the bed

and he hoped, as he hoped every night, that Ari might suddenly ring, to tell him she'd had a change of heart, that she'd been thinking it over and realized she did still love him, deeply, and wanted to find a way to make the marriage work.

But it stayed silent, tonight and every damn night.

And they'd had another row earlier. Ari was angry that he couldn't collect the kids from school tomorrow after-noon, because there was a lecture she wanted to go to in London. That sounded suspicious to him, rang alarm bells. She never went to lectures in London. Was it a guy?

Was she seeing someone?

It was bad enough coping with being apart from her. But the thought that she might be seeing someone, start another relationship, introduce that person to his kids, was more than he could bear.

And he had work to think about. Had to focus somehow.

Two cats, fighting, yowled outside. And somewhere in the distance a siren shrieked. A response unit from Brighton and Hove Division. Or an ambulance.

He rolled over, suddenly craving Ari's body. Tempted to call her. Maybe she was—

Was what?

Oh, God almighty, how much they used to love each other.

He tried to switch his mind to his work. To his phone conversation yesterday evening, with the wife of the missing skipper of the *Scoob-Eee*. A very distraught Janet Towers. Friday night had been their twenty-fifth wedding anniver-sary. They had a table booked at the Meadows restaurant in Hove. But her husband had never come home. She had not heard from him since.

She was absolutely certain he'd had an accident.

All she could tell Glenn was that she had contacted the coastguard on Saturday morning, who had reported back to her that the *Scoob-Eee* had been seen going through the lock at Shoreham Harbour at nine on Friday night, along with an Algerian-registered freighter. It was common for local fishing boats to enter the lock behind a commercial cargo vessel, enabling them to skip the locking fees. No one had paid any attention to the vessel.

Neither the boat nor Jim Towers had been seen since.

No accidents at sea had been logged by the coastguard, she had told Glenn. Jim and his boat had literally disappeared into thin air.

Suddenly, in his sleepless state, he remembered something. It might be nothing. But Roy Grace had taught him many important lessons about being a good detective and one of them was going around in his head now. *Clear the ground under your feet.*

He was thinking back to Friday morning, when he had been standing on the quay at Aldrington Basin, waiting to board the *Scoob-Eee*. To a glint of light he had seen as they cast off, on the far side of the harbour, beside a cluster of refinery tanks.

*

At half past six that morning, Glenn pulled his unmarked police Hyundai Getz up, putting two wheels on the pavement of Kingsway, opposite a row of houses. He climbed out into drizzle and breaking daylight, eased himself over the low wall, then, clutching his torch, half slid and half ran down the grassy embankment behind the cluster of white petroleum storage tanks, until he reached the bottom. Across the far side of the dark grey water he could make out the timber yard, the gantry and, further up, the lights of the

Arco Dee dredger, disgorging its latest cargo of gravel and sand. He could hear the rattle of its conveyor belt and the falling shingle.

He worked out the position where he had boarded the *Scoob-Eee* with the police diving team, right in front of that timber yard, and where he had seen that glint of light across the water, between the fourth and fifth tanks, and made his way to the gap.

A fishing boat, with its navigation lights on, was coming down the harbour, its engine *put-put-putting* in the morning silence. Gulls cried above him.

His nostrils filled with the smells of the harbour – rotting seaweed mixed with oil and rust and sawn timber and burning asphalt. He shone the beam of the torch directly at the ground beneath his feet. Then briefly up at the white cylindrical walls of the refinery storage tanks. They were much bigger now he was close up to them than they had appeared on Friday.

He checked his watch. He had just under an hour and a half before he needed to leave to get to the morning briefing in time. He pointed the beam back down on to the wet grass. Looking for a footprint that might still be there from Friday morning. Or any other clue.

Suddenly he saw a cigarette butt. Probably nothing significant, he thought. But those words of Roy Grace buzzed inside his head, like a mantra.

Clear the ground under your feet.

He knelt and picked it up with the neck of an evidence bag he had brought along – just in case. Printed around the butt were the words, in purple, Silk Cut.

Moments later, he saw a second one. It was the same brand.

To drop one cigarette butt here could have meant

someone was just passing by. But two, that meant someone was waiting here.

For what?

Maybe, if he got lucky, DNA analysis would reveal something.

He continued to look for the next hour. There were no further clues, but he headed towards the morning briefing with wet shoes and a sense of achievement.

48

'Please tell me you are joking?' Lynn begged.

She was utterly exhausted after the sleepless night she had just spent in the chair beside Caitlin's bed, in the small, claustrophobic room off the liver ward. A muted cartoon was playing on the small, badly tuned television bolted to an extension arm on the wall above the bed. A tap was dripping in the sink. The room smelled of poached eggs from breakfast trays out in the main ward, weak coffee and disinfectant.

It must have been like the kind of tense, desperate last night a prisoner spends before being executed at dawn, hoping for that last-minute reprieve, she thought.

Lights coming on and off. Constant interruptions. Constant examinations, injections and pills given to Caitlin, and blood and fluid samples being taken from her. The alarm handle dangling from a cord above her. The empty drip stands and the oxygen pump that she did not need.

Caitlin fretting, unable to sleep, telling her over and over again that she was itching and scared, and wanted to go *home*, and Lynn trying to comfort her. Trying to reassure her that in the morning everything would be fine. That in three weeks she would be leaving the hospital with a brand-new liver. If all went well, she would be home in time for Christmas, OK, not to Winter Cottage, but to the place that was now her home.

It would be the best Christmas ever!

And now this woman was standing in the room. The

transplant coordinator. Shirley Linsell, with her English rose face and her long hair, and the tiny burst blood vessel in her left eye. She was wearing the same white blouse and knitted pink top and black trousers as when she had first met her, almost a week – that seemed like a million years – ago.

The only difference was her demeanour. When they had first met, she had seemed positive and friendly. But now, at seven o'clock this morning, although apologetic, she seemed cold and distant. Lynn stood facing her, glaring in fury.

'I'm extremely sorry,' she said. 'I'm afraid these things happen.'

'Sorry? You phoned me last night to say that you had a liver that was a perfect match, and now you are telling us you were wrong?'

'We were informed a liver had become available which was a good match.'

'So what exactly happened?'

The coordinator addressed Lynn, then Caitlin. 'From the information we were given, it appeared that the liver could be split, with the right side to be given to an adult and the left side to you, Caitlin. When our consultant and his team went down to the hospital to collect the liver, in their assessment, it was healthy and suitable. We use a scale of size of liver against body weight. But this morning our senior consultant surgeon, who was to have performed the transplant, examined the liver more closely and found there was more than 30 per cent fat. He did a biopsy and made a decision that it would not be suitable for you.'

'I still don't understand,' Lynn said. 'So are you going to throw it away?'

'No,' Shirley Linsell said. 'With this amount of fat, there

is a danger it could take several weeks to function properly. Caitlin needs a liver that will function immediately. She is too ill to take the risk. It will be used for a man in his sixties with liver cancer. It will hopefully prolong his life for a few years.'

'How great is that?' Lynn said. 'You're bumping my daughter in favour of an elderly man? What is he? Some fucking alcoholic?'

'I can't discuss another patient with you.'

'Yes, you can.' Lynn raised her voice. 'Oh yes, you damn well can. You're sending Caitlin home to die so some fucking alcoholic, like that footballer George Best, can live a few more months?'

'Please, Mrs Beckett – Lynn – it's not like that at all.'

'Oh? So what is it like, exactly?'

'Mum!' Caitlin said. 'Listen to her.'

'I am listening, darling, I'm listening really hard. I just don't like what I'm hearing.'

'Everyone here cares for Caitlin, a lot. It's not just work in this unit – it's personal for us all. We want to give Caitlin a healthy liver, to give her the best chance of a normal life, Mrs Beckett. There is no point in giving her a liver that might not work or that might fail in a few years' time and put her through this ordeal a second time. Please believe me – the whole team here wants to help Caitlin. We're very fond of her.'

'Fine,' Lynn said. 'So when will this healthy liver be available?'

'I can't answer that – it depends on a suitable donor.'

'So we're back to square one?'

'Well – yes.'

There was a long silence. 'Will my daughter be at the top of the priority list?' Lynn demanded.

'The list is very complicated. There are a number of factors affecting it.'

Lynn shook her head vigorously. 'No, Shirley – Nurse Linsell. Not a number of factors, just one as far as I am concerned. My daughter. She needs a transplant urgently – correct?'

'Yes, she does, and we are working on that. But you have to understand, she is one of many people.'

'Not to me, she isn't.'

The woman nodded. 'Lynn, I appreciate that.'

'Do you?' Lynn said. 'What percentage of patients on your waiting list die before they get a liver?'

'Mum, stop being so hostile!'

Lynn sat on the side of the bed and cradled Caitlin's head in her arms. 'Darling, please let me deal with this.'

'You're talking about me like I'm some retard in a box. I'm upset! Don't you see that? I'm just as upset as you are – more – but it's not going to help getting angry.'

'Do you realize what this bitch is saying?' Lynn exploded. 'She is sending you home to die!'

'You are being, like, so dramatic!'

'I AM NOT BEING DRAMATIC!' Lynn turned to the coordinator. 'Tell me when another liver is going to be available.'

'I'd be misleading you if I gave you a time or a date, Lynn.'

'Are we talking twenty-four hours? A week? A month?'

Shirley Linsell shrugged and gave a wan smile. 'I don't know, that's the honest truth. We thought we had got lucky, getting this liver so quickly, in a week with no matching recipient higher up the priority list than Caitlin. The donor was an apparently healthy thirty-year-old man, but clearly, it turned out, he had a drink or a diet problem.'

'So this same shit could happen again, could it?'

The coordinator smiled, trying to placate Lynn and reassure Caitlin. 'We have a very good record here. I'm sure that everything will be fine.'

'You have a good record? What does that mean?' Lynn said.

'Mum!' Caitlin implored.

Ignoring her, Lynn went on, 'You mean you have a good record compared to the national average? That only 19 per cent of your patients die before they get a liver, compared to the national average of 20 per cent? I know about the National Health and your damn statistics.' Lynn started crying. 'You've gambled with my daughter's life by giving some elderly alcoholic an extra few months of life because that will tick the right boxes for your statistics. I'm right, aren't I?'

'We don't play God here, Mrs Beckett. We cannot say that one human being has more right to life than another because of their age, or because of how they may or may not have abused their bodies. We're non-judgemental. We try our best to help everyone. Sometimes we have to make difficult decisions.'

Lynn glared at her. Never in her whole life had she hated anyone as much as she hated this woman right now. She didn't even know if she was getting the truth or being fed some yarn. Had some rich oligarch with a sick child made a donation to the hospital for bumping Caitlin and getting his child saved? Or had there been a screw-up that she was trying to cover up?

'Really?' she sneered. '*Difficult decisions?* Tell me something, Shirley, did you ever lose a night's sleep in your life over a *difficult decision*?'

The nurse kept calm, her tone gentle. 'I care about all

our patients very deeply, Mrs Beckett. I take their problems home with me every night.'

Lynn could see she was telling the truth.

'OK, answer this for me – you just said that Caitlin would have got this liver, had it been OK, because there was no matching recipient higher up the list than her. That could change, right? At any moment?'

'We have a weekly meeting to decide the priority list,' Shirley Linsell replied.

'So it could all change at your next meeting, couldn't it? If someone in greater need than Caitlin – in your assessment – came along?'

'Yes, I'm afraid that's how it works.'

'That's great,' Lynn said, her blood boiling again. 'You're like a firing squad, aren't you? This weekly meeting to decide who is going to live and who's going to die. It's like you all pull the trigger, but one of you doesn't have a bullet in the gun, just a blank. Your patients die and none of you has to take the damn blame.'

49

Simona lay on the examination couch, wearing just a loose dressing gown. Dr Nicolau, a serious, pleasant-looking man of about forty, strapped a Velcro sleeve around her arm and tightened it, plugged his stethoscope into his ears and pumped the rubber bulb until the sleeve squeezed her arm tightly. Then he looked at a gauge fitted to it.

After a few moments he released the sleeve, nodding, as if everything was fine.

The German woman, who had told her that her name was Marlene, stood beside her. She was beautiful, Simona thought. She was dressed in a sleek, fur-trimmed black suede coat, over a light pink pullover, smart jeans and black leather boots. Her blonde, elegantly tangled hair cascaded around her shoulders, and she smelled of a wonderful perfume.

Simona liked and trusted her. Romeo had been right in his judgement of her, she thought. She was such a confident woman, kind and gentle. Simona had never known her mother, but if she could have chosen a mother, she would have liked her to be a person like Marlene.

'Just going to take a little blood,' the doctor said, removing the strap and producing a syringe.

Simona stared at it, cringing in fear.

'It's OK, Simona,' Marlene said.

'What are you doing?' she asked, her voice tight.

'We are giving you a full examination, just to make sure

you are healthy. It's a big investment for us to send you to England. We have to get you a passport, somehow, which is not so easy as you have no papers. And they won't allow you to work there if you are not healthy.'

Simona shrank away as the needle approached. 'No,' she said. 'NO!'

'It's OK, darling Simona!'

'Where's Romeo?'

'He's outside. He is having the same tests. Would you like him to come in here with you?'

Simona nodded.

The woman opened the door. Romeo came in, his saucer eyes becoming even wider when he saw Simona in her dressing gown.

'What are they doing?' Simona asked him.

'It's OK,' Romeo said. 'They won't hurt you. We have to have this medical.'

Simona shrieked as she felt the prick in her arm. Then she watched in terror as the doctor drew up the plunger and the plastic barrel filled, slowly and steadily, with her dark red blood.

'We have to have the certificates to get into the country,' Romeo said.

'It hurts.'

Moments later, the syringe was full. The doctor removed it, laid it on a table, then pressed an antiseptic wipe against her arm. He held it for a few seconds, then stuck on a small square of Band-aid in its place.

'All done!' he said.

'Can I go now?' she asked.

'Yes, you can go,' the woman said. 'You will be in the same place?'

'Yes,' Romeo answered for both of them.

'Then I will come and find you, if we are happy that everything is all right. You can get dressed again now. Are you sure about England, Simona? You are sure you want to go, my little Liebling?'

'You can get me a job there, can't you? Me and Romeo? And a flat to live in, in London?'

'A good job and a nice flat. You will love it.'

Simona looked at Romeo for reassurance. He shrugged, then nodded.

'Yes,' she said. 'I am sure.'

'Good,' Marlene said. She kissed Simona on the forehead.

'When do you think we will go?' Romeo asked.

'If your medical results are good, then soon.'

'How soon?'

'When do you want to go?'

He shrugged again. 'Can Valeria come with us?'

'The one who has a baby?'

'Yes,' he said.

'That's not possible now. Perhaps later, when you are settled, then we can make arrangements.'

'She wants to come with us,' Simona said.

'It is not possible,' the German woman said. 'Not at this time. If you would prefer to stay here in Bucharest to be with her, then you must say so.'

Simona shook her head vigorously. 'No.'

Romeo also shook his head, equally vigorously, as if afraid Marlene might suddenly change her mind about Simona and himself. 'No.'

*

Back in Berlin, Marlene Hartmann received a phone call from Dr Nicolau in Bucharest. Simona's blood type was AB negative. She smiled and noted the details down – it was good to have a rare blood group on her books. She was sure she would find a home for all Simona's organs very quickly.

50

After the Tuesday morning briefing meeting of Operation Neptune, Roy Grace drove to the Sussex Police headquarters, twenty minutes away, to update Alison Vosper.

Although she was leaving at the end of the year, to be replaced by a Yorkshire Detective Chief Superintendent called Peter Rigg – about whom he knew little so far – she was still fully hands on for a few weeks more and wanted the usual weekly face-time she had with Roy on any major investigation he was involved with. To his surprise, and relief, today she had been in a strangely subdued mood. He waited for her to kick off, but it hadn't happened. She listened quietly to his update and dismissed him after only a few minutes.

Now back in his office, scrolling through the endless emails on his screen, he was concentrating on his various lines of enquiry when he was interrupted by a knock on his door and Norman Potting entered, reeking of strong tobacco – no doubt having just nipped outside for quick puff or three on his pipe.

'Do you have a moment, Roy?' he asked in his rural burr.

Grace gestured for him to take a seat.

Settling down into the chair in front of the desk, loudly expelling a puff of garlicky breath in the process, Potting said, 'I wondered if I could have a word with you about Romania? I have something which I didn't think I should raise publicly at the briefing meeting.'

'Sure.' Grace looked at him with interest.

'Well, I think I might have a short cut. I know that we've sent dental records, fingerprints and DNA samples of these three individual to Interpol, but you and I know how long those desk jockeys take to get a result.'

Grace smiled. Interpol was a good organization, but the bureau was indeed full of desk-bound police officers who relied on cooperation with police forces in countries abroad and were seldom able to short-cut rigid time frames.

'We could be looking at three weeks minimum, at least,' Norman Potting said. 'I've done some more trawling on the web. There are thousands of street people in Bucharest who live on the margins. If – and it's only speculation – these three victims are street kids, then it's unlikely they'll ever have been to a dentist – and unless they've been arrested, there won't be any fingerprint or DNA records.'

Grace nodded in agreement.

'There's a chap I was on a Junior Detective Training course with at Hendon when we were young DCs. Ian Tilling. We became mates and kept in touch. He joined the Met, then after some years he got transferred to Kent Police. Rose to inspector. Long story short, about seventeen years ago his lad was killed in a motorcycle accident. His life fell apart, his marriage bust up, and he took early retirement from the force. Then he decided to do something totally different – you know the syndrome – try to make sense of what had happened and to do something useful. So he went to Romania and began working with street kids. Last time I spoke to him was about five years ago, just after my third marriage went kaput.' Potting gave a wistful smile. 'You know how it is, when you are down in your cups, you start going through your address book, phoning up old mates.'

That wasn't something Roy Grace had ever done, but all the same he nodded.

'He'd just got a gong – an MBE – for his work with these street kids, which he was proud as all hell about. With your permission I'd like to contact him – it's a long shot, but he might – just might – be able to help us.'

Grace thought for a little while. In the last few years the police had become increasingly bureaucratic, with guidelines on just about everything. Their procedures with Interpol had been strictly in accordance with these. Stepping outside was risky – and nothing was more certain to bring him into conflict with the new Chief Constable than deviating from procedure. On the other hand, Norman Potting was right that they could spend weeks waiting for Interpol to come back to them, and probably with a negative result. How many more bodies might turn up in the interim?

And he was reassured by the fact that this man, Ian Tilling, was a former police officer, which meant he was unlikely to be a flake.

'I won't put this in my policy book, Norman, but I'd be very comfortable for you to pursue this line in an off-the-record way. Thanks for the initiative.'

Potting looked pleased. 'Right away, guv. The old bugger'll be surprised to hear from me.' He started to stand up, then got halfway and sat back down again. 'Roy, would you mind if I asked you something – you know – man to man – personal?'

Grace glanced at another slew of emails that had appeared on his screen. 'No, ask away.'

'It's about my wife.'

'Li? Isn't that her name?'

Potting nodded.

'From Thailand?'

'Yeah, Thailand.'

'You found her on the Internet, right?'

'Well, sort of. I found the agency on the Internet.' Potting scratched the back of his head, then checked with his stubby, grimy fingers that his comb-over was in place. 'Did you ever think of – you know – doing that?'

'No.' Grace glanced anxiously at his computer screen, conscious of his morning running out on him. 'What was it you wanted?'

Potting looked gloomy suddenly. 'Bit of advice, actually.' He dug his hands into his jacket pockets and rummaged around, as if searching for something. 'If you could imagine yourself in my position for a moment, Roy. Everything has been just grand with Li for the past few months, but suddenly she's making demands on me.' He fell silent.

'What kind of demands?' Grace asked, dreading graphic details of Norman Potting's sex life.

'Money for her family. I have to send money every week, to help them out. Money I've got saved up for my retirement.'

'Why do you have to do this?'

Potting looked for a moment as if he had never asked this question. 'Why?' he echoed. 'Li tells me that if I truly love her, then I would want to help her parents.'

Grace looked at him, astonished at his naivety. 'You believe that?'

'She won't have sex with me until she's seen me make the bank transfer – I do it online, you know,' he said, as if proud about his technical prowess. 'I mean, I understand the relative poverty of her country and how they perceive me as rich, and all that. But . . .' He shrugged.

'Do you want to know what I think, Norman?'

'I would value your opinion, Roy.'

Grace studied the man's face. Potting looked lost, for-lorn. He didn't see it, he really did not.

'You're a police officer, for God's sake, Norman. You're a sodding detective – and a really good one! You don't see it? She's having a laugh on you. You're being led by your dick, not by your brain. She'll bleed you of every penny you have and then she'll sod off. I've read about these girls.'

'Not Li – she's different.'

'Oh yes, how? In what way?'

Potting shrugged, then looked at the Detective Superintendent helplessly. 'I love her. I can't help it, Roy. I love her.'

Roy's mobile phone rang. Almost with relief at the interruption, he answered.

It was a bright police colleague he liked a lot, Rob Leet, an inspector in the East Brighton sector.

'Roy,' he said, 'this may be nothing but I thought it might be of interest, with your current inquiry with the three bodies from the Channel. One of my team has just gone down to the beach to the east of the Marina. A guy walking his dog through the rock pools at low tide has found what looks like a brand-new outboard motor lying there.'

Thinking fast, Grace said, 'Yes, it could be. Make sure no one touches it. Can you get it forensically bagged and brought in?'

'That's under way.'

Grace thanked him and hung up. He raised an apologetic finger at Norman Potting, then dialled an internal number to the Imaging Department on the floor below him. It was answered after two rings.

'Mike Bloomfield.'

'Mike, Roy Grace. Are you guys able to get prints off an outboard motor that's been immersed in the sea?'

'Funny you should ask that this morning, Roy. We've just taken delivery of a new piece of kit we're trialling. Costs a hundred and twelve thousand quid. It's meant to be able to get fingerprints off plastic that's been immersed in any kind of water for considerable periods.'

'Good stuff. I think I may have your first challenge for you.'

Norman Potting stood up, mouthed that he would pop back later, then walked slowly out of the door, stooping a little, Grace noticed, his shoulders rounded. His heart suddenly went out to him.

51

Vlad Cosmescu stood in the arrivals hall of Gatwick Airport, along with the usual assortment of relatives, drivers and tour operators, holding a small placard. The Bucharest flight had landed just over an hour ago and the girls had not come through yet.

Good.

From the tags he had managed to read on the bags of the steady stream of passengers emerging through Customs, everyone from that flight had now gone. He saw Al Italia tags, which he reckoned must be from a flight that had come in from Turin a good thirty minutes later. And Easyjet tags, too, probably from the Nice flight. Then SAS tags, mingled with some KLM ones.

His watch told him it was 11.35 a.m. He popped a tab of Nicorette gum in his mouth and chewed. The two girls he was meeting had been given strict instructions what to do once they had disembarked and entered the passport area, and it seemed they were obeying them.

They were to hang back for an hour, let other flights land and their passengers go through, before they entered the passport queues. Although Romania was now a member of the EU, Cosmescu was well aware that it was internationally regarded as a hot zone for human trafficking. Romanian passports automatically raised a flag for the Border and Immigration Agency.

Which was why all those he came here to meet, sometimes weekly and sometimes more frequently than that, were instructed to tear their Romanian passports up and flush them down the aeroplane toilets, wait for one hour after landing and then arrive at passport control with the false Italian passports they had been given. In that way, if the agency was keeping a lookout for arrivals from the Romanian flight, they would have stopped looking by the time the girls came through.

Two girls were coming now. Good-looking young things in their late teens, cheaply dressed and towing cheap luggage. Could be them. He held up his placard with the innocuous words JACKSON PARTY on it.

One of the girls – really very sexy-looking, slender with long dark hair – raised a hand and waved at him.

'You had a good flight?' he asked in Romanian, as a greeting.

'Yeah,' she said. 'Great!'

'Welcome to England.'

'Yeah,' she said again. 'Great.'

'Great!' her companion added.

The relief on their faces was palpable.

*

Twenty minutes later, Cosmescu sat in the front passenger seat of the tired, brown E-Class Mercedes. Grubby little buck-toothed Grigore drove. He didn't actually have a hunchback, but he looked like a hunchback. He squatted over the wheel, in one of his cheap beige suits, with his greasy hair, beaky nose and eyes more on the mirror than the road ahead, shooting quick, lascivious glances at every opportunity at the two girls who were seated in the back.

Cosmescu had worked with Grigore for five years and

still he knew virtually nothing about the weirdo little creature. The man always turned up on time, did the pick-ups
and the drop-offs, but rarely spoke – and that was fine with
Cosmescu. If you got into conversation, then you had at
some point to talk about yourself. He did not want to talk
about himself to anyone. That wasn't smart. The less anyone knew about you, the more anonymous you could be.
And the more anonymous you were, the safer you were.
The *sef* had instilled that in him.

Grigore was good at fixing things. He could turn his
hand to just about anything, from plumbing to electrics to
damp-proofing, which meant he could deal with all the shit,
all the leaking pipes and blocked toilets and loose floor-
boards and busted blinds, and everything else that could go
wrong in the four brothels Cosmescu looked after in the
city. Which meant that Cosmescu did not have to worry
about gossiping tradesmen. Once a week he allowed Grigore
to take his pick of any girl, for an hour. That and the
generous pay packet were more than enough to secure
Grigore's undying loyalty.

Which meant there was one less headache for him. He
was still thinking about the bodies. About the fuck-up.
About Jim Towers. It had been stupid, killing him. But it
would have been a lot more stupid to have let him live, all
cosied up to the police, with the knowledge he had. Towers
had been up to something – maybe he just had a bad
conscience, but he could have been planning blackmail.
Like in gambling, you had to balance your risks. A small
one against a larger one.

He turned and looked at the girls. The one on the left,
Anca, she was nice. Her companion, Nusha, had a harder
face, her nose was a little big. But both of them were young,

seventeen, eighteen maximum. They were OK, they would do fine. He wouldn't kick either of them out of bed.

And he didn't intend to.

*

Cosmescu turned the privacy key and the lift ascended non-stop from the underground car park of his apartment block, behind the Metropole Hotel. The two girls stood with him, with their cheap luggage, in silence.

Then Anca asked, 'When do we start work?'

'You start now,' he said.

She raised a finger. 'We go to the bar?'

He looked at her sparkly necklace. Smelled her sweet perfume, and her companion's, which was even sweeter. He stared down her neckline. Good tits. Her friend had even better ones, which made up for her face. He pulled out a packet of cigarettes, knowing that almost certainly they would both smoke. He was right. Each accepted one.

Before he had a chance to click his lighter – his timing, as ever, perfect – the lift stopped and the doors opened.

Now they would be focusing on their unlit cigarettes more than anything else. Keeping them tantalized, he stepped forward into his apartment, then held the door until they had pulled their suitcases, containing their life's possessions, clear.

As they walked along the carpeted landing, he showed each her room. Single rooms. Divide and rule. That strategy always worked. Then he went into Anca's room and picked up her plastic handbag.

'Hey!' she said.

Ignoring her, he removed her passport and then all the cash from her purse.

'What you do?' she demanded angrily.

He produced his lighter and finally lit her cigarette. 'You know how much money you owe? How many thousands, for your journey and your passport? When you have repaid my boss, then you may have your passport.'

He went out and repeated the scenario with Nusha.

*

A few minutes later, the two girls walked sullenly into the large, modern living room. It had fine views of the Palace Pier and the blackened remains of the West Pier, the Marina, over to the east, and far out across the English Channel.

Cosmescu was sure they would never have seen anything like this place in their lives. He knew the kind of background they would have come from. And that Marlene would have cleaned them up, in preparation for their new lives.

All the girls that came here were debt-bonded, which meant they had signed up in Romania to an impossibly large loan – although they never actually saw the cash – agreeing to work off in England their one-way passage to what they thought was freedom. They would start here in Brighton. If they settled into their work, fine. But the vigilant Brighton and Hove police, along with care workers, visited the local brothels from time to time, talking to the girls, trying to find ones that were there against their will.

If either of these looked as if she might start giving out signals that she wanted help from the police, he would move her away from Brighton and up to a brothel in London, where less interest would be taken in her, by anyone.

'We go to the bar tonight?' Anca said.

'Take your clothes off,' he said. 'Both of you.'

The two girls looked at each other in surprise. 'Clothes?'

'I want to see you naked.'

'We – we did not come to be strippers,' Nusha said.

'You are not strippers,' he said. 'You are here to pleasure men with your bodies.'

'No! That's not the deal!' Anca protested.

'You know how much it cost to bring you here?' he said harshly. 'You want to go home? I will take you to the airport tomorrow. But Mr Bojin will not be pleased to see you. He will want his money back. Or would you rather I call the police? In this country false passports is a bad offence.'

Both girls fell silent.

'So tell me, which do you want? Shall I phone Mr Bojin now?'

Anca shook her head, looking terrified suddenly. Nusha bowed hers, looking ashen.

'OK.' He pulled his mobile phone from his pocket and stabbed a button on the dial pad. 'I call the police.'

'No!' Anca shouted. 'No police!'

He put the phone back in his pocket. 'So, take your clothes off. I will teach you how to pleasure a man in this country.'

Staring sullenly at the black carpet, as dark as the void of their new lives, both girls began to undress.

52

On the flat screen high on the wall, a short distance in front of her desk, Lynn read the words in large gold letters: COLLECTOR BONUSES TOP TEN.

Below was a list of names. The top was currently Andy O'Connor, on a rival team, the Silver Sharks. The screen informed her that Andy had collected a total of £9,987 in cash this week, so far. His accumulated bonus, if he maintained this position, was £871.

God, how she could do with that!

She looked enviously at the other nine names beneath his. The bottom was her friend and team-mate Katie Beale, at £3,337.

Lynn was way off the scale. But one sizeable client had just agreed to a plan. He would make a lump sum payment of £500 and a regular £50 a month, to pay off a MasterCard debt of £4,769. But that £500 – assuming it did come in – would only bring her weekly total to £1,650. Leaving her with an almost impossibly long way to go.

But perhaps she could stay late tonight and catch up on her hours. Luke had come over to see Caitlin after they'd got back from the hospital this morning, so at least she would have company. But she did not want to be away from her for too long.

Suddenly an email pinged on to her screen. It was from Liv Thomas, her team manager, asking her to have another try with one of her least favourite clients.

Lynn groaned inwardly. A golden rule of the company

was that you never actually met with your *clients*, as they were called. Nor did you ever tell them anything about yourself. But she always had a mental picture in her head of everyone she spoke to. And the image she had in her head of Reg Okuma was of a cross between Robert Mugabe and Hannibal Lecter.

He had run up a bill of £37,870 on a personal loan from the Bradford Credit Bank, putting him up among the largest debtors on their client list – the highest topping out at a whopping £48,906.

A few weeks ago she had given up on ever recovering a penny from Okuma, and had passed his debt over to the litigation department. On the other hand, she thought, if she did get a result, then it could be fantastic and would propel her into contention for this week's bonus.

She dialled his number.

It was answered by his deep, resonant voice on the first ring.

'Mr Okuma?' she said.

'Well, this sounds like my good friend Lynn Beckett from Denarii, if I am not mistaken.'

'That's right, Mr Okuma,' she said.

'And what can I do for you on this fine day?'

It may be fine inside your head, Lynn thought, *but it's pissing with rain inside my head and outside my window.* Following her long-used training script, she said, 'I thought it might be a good idea to discuss a new approach to your debt, so that we can avoid all that messy litigation business.'

His voice exuded confidence and oily charm. 'You are thinking of my welfare, Lynn, would that be right?'

'I'm thinking of your future,' she said.

'I'm thinking of your naked body,' he replied.

'I wouldn't think about that too hard, if I were you.'

'Just thinking about you makes me hard.'

Lynn was silent for a moment, cursing for falling into that one. 'I'd like to suggest a payment plan for you. What exactly do you think you could afford to pay off on either a weekly or a monthly basis?'

'Why don't we meet, you and I? Have a little tête-à-tête?'

'If you would like to meet someone from the company I can arrange that.'

'I have a great dick, you know? I'd like to show it to you.'

'I will certainly tell my colleagues.'

'Are they as pretty as you?'

The words sent a shiver rippling through her.

'Do your colleagues have long brown hair? Do they have a daughter who needs a liver transplant?'

Lynn cut the call off in terror. How the hell did he know?

Moments later her mobile rang. She answered it instantly, spitting out the word, 'Yes?' convinced it was Reg Okuma, who had somehow got hold of her private number.

But it was Caitlin. She sounded terrible.

53

There were occasions when Ian Tilling missed his life in the British police force. Plenty of moments too when he missed England, despite the painful memories it held for him. Particularly on those days when the numbing cold of the Bucharest winter froze every bone in his fifty-eight-year-old body. And on those days when the chaotic bleakness of his surroundings here in the suburban sector 6, and the bureaucracy and corruption and callousness of his adopted country, dragged his spirits down.

Whenever he felt low, his mind went back to the terrible evening, seventeen years ago, when two of his colleagues came to his house in Kent and told him that his son, John, had died in a motorcycle accident.

But he had an instant fix for coping with that pain. He would get up from his desk in the ramshackle office, filled with donated furniture, which he shared with three young female social workers, and take a walk around the hostel he had created as a sanctuary for fifty of this cruel city's homeless. And see the smiles on his residents' faces.

He decided to do just that, now.

When Ceauşescu had come to power in 1965, he had a skewed plan to turn Romania into the greatest industrial nation in Europe. To achieve that he needed to increase, dramatically, the size of the population in order to create his workforce. One of his first acts of legislation was to make it compulsory for all girls, from the age of fourteen, to have a pregnancy test once a month. If they fell pregnant they were forbidden to abort.

The result, within a few years, was an explosion in the size of families, and the offspring became known as the Children of the Decree. Many of these children were handed to government care institutions and brought up in vast, soulless dormitories, where they were brutally mal-treated and abused. Many of them escaped and took to a life on the streets. A huge number of them were now living rough in Bucharest, either in shanties built along the net-work of communal steam pipes that criss-crossed the sub-urbs, or in holes in the roads, beneath them. Tributaries of these pipes fed every apartment block in the city with their central heating, which was switched on in autumn and off in spring.

After the tragedy of John's death led to the collapse of Tilling's marriage, he had found it impossible to concen-trate on his police work. He quit the force, moved into a flat and spent his days drinking himself into oblivion and end-lessly watching television. One evening he saw a documen-tary on the plight of Romanian street kids and it had a profound effect on him. He realized that maybe he could do something different with his life. Nothing would bring John back, but perhaps he could help other kids who'd never had any of the opportunities in life that John, and most other kids in England, had. The next morning he phoned the Romanian embassy.

He remembered the first government home for children he had visited when he arrived in the country. He walked into a dormitory in which fifty handicapped children aged from nine to twelve lay in caged cots, staring blankly ahead of them or at the ceiling. They had no toys at all. No books. Nothing to occupy them.

He had gone straight out and bought several sackfuls of toys and handed a toy to each child. To his astonishment, there was no reaction from any of them. They stared at the toys blankly, and he realized in that moment that they did not know what to do with them. Not because they were mentally retarded, but because they had never been given toys before in their lives and did not know how to play with them. No one had ever taught any of these kids anything. Not even how to play with a fucking doll.

And he became determined, then and there, that he would do something for those kids.

Originally, he had figured on spending a few months out in Romania. He never thought he would still be here, seventeen years later, happily married to a Romanian woman, Cristina, and more content than he had ever been in his entire life.

Tilling looked tough and fit, despite carrying more than a few excess pounds around his midriff and he walked, exuding pent-up energy, with a copper's strut. His face was craggy and lived in, with a toothbrush moustache and topped with close-cropped grey hair. Making few concessions to the weather, he was dressed today in a blue open-neck shirt, baggy fawn trousers and old brown brogues.

He stepped out into the hallway and smiled at a group of new arrivals from a care organization who were seated on the battered armchairs and sofas. Four dark-skinned Roma kids, a boy of eight in shell-suit bottoms and a sparkly T-shirt, a youth of fourteen in a baggy top and black tracksuit trousers that were too short for him, and two girls, a long-haired twelve-year-old in a mismatched jogging suit and a girl of fifteen in jeans and a holed cardigan. Each of them held a helium-filled party balloon, which they raised in celebration.

They were all from one family who could not cope and had placed them into an institution that they had run away from two years ago. They had been living on the streets since and now had the smiles on their faces he had seen so many times before, and which broke his heart each time. The smiles of desperate human beings who could not quite believe that their luck had changed.

'How are you doing? All OK?' he said, in Romanian.

They beamed and jigged their colourful balloons. Tilling had no idea where the balloons had come from, but he knew one thing for sure. Apart from the clothes they stood up in, these were the only possessions they had in the world.

The residents of Casa Ioana ranged in age from a seven-week-old baby, with her fourteen-year-old mother, to an eighty-two-year-old woman who had been tricked out of her home and her life savings by one of the many monsters who exploited Romania's ill-thought-out laws. There was no welfare for the homeless in this country – and few shelters. The old woman was lucky to be here, sharing a dormitory room with three other elderly inmates who had met the same fate.

'Mr Ian?'

He turned at the voice of Andreea, one of the social workers, who had stepped out of his office behind him. A slim, pretty twenty-eight-year-old, who was getting married in the spring, Andreea had a deep warmth and compassion, and tireless energy. He liked her a lot.

'Telephone call for you – from England.'

'England?' he said, a little surprised. He rarely heard

from England these days, except from his mother, who lived in Brighton, and to whom he spoke every week.

'It is a policeman. He says he is old friend?' She said it as a question. 'Nommun Patting.'

'Nommun Patting?' He frowned. Then suddenly his eyes lit up. 'Norman *Potting*?'

She nodded.

He hurried back into his office.

54

Lynn cursed as she saw two flashes from the speed camera in her rear-view mirror. She always drove slowly past that sodding camera opposite Preston Park, but this afternoon it had gone completely out of her mind. She was concentrating on getting home to Caitlin as quickly as possible and on nothing else. Now she faced a fine to add to her financial woes, and another three points on her licence, but she carried on without slowing down, a steady fifty-five in the thirty limit, desperate to get to her child.

Five minutes later she pulled into her driveway, jumped out of her car, jammed her key in the front door and pushed it open. Luke was standing in the hall, limp hair slanted across one eye, wearing a baggy top and trousers that looked like they might have come from the rear of a pantomime horse. His mouth was open and he had an even more gormless expression than usual on his face, like a man on a railway platform watching the last train of the night disappearing and not sure what to do next. He raised his arms by way of a greeting to Lynn, then let them drop again.

'Where is she?' she said.

'Oh – er – right – Caitlin?' he said.

Who the fuck do you think? Boadicea? Cleopatra? Hillary Clinton? Then she saw her daughter, standing at the top of the stairs, in a dressing gown over her nightdress, swaying as if she were drunk.

Dumping her handbag on the floor, Lynn threw herself

up the stairs just as Caitlin stepped out into space, missing the top stair altogether, and tumbled forwards. Somehow, Lynn caught her, grabbing her thin frame in one arm and the banister rail in the other, and, clinging for dear life, managed to stop herself plunging backwards.

She stared into Caitlin's face, inches from her own, and saw her eyes roll. 'Darling? Darling? Are you OK?'

Caitlin slurred an incomprehensible response.

Using all her strength, somehow Lynn managed to push her back and up on to the landing. Caitlin tottered against the wall. Luke followed them, stopping halfway up the stairs.

'Have you been doing drugs?' Lynn screamed at him.

'No, no way, Lynn,' Luke protested, the shock in his voice sounding genuine.

Slurring her words, Caitlin said, 'I'm like – I'm – I'm like . . .'

Lynn steered her back into her room. Caitlin half sank, half fell backwards on her bed. Lynn sat down beside her and put an arm around her. 'What is it, my darling? Tell me?'

Caitlin's eyes rolled again.

Lynn thought, for one terrible moment, that she was dying.

'If you've given her anything, Luke, I'll kill you. I swear it. I'll tear your fucking eyeballs out!'

'I haven't, I promise. Nothing. Nothing. I don't do drugs. I wouldn't, wouldn't give her nothing.'

She put her nose to her daughter's mouth to see if she could smell alcohol, but there was only a warm, faintly sour odour. 'What's the matter, darling?'

'I just feel giddy. I've got the roundabouts. Where am I?'

'You're home, darling. You're OK. You're at home.'

Caitlin stared blankly around the room, without any recognition at all, as if she was in a totally unfamiliar place. Lynn followed her eyes as she stared at the dartboard with the purple boa hanging from it, then at the photograph of the rock star hunk, whose name Lynn had momentarily forgotten, as if she was looking at them for the first time.

'I – I don't know where I am,' she said.

Lynn stood up, gripped by a terrible panic. 'Luke, stay here with her for a moment.' Then she ran downstairs, grabbed her handbag and went into the kitchen. She pulled her address book out of her bag, then dialled the mobile phone number of the Royal South London transplant coordinator.

Please God, be there.

To her relief, Shirley Linsell answered on the third ring. Lynn told her Caitlin's symptoms.

'It sounds like encephalopathy,' she said. 'Let me speak to a consultant and either I or he will get straight back to you.'

'She's in a really bad way,' Lynn said. 'Encephalopathy? How do you spell that?'

The coordinator spelled it out. Then, promising to get back to her within minutes, hung up.

Lynn ran back up the stairs, holding the cordless phone. 'Luke, can you look up "encephalopathy" on the Net?' She spelled it out for him.

Luke sat down at Caitlin's dressing table, opened her laptop and began clicking on the keypad.

Five minutes later, Shirley Linsell rang back. 'You need to get Caitlin to move her bowels. Would you like to bring her back up here?'

'Have you found a liver for her?'

There was a hesitation that Lynn did not like.

'No, but I think it would be a good idea for her to come in.'

'For how long?'

'Until we've stabilized her.'

'When will you have a liver?'

'Well, as I said this morning, I cannot answer that. You could treat her at home for this.'

'What do I have to do?'

'Give her an enema. Usually with this condition, evacuating the bowel will regularize her.'

'What kind of enema? Where do I get one?'

'Any chemist.'

'Terrific,' Lynn said.

'Why don't you try that? Give it a few hours, then see how she is and call me. There is someone here all the time and she can come in at any hour.'

'Yes,' Lynn said. 'Fine, I'll do that.'

She hung up.

Caitlin was lying back on her bed, eyes opening and closing.

'I think I've found what you're looking for!' Luke announced.

Lynn peered over his shoulder. His hair smelled unwashed.

Reading aloud off the webpage he said, 'Encephalopathy is a neuropsychiatric syndrome which occurs in advanced liver disease. Symptoms are anything from slight confusion and drowsiness to change in personality and outright coma.'

'How fucking great is that?' Lynn said. Then she turned to Caitlin, whose eyes were now closed. Afraid, suddenly, that she might be slipping into a coma, she shook her. 'Darling? Keep awake, darling.'

Caitlin opened her eyes. 'You know what?' she slurred. 'Liver disease rocks.'

'Rocks?' Lynn said, astounded.

'Yeah, why not?' Luke retorted.

'Why does it rock?' Lynn stared quizzically at Luke, as if somehow she was going to find the answer in his inane face.

'This transplant waiting list, yeah?'

'What about it?'

'There's a way around it.'

'What way?'

'Yeah, well, I've been looking on the Net. You can buy a liver.'

'Buy a liver?'

'Yeah, it's whack.'

'Whack? I'm not sure I'm on your planet. How do you mean, *buy a liver*?'

'Through a broker.'

'A what?'

'An organ broker.'

Lynn stared at him, thinking for a moment this was his idea of humour. But he looked deadly earnest. It was the first time she had ever seen him remotely animated.

'What do you mean by an *organ broker*?'

'Someone who will get you whatever organ you want. On the Net. They're selling anything you could want for a transplant. Hearts, lungs, corneas, skin, ear parts, kidneys – and livers.'

Lynn stared at him in silence for some moments. 'You are serious? You can buy a liver on the Internet?'

'There's a whole bunch of sites,' Luke went on. 'And – this'll interest you – I found a forum about waiting lists for organs. It says the waiting list for liver transplants in some countries is even worse than in the UK. Something like 90 per cent of people on the list in the USA will die before they get a new liver. Sort of puts our 20 per cent into the shade.'

Unless one of that 20 per cent happens to be your daughter, Lynn thought, staring hard at Luke. *One of the three people a day in the UK who die waiting for a transplant.*

She was sick with worry and all twisted up inside with rage. Thinking. Thinking about Shirley Linsell. Her change from warmth to coldness. Caitlin was just another patient to her. In a year or two's time, she probably wouldn't even remember her name – she would just be a statistic.

Lynn was not going to take that chance.

'I'm going to the chemist. When I get back, I'd like you to show me about these organ brokers,' she said.

*

On the way, she stopped at a newsagent's, went inside and scanned the *Argus* for any further news on the story about the three bodies. On the third page was a long article, headlined POLICE REMAIN BAFFLED BY CHANNEL BODIES. She stared at the sanitized photographs of the three dead teenagers' faces. Read the speculation that they might be organ donors. Read the quotes from Detective Superintendent Roy Grace, whoever he was.

Something dark stirred inside her. Leaving the paper on the rack, not wanting Caitlin to see it, she bought a packet of ten Silk Cut cigarettes, then went back out to her car and smoked one, thinking again, hard, her hands shaking.

55

Some years ago, when he was a detective sergeant, Roy Grace had attended a break-in at a small wine merchant's premises up on Queens Park Road, close to the racecourse and the hideous edifice of Brighton and Hove General Hospital.

The proprietor, Henry Butler, a drily engaging, shaven-headed and impeccably spoken young man, appeared more upset at the quality of the wines the thieves had taken than at the break-in itself. While the SOCOs went about their business, dusting and spraying for fingerprints, Butler bemoaned the fact that these particular specimens of Brighton's broad church of villainy had no taste at all.

The Philistines had taken several cases of his cheapest plonk, leaving all the fine wines, which in his view would have been far better drinking, untouched. Grace had liked him instantly, and whenever he needed a bottle for a special occasion, he had always returned to this shop.

At four o'clock on Tuesday afternoon, taking a quick, late lunch break, he pulled up the unmarked Ford Focus on double yellow lines outside the small, unassuming shop front of the Butler's Wine Cellar and dashed inside. Henry Butler was in there now, head still shaved, sporting a gold earring and a goatee beard, dressed in dungarees and a collarless shirt, as if he had just been out picking grapes.

The door pinged shut behind him and Roy instantly breathed in the familiar, sour, vinous smell of the place, mixed with the sweeter scent of freshly sawn timber from the wooden cases.

'Good afternoon, Detective Superintendent Grace!' Butler said, putting down a copy of *The Latest*. 'Very nice to see you. All crimes solved now, so you're free to partake of my libations?'

'I wish.' Grace smiled. 'How's business?'

Butler gave a shrug at the empty shop. 'Well, with your arrival, I would say the day just got better. So what can I tempt you with?'

'I need a rather special bottle of champagne, Henry,' he said. 'What's the most expensive bottle you have?'

'Good man! That's what I like to hear!' He disappeared through a doorway into a tiny, cluttered back office and then clattered down some stairs.

Grace checked a text that just pinged in, but it was nothing important, a reminder about his haircut appointment tomorrow at the Point, the hair salon his self-appointed style guru, Glenn Branson, insisted he go to for his monthly close-crop. He stared around at the displays of dusty bottles flat on their sides on shelves and stacked in wooden boxes on the floor. Then he glanced at the headline of the *Argus*: BRIGHTON REGAINS DRUG DEATH CAPITAL OF ENGLAND STATUS.

A grim statistic, he thought, but at least it kept his case off the front page today.

A couple of minutes later, Henry Butler reappeared, reverently cradling a squat bottle in his arms. 'Got this rather seductive Krug. One sip and anybody's knickers will hit the ground.'

Grace grinned.

'Two hundred and seventy-five quid to you, sir, and that's with 10 per cent discount.'

Roy's smile fell into a black hole. 'Shit – I didn't actually mean *quite* that expensive. I'm not a Russian oligarch, I'm a copper, remember?'

The merchant gave him a quizzical, mock-stern look. 'I have a luscious Spanish cava at nine quid a pop. It's what we drink at home in summer. Gorgeous.'

'Too cheap.'

'There you go, Mr CID – ' which he pronounced *Sid* – 'I never did take you for a cheapskate. I do have a rather special house champagne, seventeen quid for you, sir. A massive, buttery nose, long finish, quite a complex, biscuity style. Jane MacQuitty did her tonsils over it in the *Sunday Times* a while ago.'

Grace shook his head. 'Still too cheap. I want something *very* special, but I don't want to have to take out a mortgage.'

'How does a hundred quid sound?'

'Less painful.'

The merchant disappeared down into the bowels of his emporium and re-emerged. 'This is the dog's bollocks! Roederer Cristal, 2000. Best vintage of the decade. Last one I have, bin-end price. A beaut! Normally one hundred and seventy-five – I'll flog it to you for a hundred, as it's you.'

'Done!'

'Diamond geezer!' Henry Butler said approvingly.

Grace pulled out his wallet. 'Credit card OK?'

Butler looked like he had been kicked in the nuts. 'You know how to squeeze a man when he's down – yeah, all right.' He shrugged. 'Very special occasion, is it?'

'Very.'

'Give her this and she'll love you forever.'

Roy smiled. 'That's kind of what I'm hoping.'

56

Lynn sat on Caitlin's bed, staring at the computer screen. Luke, hunched on a stool in front of the cluttered dressing table, was busily pecking away at the keyboard of Caitlin's laptop, using just one finger and, apparently, just one eye.

Caitlin, in her dressing gown, had spent much of the past hour going backwards and forwards to the toilet. But she was already looking a little better, Lynn was relieved to see, except she was scratching again. Scratching her arms so hard they looked as if they were covered in insect bites. At the moment, iPod in her ears, she was switching focus between an old episode of the *OC* playing silently on the muted TV and her purple mobile phone, on which she was texting someone, with furrowed concentration, while rubbing the itching balls of her feet on the end board of the bed.

Luke had been tapping away for nearly an hour now, working through Google, then other search engines, trying out different combinations of phrases and sentences containing the words *organs*, *purchase*, *humans*, *donors*, *livers*.

He had found a debate in the Council of Europe Parliamentary Assembly on the topic of human organ trafficking, and on another site had discovered the story of a Harley Street surgeon called Raymond Crockett, who was struck off the Medical Register in 1990 for buying kidneys from Turkey for four patients. And plenty more debates about whether organ donation should be automatic on death unless a person has opted out.

But no organ brokers.

'Are you sure it's not just an urban myth, Luke?'

'There's a website about part of Manila being called One Kidney Island,' he said. 'You can buy a kidney there for forty thousand pounds – including the operation. That site talked all about brokers—'

Suddenly he stopped.

On the screen, in clinical white against a stark black background, the words TRANSPLANTATION-ZENTRALE GMBH had appeared.

In a bar above were options for different languages. Luke clicked on the Union Jack flag and moments later a new panel came up:

Welcome to

TRANSPLANTATION-ZENTRALE GMBH

the world's leading brokerage for
human organs for transplantations

Discreet global service, privacy assured

Contact us by phone, email
or visit our Munich offices by appointment

Lynn stared intently at the computer screen, feeling an intense, giddying frisson of excitement. And danger.

Maybe there really was another option to the tyranny of Shirley Linsell and her team. Another way to save the life of her daughter.

Luke turned to Caitlin. 'Looks like we've – yeah – found something.'

'Cool!' she said.

Moments later Lynn felt Caitlin's arms around her shoulders and her warm breath on her neck, as she too peered at the screen.

'That's awesome!' Caitlin said. 'Do you think there's –

like – a price list? Like when you go online shopping at Tesco?'

Lynn giggled, delighted that Caitlin seemed to be returning to some kind of normality, however temporary.

Luke began to navigate the site, but there was very little information beyond what they had already read. No phone number or postal address, just an email one: *post@trans plantation-zentrale.de.*

'OK,' Lynn said. 'Send them an email.'

She dictated and Luke typed:

> I am the mother of a 15-year-old girl who is urgently in need of a liver transplant. We are based in the south of England. Can you help us? If so please let us know what service you can provide and what information you require from us. Yours sincerely,
> Lynn Beckett

Lynn read through it, then turned to Caitlin. 'OK, my angel?'

Caitlin gave a wistful smile and shrugged. 'Yep. Whatever.'

Luke sent it.

Then all three of them stared at the mailbox in silence.

'Do you think we should have sent a phone number?' Caitlin asked. 'Or an address or something?'

Lynn thought for a moment, her brain feeling scrambled. 'Yes. Maybe. I don't know.'

'No harm, is there?' suggested Caitlin.

'No, no harm,' her mother agreed.

Luke sent a second email, containing Lynn's mobile number and the dialling code for England.

*

Ten minutes later, down in the kitchen making a cup of tea and preparing some supper for the three of them, Lynn's phone rang.

On the display were the words, *Private number*.

Lynn answered immediately.

There was a faint hiss, then some crackle. After a fraction of a second's time delay she heard a woman's voice, in guttural broken English, sounding professional but friendly.

'May I please speak with Mrs Lynn Beckett?'

'That's me!' Lynn said. 'Speaking!'

'My name is Marlene Hartmann. You have just sent an email to my company?'

Shaking, Lynn said, 'To Transplantation-Zentrale?'

'That is correct. By chance, I have the opportunity to be in England tomorrow, in Sussex. If it is convenient, we could meet, perhaps?'

'Yes,' Lynn said, her nerves shorting out. 'Yes, please!'

'Do you happen to know your daughter's blood type?'

'Yes, it is AB negative.'

'AB negative?'

'Yes.'

There was a brief silence before the German woman spoke again.

'Good,' she said. 'That is excellent.'

57

'The time is 6.30 p.m., Tuesday 2 December,' Roy Grace announced. 'This is the tenth briefing of Operation Neptune, the investigation into the deaths of three unknown persons.'

He was seated in his shirtsleeves, tie loosened, at the table in the briefing room of Sussex House. Outside, it was a vile night. He stared, for an instant, through trails of rain slithering down the windowpanes, at the blackness beyond. Inside, it felt cold and draughty, with most of the heat coming from the bodies of his fast-expanding team, now twenty-eight strong, crammed around the table.

On the flat surface in front of him were a bottle of water, a stack of newspapers, his notebook and his printed agenda. There was a lot to work through before he could get out of here tonight – and move on to his second, and much more pleasurable, agenda of the evening. One which involved the seriously expensive bottle of champagne lying in the boot of his car downstairs.

On the wall-mounted whiteboard were sets of fingerprints and composite e-fit photographs of the three victims. He glanced up at them now. A DI colleague, Jason Tingley, currently in the Divisional Intelligence Unit, once commented that e-fits made everyone look like Mr Monkeyman and Roy had never been able to get that image out of his mind. He was looking at two Monkeymen and one Monkeywoman up there on that wall now.

Dead.

Murdered.

Depending on him to bring their killers to justice.

Depending on him to bring closure to their relatives.

He flipped open the *Independent* newspaper, which was on the top of the pile. On page three was a stark headline: BRIGHTON AGAIN CRIME CAPITAL OF ENGLAND. This was a reference back to 1934, when Brighton was in the grip of its famous razor gangs and, within a short space of time, two separate bodies were found in trunks at Brighton's railway station. Brighton had then earned the unwelcome sobriquet *Crime Capital of England.*

'The new Chief's not impressed,' Roy Grace said. 'He wants this solved, quickly.'

He looked down at the notes Eleanor had typed for him.

'OK, we now have further pathology evidence that the organs were removed from our victims under operating-theatre conditions. The labs have identified the presence of Propofol and Ketamine in the post-mortem tissues. These are both anaesthetics.'

He paused to let the implications sink in.

'I've been giving this organ-trafficking line some thought, Roy,' Guy Batchelor said. 'Purchase and sale of human organs are illegal in the UK. But because of short-ages, there are people on the heart, lung and liver waiting lists who die before an organ becomes available. And there are people who wait for years, leading miserable lives, on the kidney transplant waiting lists. How are we getting on with our search for a disgruntled transplant surgeon?'

'Nothing so far,' DI Mantle said.

'What about making every transplant surgeon in the UK a suspect?' said Nick Nicholl. 'There can't be that many.'

'What progress have we made on surgeons who have been struck off?' Lizzie Mantle queried. 'I really think that would be a good place to start. Someone angry who wants to buck the system.'

'I'm working on that,' Sarah Shenston, one of the researchers, said. 'I hope to have a full list by tomorrow. There's a lot of them.'

'Good. Thank you, Sarah.' Grace made another note. 'I think we should make a list and visit all the human organ transplant facilities in the UK.' He looked at Batchelor. 'Something important to establish is the chain of supply of organs. How does an organ get from a donor to a transplant? Are there any windows of opportunity for a rogue supplier?'

Batchelor nodded. 'I'll get that researched.'

'I think we need to assume in the first instance,' Grace said, 'that there is a Brighton – or Sussex – connection with these victims. To my thinking, the fact that they were found close to the coast of Brighton indicates that. Does everyone accept that?'

The entire team nodded agreement.

'I think an important part of this jigsaw is to establish the identities of the victims – and we are making headway here.' He looked down at his notes again. 'We have an interesting piece of information from the laboratory, Cellmark Forensics, where we sent DNA samples of the victims. Their US laboratory, Orchid Cellmark, has done an enzyme and mineral analysis of the DNA from the three victims. It indicates they had a diet compatible with that of south-eastern Europe.'

He took a swig from his bottle of water, then went on.

'Now, this tallies with the toxicology report from the path labs. All three victims have small traces of a Romanian-manufactured metallic paint, known as Aurolac, in their blood. According to the pathologist's information, this substance is inhaled by Romanian street kids, having an effect similar to sniffing glue. Now, supporting this, Nadiuska returned to the mortuary last night to carry out a further examination and discovered traces of metallic paint in the nostrils of the victims.' He looked at Potting. 'Norman, would you like to bring us up to speed on Romania?'

Potting, looking pleased as punch at being given the floor, puffed up his chest. 'Well, I've briefed Interpol, but same as usual with those desk jockeys. No blooming sense of urgency. Could be looking at three weeks for a response – longer with Christmas coming up.' Then he hesitated and looked at Roy Grace. 'Can I mention Ian Tilling in Bucharest, sir?'

Grace nodded, then said, 'Norman has a contact in Romania, a very well-respected former UK police officer who is running a charity helping to shelter street people there. Taking into account the imperative to move this case forward, I have given DS Potting permission to bypass Interpol on an exploratory basis. Can you update us please, Norman?'

'I've tasked him with looking for anyone with the name Rares who might have come to England recently. I only spoke to him a few hours ago, but he promised to get on the case right away, and I hope to hear back from him with his first report tomorrow. That's all I have at this point.'

Grace then turned to Bella Moy. 'What progress have you made with dentists?'

'None,' she said, and held up several sheets of paper. 'These are the ones I have seen so far. All have said the same thing. The victims show signs of poor nutrition and probably drug abuse, but no signs of any dental work. I'm not sure there's any point in pursuing dentists, Roy. I don't think any of these three victims had ever been to a dentist, and certainly not in the UK.'

'Yes, doesn't sound like it's getting us anywhere. You can cease that line.' He turned to DC Nick Nicholl. 'What do you have to report on Mispers?'

'Nothing so far, chief.'

Nicholl then outlined the progress he had made. He reported that he had circulated the e-fit photographs widely around Sussex and the neighbouring counties, with no hits. There had been no result, either, from the newspapers. The *Crimewatch* television show was another option, but that was still a week away.

Grace looked down at his notes again.

'Ray Packham, from the High-Tech Crime Unit, has something to tell us.'

Seated opposite him, the computer analyst was nothing like the traditional image of the geek. Packham reminded him of the original 'Q' in the Bond films. In his early forties, he was keenly intelligent and always bursting with enthusiasm, despite the grim nature of his work, much of it studying photographs on seized computers of horrific sexual abuse of children, day in and day out. Anyone meeting him for the first time, finding him in a grey suit and club tie, might have mistaken him for an avuncular, old-school bank manager.

'Yes, we've been checking out the countries that are party to the global trafficking of human organs, sir, and Romania is one of them,' Packham said. 'This confirms what DS Potting told us previously. We are continuing with our searches.'

Grace thanked him, then he said, 'OK, I spoke this afternoon to several members of the team behind Operation

Pentameter, which is investigating human trafficking. Jack Skerritt at HQ CID and DI Paul Furnell and DS Justin Hambloch at Brighton nick have given me a list of names that have south-east European connections, including a couple of Romanian ones. There are a number of Romanian girls working in Brighton brothels. We need to check all of them out, see if any recognize any of these three teenagers. And see if we can get any of them to talk about their contacts, either in Romania or here.'

Grace turned to DS Branson. 'Do you have anything to report, Glenn?'

'Yeah, there is still no news on the missing fishing boat. I have an appointment to interview the wife of the owner of the *Scoob-Eee* tonight, after this meeting. As agreed at this morning's briefing, I've asked the Scientific Support Unit to send the two cigarette butts I retrieved from Shoreham Harbour out for DNA analysis.'

Grace nodded, then checked his notes again and said, 'There may be no connection at all, but a brand-new five-horsepower Yamaha outboard motor was found earlier today on the beach at low tide, between the Marina and Rottingdean, at Black Rock. I'm having it analysed with some new fingerprint technology that the labs here are testing. Glenn, I'd like you to get a list of all Yahama outboard motor dealers in the area and find out who's sold one recently.'

'Where's it now, Roy?'

'In the evidence store.'

'OK.'

Roy surreptitiously glanced at his watch, momentarily allowing himself a pleasant distraction. He'd told Cleo he hoped to be at her house by eight. Then he focused back on the meeting.

'I'm taking the view that we are dealing with human trafficking here, until I'm persuaded otherwise. From what DI Furnell has told me, all of the known trafficking to date has been for the sex trade. The girls brought into Brighton for this purpose are handled by a number of Mr Bigs here. Some are under surveillance by his team, but he believes there are several others not yet on his radar. I think a key line of enquiry is going to be to talk to the girls employed in Brighton's brothels and see if we can broaden our lists of Mr Bigs.'

Recognizing that the sex trade flourished in every town and city, Brighton Police preferred the working girls to be inside, rather than out on the streets, principally for their own safety. It also made it easier to monitor them for underage, trafficked girls.

'Bella and Nick, I think you two would get the best out of them,' Grace said.

He felt the prostitutes might feel comfortable with a woman present, and as Nick Nicholl was the doting father of a young baby, he was unlikely – as opposed to someone like Norman Potting – to be swayed by any sexual allure.

'I was on brothels for a time when I was in uniform,' Bella said.

Nick Nicholl blushed. 'Just so long as someone explains to my wife – you know – what I'm doing in these places.'

'Women lose their sexual drive after they've sprogged,' Norman Potting interjected. 'Take it from me. You'll be in need of a bit on the side soon enough.'

'Norman!' Grace cautioned.

'Sorry, chief. Just an observation.'

Glaring at him, wishing the man could shut up and just get on with doing what he was good at, Grace went on. 'Bella and Nick, I want you to talk to as many working girls as you can. We know that a lot of them are making good money and are quite happy with their lot. But there are some who are debt-bonded.'

'Debt-bonded?' Guy Batchelor asked.

'Rescued from poverty by scumbags who tell them they can get them a wonderful new life in England. Passport, visa, job, flat – but for a price they will never be able to pay back. They arrive in England, tens of thousands of pounds in debt, and some Mr Big will be licking his slimy lips. He'll put them in a brothel, even if they are thirteen, and tell them it's the only way they can pay the interest on the bond. If they refuse, they will be told that their families or friends will be harmed. But these Mr Bigs over here usually have their fingers in more than one pie. They'll be into the drugs market – and some, it seems, into the human organ market.'

He had everyone's attention.

'I think that's likely to be our number one suspect. A local Mr Big.'

58

Glenn Branson halted the unmarked black Hyundai at the roundabout and glanced up at the curved front of a modern building that he particularly liked, Shoreham's Ropetackle Centre for the Arts. Then he took the first exit and drove along a wide street that was lined on both sides with shops, restaurants and pubs, all glittering with Christmas lights and decorations. Although it was half past eight on a rain-lashed Tuesday night, the place seemed vibrant and thrumming with people. Office-party season was in full swing. Not that he cared.

He felt terrible.

Christmas was looming. Ari didn't even want to discuss it with him. Was he going to spend it alone, in Roy Grace's lounge?

There were three missed calls from Ari on his mobile, which had come in during the briefing meeting, but when he had called her back afterwards, a man had answered.

A *man* in his house, telling him that his wife was out.

When Glenn had asked him who the hell he was, the man, with a creepy, arrogant voice, had told him he was the babysitter and that Ari was at an English literature class.

A male babysitter?

If he had sounded like a teenager, that would have been one thing. But he didn't; his voice was older, like someone in his thirties. Who the fuck was he? When he had asked that question, the little shit had replied snidely that he was a *friend*.

What the hell did Ari think she was doing leaving his kids, Sammy and Remi, in the hands of a man he had never met or vetted? Jesus, he could be a paedophile. He could be *anything*. The moment the interview was over, Glenn determined to drive straight over there and see him for himself. And throw the fucker out of his house.

The turn-off was coming up, according to the directions he had memorized. He slowed, indicated left, then turned into a narrow, residential street. Driving slowly, he passed a crowded fish and chip shop, trying with difficulty to read the numbers of the terraced houses. Then he saw No. 64. Fifty yards or so on, there was a tight, empty space between two parked cars. He manoeuvred the little Hyundai into it, touching bumpers with the car behind once, and climbed out. Hurrying through the rain, the collar of his cream mackintosh turned up, he rang the doorbell.

The woman who answered was in her mid-fifties, tall and buxom, with a crown of reddish hair that looked as if it had been freshly styled today. She wore a loose grey smock over blue jeans and clogs. Dark rings under her eyes and mascara stains gave away her misery.

'Mrs Janet Towers?' he asked, holding up his warrant card.

'Yes.'

'Detective Sergeant Branson.'

'Thank you for coming.' She moved aside to let him in and then, in a sudden spurt of hope, she asked, 'Do you have any news?'

'Nothing so far,' he said. 'I'm sorry.'

He stepped inside, squeezing past her into a narrow hallway lined with framed antique nautical prints of Brighton. The house felt hot and stuffy, and smelled of cigarette smoke and damp dog. Something he had noted from past experience was that when people were in shock or mourning, they tended to keep their curtains drawn and turn the heating up high.

She ushered him into a tiny, sweltering lounge. Most of the space was taken up by a brown velour three-piece suite, and the rest by a large television set, a coffee table fashioned from a ship's wheel, on which sat an ashtray filled with lipsticky butts, and several display cabinets filled with ships-in-bottles in varying sizes. An old-fashioned three-bar heater with fake coals blazed in the fireplace. On the mantelpiece above it were several family photographs and a large greetings card.

'Can I get you a drink, Detective – er – Detective Sergeant Branson, you said? Like the Virgin guy, Richard Branson?'

'Yeah, 'cept I'm not as rich as him. Coffee would be lovely.'

'How do you take it?'

'Muddy, no sugar, thank you.'

'Muddy?'

'Strong, with just a tiny dash of milk.'

She went out of the room and he took the opportunity to look at the photographs. One showed a couple outside the front of a church – All Saints, Patcham, he recognized, because it was the same church where he and Ari had been married. The husband, whom he presumed was Jim, wore a narrow-cut suit with a shirt that looked too big for him, bouffant frizzy hair and a quizzical smile. The bride, a much skinnier Janet, had ringlets down to her shoulders and a lace gown with a long train.

Ranged alongside it were several photographs of two children in varying stages of childhood and one of a shy-looking young man in a mortar board and graduation gown.

Graduation, he thought gloomily. Would he ever get to

go to either of his kids' graduations? Or would his bitch wife exclude him?

He pulled out his personal mobile and checked the display. Just in case.

In case what? he thought, pocketing it miserably and wondering again about the man who had answered the phone. The man who was alone with his children.

Was the little turd going to screw Ari when she came home?

He heard wheezing and turned to see an elderly, overweight golden retriever peering at him through the doorway.

'Hello!' Glenn said, holding out a beckoning hand.

The dog deposited a slick of slobber on to the carpet, then waddled towards him. He knelt and patted it. Almost immediately the dog rolled over on to its back.

'Well, you're a great guard dog, aren't you?' he said. 'And you're a tart too, showing me your tits!'

He stroked its belly for some moments, then got to his feet again and picked up the greetings card.

On the front, in gold, was printed: *'TO MY DARLING.'*

Inside was written, *To Janet, the love of my life. I adore you and miss you every second that we are apart. Thank you for the happiest twenty-five years of my life. All my love. Jim XXXXXXXX*

'Hope it's the right strength for you!'

Glenn closed the card and replaced it. 'Nice card,' he said.

'He's a nice man,' she replied.

'I can tell from reading it.'

She placed a tray, with two cups of coffee and a plate of chocolate digestive biscuits on the coffee table, then sat on the sofa. The dog pressed its nose against the plate.

'Goldie! No!' Janet Towers said sternly.

The dog waddled away reluctantly. Glenn chose the armchair that was furthest away from the fire and looked at the biscuits, suddenly realizing he was feeling hungry. But he felt it might seem rude to start eating at such a sensitive time for this poor woman.

'I have a few questions for you, further to our telephone conversation yesterday,' he said. 'If you don't mind?'

'I'm desperate,' she said. 'Anything, anything at all.'

He turned to the mantelpiece. 'Are those your children? How old are they?' Then he watched her eyes very closely.

They swung to the right, then centred as she stared at him, frowning. 'Jamie, twenty-four and Chloe, twenty-two. Why?'

Without answering, he said, 'I take it you've still heard nothing?'

Roy Grace had taught him, some while back, that you could tell if a person was lying or telling the truth by watching their eye movements. It was an area of neurolinguistic programming. The human brain was divided into left and right parts. Although it was more complicated than Grace taught, essentially with right-handed people, the imagination – or *construct* – took place in the left-hand side, and the long-term memory and factual stuff took place in the right-hand side. When you asked someone a question, their eyes often moved either to the construct or to the memory side, depending on whether they were lying or telling the truth.

Glenn had already established, by watching her, that she was right-handed. If he now observed her eyes carefully, he should see them move to the left if she was lying or to the right if telling the truth.

Her eyes moved sharply to the right. 'Not a word,' she said. 'Something has happened to him, please believe me.'

He pulled out his notebook and pen. 'Am I right that you've had no word from your husband since Friday night?'

Again her eyes flicked distinctly to the right.

'Yes.'

'Has Jim ever been absent for a period like this before?'

'No, never.'

She still appeared to be telling the truth. He made a note, then sipped his coffee, but it was too hot, so he put it back down.

'Forgive me if I sound insensitive, Mrs Towers – did you and your husband have any kind of argument before he – disappeared?'

'No, absolutely not! It was our wedding anniversary – our twenty-fifth. The night before, he told me that he wanted us to renew our wedding vows. We were – are – extremely happy.'

'OK.' He looked at the biscuits longingly, but continued to resist. 'How much did he tell you about his clients?'

'He told me lots about them, if they were interesting – or odd.'

'Odd?'

'He had one guy this summer who hired him to go out deep-sea fishing who turned out to have a penchant for fishing naked.' She managed a grin.

'Whatever floats your boat,' he said, grinning back.

Then, in the awkward silence that followed, he realized that was probably not the best analogy to have used at this moment.

'So what are the police doing about – about trying to find him?' she asked.

'Everything we can, Mrs Towers,' Glenn replied, his face burning from his faux-pas. 'The coastguards have launched a full air-sea rescue team, with support from the RAF, out looking for the boat. They've stopped tonight but will resume again at first light. All UK and overseas Channel ports have been alerted. All shipping has been alerted to be on the watch for the *Scoob-Eee*. But so far, I'm afraid, there has been no reported sighting.'

'We had a table booked for dinner at eight o'clock on Friday night. Jim told me the boat had been chartered for the day by the police diving unit, and that all he had to do was move it back to its mooring, when they returned, and he'd be home by about six.' She shrugged. 'Then at nine o'clock his boat was seen going through the Shoreham Harbour lock and heading out to sea. That doesn't make any sense.'

'Perhaps he got a last-minute charter?'

She shook her head vigorously. 'Jim's very romantic – he's been planning this evening for weeks – months. He wouldn't have taken a charter that night, absolutely no way.'

Glenn finally succumbed, took a biscuit and bit a chunk. Chewing, he said, 'I don't want to sound insensitive, but we know that a lot of smuggling, both of humans and of drugs, goes on in this city. Is it possible that your husband could have been involved in some kind of shipment?'

Again she shook her head vigorously. 'Not Jim, no.'

Still happy that she was being truthful, he asked, 'Does Jim have any enemies?'

'No. None that I'm aware of, anyway.'

'What do you mean by that, Mrs Towers?'

'Do you mind if I smoke?' she asked.

'Go ahead.'

She pulled a packet of Marlboro Lites from her handbag, took out a cigarette and lit it.

'Everyone loves Jim,' she said. 'He is that kind of man.'

'So in all his time as a private eye he never made an enemy?'

'It's possible. I keep thinking about all his old clients. Yes, he might have upset someone, but he's been out of that game for a decade.'

'Could it be someone he put inside who's just been released?'

'He didn't put people in prison. He was more – you know – following unfaithful spouses around, doing a bit of industrial espionage. He just snooped around, followed people, that sort of thing.'

Glenn made another note. Then he asked, 'I presume Jim has a mobile phone?'

'Yes.'

'It's not here?'

'No, he always has it with him.'

'Could I have the number?'

She reeled it off from memory and he wrote it down.

'Who is the provider?'

'O2.'

'When was the last time you spoke to him?'

'About quarter past five on Friday. He'd just picked up the boat from the police diving unit and was back in his berth. He said he was going to tidy her up and then he'd be home.'

'That was the last conversation you had?'

'Yes.'

She started sobbing.

Glenn sipped his coffee and waited patiently. When she had quietened down he asked, 'Presumably you've tried ringing him?'

'About every five minutes. Nothing happens. It just goes straight to voicemail.'

Glenn noted that down. He looked up at Janet Towers and his heart went out to her.

Then he thought again about the man who had answered the phone at his home. The man who was baby-sitting his son and his daughter.

The man he had never met, but at this moment hated more than he had ever believed it was possible to hate anyone.

If you are sleeping with Ari, he thought, *then God help you. I'll rip your testicles out of your scrotum with my bare fingers.*

He forced a smile at Janet Towers and handed her his card.

'Call me if you hear anything. We'll find your husband,' he said. 'Don't worry about it. We'll find him.'

Through her sobs her voice suddenly turned to anger. 'Yes, well, I hope to hell you find him before I do, that's all I can say.' She began sobbing again.

59

Roy Grace, holding tightly on to the most expensive bottle of champagne he had ever bought in his life, slipped his key into the front door lock of Cleo's gated townhouse.

As he did so his phone rang.

Cursing, he dug it out of his pocket and answered it. 'Detective Superintendent Grace.'

It was ACC Alison Vosper. Just the person he did not want to speak to at this moment. And to cap it, she sounded in a characteristically sour mood.

'Where are you?' she asked.

'I just got home,' he said, hoping she might be impressed that it was after nine o'clock.

'I want to see you first thing in the morning. The chief's been talking with the Chief Executive of Brighton and Hove Council about all the bad press Brighton is getting over your case.'

'Sure,' he said, doing his best to mask the reluctance in his voice.

'Seven o'clock.'

Inwardly he groaned. 'Fine!' he said.

'I hope you have some progress to report,' she added before hanging up.

Have a nice evening, he mouthed. Then he opened the door.

Cleo, in a man's shirt over ripped jeans, was on her hands and knees on the wooden floor, playing *who owns the sock* with Humphrey. The dog was snarling, growling, whining, tugging away at the sock as if his life depended on it.

'Hi, darling!' he said.

She looked up at him, without stopping her tug-of-war and without noticing the bottle he was brandishing.

'Hi! Look, Humphrey, look who's here. It's Detective Superintendent Roy Grace!'

He knelt and kissed her.

She gave him a quick peck, but her concentration was on the dog. 'Champagne!' she said. 'How nice!' Then, squinting at the black ball of yapping fluff, she said, 'What do you think of that, Humphrey? Detective Superintendent Roy Grace has brought us champagne! Do you think it's a peace offering?'

'Sorry I'm late – got held up after the briefing meeting.'

She tugged the sock, hard. Humphrey slithered towards her, his paws failing to get traction on the polished oak boards. His jaws released the sock, then snapped back on it. Cleo looked up at Roy. 'I've made you the best martini of your life! A fantastic new vodka I've discovered – Kalashnikov. It's in the fridge.' Then she added, 'Lucky bastard, you'll have to drink it for both of us!'

She turned back to the dog. 'He's lucky, isn't he, Humphrey? He gets here an hour later than he promised and he still gets a nice drink. And you and I have to drink water. What do you think of that?'

Grace felt awkward suddenly. She seemed in a slightly distant mood.

'It'll go down nicely while I'm waiting for the champagne to chill!' he said, trying to placate her.

He showed her the bottle.

Examining the label while continuing to tease Humphrey, she said, 'Detective Superintendent, do you have wicked designs on me tonight?'

'Very wicked!' he said.

'You know I shouldn't drink.'

'I checked on the Internet. The new thinking is that the occasional glass doesn't do pregnant women any harm.'

'And two?'

'Two would be even better. One for you, one for the Bump.'

She grinned, then looked down and patted her stomach. 'What a thoughtful daddy!' she said, mocking.

Grace slung his jacket and his tie on to a sofa, then put the bottle into the freezer and opened the fridge door. A martini glass, filled to the brim, with an olive on a stick, sat there. He took it out, carried it through into the living room and drank some, then sat down on the edge of a sofa. The alcohol hit him like rocket fuel, giving him an instant lift.

Humphrey let go of the sock and bounded towards him in a series of short hops.

'Hey, you!' He knelt and stroked the dog, which immediately responded by biting his hand playfully. 'Ouch!' He withdrew it.

Humphrey looked at him, then jumped up and bit him again.

Holding his martini clear, he said, 'Fellow, you've got sharp teeth! You're hurting me!'

'Do you know what my father says about martinis?' Cleo said.

Humphrey ran back to the sock, tore it free from Cleo and began shaking it furiously, as if he was trying to kill it.

'No. What?'

'*Ladies, beware of the dry martini, have two at the very*

most. For with three you will be under the table – and with four, you will be under your host!'

Grace grinned. 'So what does he say about vintage champagne?'

'Nothing – he's usually off his face with martinis before he gets to the champagne!'

'I'm looking forward to meeting him.'

'You'll like him.'

'I'm sure,' Grace said, not at all sure how her posh father would take to a humble copper.

He sipped again, and now the sharp, dry alcohol was really kicking off inside his head. Then his phone rang, again. Nodding an apology to her, he tugged it from his jacket.

'Roy Grace,' he answered.

'Yo, old-timer!'

It was Glenn Branson.

'Hi,' he said. 'What do you want?'

'Is this a good moment?'

'No,' he said. 'What's up?'

'It's OK,' the DS said. 'Just wanted to talk to you, about Ari.'

'Can it wait until the morning?'

'Yeah, tomorrow. No worries.'

'Are you sure?'

'Tomorrow's good,' Glenn said, sounding terrible.

'Tell me?'

'Nah, tomorrow's fine. Have a good one!'

'I can talk.'

'No. No, you can't. Tomorrow's good.'

'Listen, mate, what is it?'

The line went dead.

Grace tried to phone his friend back, but got straight

through to voicemail. He tried his own home number, in case he was there, but that went to the answering machine after eight rings. He jammed his phone into his trouser pocket, then knelt down.

For several minutes Cleo continued playing with Humphrey, again barely acknowledging his existence. Then, after a while, tiring of the game, she let go of the sock. Humphrey dragged it over to the beanbag that was his bed and continued to wrestle with it, snarling and yapping, as if he was fighting a dead rat.

'Want to eat something?' Cleo asked. 'I made one of your favourite meals. Just in case you deigned to turn up.'

She had chosen almost exactly the same words as Sandy. Sandy used to get angry at the hours he worked, and especially on the occasions when he was called out in the middle of a meal with her.

'Hey!' he said. 'What do you mean by that? *In case I deigned to turn up!*'

'You're the boss man,' Cleo said. 'You could be home on time if you really wanted to, couldn't you?'

'You know I can't. Come on, let's not have an argument about it. I've got three young murdered teenagers and a lot of people wanting answers. You've seen the kids – I want to find out who did this, and fast, before it happens again. And I have a ton of people on my back wanting answers before Christmas. Me included. I have to give it all I've got.'

'I get people brought into the mortuary every day, and I give them and their relatives all I've got. But I manage to keep a separate compartment for my life. You don't do that, Roy. Your work is your life.'

Feeling that he was pedalling in a vast, dark void, Grace said, 'When you're on call, you have to go out – sometimes 24/7 – don't you?'

'That's different.' She shrugged and gave him an odd stare.

Grace felt a sudden stab of panic. He took a long sip on his drink, but the alcohol had stopped working. For the first time since they had started dating, she seemed a stranger, and he was scared that he might be losing her.

'It's always going to be like this, isn't it, Roy?'

'Like what?'

'Hanging around, waiting for you. You're in love with your work.'

'I'm in love with you,' he said.

'I'm in love with you too. And I'm not stupid enough to think that I can change you. I wouldn't want to change you. You're a good man. But . . .' She shrugged. 'I feel very proud to be carrying your – our – child. But I worry about what kind of a father you might be.'

'My father was a police officer,' Grace said. 'He was a terrific dad to me. I was always very proud of him.'

'But he was a sergeant, wasn't he?'

'What's that supposed to mean?'

'Shit, I need a drink. How long before we can open that bottle?'

'Maybe another ten minutes?'

'I'll get supper ready. Can you take Humphrey out on to the patio? He needs to do a pee and a dump.'

Grace dutifully took the dog up on to the roof garden and walked him around in circles for ten minutes, during which Humphrey did nothing except nip his hand several more times. Then, when he let him back indoors, the dog trotted down the stairs, peed on the living-room floor, then squatted and proudly delivered a massive turd on a white rug.

By the time he had cleaned up the mess, the Roederer

Cristal was perfectly chilled. Two bowls of prawns, diced avocado and rocket salad were laid out on the small kitchen table. He pulled two crystal flutes from a cabinet, opened the bottle as carefully as if he was tending to a baby, then poured it.

They clinked glasses.

Cleo, seated at the table, looked stunning. So beautiful, so vulnerable. It was utterly incredible to him that she was carrying their baby. She took a tentative sip, then closed her eyes for a moment. When they opened again, they were sparkling, like the drink.

'Wow! That is amazing!'

He stared into her eyes. 'Look,' he said, 'I know I haven't yet met your father, and there are protocols that need to be observed in your world – but – Cleo – will you marry me?'

There was a long, agonizing silence, during which she just stared back at him with an unreadable expression. Finally she took another long sip, then said, 'Roy, my darling. I don't want this to sound –' she hesitated – 'sort of weird or anything, OK?'

He shrugged, having no idea what was coming next.

She twisted the glass in her hand. 'I just thought to myself that if you proposed to me, one day, because I was pregnant, I would never marry you.' She gave him a helpless, lost-child look. 'That's not the kind of life I want – for either of us.'

There was an even longer silence. Then he said, 'Your being pregnant has nothing to do with this. That's just a very big bonus. I love you, Cleo. You are the most beautiful person, inside and out, that I've ever been lucky enough to meet in my life. I love you with all my heart and soul. I will love you to the ends of the earth and back. And more. I want to spend the rest of my life with you.'

Cleo smiled, then nodded pensively. 'That's not bad,' she said. Then she gave a rolling motion with her hand. 'More?'

'I love your nose. Your eyes. I love your humour. I love the way you look at the world. I love your mind. I love your kindness to people.'

'So it's not about me being a good shag?' she said, in mock disappointment.

'Yep, that too.'

She drank some more, then putting her elbows on the table, held her glass in the fingers of both hands and peered at him over the top of it. 'You know, you're not a bad shag either.'

'Slapper!'

She wrinkled her nose. 'Horny bastard.'

'You like it!'

Puffing herself up haughtily, she said, 'No, I don't. I only do it to please you.'

He grinned. 'I don't believe you.'

*

Later, Humphrey sat on the bedroom floor, barking and whining while they made love, until he got bored and went to sleep.

Lying in each other's arms, Cleo kissed Roy on the nose, then on each eye, then on the lips. 'You know, you're an incredible lover. You are so amazingly unselfish.'

'Are most men selfish?'

She nodded. Then she grinned. 'Talking from experience, of course, all the hundreds of lovers I've had – not!'

'I take that as a compliment, coming from an expert.'

She thumped him. Then she kissed him again. 'There's something else about you, Detective Superintendent – you make me feel safe.'

'You make me feel horny.'

She slid her hands down his hard, muscular body. Then stopped. 'Bloody hell, you want more?'

'Did we just do it?'

'About five minutes ago.'

'Must be my premature Alzheimer's kicking in. I thought that was just – you know – foreplay!'

She grinned. 'You are the horniest man I ever met!'

'You make me horny,' he said, and kissed her lightly on the lips, and then on her neck, her shoulders and then on every inch of her arms, legs, ankles, toes. Then they made love again.

*

A long time later, in the flickering glow of an almost burnt-down candle, Cleo, wrapped around him and dripping with perspiration, said, 'OK, I surrender. I'll marry you.'

'You will?'

'Yes, I will. I want to, more than anything in the world. But isn't there a complication?'

'What?'

'You already have a wife.'

'I've just started the process to have her declared dead, under the seven-year rule. My sister's been trying to persuade me to do that for a long time.'

'*Cleo Grace*,' she murmured. 'Mmm, that has a nice ring to it.'

She kissed him again, then, clinging tightly to him, fell asleep.

60

Glenn Branson sat in silence behind the wheel of the black Hyundai, staring wretchedly at his house. He had been here for five hours.

The small, 1960s semi was on a steep street in Saltdean, inland from the cliff top and a real wind trap. In the hooley that was blowing, the car rocked constantly and rain thwacked on to the body panels.

Tears streamed down his face. He was oblivious to the freezing cold, to his hunger, to his need to pee. He just stared across at the little house with its bright yellow front door that was his home. Stared at the front façade that was now like some kind of a Berlin Wall between himself and his life. It was all a sodding blur. His eyes blurred by his tears. The car windows blurred by the driving rain. His mind blurred by love, by anger and by pain.

He'd watched Ari arrive home shortly after ten and she hadn't spotted him in this car. Then he'd waited for the male babysitter, whoever the arrogant bastard was, to leave. It was now twenty past two in the morning and he still had not left. Over two hours ago, the lights had gone off downstairs, then had come on in her bedroom. After a while, they had gone off there too. Which meant she was sleeping with this babysitter. Screwing him in *their* house.

Were Sammy and Remi going to run into the bedroom in the morning, as they always did, excitedly calling out, 'Mummy! Daddy!', only to find a strange man in the bed?

Or had they stopped running in now? How much had changed in his home during these past few weeks?

The thought was like a knife twisting in his soul.

He looked at the car clock. 2.42. He looked at his watch, as if hoping the car clock was wrong. But his watch said 2.43.

A plastic dustbin lid rolled along the pavement. Then he saw a flurry of ice-blue splinters in his mirrors and moments later a police patrol car shot by, roof spinners on but siren off. He saw it turn right at the top of the road and disappear. It might be going to a domestic, or an accident, or a break-in – or anything. Reluctant to risk getting called away from here, he hesitated before phoning in. But he was using a police pool car and that obliged him to be on call. And, despite all that was happening in his private life, he was still grateful to the police force for giving him the chances in life it had.

On his mobile, he phoned through to the control room at Southern Resourcing Centre.

'Glenn Branson here. I'm the on-call DS for the Major Crime Branch. I've just seen the boys go by in Saltdean on a shout – anything for us?'

'No, they're on their way to an RTC.'

Relieved, he ended the call. Within moments his full focus was again on his house. His anger was growing. He did not care about anything except what was going on inside his house.

And finally he could not restrain himself any longer. He climbed out of the car, crossed the road, walked up to his front door, feeling furtive, a stranger, as if he should not be here, should not be walking up the path to his own front door.

He pushed the key into the lock and tried to turn it.

But it would not move. He took it out, puzzled, wondering for an instant whether he had used the key to Roy Grace's front door in error. But it was the right key. He tried again and still it would not turn.

Then it dawned on him. She had changed the lock!

Oh shit! No, you don't, lady!

Memories of a hundred movie scenes of spouses fighting flashed through his mind. Then, in an explosion of rage, he rang the doorbell, a long ring, a good ten seconds of jangling noise from inside the house. And he realized, through his red mist of anger, that he had never in his life before rung his own doorbell. He followed it by hammering on the door.

Moments later he sensed light above him and looked up. Ari was standing at the bedroom window, the curtains parted. She pushed the window open and looked down, her face peering out of the top of her pink dressing gown, her sleek, straightened black hair looking immaculate, the way it always did, as if she had just stepped out of a hair salon. It even looked that way after they'd gone white-water rafting, one time.

'Glenn? What the hell are you doing? You'll wake the kids!'

'You've changed the fucking locks!'

'I lost my keys,' she shouted back, defensively.

'Let me in!'

'No.'

'Fuck you, this is my home too!'

'We agreed to be apart for a while.'

'We didn't agree you could bring men home and fuck them.'

'I'll talk to you in the morning, OK?'

'No, you let me in and we talk now!'

'I'm not opening the door.'

'I'll break a fucking window if that's what you want.'

'Do that and I'm calling the police.'

'I am the police, in case you'd forgotten.'

'Do what the hell you want,' she said. 'You always have done!'

She slammed the window shut. He stepped back to get a better view, saw the curtains being pulled tightly shut and the light go off.

He clenched his fists, then unclenched them, his mind a maelstrom. He walked some yards up the street. Then down again. A car drove past, some small custom job with rap playing on boom-box speakers, shaking the already shaken air. He stared up at his house again.

For a moment, he was tempted to smash a window and let himself in – and break the fucking babysitter's neck.

The problem was, he knew that's exactly what he would do if he went in.

Reluctantly, he turned away, climbed back into the Hyundai and drove down to the main coast road. He halted at the T-junction, signalling right. As he was about to pull out, he noticed a tiny pinprick of light a long way off in the murky darkness. A ship of some kind, out at sea.

And suddenly he had a thought that momentarily pushed his anger to one side.

The thought stayed with him, developing more in his mind, as he drove along the gusty road, through Rotting-dean and Kemp Town, and then along Brighton seafront.

Back in Roy's house, he poured himself a large whisky, then sat down in an armchair and thought some more.

He was still shaking with anger about Ari.

But the thought stayed with him.

And it was there when he woke, three hours later.

He had been rubbish at most subjects at school, because his dad, who was either drunk or stoned, and beat up his mother, consistently told him he was no good, the way he told his two brothers and his sisters they were no good either. And Glenn had believed him. He'd spent his childhood being moved from one care home to another. Geometry was the one subject he had liked. And there was one thing he remembered from that, and it had stuck in his head all night.

Triangulation.

61

At nine o'clock in the morning, Ian Tilling sat at his desk in his office in Casa Ioana, in Bucharest, and enthusiastically studied the lengthy email and scanned photographs that had come in from his old mate Norman Potting. Three sets of fingerprints, three e-fit photographs, two of young males and one of a young female, and several photographs, the most interesting of which was the close-up of a primitive tattoo of the name *Rares*.

It felt good to be involved in some detective work again. And with the briefing meeting about to start, it was really going to feel like the old days!

He sipped his mug of Twinings English Breakfast tea – his elderly mother in Brighton posted him regular supplies of the tea bags, as well as Marmite and Wilkin & Sons Tiptree Medium Cut Orange Marmalade. Just about the only things he missed from England that he could not easily obtain out here.

Seated on wooden chairs in front of his desk were two of his female social workers. Dorina was a tall twenty-three-year-old with short black hair who had come to Romania from the Republic of Moldova with her husband. Andreea was an attractive girl. She had long brown hair and was dressed in a V-neck brown jumper over a striped shirt and jeans.

Andreea reported first, giving the general consensus that Rares was quite a posh name, and was unusual for a street kid. She opined that the tattoo was self-inflicted, which indicated the girl might be a Roma – or Tigani – a gypsy. She added that a Roma girl and a non-Roma boyfriend would be very uncommon.

'We could put an announcement up on the main notice-board,' Dorina said, 'with the photographs. See if any of our homeless clients have any information who these people might be.'

'Good idea,' Tilling said. 'I'd like you to contact all the other homeless charities. Andreea, if you could get these to the three Fara homes, please.'

There were two Fara homes in the city and a farm out in the country, charitable institutions set up by an English couple, Michael and Jane Nicholson, which took in street kids.

'I'll do that this morning.'

Tilling thanked her, then glanced at his watch. 'I have a meeting at the local police station at half past nine. Can the two of you contact the placement centres in all six local authority areas?'

'I already started,' Dorina said. 'I'm not getting a good response. I just spoke to one, but they refused to assist. They're saying that they cannot share confidential infor-mation – and that it's the police who should be making the enquiries and not some director of a charity.'

Tilling thumped his desk in frustration. 'Shit! We all know what kind of help to expect from the bloody police!'

Dorina nodded. She knew. They all knew.

'Just keep trying,' Ian Tilling said. 'OK?'

She nodded.

Tilling sent a brief email back to Norman Potting, then left the room for the short walk to Police Station No. 15. To the only police officer he knew who might be helpful. But he was not optimistic.

62

Glenn Branson, feeling alert and wired despite his ragged night, stood in the corridor outside the briefing room, holding a cup of coffee in one hand and an All-Day Breakfast egg, bacon and sausage sandwich in the other. Members of the team were filing in through the doorway for the Wednesday morning briefing meeting.

Bella Moy stepped past him, giving him a wry smile. 'Good morning, Mr Healthy Eating!' she said.

Glenn mumbled a reply through a mouthful of his sandwich.

Then Bella's phone rang. She glanced at the display before stepping to one side to answer it.

Moments later, the man Glenn was waiting for, Ray Packham, from the High-Tech Crime Unit, appeared.

'Ray! How are you doing?'

'I'm tired,' he said. 'The wife had a bad night.'

'I'm sorry.'

'Jen's diabetic,' he said, nodding. 'We went out for a Chinese. Her blood sugar was off the scale this morning.'

'Diabetes is a bummer.'

'That's the problem with Chinese restaurants – you don't know what they put in their food. All tickety-boo in your neck of the woods?'

'My wife's got a medical condition too.'

'Oh blimey, I'm sorry to hear that.'

'Yeah, she's developed an allergy to me.'

Packham's eyes gleamed behind the thick lenses of his

spectacles. He raised a finger. 'Ah! I know just the chap! I'll give you his number. Top allergist in the country!'

Glenn smiled. 'If you'd said he was the top divorce lawyer, I might be interested. Look, before we get into the briefing, I need to ask you a quick technical question.'

'Fire away. Divorce. Sorry to hear that.'

'Not if you'd met my wife, you wouldn't be. But hey! I need to pick your brains about mobile phones. Yeah?'

More people squeezed past them. Guy Batchelor greeted Glenn with a cheery, 'Good morning.' The DS waved his sandwich at him by way of a reply.

'You're a film buff, Glenn, aren't you?' Packham asked. 'Did you ever see *Phone Booth*?'

'Colin Farrell and Keifer Sutherland. Yeah. What about it?'

'Crap ending, didn't you think?'

'It was all right.'

Ray Packham nodded. In addition to being one of the most respected computer crime experts in the force, he was the only other film buff Glenn knew.

'I need some help on mobile phone masts, Ray. Is that your terrain?'

'Masts? Base station masts? I'm your man! I actually do know quite a bit about them. What exactly are you after?'

'A guy who disappeared – on a boat. He always had his phone with him. Last time he was seen was on Friday night, sailing out of Shoreham Harbour. The way I figure it is that I might be able to plot the direction he was heading in from his mobile phone signals. Through some kind of triangulation. I know it's possible on land – what about out at sea?'

More people filed past them.

'Well, it would depend on how far out and what kind of boat.'

'What kind of boat?'

Packham launched into an explanation, his whole body becoming animated. It seemed that nothing in the world pleased him more than to find a home for some of the vast repository of knowledge that was stored in his head.

'Yes. Ten miles and more, out at sea, and you can still be in range, but it depends on the structure of the boat, and where the phone is situated. You see, inside a steel tub, the range would be drastically reduced. Was this particular phone on deck, or at least in a cabin with windows? Also the height of the masts would be a big factor.'

Glenn thought hard back to his time on board the *Scoob-Eee*. There was a small cabin at the front that you accessed via steps, where the toilet, kitchenette and seating area were. When he had been down there, he had the impression it was mostly below the waterline. But if Jim Towers had been driving the boat, he would have been up on deck, in the partially covered wheel-house area. And if he was heading out to sea, there would have been a direct line-of-sight behind him to the shore. He explained this to Packham.

'Super!' he said. 'Do you know if he made any calls?'

'He didn't bell his wife. I don't know if he called anyone else.'

'You'd need to get access to the mobile phone records. On a major crime investigation, that shouldn't be a problem. I take it this is connected to Operation Neptune?'

'It's one of my lines of enquiry.'

'So here's the thing. If on standby, a mobile phone registers with its network every twenty minutes or so – it sort of checks in, saying, *Here I am, chaps!* If you've ever left your phone lying near your car radio you can sometimes hear that *beeditty-beeditty-beep* noise as interference with the radio, yes?'

Branson nodded.

'That's when it's radioing in!' Packham beamed, as if the sound was a trick he had taught all phones to perform. 'Now, from the records, you could work out where the last registration occurred, to within a few hundred yards.'

He glanced around, conscious that almost everyone had now gone into the briefing room.

'It would probably be in contact with, say, two or three coastal base stations and would be talking to a known sector, about a third of the circle on each.'

He glanced around again.

'Very quickly, there is a thing called *timing advance*. Without getting too technical, the signal travels to and from the base station at the speed of light – three hundred thousand kilometres per second. That *timing advance* – depending on which network we are talking about – allows you to calculate a distance to the phone from each base station. Are you still with me?'

Glenn nodded.

'Thus you have some approximate bearings – but, more importantly, distances from each, which together should allow you to triangulate a location within a few hundred yards. But you have to remember, this is only the place where the last registration took place. The boat could have moved twenty minutes on.'

'So at least I would get its last known position and roughly the course it was steering?'

'Spot on!'

'You're a star, Ray!' Glenn said, writing down notes on his pad. 'You're a fucking star!'

63

At half past eight in the morning, two people, looking to the outside world like a mother and son, stood in line at one of the dozen EU Passport Holders immigration queues at Gatwick Airport.

The woman was a confident, statuesque blonde in her forties, with hair just off her shoulders in a chic, modern style. She wore a fur-trimmed, black suede coat and matching boots, and towed behind her a Gucci overnight bag on wheels. The boy was a bewildered-looking teenager. He was thin, with ruffled black hair cut short, and with a hint of Romany in his features, dressed in a denim jacket that looked too big for him, crisp blue jeans and brand-new trainers with the laces trailing loose. He carried nothing, except a small electronic game he had been given to occupy him, and the hope in his heart that soon, hopefully this morning, he would be reunited with the only person he had ever loved.

The woman made a series of phone calls in a language the boy did not speak, German, he presumed, while he played with his game, but he was bored with it. Bored with the travelling. Hoping against hope the journey would soon be over.

Finally, it was their turn next. A businessman in front handed his passport to the female, Indian-looking immigration officer, who scanned it, looking faintly bored, as if she was coming to the end of a long shift, and handed it back to him.

Marlene Hartmann stepped forwards, squeezed the boy's hand, her leather gloves masking the clamminess of her own hands, then handed over the two passports.

The officer scanned Marlene's first, looked at the screen, which flagged up nothing, and then scanned the boy's. *Rares Hartmann.* Nothing. She handed the passports back.

Outside, in the Arrivals hall, among the plethora of drivers holding up printed or handwritten name-boards, and anxious relatives scanning everyone coming through the door, Marlene spotted Vlad Cosmescu.

They greeted each other with a formal handshake. Then she turned to the boy, who had never been outside of Bucharest in his life and was looking even more bewildered now.

'Rares. This is Uncle Vlad. He will look after you.'

Cosmescu greeted the boy with a handshake and, in his native Romanian tongue, told him he was happy to welcome him to England. The boy mumbled a reply that he was happy to be here and hoped to see his girlfriend, Ilinca, soon – this morning?

Cosmescu assured him Ilinca was waiting for him and longing to see him. They were going to drop Frau Hartmann off, then go on to see Ilinca.

The boy's eyes lit up and, for the first time in a long time, he smiled.

*

Five minutes later, the brown Mercedes, with grubby little buck-toothed Grigore at the wheel, pulled out of Gatwick Airport and on to the link road to the M23 motorway. Minutes later they were heading south towards the city of Brighton and Hove. Marlene Hartmann sat in the front passenger seat. Rares sat quietly in the back. This was the start of his new life and he was excited. But more than anything, he could scarcely wait to see Ilinca again.

It had only been a few weeks since they parted company, in a flurry of kisses and promises and tears. And less than a couple of months since this angel, Marlene, had come into their lives to rescue them.

It felt like a dream.

His real name was Rares Petre Florescu and he was sixteen years old. Some time back, he could not remember exactly when but it was shortly after his seventh birthday, his mother had run away from his father, who drank and hit her constantly, taking him with her. Then she had met another man. This man did not want a family, she had explained sadly to Rares, so she was putting him in a home where he would have lots of friends, and would be with people who loved and cared for him.

Two weeks later a silent old woman, with a face as flat and hard as a steam iron, led him up four flights of stone stairs, into a crowded, flea-infested dormitory. His mother was wrong. No one loved or cared for him there, and at first he was bullied. But eventually he made friends with other children his own age, though never with older boys, who regularly beat him up.

Life was hell. Early every morning they were forced to sing national songs, and like all the others, boys and girls, if he did not stand up straight, he was beaten. When he was ten he started wetting his bed and was beaten regularly for that. Gradually, he learned to steal from some of the older boys, who seemed to be able to get extra food. One day he was caught with two chocolate bars he had taken.

To escape retribution, he ran away. And stayed away, joining a community who hung out at Bucharest's main railway station, Gara de Nord, begging and doing drugs.

They slept wherever they could, sometimes in doorways, sometimes in tiny one-room shacks built along the overland steam pipes, and sometimes in cavities beneath the roads.

It was meeting pretty, lost Ilinca, in a hole beneath the road when he was fourteen, that had brought Rares alive for the first time. She had given him a reason to go on living.

Dragging their bedding further up the tunnel beneath the hot pipeline, away from their friends, they made love and they dreamed.

They dreamed of a better life.

Of a land where they could have a home of their own.

And then one day, on the street, fresh from stealing several bottles of Aurolac, he met the angel he had always believed – but had never dared to hope – would visit him.

Her name was Marlene.

And now he was in the back seat of her Mercedes car, and in a short while he would meet his beloved Ilinca.

He was in a state of bliss.

The car was stopping in a residential street. It was so clean. It was like one of the rich sectors of Bucharest where he sometimes went begging.

Marlene turned round and said to him, 'Vlad and Grigore will look after you now.'

'Will they take me to see Ilinca?'

'Exactly,' she replied. Then she climbed out of the car and walked to its rear.

Peering through the rear windscreen, Rares saw the boot lid pop open. A few moments later, she slammed it shut and walked up the path to the front door of a house, holding an attaché case. He watched her, waiting for her to turn and wave at him. But she just kept looking straight ahead.

The Mercedes pulled away, sharply, jerking him against the seat back.

64

Roy Grace sat in his office, reading through his notes from the briefing meeting. Despite the damp, grey day outside, he was in a sunny mood. In fact, he was feeling happier and more positive about life than he could ever remember. He was on a total high. His 7 a.m. meeting with an even more sour than usual ACC Vosper had not made even the slightest dent in his mood.

This afternoon he was meeting with a solicitor to work out the details of having Sandy declared legally dead. Finally he felt as if the past really was behind him, that he could close the door and move on. He was going to marry Cleo. They were going to have a baby.

Everything else suddenly seemed unimportant this morning – and that was a luxurious feeling he knew he could not allow himself to revel in. He had a ton of work ahead of him. His job was to serve the public, to catch criminals, to make the city of Brighton and Hove a safer place. He viewed any serious crime in this city as a failing by the entire police force and therefore a failing in some part by himself. He couldn't help it, that was the way he was.

Three dead teenagers lay in fridges in the mortuary because the police had failed in some way to protect them. Now at least that wrong could be partially redressed by capturing whoever did this, and hopefully depriving them of their liberty – and ability ever to do this again – forever.

In front of him were the names of doctors in the UK

who had been struck off the medical register. As he read down the very long list, looking for anyone who might be capable of organ transplantation work, he was amazed at the variety of offences.

He had always loathed the idea of bent doctors, almost as much as he loathed the idea of bent coppers – of whom he had encountered mercifully few. He hated anyone in public service, in a position of trust, who exploited it through either corruption or incompetence.

The first name on the list was a detox doctor struck off for negligence leading to the death of a heroin addict. Not a likely candidate, Grace thought.

Next were a husband and wife GP team who ran a private nursing home. He read more. They had been struck off for the disgusting condition of the place and leaving elderly patients in a state of distress. Not likely either.

A junior doctor who failed his training was struck off after lying to get a job as a consultant. Grace read on, with interest. This was just the kind of person – while not actually a transplant surgeon – who might get taken on to assist in illegal operations at a private clinic. He wrote the man's name down in his policy book: Noah Olujimi.

Then he had a sudden thought, and wondered why it had not occurred to him sooner. What procedures were in place at UK hospitals, and UK Transplant, the national transplant centre, where transplants were coordinated, to prevent an illegally acquired organ entering the system? Plenty of rigorous ones, he was sure, but he made a note for this to be followed up.

He continued reading down the list.

A GP struck off for downloading child porn. No.

The next held his interest. A GP who was struck off for committing euthanasia on a cancer victim patient. Euthanasia was something Grace had sympathy with. He remembered, as a child, visiting his beloved, dying grandfather, a tall bear of a man who had lain in bed, screaming in pain, begging for someone to help him, to do something, and then sobbing, while everyone in the room looked on helplessly, except his mother who sat by his bed, holding his hand, praying. He had never forgotten that visit, the last time he had seen him. Nor the uselessness of his mother's prayers.

Euthanasia, he thought again. There were doctors who broke the rules because they didn't agree with the system. For sure there would be transplant surgeons who did not agree with it either. But the list of surgeons the researcher, Sarah Shenston, had come up with was far longer than he had expected.

His computer pinged, as it did every few minutes, with yet another incoming email or batch of emails. He glanced up at the screen. Some new Health and Safety crap that he and every other serving police officer was being copied in on. In recent months he had started to hate Health and Safety even more than the whole political correctness ethos. The latest rubbish to come through was a warning that any police officer climbing up more than six feet would be deemed to be *working from a height*, and only allowed to go higher if properly qualified in working at heights.

How sodding great is that? he thought. If an officer was in pursuit of a criminal, was he going to have to shout out, *Oi! Don't climb higher than six feet or I'll have to let you go?*

There was a rap on his door and Glenn Branson came in.

Grace nodded at his shiny tie. 'You need to replace the batteries. It's not glowing so brightly.'

'Very witty, old-timer.' Then he looked at the Detective Superintendent. 'You got new batteries in? You're glowing!'

'Want a coffee?' Grace gestured for him to sit.

'Nah, I'm OK. Just had one.' Branson eased himself on a chair, gave his friend a curious look, then leaned forward, plonking his massive arms on Grace's small desk. 'How do you find anything, working in such a mess?'

'Well, normally I'd take my files home and sort them at night, but I loaned my house to a nine-hundred-pound gorilla who swings around it, dangling from the light cords, and trashes it.'

The DS suddenly looked a tad sheepish. 'Yeah, well, I'm actually planning to do a big tidy-up – you know, like a spring clean – this weekend. You won't recognize the place.'

'I don't at the moment.'

'You know, half your CDs were in the wrong sleeves – I'm sorting it all out for you. Problem is, it's such a rubbish collection.'

'How can a man who worships Jay-Z say that with a straight face?'

'Jay-Z's the man! He's, like, God! You are so much on another planet with your taste.' Then he grinned. 'One good thing about your car wreck, that awful music you had in there will have gone with it!'

Grace opened a drawer in his desk, removed a small, grimy-looking Jiffy bag and tipped six CDs on to his desk. 'Sorry to disappoint you!'

'I thought your Alfa plunged eight hundred feet?'

'It did, but the tide was out – I managed to get these back when they recovered the wreckage.'

Branson shook his head disappointedly. 'So anyway, when are you getting new wheels?'

'Still waiting on the insurance. Nick Nicholl's wife's got a little motorbike she never uses now – a Yamaha – I think it's an SR 125. I thought I might buy it from them and use that for a while. Do my bit for the environment. Except Cleo's not too happy about the idea.'

Branson grinned.

'What's funny?'

'*Electra Glide in Blue* – you ever see that film? About a motorcycle cop?' Then his phone rang.

He answered immediately, standing up and moving away from the desk. 'Glenn Branson.' Nodding an apology to Grace, he continued, 'Brian – hi – I'm actually just across the corridor from you, in Roy Grace's office. Yeah, both cigarette butts, cos I want to know if it's the same person, which would indicate he was there for a while, or two different persons. OK, brilliant. Thanks!'

He sat back down again, then gave Grace another curious look. 'You can't hide it, mate.'

'Hide what?'

'You look like the cat that's got the cream. What's up?'

Roy shrugged, then couldn't stop himself from grinning.

'You and Cleo?'

He shrugged again, grinning even more.

'You're not – not – not . . . ' he asked, his eyes widening. 'Is there something I should know? As your friend, right?'

Grace suppressed a smile. Then he nodded. 'We got engaged last night. I think.'

Branson almost vaulted his desk. He threw his arms around his friend and gave him a massive bear hug.

'That's just wicked! The best news! You got yourself a great lady! I'm really happy for you!' He released Grace, shaking his head, beaming. 'Like, wow!'

'Thanks.'

'So, have you set a date?'

He shook his head. 'I've got to go and do the *meet daddy* bit and formally ask him. Her family's all a bit posh.'

'So you'll be able to retire and help run the family estates?'

Grace grinned. 'They're not *that* posh!'

'Wicked!' Branson said.

'And you? What's happening?'

Glenn's face fell like a dropped barometer. 'Don't ask. She's shagging someone. Just don't go there. I need to talk to you, man, I need your help, but later. We'll have a drink to celebrate – and perhaps a chat?'

Grace nodded. 'What are you going to do about Christmas?'

'I don't know. I don't frigging know.' He suddenly turned away sharply, and Roy could hear his voice break. 'I – I can't – I can't not spend it with Sammy and Remi.'

Roy realized that Glenn had turned away so that he could not be seen crying.

'Catch you later,' Branson said, choked, and headed for the door.

'Want to stay and chat?'

'No, later. Thanks.'

He pulled the door shut behind him.

Grace sat still for a few moments. He knew that what Glenn was going through must be hell, made all the worse by this time of year, with the dark, gloomy nights and Christmas looming. But it sounded, from all he had heard, that the marriage problems were terminal. Once Glenn accepted that, however bad the pain, then at least he could start the process of moving forward again with his life, instead of living in a hopeless limbo.

He was tempted, for a second, to go after his friend, who clearly needed to talk. But at this moment, he had to get on with his job. Ignoring another ping from his computer, he turned his attention back to his notes from the briefing meeting.

He stared at the list he had started making, beneath the heading *Lines of Enquiry*.

Then his internal phone rang. He picked up the receiver. 'Roy Grace.'

It was Ray Packham, from the High-Tech Crime Unit. 'Roy,' he said. 'You asked me to do a trawl on the Net for organ brokers?'

'Yup.'

'Well, I've got something that may be interesting for you. There's an outfit in Munich, in Germany, called Transplantation-Zentrale GmbH. They're advertising themselves as the world's largest brokers of human organs. My boss here, Sergeant Phil Taylor, did a spell in the Interpol office a few years ago. He knows the guy on the German desk, so we were able to get a quick check done. I think you're going to like this!'

'Yes?'

'The LKA – the Landeskriminalamt – sort of the Bavarian equivalent of the FBI – have had them under surveillance for some time, on suspicion of human trafficking. Now, this is the bit you will like most. One of the countries they have a link with is Romania!'

'Brilliant, Ray!' Grace said. 'I have a very good contact at the LKA in Munich.'

'Yes, well, I thought, you know, for what it's worth.'

Grace thanked him, then hung up. Immediately, he spun his Rolodex and retrieved a card from it. It was printed *Kriminalhauptkommissar Marcel Kullen.*

Kullen was an old friend, from when he had spent six months on an exchange, about four years ago, at Sussex

House. Marcel had helped him a while back, when there had been a possible sighting of Sandy in Munich, and Grace had gone over there for a day, on what had turned out to be a wild-goose chase.

He dialled Kullen's mobile number.

It went to voicemail and he left a message.

65

Lynn wished more than ever, now that she was expecting an important visitor, that she had been able to afford to make the downstairs of the house look better. Or at least to have replaced the horrible patterned curtains in the living room with modern blinds and to have got rid of the manky carpet.

She had done her best to make the house look presentable this morning, putting fresh flowers around the hall and living room, and laying out *Sussex Life*, *Absolute Brighton*, and a couple of other classy magazines on the coffee table – a trick she had learned from a home-makeover show on television. She had made herself look smart too, putting on a navy two-piece she had bought in a second-hand shop, a crisp white blouse and black court shoes, as well as a few liberal squirts of the Escada eau de toilette Caitlin had given her for her birthday, in April, and which she rationed carefully.

As the minutes ticked by, she was starting to become increasingly afraid that the German woman was not going to show up. It was now quarter past ten and Marlene Hartmann had said, yesterday afternoon, that she anticipated being at the house by half past nine. Weren't Germans supposed to always be punctual?

Maybe her flight was late.

Shit. Her nerves were shot to hell. She'd barely slept a wink all night, fretting about Caitlin, getting up every hour, almost on the hour, to check she was OK. And thinking angrily about that transplant coordinator, Shirley Linsell, at the Royal.

And wondering what she was getting herself and Caitlin into by seeing this broker.

But what alternative did she have?

She gave the living room a final check and suddenly noticed, to her horror, a cigarette butt stubbed out into the earth of her potted aspidistra. She retrieved it, feeling a flash of anger towards Luke. Although of course it might have been Caitlin. She knew, from the smell on her sometimes, that Caitlin smoked occasionally. That had started since she met Luke. Then she noticed a stain on the beige carpet, and was about to hurry and put some Vanish on it when she heard the slam of a car door.

With a beat of excitement, she darted across to the window. Through the net curtains she saw a brown Mercedes, with tinted windows, parked outside. Hastily, she moved away, walked through into the kitchen, deposited the offending butt in the bin and turned down the volume on the television. On the screen, a couple were showing two presenters around a small semi that was not dissimilar to her own – from the outside, at any rate.

Then she hurried upstairs and entered Caitlin's room. She had woken her up early, and made her shower and get dressed, unsure whether the German woman might want to examine her medically. Caitlin was now asleep on top of her bed, with her iPod earpieces plugged in, her complexion even more yellow today. She was dressed in ragged jeans, a green hoodie over a white T-shirt, and thick, grey woollen socks.

Lynn touched her arm lightly. 'She's here, darling!'

Caitlin looked at her, a strange, unreadable expression in her eyes, a mixture of hope, despair and bewilderment.

Yet somewhere in the darkness of her pupils lurked her old defiance. Lynn hoped she would never lose that.

'Did she bring a liver with her?'

Lynn laughed and Caitlin managed a wry grin.

'Do you want me to bring her up here, darling, or are you going to come down?'

Caitlin nodded pensively for some moments, then said, 'How ill do you want me to look?'

The doorbell rang.

Lynn kissed her on the forehead. 'Just be natural, OK?'

Caitlin lolled her head back and let her tongue fall out of her mouth. 'Yrrrrrr,' she said. 'I'm dying for a new liver and a nice glass of Chianti to wash it down with!'

'Shut up, Hannibal!'

Lynn left the room, hurried downstairs, and opened the front door.

The elegance of the woman standing in the porch took her by surprise. Lynn had not known what to expect, but had imagined someone rather dour and formal, perhaps a little creepy. Certainly not the tall, beautiful woman – early forties, she guessed – with wavy, shoulder-length blonde hair and a fur-trimmed black suede coat to die for.

'Mrs Lynn Beckett?' she quizzed in a deep, sensual, broken English accent.

'Marlene Hartmann?'

The woman gave her a disarming smile, her cobalt blue eyes full of warmth.

'I am so sorry to be late. There was a delay because of snow in München. But now I am here, *alles ist in Ordnung, ja*?'

Thrown for a second by the sudden switch of language, Lynn mumbled, 'Um, yes, yes,' then stepped back and ushered her into the hall.

Marlene Hartmann strode past her and Lynn noted, with dismay, the faintest hint of a frown of disapproval on her face. Directing her into the sitting room, she asked, 'May I take your coat?'

The German woman shrugged it off her shoulders with the haughtiness of a diva, then handed it to Lynn, without looking at her, as if she were a cloakroom attendant.

'Would you like some tea or coffee?' Lynn was cringingly conscious of the woman's roaming eyes, clocking every detail, every stain, every chip in the paintwork, the cheap furniture, the old telly. Her best friend, Sue Shackleton, had once had a German boyfriend and had briefed her that Germans were very particular about coffee. At the same time as buying the flowers last night, Lynn had bought a packet of freshly ground roasted Colombian beans.

'Do you have mint tea, perhaps?'

'Er – mint tea? Actually – yes, yes, I do,' Lynn said, masking her disappointment at her wasted purchase.

A few minutes later she came into the living room, carrying a tray with a mint tea and a milky instant coffee for herself. The German woman was standing at the mantelpiece, holding a framed photograph of Caitlin, who was dressed as a Goth, with spiky black hair, a black tunic, a chin stud and a ring through her nose.

'This is your daughter?'

'Yes, Caitlin. It was taken about two years ago.'

She replaced the photograph, then sat down on the sofa, placing her black attaché case beside her.

'A very beautiful young lady. A strong face. Good bone structure. She could model, maybe?'

'Maybe.' Lynn swallowed, thinking, *If she lives.* Then she put on her most positive smile. 'Would you like to meet her now?'

'No, not yet. Give to me first a little of her medical history.'

Lynn put the tray down on the coffee table, handed the woman her cup, then sat in an armchair beside her.

'Well, OK – I'll try. Up until nine she was fine, a normal, healthy child. Then she started having bowel problems, strong occasional stomach pains. Our GP diagnosed it initially as indeterminate colitis. That was followed by diarrhoea with blood in it, which persisted for a couple of months, and she felt tired all the time. He referred her to a liver specialist.'

Lynn sipped her coffee.

'The specialist said that her spleen and liver were enlarged. She had a distended stomach and she was losing weight. Her tiredness was getting worse. She was always falling asleep, wherever she was. She was going to school, but needed four or five naps a day. Then she started getting stomach pains that went on all night. The poor kid was really distressed and kept asking, "Why me?"'

Suddenly, Lynn looked up and saw Caitlin entering the room.

'Hi!' she said.

'Angel – this is Mrs Hartmann.'

Caitlin shook the woman's hand warily. 'Nice to meet you.' Her voice was quavering.

Lynn saw the woman studying her daughter closely. 'It is very nice to meet you, Caitlin.'

'Darling, I was just telling Mrs Hartmann about your stomach pains that used to keep you awake all night. Then the doctor put you on antibiotics, didn't he? Which worked well, for a time, didn't they?'

Caitlin sat down in the opposite sofa. 'I can only sort of remember.'

'You were very young, then.' Lynn turned back to Marlene Hartmann. 'Then they stopped working. That was when she was twelve. She was diagnosed with a condition called PSC – primary sclerosing cholangitis. She spent almost a year in hospital – first down here, then in London, in the liver unit at the Royal South London. She had an operation to put stents inside her bile ducts.'

Lynn looked at her daughter for confirmation.

Caitlin nodded.

'Can you understand what it is like for an active teenager to spend a year in a hospital ward?'

Marlene Hartmann smiled sympathetically at Caitlin. 'I can imagine.'

Lynn shook her head. 'No, I don't think you can imagine what it is like in an English hospital, I really don't think so. She was at the Royal South London, one of our top hospitals. At one point, because of overcrowding, they put her, a teenage girl, in a mixed ward. No television. Surrounded by deranged elderly people. She had to put up with confused women and men climbing into bed with her, day and night. She was in a terrible state. I used to go up and sit with her until they threw me out. I'd then sleep in the waiting room or in the corridor.' She looked at Caitlin for corroboration. 'Didn't I, darling?'

'It wasn't that great in that ward,' Caitlin confirmed, with a wistful smile.

'When she came out, we tried everything. We went to healers, priests, tried colloidal silver, a blood transfusion, acupuncture, the lot. Nothing worked. My poor angel was like a little old person, shuffling along, falling over – weren't you, darling? If it wasn't for our GP, I don't know what would have happened. He's been a saint. Dr Ross Hunter. He found a new specialist who put Caitlin on a different regime of drugs, and he got Caitlin's life back – for a while. She returned to school, was able to swim, play netball, and she took up music again, which had always been a big love of hers. She started playing the saxophone.'

Lynn drank some more of her coffee, then noticed, to her irritation, that Caitlin's concentration had gone and she was texting on her phone.

'Then about six months ago, everything went pear-shaped. She started finding her breathing difficult on the saxophone, didn't you, darling?'

Caitlin raised her head, nodded, and returned to her texting.

'Now the specialist has told us that she needs to have a transplant – as a matter of urgency. They found a matching donor and I took her up to the Royal for the operation a couple of days ago. But at the last minute they said there were problems with the donor liver – although they never explained exactly what those problems were – not to my satisfaction. Then we were told – or at least, it was hinted to us very strongly – that she was not being treated as a priority. Which meant that she could be in that group of 20 per cent of those waiting for a liver transplant who . . .'

She hesitated, looking at Caitlin. But Caitlin completed the sentence for her.

'Who die before they get one, is what my mother is saying.'

Marlene Hartmann took Caitlin's hand, and looked deeply into her eyes. 'Caitlin, *mein Liebling*, please trust me. In today's world, no person needs to die because they cannot get the organ they need. Look at me, OK?' She tapped her chest and pouted her lips. 'You see me?'

Caitlin nodded.

'I had a daughter, Antje, who was thirteen, two years

younger than you, and needed a liver transplant in order to live. It was not possible to find one. Antje died. On the day that I buried her I made a promise, that no one would ever die again, waiting for a liver transplant. Nor for a heart-lung transplant. Nor a kidney transplant either. That was when I set up my agency.'

Caitlin pushed her lips out, the way she always did when she agreed with something, and nodded approval.

'Could you guarantee finding a liver for Caitlin?' Lynn asked.

'*Natürlich!* That is my business. I guarantee always to find a matching organ and to effect the transplant within one week. In ten years I have not had one failure. If you would like reassurance from my past clients, there are some who would be willing to contact you and tell you their experiences.'

'One week – even though she's an AB negative blood group?'

'The blood group is not important, Mrs Beckett. Three thousand five hundred people die on the roads, around the world, every day. There will always be a matching donor somewhere.'

Lynn suddenly felt overwhelmed with relief. This woman seemed credible. Her years of experience in the world of debt collecting had taught her a lot about human nature. In particular, telling the genuine people from the bullshitters.

'So what would be involved in finding a matching liver for my daughter?'

'I have a worldwide network, Mrs Beckett.' She paused to sip some of her tea. 'It will not be a problem to find an accident victim, somewhere on this planet, who is a type match.'

Then Lynn asked the question she was dreading. 'How much do you charge?'

'The complete package, which includes all surgical fees for a senior transplant surgeon and a second surgeon, two anaesthetists, nursing staff, six months' unlimited post-operative care, and all drugs, is –' she shrugged, as if aware of the impact this was going to have – 'three hundred thousand euros.'

Lynn gasped. '*Three hundred thousand?*'

Marlene Hartmann nodded.

'That's –' Lynn did some quick mental arithmetic – 'that's about two hundred and fifty thousand pounds!'

Caitlin gave her mother a *forget-it* look.

Marlene Hartmann nodded. 'Yes, that is about right.'

Lynn raised her hands in despair. 'That – that's a huge sum. Impossible – I mean, I just don't have that kind of money.'

The German woman sipped her tea and said nothing.

Lynn's eyes met her daughter's, and she saw all the earlier hope in them had gone.

'I – I had no idea. Is there any – any – payment plan that you offer?'

The broker opened her attaché case and pulled out a brown envelope, which she handed to Lynn.

'This is my standard contract. I require half upfront and the balance immediately before the transplant takes place. It is not a big sum, Mrs Beckett. I never went to see anyone who could not raise this amount.'

Lynn shook her head in dismay. 'So much. Why is it so much?'

'I can go through the costs with you. You have to understand that a liver starts to deteriorate if it is more than half an hour out of a body. So the person this comes from will have to be flown here in an air ambulance on life support. As you know, it is illegal in this country to do this. All the medical team take a great risk, and of course we have to use top-quality people. There is one private clinic here in Sussex, but they are extremely expensive. I person- ally make very little out of this, after covering my costs. You could save some money by flying with your daughter to a country where legal issues are not such a problem. There is a clinic in Mumbai, in India, and also one in Bogotá, in Colombia. That would be perhaps fifty thousand euros less.'

'But would we have to stay there for a long time?'

'For some weeks, yes. Perhaps longer in case of compli- cations, like an infection. Or rejection, of course. You must also think financially, beyond our six-month period, of the cost of anti-rejection drugs, which your daughter will have to take for life.'

Lynn shook her head, feeling in total despair.

'I – I don't want us to be somewhere we don't know. And I have to work. But it's impossible, anyway. I don't have that kind of money.'

'What you have to think of, Mrs Beckett – may I call you Lynn?'

She nodded, blinking away tears.

'What you have to think of are the alternatives. *What are Caitlin's chances otherwise?* That is what you must be thinking, no?'

Lynn sank her head into her hands and felt tears rolling down her cheeks. She was trying to think clearly. A quarter of a million pounds. Impossible! She thought for an instant about some of her clients at work. She offered them pay- ment plans spread over years. But an amount this large?

'Perhaps you could raise a mortgage on this house?' Marlene Hartmann said helpfully.

'I'm mortgaged up to the hilt already,' Lynn replied.

'Sometimes my clients get help from family and friends.'

Lynn thought about her mother. She lived in a rented council flat. She had some savings, but how much? She thought about her ex-husband. Malcolm earned good money on the dredger, but not this kind of money – and he had a new family to take care of. Her friends? The only one who had money was Sue Shackleton. Sue was divorced, from a wealthy guy, and had a nice house in one of Brighton's smartest districts, but she had four children in private school and Lynn had no idea what her finances were like.

'There is a bank in Germany that I work with,' Marlene said. 'They have arranged finance in the past for some of my clients. Five-year-term loans. I can put you in touch.'

Lynn stared at her bleakly. 'I work in the world of finance. At the tragic end of it, the debt-collecting end. I know that no one is going to lend me that kind of money. I'm sorry, I'm desperately sorry, but you've had a wasted journey. I feel so stupid. I should have asked you on the phone yesterday and that would have been the end of it.'

Marlene Hartmann sipped some more tea, then put her cup down.

'Mrs Beckett, let me tell you something. It is ten years now that I am doing this work. Not once, in all this time, have I made a wasted journey. This may seem a lot of money to you at this moment, when you have not had time to think clearly. I will be here in England for a couple of days. I want to help you. I want to do business with you.' She handed Lynn a business card. 'You can reach me on this number 24/7.'

Lynn stared at it, through her blur of tears. The printing was tiny. And her hopes of raising the money were even smaller.

66

Rares clutched the electronic game in his hands, staring out of the rear window of the Mercedes at the passing English countryside. It was a windy day, with fat, puffball clouds shunting across the blue sky. In the distance he saw a range of tall, green hills that reminded him a little of the countryside where he had lived for his first few years as a child, in Romania.

They drove across a roundabout, past a signpost to a place called Steyning, and he mouthed this name to himself. The car accelerated hard and he felt the seat back pressing against him. He was excited. Soon he would see Ilinca again. He was thinking about her smile. The soft feel of her skin. The trust in her nut-brown eyes. Her confident, independent spirit. She was the one who had found this German woman, who had arranged for their new lives. He loved that about Ilinca. The way she could make things happen. The way she seemed to be able to take care of herself. And he loved the way she told him he was the only person in her life who had ever looked after her.

He wished they could have travelled together, but the German woman had been adamant. Ilinca first, then him. There were reasons why they could not travel together, good reasons, the German woman had assured them. They had trusted her.

And now they were here!

The two men in front were silent, but that was fine.

They were his saviours. It was good to be quiet, to have time to think, to look forward.

The road narrowed. Tall, green hedgerows on either side. Music played on the car radio. A woman singer he recognized. Feist.

He was free!

In a short while they would be together again. They would earn the good money they had been promised. Live in a nice apartment, perhaps even with a view of the sea. With every passing tree, hedge, road sign, his heart beat faster.

And the car was slowing now. It made a left turn through a grand, pillared gateway, past a sign which read WISTON GRANGE SPA RESORT. Rares stared at the name, wondering how it was pronounced and what it meant.

They were winding up a narrow tarmac driveway, past several warning signs, which he could not read:

PRIVATE PROPERTY

NO PARKING

NO PICNICKING

STRICTLY NO CAMPING

The hills lay ahead of them. One of them had a clump of trees on the summit. They wound past a large lake on the left, then entered a long, straight avenue of overhanging trees, the verges covered in fallen leaves. The car slowed, went over a sharp bump, then accelerated. Rares could see manicured grass to the left of them, with a flag on a pole in the centre. Two women were standing on the grass, one of them holding a metal stick, about to tap a small white ball. He wondered what they were doing.

The car slowed again, went over another sharp bump,

then accelerated again. Finally, at the end of the drive they stopped outside an enormous, grey-stone house, with a circular tarmac driveway in front. Rares had no concept of architecture, but it looked old, and very grand.

All kinds of smart cars were parked here. He wondered if it was a very expensive hotel. Was this where Ilinca was working? Yes, he decided, that must explain it, and he would be working here too.

It seemed isolated, but that would not matter so long as he was with Ilinca, and they had a place to sleep and be warm and food to eat, and no police threatening them.

The Mercedes turned sharply right, passing under an archway, then pulled up at the rear of the house, which looked less smart, beside a small white van.

'Is Ilinca here?' Rares asked.

Cosmescu turned his head. 'She's here, waiting for you. You just have to have a quick medical and then you will meet her again.'

'Thank you. You are so kind to me.'

Uncle Vlad Cosmescu turned back in silence. Grigore looked over his shoulder and smiled, revealing several gold teeth.

Rares pressed down on the door handle, but nothing happened. He tried again, feeling a sudden stir of panic. Uncle Vlad climbed out and opened the rear door. Rares stepped out and was then steered by Uncle Vlad up to a white door.

It was opened, as they reached it, by a big slab of a woman in a white medical tunic and white trousers. She had a square, unsmiling face with a flat nose and her black hair was cut short, like a man's, and gelled back. Her name tag read *Draguta*. She looked at him with stern, cold eyes, then her tiny, rosebud lips formed the thinnest of smiles. In his native Romanian tongue she said, 'Welcome, Rares. You had a good journey?'

He nodded.

Flanked by the two men, he had no option but to step forward, into a clinical-feeling, white-tiled corridor. It smelled of disinfectant. And he felt a sudden, deep unease.

'Ilinca?' he said. 'Where is she?'

The puzzled look in the woman's small, dark, hooded eyes instantly deepened his unease.

'She is here!' Uncle Vlad said.

'I want to see her now!'

Rares had lived by his wits on the streets of Bucharest for years. He had learned to read expressions in faces. And he did not like the exchange of glances between this woman and the two men. He turned, ducked under Cosmescu's arms and ran.

Grigore grabbed the collar of his denim jacket. Rares wriggled free of it, then was felled, unconscious, by a single chop on the back of his neck from Cosmescu.

The woman hoisted his limp body over her shoulders and, followed by the two men, carried him on down the corridor a short distance, then through double doors into the small, pre-op room. She laid him out on a steel trolley.

A young Romanian anaesthetist, Bogdan Barbu, who had graduated five years ago from medical school in Bucharest, on a salary of 3,000 euros a year, was waiting to receive him.

Bogdan had thick black hair, brushed forward into a fringe, and designer stubble. With his tanned, lean features, he could have passed for a tennis pro, or an actor. He already had the syringe, filled with a bolus of Benzodiazepine, prepared. Without needing instructions, he injected the pre-med into the upper arm of the unconscious Rares.

It would be enough to keep him out for several more minutes.

Between them, they used the time to remove all of the young Romanian's clothes and insert an intravenous cannula in his wrist. They then connected it to a drip-line of Propofol, fed by a pump.

This would ensure that Rares did not regain consciousness – but without causing any harm to his precious internal organs.

In the adjoining room, the main operating theatre of the clinic, an anaesthetized twelve-year-old boy, with a liver so diseased he had only weeks to live, was already being opened up by the junior surgeon, a thirty-eight-year-old Romanian liver transplant specialist, Razvan Ionescu. In his home country, Razvan could take home just under 4,000 euros a year – augmented a little with bribes. Working here, in this clinic, he was taking home more than 200,000. In a few minutes, dressed in green surgical scrubs, with magnifying glasses over his eyes, he would be ready to start removing the boy's failed liver.

Razvan was assisted by two Romanian nurses, who placed the clamps, and every step was scrutinized, in microscopic detail, by one of the most eminent liver transplant surgeons in the UK.

The first rule of medicine which this surgeon had learned many years ago as a young student was, *Do no harm*.

In his view at this moment, he was doing no harm.

The Romanian street kid had no life ahead of him. Whether he died today or in five years' time from drug abuse was of little consequence. But the English teenager who would receive his liver was altogether different. He was a talented musician, he had a promising future ahead of him. Of course, it was not up to doctors to play God, to decide who lived and who died. Nor was it up to them to value one human life over another. But the stark reality was that one of these two young men was doomed.

And he would never admit to anyone that the £50,000, tax-free, deposited into his Swiss bank account for each transplant he performed swayed his judgement in the slightest.

67

Shortly after half past twelve – half past one in Munich, Grace calculated – Kriminalhauptkommissar Marcel Kullen returned his call.

It was good to speak to his old friend and they spent a couple of minutes catching up on the German detective's family and career news, from when they had last seen each other, all too briefly, in Munich.

'So, no more information you have of Sandy?' Kullen said.

'Nothing,' Grace replied.

'Her photographs are still in every police station here. But so far, nothing. We are keeping trying.'

'Actually, I'm starting to think it is time to wind down,' Grace said. 'I'm beginning the legal process to have her declared dead.'

'*Ja*, but I am thinking – your friend who has seen her in the Englischer Garten. We should look longer, I think, no?'

'I'm getting married, Marcel. I need to move on, to have closure.'

'Married? You have a new woman in your life?'

'Yes!'

'OK, good, so – I am happy for you! You want now that us stop to look for Sandy?'

'Yes. Thank you for all you've done. But that's not why I called you. I need help in a different direction.'

'*Ja*, OK.'

'I need some information on an organization in Munich called Transplantation-Zentrale GmbH. I understand it is known to your police force.'

'How are you spelling this?'

It took Grace several minutes, working patiently with the German detective's broken English, to get the name across correctly.

'Sure, I will check,' Kullen said. 'I call us back, yes?'

'Please, it's urgent.'

*

Kullen called him back thirty minutes later. 'This is interesting, Roy. I am talking with my colleagues. Transplantation-Zentrale GmbH is under observation by the LKA for some months now. There is a woman who is the boss, her name is Marlene Hartmann. They have links with the Colombian mafia, with factions of the Russian mafia, with organized crime too in Romania, with the Philippines, with China, with India.'

'What does the LKA know about them?'

'Their business is the trafficking, internationally, of humans, and in particular in human organs. So it would seem.'

'What action are you taking against them?'

'At this stage, we are just information gathering, observing. They are on the LKA radar, you would say. We are looking to connect them with specific offences in Germany. Do you have information about them you can give to me for my colleagues?'

'Not at the moment – but I'd like to interview Marlene Hartmann. Perhaps I could come over and do that?'

The German sounded hesitant. 'OK.'

'Is there a problem with that?'

'Only – at this moment, according to the surveillance file, she is not in München – she is travelling.'

'Do you know where?'

'Two days ago she flew to Bucharest. We don't have more information.'

'But you will know when she is back in Germany?'

'Yes. And we do know that she goes regularly to England.'

'How regularly?' Grace asked, his suspicions suddenly rising.

'She flew into München from London last week. And also the week before.'

'Presumably she was not on a winter-break holiday.'

'Perhaps. Is possible,' the German said.

'No one in their right mind comes to England at this time of year, Marcel,' Grace said.

'Not to see the Christmas lights?'

Grace laughed. 'She doesn't sound the type.'

He was thinking hard. The woman was in England last week, and the week before. At some point in the past week to ten days three teenagers had been killed and their organs harvested.

'Is there any possibility of obtaining this woman's phone records, Marcel?' he asked.

'Her fixed lines or handy?'

Handy, Grace knew, was the German word for a mobile phone.

'Both?'

'I will see what I can do. Do you want all calls, or just those to the UK?'

'Those to the UK would be a very good starting point. Do you have any plans to arrest her any time soon?'

'Not just now. They want to keep watching her. There

are other German human trafficking connections that she is linked to.'

'Shame. It would have been good to have her computers looked at.'

'I think on this we can help you.' Grace could almost feel the Kriminalhauptkommissar smiling down the phone.

'You can?'

'We have a warrant issued by an *Ermittlungsrichter* for phone and computer records.'

'By who?'

'It is an investigating judge. The warrant is – how is it you say – *in camera*?'

'Yes – without the other party knowing.'

'Exactly. And you know now in the LKA we have good technology for computer surveillance. I understand we have duplicates of all computer activity, including laptop away from the office, of Frau Hartmann and her colleagues. We have implanted a servlet.'

Grace knew all about servlets from his colleagues, Ray Packham and Phil Taylor in the High-Tech Crime Unit. You could install one simply by sending a suspect an email, provided he or she opened it. Then all activity on the suspect's computer would be automatically copied back to you.

'Brilliant!' he said. 'Would you let me see them?'

'I would not be permitted to send them to you, despite the EU cooperation treaty – it will be a long process of bureaucracy.'

'Any way of short-circuiting that?'

'For my friend Roy Grace?'

'Yes, for him!'

'If you are coming over – perhaps I could leave copies of them by accident – on a restaurant table? But they are for information only, you understand? You must not reveal their source, and you will not be able to use the information in evidence. Is that OK?'

'That is more than OK, Marcel!'

Grace thanked him and hung up with a real lift of excitement.

68

Subcomisar Radu Constantinescu had a swanky office in Police Station No. 15 in Bucharest – at least, swanky by Romanian police standards. The four-storey building had been put up in 1920, according to an engraved plaque on the wall, and did not appear to have been dusted or redecorated since. The staircases were bare stone and the floors covered in cracked linoleum. The pastel-green walls were chipped and scored, with plaster crumbling from some of the cracks. It always reminded Ian Tilling of his old school in Maidenhead.

Constantinescu's room was large, dark and dingy, and shrouded in a permanent blue-grey fug of cigarette smoke. It was starkly furnished, with a wooden desk that was bland and old, but almost as big as his ego, and a conference table of indeterminate vintage, surrounded by mismatched chairs. Proudly displayed, high up, beneath the nicotine-stained ceiling, were the policeman's hunting trophies – the mounted heads of bears, wolves, lynxes, deer, chamois and foxes. Framed certificates and photographs of Constantinescu rubbing shoulders with various dignitaries filled a little of the wall space, along with a couple of photographs of him in hunting kit, kneeling by a dead boar in one and holding up the horned head of a stag in the other.

The Subcomisar sat behind his desk, dressed in black trousers, a white shirt with braided epaulettes, and a slack green tie. He busied himself for a moment, lighting a fresh cigarette from the stub of the previous one, which he then crushed out, ineffectually, in a huge overflowing crystal ashtray. Several screwed-up balls of paper, which had clearly missed the waste bin, littered the floor around the desk.

Constantinescu was forty-five years old, short and wiry, with a gaunt face, jet-black hair and piercing dark eyes with dark, heavy rings beneath them. Ian Tilling had got to know him when the officer had started to visit Casa Ioana on a regular basis.

'So my friend, Mr Ian Tilling, Member of the British Empire for services to the homeless of Romania!' Constantinescu said, through a fresh cloud of noxiously sweet blue smoke. 'Yes? You have met your queen, no?'

'Yes, when I got my gong.'

'Gong?'

'Slang,' Tilling said. 'It's English slang for a medal.'

Constantinescu's eyes widened. '*Gong*!' he said. 'Gong! Very good. Maybe we should drink! To celebrate?'

'It was a few months ago.'

The police officer reached under his desk and produced a bottle of Famous Grouse whisky and two shot glasses. He filled them both with a clear liquid and handed one to Tilling.

'*Spaga*!' he said, indicating shamelessly that he had been given the whisky as a bribe. 'Good whisky, yes? Special?'

Tilling did not want to disillusion him that it was a basic blended whisky. 'Special!' he agreed.

'To your – *gong*!'

Reluctantly, but understanding the protocol, Ian Tilling drained his glass, the alcohol hitting him almost instantly on his empty stomach, sending his head reeling.

The police officer set his empty glass down. 'So, how can I help my *important* friend? All the more important now that Romania and England are partners in the EU together!'

Ian Tilling placed the three sets of fingerprints, the three e-fit photographs and the close-up of a primitive tattoo of the name *Rares* on the man's desk.

Looking at them, Constantinescu suddenly asked, 'And how, by the way, are all your pretty girls working for you?'

'Yep, they are fine.'

'And the beautiful Andreea, she is still working with you?'

'Yes, but she's getting married in a month's time.'

His face fell. 'Ah.' He raised his head, looking disappointed.

The Subcomisar occasionally popped into Casa Ioana on some pretext or another. But Tilling always knew the real reason was to chat up the girls – the man was an inveterate womanizer, and every time he came, he tried, unsuccessfully, to hassle one or other of them for a date. But being good diplomats, they were always polite to him, always leaving a faint window of hope open, just to keep him onside for the hostel.

Trying to steer the meeting on to business, Ian Tilling pointed at the E-Fit and fingerprint sets, then explained their provenance. The Romanian was distracted twice by internal calls, and once by what was a clearly personal call from his current squeeze, on his mobile.

'Rares,' he said, when Tilling had finished. 'Romanian, sure. Interpol have the fingerprints?'

'Would you do me a favour and run them yourself? It will be quicker.'

'OK.'

'And could you get copies of these photos of the three kids circulated to your other police stations in Bucharest?'

Constantinescu lit his third cigarette since the meeting had started and then had a bout of coughing. When he finished, he poured himself another slug of whisky and offered the bottle to Tilling, who declined.

.   'Sure, no problem.'

He burst again into a series of deep, racking coughs, then, when he had finished, he slipped the photographs and fingerprints into a large brown envelope and, to Tilling's dismay, slid them into a drawer in his desk.

From long experience dealing with the man, Tilling knew he had a habit of forgetting things very quickly. He sometimes suspected that once something entered that drawer it never came out again. But at least Constantinescu was a man who actually did care about the plight of the city's street kids – even if his motivation was to try and bed the women who looked after them.

And hey, better safe in that drawer than lying, screwed up, amid those other balls of paper littering the floor in front of his desk.

In seventeen years of battling the authorities in this country, Ian Tilling had learned to be grateful for small mercies.

69

Mal Beckett never found it easy talking to his ex-wife, and sitting opposite her now, in the quiet café on Church Road, despite the new shared bond of their daughter's plight, he felt as awkward as ever.

The problem went back to the early days of their separation, when he had left her for his then mistress – and now wife – Jane. Out of guilt, and concerned for her mental stability, he had made a point of seeing Lynn every few months for lunch. And she would always begin with the same question, *Are you happy?*

It left him in a *damned-if-you-do* and *damned-if-you-don't* situation. If he told her that yes, he was happy, he sensed that would make her even more miserable. So during those first meetings he would reply that no, he was not happy. Whereupon Lynn would immediately relay this to her friends. With Brighton being both a big city and a tiny village at the same time, word would rapidly get back to Jane that he was not happy being with her.

So he had learned to parry the question by replying with a very neutral, *I'm OK.* But now, as he spooned the creamy froth from his cappuccino into his mouth and stared across the plastic table, he realized they had both outgrown this game. He felt genuinely sorry for Lynn, still being alone, and was shocked by how much weight she had lost since they had last seen each other, a couple of months ago.

Lynn never found it easy seeing Mal either. Looking across at him, dressed in a faded blue sweatshirt, with a chunky anorak slung over his seat back, she saw he was ageing well; if anything, he was getting even better-looking, more rugged and manly with every passing year. If he asked her to come back to him, she would have done so in a blink. That was not going to happen, but God, how she needed him!

'Thanks for making the time, Mal,' she said.

He glanced at his watch. 'Of course. I need to be away at one sharp to catch the afternoon tide.'

She smiled wistfully, and without any malice said, 'Gosh, how many times did I hear you say that over the years. *Off to catch the tide.*'

Their eyes met, in a moment of genuine tenderness between them.

'Maybe I should have that on my gravestone,' he said.

'Wouldn't that be a bit difficult? I thought you were going to be buried at sea?'

He laughed. 'Yeah, that was . . .'

Then he suddenly halted in mid-sentence. She would not be impressed to know that Jane had talked him out of that. Lynn had tried to do the same herself, unsuccessfully, for all the years of their married life.

It was quiet in the café. Just past midday, the lunchtime rush had not yet started. They waited for a moment as the waitress brought them over their food, a doorstep of a hot corned beef sandwich for Mal and a small tuna salad for Lynn.

'Two hundred and fifty-two thousand pounds?' he said.

Lynn nodded.

'You know we pulled up a dead body – caught in the drag head – the one that is in all the papers right now?'

'I read about it,' she said. 'That must have been a shock for you.'

'You've heard the rumours?'

'I've been so preoccupied, I've barely glanced at the papers,' she lied.

'It was a teenage boy. They don't know where he's from, but there's speculation that he was killed for his organs. Some kind of trafficking ring.'

Lynn shrugged. 'Horrible. But that doesn't have anything to do with our situation with Caitlin, does it?'

His worried expression unsettled her further. 'There were two other bodies found subsequently. All missing their internal organs.'

He spooned some more froth into his mouth, leaving a ring of white foam, dusted with cocoa powder, around his top lip. A few years ago, she would have leaned forward with a napkin and wiped it.

'What are you saying, Mal?'

'You want to buy a liver for Caitlin. Do you know where it's going to come from?'

'Yes, someone killed in an accident abroad somewhere. Most likely a car or motorcycle accident, Frau Hartmann said.'

He looked down at his sandwich, lifted the top piece of bread and squeezed mustard across the meat and gherkin from a plastic bottle. 'You can be sure that liver's kosher?'

'You know what, Mal,' she said, with rising irritation at his attitude, 'so long as it is a match and healthy, I don't actually care where it comes from. I care about saving my daughter's life. Sorry,' she corrected herself, looking at him pointedly, '*our* daughter's life.'

He put the mustard dispenser down and laid the bread back across the pink beef. Then he picked the sandwich up, opened his jaws, sizing up where to take the first bite, then put it back down on the plate, as if he had suddenly lost his appetite.

'Shit,' he said, shaking his head.

'I know you have other priorities, Mal.'

He shook his head again. 'Two hundred and fifty-two thousand pounds?'

'Yes. Well, it's down to two hundred and twenty-seven thousand since an hour ago. My mother has got twenty-five thousand life savings in a building society account she's letting me have.'

'That's decent. But two hundred and twenty-seven thousand. That's an impossible sum!'

'I'm a debt collector. I hear that line twenty times a day. That's what almost every single one of my clients tells me, *Impossible. Impossible*. You know what? No sum is impossible, it's just a question of attitude. There's always a way. I haven't come here to listen to you telling me you are going to let Caitlin die because we can't find a lousy two hundred and fifty-two thousand pounds. I want you to help me find it.'

'Even if we did find it, what guarantees do we have – you know – that this woman will deliver? That it will work? That we aren't faced with this same situation in six months' time?'

'None,' she said baldly.

He stared at her in silence.

'There's only one guarantee I can give you, Mal. That if I – we – don't find this money, Caitlin will be dead by Christmas – or soon after.'

His big shoulders went limp suddenly. 'I have some savings,' he said. 'I've got just over fifty thousand – I increased my mortgage a couple of years ago, to free up some cash to pay for an extension. But we had planning problems.' He was about to add that Jane would go nuts if he gave it to Lynn, but he kept quiet about that. 'I can let you have that if it helps.'

Lynn leapt across the table, almost knocking their drinks over, and kissed him clumsily on the cheek.

Only one hundred and seventy-five thousand to go! she thought.

70

The fine architectural heritage of the city of Brighton and Hove had long been one of its major attractions, to residents and visitors alike. Although it had been blighted in parts by functional, drab modern buildings, anyone turning a corner in its sprawling downtown and mid-town areas would find themselves in a street, or a twitten, of Georgian, Victorian or Edwardian terraced houses or villas, some in fine condition, others less so.

Sillwood Road was a typical such gem that had seen better times. Visitors with an eye for architecture, heading south to the seafront from the bland shopping precinct of Western Road, might choose Sillwood Road, then stop and stare, but it wasn't so much from a sense of visual joy, as shock that such a perfect row of canopied Victorian terraced houses could be in such shabby company.

Shrouded by a forest of estate agency letting signs, it remained steadfastly a downmarket area, not helped by the fact that in recent years it had become part of the city's discreet red-light district.

At five o'clock in the afternoon, and already pitch dark outside, Bella Moy said to Nick Nicholl, who was driving, 'Pull over anywhere you can.'

The DC pulled the unmarked grey Ford Focus estate into a parking bay beneath a Resident's Parking sign and switched off the engine.

'Ever been to a brothel before?' she asked.

House of Babes was going to be their first call.

Blushing, he replied, 'No, I haven't actually.'

'They have a unique smell,' she said.

'What kind of smell?'

'You'll see what I mean. You could blindfold me and I'd know I was in a brothel.'

They climbed out of the car and walked a short distance down the street in the blustery wind, the DC carrying his notebook. Then he followed Bella to the front door of one of the houses and stood, beneath the silent eye of a surveillance camera, patiently waiting as she rang the bell. Bella was dressed in a brown trouser suit that looked one size too big for her and clumsy black shoes.

'Hello?' A chirpy woman's voice, with a Yorkshire accent, came through the intercom.

'Detective Sergeant Moy and DC Nicholl from Sussex CID.'

There was a sharp rasp from the entryphone buzzer, then a loud click. Bella pushed the door open and Nick followed her in, nostrils twitching, but all that greeted him was a reek of cigarette smoke and takeaway food.

The dingy hallway was lit with a low-wattage red bulb. There was badly worn pink wall-to-wall carpeting and the walls were papered in a magenta flock. On a plasma screen on the wall, a black woman was giving oral sex to a tattooed, muscular white man who had a penis bigger than Nick Nicholl could have ever thought possible.

Then a woman appeared. She was short, in her mid-fifties, dressed in shell-suit trousers and wearing a blouse that revealed an acreage of cleavage. Her face, beneath a fringe of long brown hair, must have been pretty when she was younger and ten stone slimmer, Nick Nicholl thought.

'DS Moy!' she said in a little-girl voice. 'Nice to see you. Always good to see you!'

'Good evening, Joey. This is my colleague, DC Nick Nicholl,' Bella replied curtly, a little harshly, Nick thought.

'Nice to meet you, DC Nicholl,' she said deferentially. 'Nice name, Nick. I got a son called Nick, you know!'

'Ah,' he said. 'Right.'

She led them through into a reception area that surprised Nick. He had been expecting to see, from images in books and films, a gilded, mirrored, velour-draped parlour. Instead he was in a tip of a room, with two battered sofas, a cluttered desk on which sat a steaming, opened pot-noodle carton with a plastic fork sticking out of it, an array of grimy-looking mugs and several unemptied ashtrays, overflowing with butts. An old phone sat on the desk, alongside an elderly-looking fax machine. On the wall above he saw a price list.

'Can I offer either of you a drink? Coffee, tea, Coca-Cola?' She sat back down, glanced at her pot-noodle meal, but left it steaming, half eaten.

'No, we're fine,' Bella said stiffly, to Nicholl's relief as he stared again at the grimy mugs.

There was an unwritten understanding between the city's brothels and the police that, provided those running them did not use under-age or trafficked girls, they were left alone – subject to them allowing random, unannounced inspections from police officers. Most brothel owners and managers, including this woman, respected this, but Bella had learned never to let anyone confuse tolerance with friendship.

She showed the woman, Joey, the three e-fit photographs.

'Have you seen any of these people before?'

She studied the picture of the dead girl closely, then each of the two boys and shook her head.

'No, never.'

'How many girls do you have here this evening?' Bella asked.

'Five at the moment.'

'Any new ones?'

'Yes, two new arrivals from Europe. A girl called Anca and one called Nusha.'

'Where are they from?'

'Romania,' she said, adding, 'Bucharest,' as if trying to show her willingness to be helpful.

'Are they – um – free?' said Bella, delicately.

'I've seen their ID,' the madame said anxiously. 'Anca's nineteen, Nusha's twenty.'

There was a sharp, rasping ring. The woman's eyes went up to a wall-mounted television monitor. On the poor-quality colour screen they could see a balding, bug-eyed man in a suit and tie.

She winked at the two police officers and said, a tad awkwardly, 'One of my regulars. Would you like to see them separately or together?'

'Separately,' Bella said.

She ushered them hastily down the hall and through a doorway into a small room.

'I'll go and fetch them.'

She closed the door. And now Nick Nicholl noticed the smell Bella meant. There was a sharp, hygienic tang of disinfectant, mixed with a potent, cheap-smelling, musky scent. He stared in shock at the small, pink-painted room they were in. There was a double bed with a leopard-skin-patterned bedspread and a folded white towel, a television monitor on which a pornographic film was playing, a bed-side table with some toiletries and a roll of lavatory paper on it, a wide mirror on the wall and a pile of erotic DVDs.

'This is so tacky,' he said.

Bella shrugged. 'Normal. See what I mean about the smell?'

He nodded, breathing it in, slowly, again.

A few moments later the door opened again and Joey showed in a pretty girl, with long dark hair, dressed in a flimsy, pink see-through nightdress over dark underwear. She looked sullen and nervous.

'This is Anca – I'll be back!' the madame mouthed, closing the door.

'Hello, Anca,' Bella said. 'Take a seat.' She indicated the bed.

The girl sat down, her eyes darting between them. She was holding a pack of cigarettes and a lighter, as if they were stage props.

'We are police officers, Anca,' Bella said. 'Do you speak English?'

She shook her head. 'Little.'

'OK, we are not here to cause you trouble, do you understand?'

Anca stared blankly.

'We just want to make sure you are all right. Are you happy to be here?'

Anca had been well briefed. She had been told by Cosmescu that the police might ask questions. And she had been warned of the consequences of saying anything negative.

'Yes, is good here,' she replied in a guttural accent.

'Are you sure about that? Do you want to be here?'

'Want, yes.'

Bella shot a glance at her colleague, who appeared to not know where to put himself.

'You just came over from Romania? Is that right?'

'Romania. Me.'

Bella showed her the three e-fits, then watched her face closely.

'Do you recognize any of these?'

The Romanian girl looked at them, with no glimmer of a reaction, then shook her head. 'No.'

She appeared, to Bella, to be telling the truth.

'OK, what I want to know is who brought you here.'

Anca shook her head and delivered a line that Cosmescu had drummed into her. 'No understand.'

Patiently, and very slowly, gesticulating with sign language, Bella asked her, 'Who brought you here?'

The girl shook her head blankly.

Nick suddenly flipped through the pages of his notebook for some moments, then stopped. Reading out aloud, slowly, in Romanian, he asked, 'You have a contact here in England?'

Anca looked startled to hear her native language, however badly pronounced it was.

Bella looked equally astonished – and had no idea what he had said.

The girl shook her head.

Nick turned a page and looked at his notes. Then, harshly, he read out in Romanian, 'If you are lying we will know. And we will send you back to Romania. Tell me the truth now!'

Startled, and looking scared, the girl said, 'Vlad. His name.'

'Vlad, what?'

'Coz, er Cozma, Cozemec?'

'Cosmescu?' Bella suggested.

The girl was silent for some moments, looking at her with scared eyes. Then she nodded.

*

Twenty minutes later, after having interviewed both girls, they got back into the car.

Bella said, 'Do you mind telling me what that was all about?'

'I checked with the UKHTC.'

'The what?'

'The United Kingdom Human Trafficking Centre. I wanted to establish where the girls were most likely to have come from. Romania was high on the list. And Romania was our brief.'

'So you learned fluent Romanian in an afternoon?'

'No, just the phrases I thought I might need.'

Bella grinned. 'I'm impressed.'

'Not as impressed as my wife will be – not – when she finds out where I spent my afternoon.'

'Don't all men visit brothels?' she said.

'No,' he said, fervently and indignantly. 'Actually, no.'

'You've really never been to one before?'

'No, Bella,' he said snarkily. 'I really haven't. Sorry to disappoint you.'

'I'm not disappointed. It's good to know there are some decent guys out there. I just don't seem to be able to find one.'

'Maybe that's because my wife found the only one!' he said.

Bella looked at him, at his thin, elongated, grinning face in the glare of the street light. 'Then she's a lucky woman.'

'I'm the lucky one. What about you? You're an attractive lady. You must have tons of opportunities.'

'No, I've had tons of disappointments. And you know what? I'm actually content being on my own. I look after my mum, and when I'm not looking after her, I'm free. I like that feeling.'

'I love my kid,' he said. 'It's an incredible feeling. You can't describe it.'

'I should think you'll be a great father, Nick.'

He smiled again. 'I would like to be.' Then he shrugged. 'Can you imagine what kind of father Anca had? Or the other girl, Nusha?'

'No.'

'For life for them in a crummy Brighton brothel to be better than whatever they left behind, I find that incredible.'

'I find it incredible that you bothered to learn their language, Nick. I'm blown away by that.'

'I didn't learn their language. Just a few phrases. Enough so that we could get through to them.'

She looked down at her notes. 'Vlad Cosmescu.'

'Vlad the Impaler.'

'Vlad who?'

'He was the Transylvanian emperor that Dracula was based on. A charmer who used to impale his enemies on a spike up their rectums.'

'Too much information, Nick,' she said, wincing.

'You're a police officer, Bella. We can never have *too much* information.'

She smiled, then said, 'Vlad Cosmescu.'

'Do you know him?'

'By name. He's a pimp. Was active a few years ago when I was on brothels. He's a kind of gatekeeper for Romanian, Albanian and other eastern European contraband. Drugs, pirated videos, cigarettes, you name it. He's been a Person of Interest for the drugs teams for years, but I heard he always managed to keep out of trouble himself. Interesting that he's still around.' She made a note on her pad, then said breezily, 'Right! One down. There are only about twenty-eight more brothels in Brighton to cover before we're done. How's your stamina?'

With a baby needing feeding every few hours, around the clock, probably a lot better than my libido at this point, he thought.

'My stamina? Terrific!'

71

It was just gone seven in Bucharest and Ian Tilling had promised Cristina that he would be home early tonight. It was their tenth wedding anniversary and for a rare treat they had booked a table at their favourite restaurant, for a feast of traditional Romanian food.

He had developed a liking for the heavy, meat-based diet of his adopted country. All except for two specialities, cold brain and cubes of lard, which Cristina loved, but he still could not stomach, and doubted he ever would.

He looked up at the useless clock hooked to the huge noticeboard on the wall in front of his desk. TIME IS MONEY was printed on the face, but there were no numerals, making it easy to be an hour out either way. Pinned next to it was a splayed-out woman's fan, which had been there for so long he couldn't remember who had put it up, or why. Below it, sandwiched between several government pamphlets for the homeless, was a sheet of paper bearing his favourite quotation, from Mahatma Gandhi: *First they ignore you, then they ridicule you, then they fight you, then you win.*

That summed up his seventeen years in this strange but beautiful city, in this strange but beautiful country. He was winning. Step, by step, by step. Little victories. Kids and sometimes adults saved from the streets, and housed here in Casa Ioana. Before he left, he would do his rounds of the little dormitory rooms, as he did every night. He planned to take with him the photographs of the three teenagers Nor-

417

man Potting had sent him, to see if any of the faces jogged someone's memory. It had been good to hear from that old bugger. Really good to feel involved in a British police inquiry once more. So good, he was determined to deliver what he could.

As he stood up, the door opened and Andreea came in, with a smile on her face.

'Do you have a moment, Mr Ian?' the social worker asked.

'Sure.'

'I went to see Ileana, in Sector Four.'

Ileana was a former social worker at Casa Ioana who now worked in a placement centre in that sector, called Merlin.

'And what did she say?'

'She has agreed to help us, but she's worried about being caught out. Her centre has been told not to talk to any outsider – and that includes even us.'

'Why?'

'The government is upset, apparently, about the bad press abroad on Romanian orphanages. There is a ban on visitors and on all photography. I had to meet her in a café. But she told me that one of the street kids has heard a rumour going around that if you are lucky, you can get a job in England, with an apartment. There is a smart woman you have to go and see.'

'Can we talk to this kid? Do we have her name?'

'Her name is Raluca. She is working as a prostitute at the Gara de Nord. She's fifteen. I don't know if she has a pimp. Ileana is willing to come with us. We could go tonight.'

'Tonight, no, I can't. How about tomorrow?'

'I will ask her.'

Tilling thanked her, then fired off a quick email to Norman Potting, updating him on his progress today. Then he balled his fists and drummed them on his desk.

Yes! he thought. *Oh yes!* He was back in the saddle! He'd loved his days as a police officer and being involved now felt so damn good!

72

Lynn sat at her Harrier Hornets work station, aware it was eight at night, working through her call list, trying to make up for the time she had lost earlier today at home and then seeing Mal.

Her mother had been at the house earlier, then Luke had come over, so Caitlin had company – and, more crucially, someone to keep an eye on her. Even moronic Luke was capable of that.

Few of her colleagues were still at work. Barring a couple of stragglers, the Silver Sharks, Leaping Leopards and Denarii Demons work stations were all deserted. The COLLECTED BONUS POT sign was now reading £1,150. No way she was going to get near it this week, the way things were progressing.

And her heart was not in it. She stared up at the photograph of Caitlin that was pinned to the red partition wall. Thinking.

One hundred and seventy-five thousand pounds would determine whether Caitlin lived or died. It was a huge sum and yet a tiny sum at the same time. That kind of money, and much more, passed through these offices every week.

A dark thought entered her mind. She dispelled it, but it returned, like the determined knock of a double-glazing salesman: *People regularly stole money from their employers.*

Every few days in the paper she would read about an employee in a solicitor's office, or a hedge fund, or a bank, or any other kind of place which big sums passed through, who had been siphoning off money. Often, it had been going on for years. Millions taken, without anyone noticing.

All she needed was a lousy £175,000. Peanuts, by Denarii's standards.

But how could she *borrow* the money from here without anyone knowing? There were all kinds of controls and procedures in place.

Suddenly she saw a light flashing on her phone. Her direct line. She answered it, thinking it might be Caitlin. But, to her dismay, it was her least favourite client of all, the ghastly Reg Okuma.

'Lynn Beckett?' he said, in his lugubrious voice.

'Yes,' she said stiffly.

'You are working late, beautiful one. I am privileged to have connected to you.'

The pleasure's all mine, she nearly said. But instead she answered, 'What can I do for you?'

'Well,' he said, 'here is the situation. I applied yesterday to buy myself a new motor car. I need wheels, you know, for my work, for my new company I am setting up, which will revolutionize the Internet.'

She said nothing.

'Are you hearing me?'

'I'm listening.'

'I would still like to make beautiful sex with you. I would like to make love with you, Lynn.'

'Do you understand that this call is being recorded for training and monitoring purposes?'

'I understand that.'

'Good. If you are calling to tell me you want to make a payment plan, I will listen. Otherwise I'm going to hang up, OK?'

'No, please, listen. I was turned down, rejected, for the

hire purchase yesterday. When I asked why they told me it was because Experian gave me a bad credit rating.'

'Are you surprised?' she retorted. Experian was one of the leading companies in the UK for providing credit ratings. All of the banks and finance houses used these companies to check out customers. 'You don't pay your debts – so what kind of credit rating do you expect?'

'Well, listen, hear me out. I contacted Experian – I have rights under the Data Protection Act – and they have informed me it is your company that is responsible for this bad rating I have.'

'There's a simple solution, Mr Okuma. Enter into a payment plan with us and I can get that amended.'

'Well, yes, of course, but it is not that simple.'

'I think it is. What part of that do you not understand?'

'Do you need to be so hostile to me?'

'I'm very tired, Mr Okuma. If you would like to come back to me with a payment plan, then I will see what I can do with Experian. Until then, thank you and goodnight.'

She hung up.

Moments later, the light was flashing again. She ignored it and left the office to go home. But as she stepped out of the lift on the ground floor, she suddenly had the glimmer of an idea.

73

Roy Grace sat alone in his office, with the rising south-westerly wind shaking the windowpanes and rain falling. It was going to be another stormy night, he thought, with even the street lighting and the glow from the ASDA car-park lights dimmer than usual. It was cold too, as if the damp draught was blowing through the walls and into his bones. His watch told him it was five past eight.

He had excused Glenn Branson from this evening's briefing. The DC's wife had agreed that he could come over and help bathe the kids and put them to bed – no doubt on the advice of her solicitor, he thought cynically.

He read carefully through the notes he had jotted down during the meeting, then glanced through the typed *Lines of Enquiry* notes. A phone line was winking, but it wasn't his direct line so he left it for someone else to pick up – if there was anyone else in the building other than the ever-cheerful Duncan, one of the security guards downstairs on the front desk. It felt like the *Marie Céleste* up here, although he knew several of his team would be working long into the night in MIR One – in particular two typists and Juliet Jones, the HOLMES analyst.

Juliet was still occupied with her scoping exercise of all potentially relevant crimes, solved and unsolved, commit-ted in the UK. It was an arduous, but essential task, com-parable to fishing, Grace sometimes thought. Typing endless key words and phrases, searching for similar victims turning up elsewhere in the UK, or for any instances of organ theft. As of this evening, her trawl, which had been going on since Saturday, had yielded nothing.

During the past nine years, Grace had had many solitary hours to fill with just his own company, and he had been through one phase of educating himself on the history of detection and forensics. One man he particularly admired was a French medic, Dr Edmond Locard, who was born in 1877 and became known as the Sherlock Holmes of France. It was Locard who established the founding principle of forensic science, which was that *every contact leaves a trace*. It became known as Locard's Exchange Principle.

What, Roy Grace wondered, was he missing in the contact that had taken place with these three bodies? Where were the surgical instruments that had come into contact with the bodies? All sterilized now, for sure. Maybe there would be enough microscopic traces to get a match – but first they had to find them. Where? Similarly, it was likely that whoever had removed the organs of the teenagers – unless again it was a lone madman – had been surgically gowned up. Those clothes, their rubber gloves, especially, would carry traces. But they still had no clue where to start looking, and sifting through the waste bins and laundry carts of every hospital and clinic in the south of England was not an option at this stage.

If the fingerprint department successfully pulled prints off the outboard motor with the new technology they were trying out, then perhaps they could get them off the plastic sheeting that had wrapped the bodies?

He made another note, then quickly read through the three typed pages of the *Lines of Enquiry* document, of which every member of his team had a copy. It needed updating, and he had some important additions to make. But he also had a deep longing to see Cleo. He could do what he had to do now just as easily at her place as in his cold, lonely office.

*

The temperature was dropping and the wind was rising to a gale again, as he parked the Ford on a yellow line outside an antiques shop. Hurrying across the street, through hard pellets of rain, he caught a snatched, raucous strain of 'God Rest Ye, Merry Gentlemen' being sung, badly, somewhere nearby. Early carol singers, he wondered, or just a drunken office party?

He still had not got his head around the fact that Christmas was looming. He didn't know what to buy Cleo – other than a ring, of course, but that wasn't a Christmas present – and he wanted to get her something special.

It had been so long since he had bought presents for a woman he loved, he was at a loss what to get. A handbag? Another piece of jewellery, in addition to the ring? He would ask his sister for advice. She was practical and would know. So would DI Mantle.

Quite apart from the issue of presents, he had decisions to make about where to spend Christmas. He had been with his sister every year since Sandy's disappearance, but Cleo had suggested they go to her family in Surrey. For sure, he wanted to be with Cleo over the Christmas holidays, but he had not yet met her parents. He knew his sister would be happy to hear they were engaged – she had been urging him to move on for years – but he needed to work out the logistics. And if Operation Neptune was not resolved by then, it was likely to be a short Christmas for him, in any event.

Lugging his heavy briefcase across the cobbled court-yard, he fumbled in his pocket for the key, then let himself in Cleo's front door. Instantly, his spirits soared as he entered the warm, open-plan living area and saw Cleo's huge, happy smile. There was a tantalizing, garlicky cooking smell, and rousing opera music filled the room – the Overture from Bizet's *Carmen*, he thought, pleased he was able to recognize it. Cleo had tasked herself with broadening his musical tastes and, to his surprise, he was developing a real liking for opera.

Humphrey came bounding towards him, towing several yards of loo paper behind him, then leapt up, yapping loudly.

Grace knelt and stroked his face. 'Hey, fellow!'

Still jumping up and down with excitement, Humphrey licked his chin.

Cleo was curled up on one of the huge sofas, surrounded by paperwork and holding a book – no doubt one of the tomes on philosophy she was studying for her Open University degree.

'Look, Humphrey!' she said, with a puppy-dog squeal in her voice. 'Detective Superintendent Roy Grace is home! Your master! Somebody's pleased to see you, Roy!'

'Only the dog?' he said, in mock disappointment, standing up and walking across to her, with Humphrey tugging at his trouser legs.

'He's been a very good boy today!'

'Well, that's a first!'

'But I'm even more pleased to see you than he is!' she said, putting down the book, which was entitled *Existentialism and Humanism* and had several pages tagged with yellow Post-it notes.

Her hair was clipped up and she was wearing a thigh-length, loose-knit brown top and black leggings. For an instant he just stood and stared down at her in utter joy.

He felt the music soaring into his soul, he savoured the cooking smells again and he was overwhelmed by happiness, by a sense of belonging. A sense that he had finally, after so many nightmare years, arrived in a place – a place in his life – where he felt truly contented.

'I love you,' he said, lowering himself, putting his arms around her neck and kissing her longingly on the lips. He pulled back briefly and said, 'Like, I really love you.'

Then they kissed again, for even longer.

When they finally broke away from each other she said, 'Yeah, I quite like you too.'

'You do?'

She screwed up her face in thought, looked very pensive for some moments, as if performing some massive mental calculation, then nodded. 'Uh huh. Yep!'

'I'm going to buy you a ring, this weekend.'

She looked at him, with her big round eyes, like an excited schoolgirl. Then she grinned and nodded.

'Yes, I want a big, fuck-off bling thing, covered in rocks!'

'I'll buy you the biggest, most fuck-off bling thing in the world. If the Queen ever sees you, she'll eat her heart out!'

'Talking of eating, Detective Super, I'm cooking you stir-fried scallops.'

That was just his favourite dish. 'You're amazing.'

She raised a finger. 'Yeah, you're right. Never forget that!'

'And so modest.'

'That too.'

He glanced down at the tome beside her and read the author's name. Jean-Paul Sartre.

'Good book?'

'Actually yes. I just read something he wrote that could apply to both of us – before we met.'

'Uh huh?'

Cleo picked the book up and flicked back to one of the tagged pages.

'Tell me.'

'It was something about if someone is lonely when they are on their own, then they're keeping bad company.' She looked at him. 'Yes?'

He nodded. 'Very true. I was. I was in totally crap company!'

'So,' she said, 'at what time does my darling fiancé want to eat?'

He pointed at his briefcase. 'Somewhere this side of midnight?'

'I'm feeling rather horny. I had in mind a bit of an early night . . .'

'Half an hour?'

Pouting her lips seductively, she stopped at one of the tagged pages. 'Did you read this passage, about satiating desires? Apparently if you refuse to satisfy them, then your soul can become infected.' She put the book down. 'I'm sure you wouldn't like me to have an infected soul, would you, Detective Superintendent?'

'No, I really wouldn't want you to have one of those at all.'

'I'm glad we're on the same page.'

Reluctantly dragging himself away from her, Roy lugged his bag up the wooden stairs and went into Cleo's den, which he had now more or less seconded as his office-away-from-the-office. On the desk sat a *City Books* plastic carrier. Stuck to it was a Post-it note with his name scrawled on in Cleo's writing. He removed a book with a picture of a racehorse on the cover. It was entitled *Eclipse*.

He remembered Cleo telling him her father was mad on

horseracing and she was ordering a book for him to give as a present.

He put it carefully to one side, then from his bag he took out a wodge of papers, the first of which bore the Sussex Police shield and the wording, beneath, SUSSEX POLICE. HQ CID. MAJOR CRIME BRANCH. OPERATION NEPTUNE. LINES OF ENQUIRY. Next he took out his red ring-binder STRATEGY FILE, followed by his pale blue, A4-sized INVESTIGATOR'S NOTEBOOK, in which he had written up his notes from all the briefing meetings on *Operation Neptune*, including this evening's.

Five minutes later, Cleo came silently into the room, kissed him on the back of his neck and placed a cocktail glass, filled to the brim with a vodka martini, on the desk beside him.

'Kalashnikov,' she said. 'It will make you very fiery.'

'I already am! How's your soul?' he whispered.

'Fighting off infection.' She kissed him again, in the same place, and went out.

'This book, *Eclipse* – is it the one I'm giving to your father for Christmas?' he called after her.

She came back in. 'Yes. It will get you about a thousand brownie points with him. *Eclipse* was the most famous racehorse ever. He'll think you're very smart knowing that.'

'You'd better brief me some more.'

She smiled. 'Why not read the book?'

'Duh!' he said, slapping his forehead. 'Hadn't thought of that!' He peered more closely at the cover, at the author's name. 'Nicholas Clee. Was he a famous jockey?'

She shook her head. 'No, I have a feeling he was a tennis player originally, but I may be wrong.' She went out again.

He read through his notes from the briefing, marking up significant new developments for his MSA, from which she would amend the *Lines of Enquiry*, prior to tomorrow morning's briefing meeting.

They still had no suspect, he thought. Feedback from the United Kingdom Human Trafficking Centre was that there was no evidence of any persons being trafficked into the UK for their organs – something that had been confirmed, so far at any rate, from the HOLMES analyst's scoping.

Trafficking of humans for organ transplantation was one of the major lines of enquiry on the list. But in the absence of any evidence that this practice had happened before in the UK, Grace was concerned not to throw all his resources into this one line, despite all the pointers to it.

It could simply be some kind of maniac killer.

Someone with surgical skills.

But then why would that person have just stopped with those four organs. The high-value ones?

What would Brother Occam have done? What is the most obvious explanation here? What would the great philosopher monk cut through with his razor?

Then Cleo cut through his thoughts. Dinner, she called up sweetly to him, was on the table.

74

Lynn heard the sound of music blasting out from the living room as she arrived home, shortly before nine. She slammed the door behind her against the icy wind and unwound the Cornelia James shawl she had bought on eBay – where she bought most of her accessories – a few weeks earlier.

Then, with her coat still on, she peered around the living-room door. Luke was lounging on the sofa, drinking a can of Diet Coke, his hair looking even more stupid than ever, most of it hanging in one big, gelled, lopsided spike over his right eye. But he did not look as stupid as the two slender girls dancing on the screen, in the pop video that was playing.

Clad only in black bras and briefs, wearing silver boxes on their heads, they were gyrating in jerky, mechanical movements to a hard, repetitive beat. Various phrases were stencilled in crude black letters on different parts of their arms, legs and midriffs. DO IT! MAKE IT! WORK HARDER! EVER BETTER!

'Daft Punk?' Lynn said.

Luke nodded. 'Yeah.'

Jabbing the remote, she turned the volume down. 'All OK?'

He nodded. 'Caitlin's sleeping.'

With this fucking racket? she nearly said. Instead she thanked him for looking after her, then asked, 'How is she?'

He shrugged. 'No change. I checked on her a few minutes ago.'

Still with her coat on, Lynn hurried up the stairs and went into her daughter's bedroom. Caitlin was in bed with her eyes closed. In the weak glow of the bedside lamp, she was looking even more yellow. Then she opened one eye and peered at her mother.

'How are you, angel?' Lynn leaned down and kissed her, stroking her hair, which felt damp.

'I'm quite thirsty actually.'

'Would you like some water? Fruit juice? Coke?'

'Water,' Caitlin said. Her voice was small, and reedy.

Lynn went to the kitchen and poured out a glass of cold water from the fridge. She noticed, to her dismay, a build-up of ice at the back of the fridge – a sure sign, she knew from past experience, that the appliance was on its last legs. Yet another expense looming up which she could not afford.

As she closed the door, Luke came in, barefoot, in a grey cardigan over a ragged shirt and baggy jeans.

'How did you get on today, Lynn?'

'Raising money?'

He nodded.

'My mother's come up with some. And Caitlin's father has offered his life savings. But I still need to find one hundred and seventy-five thousand.'

'I'd like to help,' he said.

Surprised, she said, 'Well, thank you – that's – that's very kind of you, Luke. But it's an impossible sum.'

'I've got some money. I dunno if Caitlin ever told you about my dad – not my stepfather – my real father.'

Holding the glass of water in her hand, and anxious to take it up to Caitlin, she said, 'No.'

'He was killed in an accident at work. On a building site

– a crane toppled on to him. My mum got a big compensation payment, and she gave most of it to me, because she didn't want my stepdad getting it – he has a gambling habit. I'd be happy to contribute it.'

'That really is very kind of you, Luke,' she said, genuinely touched. 'All contributions are more than welcome. How much could you spare?'

'I've got one hundred and fifty thousand pounds. I want you to have it all.'

She dropped the glass.

75

Sometimes, Roy Grace thought, it was easy to become over-confident and forget the most elementary stuff. It was good, occasionally, to go back to basics.

Seated in his office at quarter to seven in the morning, drinking his second cup of coffee of the day, he pulled down from his bookshelves the *Murder Investigation Manual*, a massive but definitive tome, compiled by the Centre for Policing Excellence for the Association of Chief Police Officers.

Updated regularly, it contained every procedure for every aspect of a murder investigation, including a well-mapped-out Murder Investigation Model, which he turned to now. The Fast Track Menu, which he read through again now to refresh himself, contained ten points which were ingrained in every homicide detective's brain – and precisely because they were so familiar, some of them could easily be overlooked.

The first on the list was Identify Suspects. Fine, he could tick that box. That was in progress.

Second was Intelligence Opportunities. He could tick that one too. They had Norman Potting's man in Romania, his own contact, Kriminalhauptkommissar Marcel Kullen in Munich, DS Moy and DC Nicholl intelligence gathering in the brothels, Guy Batchelor trawling through struck-off surgeons and the HOLMES analyst's scoping operation.

Scene Forensics was third on the list. The bottom of the Channel didn't give them much to go on there. The plastic sheeting was their best hope, as well as the new fingerprint technology on the outboard, and the long-shot of the cigarette butts Glenn had sent to the DNA labs.

He moved on to Crime Scene Assessment. They had the dump site, but as yet no crime scene. Fifth was Witness Search. Who would have seen these three teenagers? Staff at whatever hospital or clinic they had been operated on? Passengers and staff at whichever airport, or seaport, or station through which they had entered the UK? They would probably have been picked up on CCTV cameras at their point of entry, but he had no idea how long they had been in the UK. It could have been days, weeks or months. Impossible at this stage to start looking through that amount of footage. Another thought he noted down, under this heading, was *Other Romanians working here who might have known them?* The e-fits had been circulated widely and been featured in the press, but no witnesses had come forward.

Sixth was Victim Enquiries. His best source on those was DS Potting's man in Romania. And perhaps Interpol, but he wasn't holding his breath on them.

Possible Motives, the seventh point on the list, was where he stopped to think long and hard. He was fond of telling his teams that *assumptions were the mothers and fathers of all fuck-ups.* As he had mulled over last night, was there a danger they were being led down a blind alley by assuming human trafficking for organs was behind these three murders? Was there some sicko out there who enjoyed filleting people?

Yes, possibly, but less so if he applied the principles of Occam's Razor. There was a world shortage of human organs. Fact. Romania was a country involved in human traffficking for, among other purposes, the international trade in human organs. Fact. Skilled medical and surgical work had been carried out on these three victims. Fact. Supporting that was the information that an eminent British surgeon, Dr Raymond Crockett, had at one time been struck off for illegally purchasing four kidneys from Turkey for patients. Against was that there was no other history of human organ trafficking in England.

But there was always a first time.

And, it occurred to him, Dr Crockett had been caught. Was he a lone maverick, or had he just been unlucky to be found out? Were there dozens of other specialists like him in the UK who were using illegal organs and had not yet been caught? Was Crockett working again? He needed to be interviewed and eliminated.

Media was next. They were using the media as best they could, but the most important resource, the television programme *Crimewatch*, did not air for almost a week – even assuming they could get on it.

Then there was Post-mortems. At the moment he had all the information he required from these. If they found the surgical instruments, then further work might be required. For the moment, the bodies were being held in the mortuary.

He yawned, shaking off his tiredness and took another long sip of his coffee. When he had woken, at half past five, his brain had been whirring. He should have gone for his early-morning run, which always helped him to think clearly, but he was feeling guilty that he hadn't finished his work last night, so instead had come in even earlier than usual.

Last on the list was Other Significant Critical Actions. He thought for some moments, then read through the list he had already noted in his policy book. Then he added, in his notebook, *Outboard? Missing Scoob-Eee?*

He leaned back in his chair until it struck the wall. Dawn was starting to break outside his window. The storm had died down overnight and it was a dry morning. But the forecast was bad. Red and pink streaks speared the dark grey sky. How did that old adage go? *Red sky at night, sailor's delight. Red sky in the morning, sailor take warning!*

What do I need to take warning of? What am I missing? he challenged himself. *There must be something. What? What the hell is it?*

He stared silently into his coffee cup, as if the answer might lie there in the steaming blackness.

And then, suddenly, it came to him.

Sandy used to like pub quiz nights. She was brilliant at general knowledge – far better than he was. He remembered a quiz they had attended, eleven or twelve years ago, and one of the questions had been to guess the size of the English Channel in square miles. Sandy had won, with a correct answer of 29,000.

He clicked his finger and thumb.

'Yes!'

76

'We are looking in the wrong place,' Roy Grace announced to his team. 'And we might be looking at the wrong people. That's what I think.'

Instantly, he had the full attention of all twenty-eight police officers and support staff at the morning briefing. Then he tapped the side of his head.

'The wrong place, mentally, not geographically.'

Twenty-eight pairs of curious eyes locked on to his.

It was the fourth item on the Fast Track menu of the *Murder Investigation Manual* that had sparked him.

'I want you all to stop thinking about your own lines of enquiry, for a moment, and focus on Crime Scene Assessment. OK? Now, we've been assuming that this choice of dump site was an unlucky or an ignorant one. But think about this. The English Channel covers twenty-nine thousand square miles. That licensed dredge area is a hundred square miles.'

He looked at Glenn, Guy Batchelor, Bella, E-J and several others.

'Anyone here good at maths?'

The HOLMES analyst put up her hand.

'What percentage of the Channel is that dredge area, Juliet?' he asked.

She did some fast mental arithmetic. 'Approximately 0.34 per cent, Roy.'

'Small odds,' Grace said. 'A third of 1 per cent. We're

talking needle in a haystack percentages. If I was going to dump a body at random out in the Channel, I'd consider myself pretty unlucky to dump it on the dredge area. Actually, I'd rate the chances of that happening to be so slim as to be not worth worrying about. Unless of course I chose that area deliberately.'

He paused to let this sink in.

'Deliberately?' Lizzie Mantle queried.

'Hear my reasoning,' he said. 'If we take the line that we are dealing with international human trafficking – the fastest-growing criminal business in the world – we can be reasonably sure of one thing: the calibre of the criminals we are dealing with. If they're sufficiently well organized to be able to bring teenage kids into this country, and to have an effective medical organ transplant facility here, they are likely to be as professional about disposing of the bodies. They wouldn't just go out to sea in a rubber dinghy and lob them over the side.'

He saw a general nod of approval.

'I know we've been over this ground before, and we concluded the bodies were taken by either private boat or private plane or helicopter. But whatever the perps used, they would have hired a professional skipper or pilot. That person would have had charts, and been aware of the different depths of the Channel, and in all probability would have known these waters like the back of their hand. The dredge area may not be marked on all charts, but even so it is relatively shallow. If you are going to dump bodies, and you've got the whole of the Channel, wouldn't you go for depth? I would.'

'What's the deepest point, Roy?' Potting asked.

'There are plenty of places where it is over two hundred feet. So why dump them in sixty-five?'

'Speed?' Glenn Branson suggested. 'People panic with bodies sometimes, don't they?'

'Not the kind of people we're looking at here, Glenn,' the Detective Superintendent said.

'Maybe they genuinely didn't see it on their chart,' Bella Moy said.

Grace shook his head. 'Bella, I'm not ruling that out, but I'm postulating they might have been put there deliberately.'

'But I don't get why, Roy,' DI Mantle said.

'In the hope that they would be found.'

'For what reason?' Nick Nicholl asked.

'Someone who doesn't approve of what they are doing?' Grace replied. 'He dumped the bodies there, knowing there was a chance they'd get found.'

'If he didn't like what they were doing why didn't he just call the police?' Glenn Branson asked.

'Could be any number of reasons. Top of my list would be a pilot or skipper who liked the money but had a conscience. If he shopped them, his nice little earner would stop. This way his conscience was salved. He dropped them in an easy depth to dive. If the dredger didn't bring them up at some point, he could tip the police off – but not for a good long while.'

The team were quiet for a moment.

'I accept I may be off beam here, but I want to start a new line of enquiry – starting with Shoreham Harbour, we need to check out all the boats. We can get help from the harbourmaster, the lock operators and the coastguard. The boats we should look at closest are fast cruisers and fishing boats – and all the rental boats. Glenn, you're on the case on that missing fishing boat, the *Scoob-Eee*. Anything to report?'

The DS raised a padded brown envelope in the air. 'Just arrived, five minutes ago from O2, the phone company, Roy. It's a plot of all the mobile phone masts the skipper's phone made contact with on Friday night. It's unlikely he crossed the Channel, so with luck we may be able to track his movements along the south coast. Me and Ray Packham are going to work on them straight after this meeting.'

'Good thinking. But we can't be sure the *Scoob-Eee* had any involvement, so we should look at the other boats.'

Grace delegated two detective constables at the meeting to do this. Then he looked at Potting.

'OK, Norman, I said we might be looking at the *wrong* people.'

Potting frowned.

'I asked you to contact all transplant coordinators to see if any of these three were familiar to them, but you've still had no positive hit?'

'That's right, chief. We've spread pretty far on this now.'

'I have something that might be better. I don't know why we didn't think of it. What we need is to check all the people who have been on a transplant waiting list, waiting either for a heart/lung transplant, a liver or a kidney, who did not receive a transplant but dropped off the waiting list.'

'Presumably there are a number of reasons why people would drop off a waiting list, Roy?' Potting said.

Grace shook his head. 'From what I understand, no one on a waiting list for a new kidney or liver gets better by themselves, bar a miracle. If they drop off the list it is for one of two reasons. Either they had the transplant done elsewhere – or they died.'

His mobile phone began ringing. He pulled it out and glanced at the display. Instantly, he recognized the German dialling code, +49, in front of the number that appeared. It was Marcel Kullen calling from Munich.

Raising an apologetic hand, he stepped out of the briefing room, into the corridor.

'Roy,' the German detective said, 'you wanted me to call us when the organ broker, Marlene Hartmann, arrived back in Munich, yes?'

'Thank you, yes!'

Grace was amused by how the German constantly confused 'you' and 'us'.

'She flew back late last night. Already, this morning, she has made three phone calls to a number in your city, in Brighton.'

'Brilliant! Any chance you could let me have that number?'

'You don't reveal its source?'

'You have my word.'

Kullen read it out to him.

77

At quarter to nine in the morning, Lynn sat in the kitchen, with her laptop open, studying the five emails that had come in overnight. Luke, who had spent some of the night with Caitlin, then had crashed on the sitting-room sofa, sat beside her. All of the emails were testimonials from clients of Transplantation-Zentrale.

One was from a mother in Phoenix, Arizona, whose thirteen-year-old son had received a liver through the organ broker two years ago and she provided a phone number for Lynn to call her on. She was, she said, utterly delighted with the service, and was certain her son would not have been alive today without Marlene Hartmann's help.

Another was from a man in Cape Town who had received a new heart through the company just eight months ago. He too claimed he was delighted and provided a phone number.

The third was again from America, a particularly touching one, from the sister of a twenty-year-old girl in Madison, Wisconsin, who had received a kidney and said Lynn could call any time. The fourth was from a Swedish woman, in Stockholm, whose thirty-year-old husband had been provided with a new heart and lungs. The fifth was from a woman in Manchester, whose eighteen-year-old daughter had received a liver transplant this time last year. There were home and mobile numbers provided for her.

Lynn, still in her dressing gown, sipped her mug of tea. She had barely slept a wink all night, she had been so wired.

Caitlin had come into her room at one stage, crying because she was in agony from where she had scratched the skin on her legs and arms raw. Then when she had settled her, Lynn had just lain awake, trying to think everything through.

The enormity of taking Luke's money was weighing heavily. So was taking her mother's nest egg. Taking the contribution from Mal worried her less; after all, Caitlin was his daughter too. But what if the transplant did not work? In the contract she had been through with Frau Hartmann, which the woman had left here, failure of the transplanted liver was covered. In the event of failure or rejection within six months a further liver would be provided at no charge.

But there was still no damn guarantee the transplant would work.

And, assuming it did, there was the further problem of finding several thousand pounds a year to pay for the anti-rejection drugs, for life.

But, more to the point, there wasn't an alternative. Except for the unthinkable.

What if Marlene Hartmann was a con woman? She would have handed over every penny she could cobble together in the world and still be nowhere. OK, the company checked out from the credit enquiries she had made, surreptitiously, from work yesterday, and now she had the references, which she would contact for sure. But all the same she was worried sick about taking the next step – to sign and fax the contract and transfer 50 per cent of the fee, 150,000 euros, to Munich.

Breakfast was on the television, with the sound turned down to silent. The host and the hostess were seated on a sofa, chatting and laughing with a guest, some beautiful young woman in her twenties she vaguely recognized but couldn't place. She had dark hair and was similar in build to Caitlin. And suddenly she had an image of Caitlin sitting there on that sofa, chatting and laughing with those hosts. Telling them about how she nearly died, but beat the system, yeaaaahhhhh!

Maybe Caitlin would become a huge star. It was possible. She was beautiful; people noticed her. She had personality. If she had her health back, she could be anything she wanted.

If.

Lynn glanced at her watch and did a quick calculation.

'Wisconsin must be six or seven hours behind the UK, right?'

Luke nodded pensively. 'Phoenix will be about the same.'

'So it would be the middle of the night. I would particularly like to talk to the mother there – I'll call her this afternoon.'

'The one in Manchester has a daughter of a similar age. You should be able to get hold of her. I think you should kick off with her.'

Lynn looked at him and, through her tiredness and her frayed emotions, suddenly felt a deep affection for him.

'Good thinking,' she said, and dialled the woman's home number. After six rings it went to voicemail. Then she tried the mobile.

Almost instantly there was a click, followed by a loud background roar, as if the woman was driving.

'Hello?' she said in a thick Mancunian accent.

Lynn introduced herself and thanked the woman for emailing her.

'I'm just dropping the young ones off,' she replied. 'I'll be home in twenty minutes. Can I call you back?'

'Of course.'

'And listen, love, don't worry. Marlene Hartmann is a star. You can come up here and meet my Chelsey. She'll chat to you, tell you the nightmare she went through with the National Health. I can show you the photos too. Twenty minutes all right for you, love?'

'Absolutely fine, thank you!' Lynn said.

She put the phone down with hope suddenly soaring in her heart.

78

As Glenn Branson drove along the perimeter road of Shore-ham Airport, the strong wind buffeted the small Hyundai. He passed a cluster of parked helicopters, then glanced at a small, twin-engined plane that was coming in to land on the grass runway. He turned right, beyond the end of the hangars, and drove up to the converted warehouse, inside a mesh-fenced compound, that housed the Specialist Search Unit. The car clock read 12.31 p.m.

A few minutes later he was in the cluttered conference room, which doubled as the canteen and shared communal office, with a mug of coffee beside him, carefully spreading out the photocopy of an Admiralty chart, which Ray Packham had helped him to prepare, on the large table.

There were charts on the walls, wooden shields, a whiteboard, some framed photos of the team, as well as a bravery award certificate. The view through the window was on to the car park and the featureless grey metal wall of the warehouse beyond. On the windowsill was a goldfish bowl, containing a solitary fish and a toy deep-sea diver.

Smurf, Jonah, Arf and WAFI were already seated. The young woman sergeant wore a black, zippered fleece, embroidered with the word POLICE and the Sussex Police shield above it. The three men wore blue, short-sleeved shirts, with their numbers on the epaulettes.

Gonzo, also wearing a fleece, came in and handed Glenn Branson a stiff paper bag. 'In case you need it.'

The other four grinned.

Glenn looked puzzled. 'Need it for what?'

'To throw up in,' Gonzo said.

'It's quite rough outside!' Jonah said.

'Yeah, and this whole building moves a bit on a windy day,' said WAFI, 'so we thought – you know – bearing in mind last time you were with us . . .'

Tania Whitlock gave Glenn a sympathetic smile as her team ribbed him.

'Yeah, very witty,' he retorted.

'Heard you applied for a transfer to this unit, Glenn,' Arf said. 'Cos you enjoyed being with us so much last time.'

'*Mutiny on the Bounty* springs to mind,' Glenn said.

'So, Glenn,' Tania Whitlock said, 'tell us what you have.'

The chart showed a section of coastline from Worthing to Seaford. There were three crude red ink rings drawn on it, marked *A*, *B* and *C*, with a sizeable space between each. A green dotted line plotted a course out to sea from the mouth of Shoreham Harbour, with a childlike drawing of a boat at the end of it, beside which someone had written *Das Boot*. There was also a large blue arc.

'OK,' Branson said. 'The skipper of the *Scoob-Eee*, Jim Towers, had a mobile phone on the O2 network. These three red circles indicate the O2 base stations and masts covering this section of coast. The phone company has given us a plot, which is all marked on here, of base station signals received from Towers's mobile phone on Friday evening, between 8.55 p.m., when it was noticed by a harbour pilot and by a shore boatman passing through the lock, and 10.08 p.m., when the last signal was received.'

'Glenn, are these calls that Jim Towers made?' Sergeant Whitlock asked.

'No, Tania. When the phone is in standby mode, once

every twenty minutes it sends out a signal to a base station, a bit like the way, when I was with you, you radioed the coastguard from time to time and gave him your position, yeah?' he explained, pleased with his analogy. 'It's like checking in – calling home. It's called, technically, a location update.'

They all nodded.

'The signal gets picked up by the nearest base station – unless it's busy, and then it gets passed to the next one. If there's more than one base station in range, it could be picked up by two or even three.'

'Blimey, Glenn,' said Arf. 'We didn't realize you were a telephone scientist as well as a master mariner.'

'Piss off!' he retorted with a big grin. Then, continuing, he said, 'So this is what was happening here. After the boat left Shoreham Harbour, the first location update was picked up by this Shoreham base station and this Worthing one.' He pointed at the ones marked *A* and *B*. 'Twenty minutes later, the second signal home was also picked up by these two. But the third one, approximately one hour after leaving harbour, was picked up by this third one as well, just east of Brighton Marina.' He pointed at *C*. 'That tells us Towers was steering a south-easterly course – which we've marked, as a best guess, with this green dotted line.'

'Good film, *Das Boot*,' Gonzo said.

'Now here's where it gets interesting,' said Glenn, ignoring him.

'Oh, great!' WAFI said. 'We've been waiting for it to get interesting, because it's been pretty boring so far!'

The DS waited patiently for them all to stop laughing.

'The timing advance can be anything from zero to sixty-three for a given link with a phone,' Glenn went on, ignoring their barracking. 'So if the maximum range is about twenty miles, then divide that into sixty-three slots and you can work out distance to within about eighteen hundred feet.'

'OK,' Gonzo said. 'If I'm understanding this correctly, you said this shows the direction the boat was heading. So this is its last known position before it went out of range?'

Glenn Branson shook his head.

'No, I don't think it went out of range.'

He looked up. The others all frowned.

'This is where the fourth and last signal – the last location update – was transmitted from,' he continued. 'Now, the seaward range from standard base stations is about twenty miles. But I was told that the mobile phone companies, where possible, build their coastal masts exceptionally high to increase range, so they can pick up lucrative roaming charges from foreign ships passing, so the range here is probably quite a bit further than that – could be as much as thirty miles.'

Gonzo scrawled some calculations down on a notepad.

'Right,' Glenn said, 'you all know the *Scoob-Eee*. It's not a fast boat – its maximum speed is ten knots – roughly twelve miles an hour. When this last signal was picked up, she had only been out for less than ninety minutes – and she was sailing at an angled course, putting her approximately ten miles out to sea – well within range.'

There was a few moments' silence while they all reflected on this. It was Tania Whitlock who broke it.

'Perhaps his phone battery died, Glenn?' she suggested.

'It's possible – but he was an experienced skipper and the phone was one of his lifelines. Don't you think it's unlikely he'd have put to sea either without a charger or with an uncharged battery?'

'He could have dropped it overboard,' said Gonzo.

'Yep, he could,' Glenn agreed. 'But again unlikely for an experienced skipper.'

Gonzo shrugged. 'Yeah, Towers knew what he was doing, but it's easily done. You think something else happened?'

Branson stared at him levelly. 'What about the possibility that it sank?'

'Ah, now I get it!' Arf said. 'You want us to go out there and take a look for it, scan the bottom?'

'You guys are catching on quick!' Branson said.

'She's a solid boat, built to take heavy seas,' WAFI said. 'She's unlikely to have sunk.'

'What about an accident?' Branson said. 'A collision? A fire? Sabotage? Or something more sinister.'

'Like what, Glenn?' Tania asked.

'The voyage doesn't make sense,' Branson said. 'I've interviewed his wife. Friday night was their wedding anniversary. They had a restaurant reservation. He had no clients booked for any night fishing trip. Yet instead of going home, he got on the boat and headed out to sea.'

'Yep, well, I can sympathize with him,' Arf said. 'The choice of dinner with your missus or being out at sea on your own – no contest.'

They all grinned. Tania, who was newly married, less humorously than her colleagues.

Gonzo pointed out of the window. 'There's a Force Nine hooley blowing out there. Do you know what the sea's like at the moment?'

'A bit choppy, I should imagine.' Glenn looked back at Gonzo quizzically.

'If you want us to go out there, mate, we'll go,' WAFI said. 'But you're coming with us.'

79

Lynn sat impatiently at her desk at the Harrier Hornets work station with her phone headset on. She glanced at the calendar, tacked to the red partition wall, to the right of her computer screen.

Three weeks to go till Christmas, she thought. She had never felt so unprepared – or uninterested – in her life. There was only one Christmas present she wanted.

Her friend Sue Shackleton had told her she could come up with £10,000 quickly. That now left a shortfall of £15,000.

Right at this moment, Luke was at his bank, setting up everything for the wire transfer of 150,000 euros to Marlene Hartmann at Transplantation-Zentrale. But he would not actually make the transfer until they'd checked out all the references.

So far it was so good on that score. She had spoken to the woman in Manchester, whose name was Marilyn Franks. Her daughter's liver transplant had been done at a clinic in Sussex, near Brighton, and it had been a complete success. Marilyn Franks could not praise Marlene Hartmann highly enough.

It was the same with the man in Cape Town. He'd had initial complications, but the aftercare, he assured Lynn, was far more thorough than he had imagined was possible. The Swedish woman in Stockholm, whose husband had had a new heart and lungs, was equally emphatic in her praise. With both the last two cases, the operations were carried out in local clinics.

It was still too early to phone America, but in her own mind, from what she had now heard, Lynn was already convinced. Still, she owed it to Luke, especially, to complete the checks. And there was not going to be any second chance.

Hopefully, some time this afternoon, or tomorrow at the latest, after she had spoken to the other two references, the transfer of the first half of the money would be done. The remaining 50 per cent would have to be handed over, cash on delivery, on the day of the transplant. Which gave her days, at most, to find the last £15,000.

She had tested the German woman out on what would happen if she had a shortfall and Marlene had been firm. It was all or nothing. She could not be more clear.

Fifteen thousand. It was still a lot of money to find – and even more so to find inside a week, maybe less. Further, the exchange rate of the pound against the euro was predicted to worsen. Which meant the shorfall might get even bigger.

From the moment Luke made the transfer, the clock would start ticking. At any time in the following days, Lynn could get a phone call from the German woman, giving her and Caitlin as little as two hours' notice before they were picked up and transferred to the clinic. As Marlene had explained so clearly, you could not predict when an accident was going to happen that would provide a suitable matching organ.

She glanced around. Christmas cards were starting to appear on desks in the office, and tiny bits of tinsel here and there, and sprigs of mistletoe. But the company had a number of Muslims working for it and there was an edict that Christmas was not to be openly celebrated by employees for fear of offending the non-Christians. So yet again there would be no proper decorations going up – nor an official office Xmas lunch.

Last year that had made her blood boil, but this year Lynn didn't care. At this moment she cared only about one thing. The time. It was five minutes to one. At one there was a lunch-break exodus, as regular as clockwork, from several of her Harrier Hornet colleagues. Crucially, Katie and Jim, who sat either side of her and could hear everything she said, if they chose to listen, and her team manager, Liv Thomas.

On the screen on the wall, the COLLECTED BONUS POT had risen to £1,450 this morning. The big pre-Christmas grab was on, to pull money in before clients blew it all on presents and booze.

Making a big effort to focus on work, but without hope of scooping this week's pot, she dialled the next number on her call list. It was answered a few moments later by a slurred, female voice.

'Mrs Hall?' Lynn asked.

'Who's that?'

'It's Lynn, from Denarii. We just noticed that you didn't make your payment on Monday this week.'

'Yeah, well, it's Christmas, innit? I got stuff to buy. What do you want me to tell my kids? They're getting no presents this year cos I got to pay Denarii?'

'Well, we did have an agreement, Mrs Hall.'

'Yeah, well, you sodding come here and explain that to my kids.'

Lynn closed her eyes for an instant. She heard a gulp as if the woman was swigging something. She didn't have the energy to deal with this right now.

'Can you tell me when we might be able to expect you to resume your payment plan?'

'You tell me. Tell me about the social housing, yeah? You know, what about the Welfare? Why don't you speak to them?'

The woman's slurring was getting worse and what she was saying made no sense.

'I think I'll call you back tomorrow, Mrs Hall.'

Lynn hung up.

Jim, to her right, a short, wiry Geordie of thirty, pulled off his headset and exhaled sharply.

'Bloody hell,' he said. 'What's with people today?'

Lynn gave him a sympathetic smile. He stood up.

'I'm off. Think I need a liquid lunch today. Fancy a drink? I'm buying.'

'Sorry. No thanks, Jim. I have to work through.'

'Suit yourself.'

To Lynn's relief, she saw Katie, a tubby red-haired woman in her forties, remove her headset and pick up her handbag.

'Right,' she said. 'Off to do battle with the shops!'

'Good luck,' Lynn said.

A few minutes later she saw her team manager wrestling her coat on. Lynn pretended to busy herself checking her emails, as she waited for all three of them to leave the room, then pulled up the client file and jotted down a number.

As soon as they were gone, she pulled off her headset, took her mobile phone from her bag, altered the setting to *Number Withheld*, then dialled the mobile phone of her most loathsome client of all.

He answered warily, after the third ring, in his deep, treacly voice.

'Hello?'

'Reg Okuma?'

'Who is this, please?'

Keeping her voice down to barely above a whisper, she said, 'Lynn Beckett, from Denarii.'

Suddenly his whole tone changed. 'My beautiful Lynn! Are you phoning me to tell me that we can now make beautiful love together?'

'Well, I'm actually calling to see if I can help you with your credit rating. We're making some special Christmas offers to our clients. You owe thirty-seven thousand, eight hundred and seventy pounds, plus accruing interest, to the Bradford Credit Bank, yes?'

'If that's what you tell me.'

'If you could raise fifteen thousand pounds right away, in cash, I think we'd be prepared to write off the rest of the debt for you, and give you a clean bill of health to kick off the New Year.'

'You would?' He sounded incredulous.

'Only because it's Christmas. We're thinking about our year-end figures. It would be good for us to have closure with some key clients.'

'This is a most interesting proposition for me.'

Lynn knew he had the money. He had a history of defaulting on debts that went back more than a decade. He operated cash businesses – ice-cream vans and street-food stalls – then would obtain credit cards, max them out and plead he had no money. Lynn calculated he probably had hundreds of thousands of pounds stashed away in cash. Fifteen thousand would be small beer to him. And a bargain.

'You told me yesterday you need to buy a car, for your new business venture, and that you can't get any credit.'

'Yes.'

'So this could be a good solution for you.'

He was silent for a long while.

'Mr Okuma, are you still there?'

'Yes, my beautiful one, I like listening to your breathing. It helps to clarify my thinking, and it so arouses me. So, if it were – ah – possible for me to find this sum for you—'

'In cash.'

'It must be cash?'

'I'm doing you a big favour. I'm putting my neck on the block on this one, to help you.'

'I would like to reward you for this, beautiful Lynn. Perhaps I can reward you in bed?'

'First I need to see the money.'

'I think this kind of money – it will be possible. Oh yes. How much time can you give me?'

'Twenty-four hours?'

'I will call you back shortly.'

'Call me on this number,' she said, and gave him her mobile.

When she hung up, she began shaking.

80

Grace logged the date and time in his notebook – 6.30 p.m., Thursday 4 December – then he glanced down the lengthy agenda his MSA had typed for the fourteenth briefing of Operation Neptune.

Several of his inquiry team, including Guy Batchelor, Norman Potting and Glenn Branson, were in a vociferous discussion about a disputed referee's decision in last night's big football game. Grace, who preferred rugby, had not seen it.

'OK,' he said, raising his voice and his hand, 'let's kick off.'

'Very witty,' Glenn Branson said.

'Do you want a yellow card?'

'I don't think you'll give me one when you hear my result. Two results, in fact. Want *me* to *kick off* first?'

Grinning, Roy Grace said, 'Fill your boots.'

'Yeah, right, well –' Branson picked up a sheaf of notes – 'first thing is that the Specialist Search Unit boys went out this afternoon to scan the area where the *Scoob-Eee* was last heard from. Despite the crap weather, they've found an anomaly on the seabed which is approximately the same dimensions as the *Scoob-Eee*. It's the shape of a boat, lying in about a hundred feet of water, approximately twelve miles due south of Black Rock. It could of course be an old wreck, but they're going to dive on it tomorrow, weather permitting, to take a look.'

'Are you going with them, Glenn?' DI Mantle asked.

'Well . . .' He sounded hesitant. 'Given the choice, I'd rather not.'

'I think you should,' she said. 'In case they find something.'

'I'll be a lot of use to them, flat on my back, puking.'

'Always lie on your side or on your stomach if you're throwing up,' Potting said. 'That way you won't choke.'

'Very helpful advice, Norman. Thanks, I'll bear it in mind,' Glenn replied.

'I'm just concerned about *resourcing*,' Grace said, cutting in. 'Beyond the *Scoob-Eee* being used as the recovery boat for two of the bodies, do we have anything to link its disappearance to our investigation, to justify Glenn's time in going out again?'

Glumly, like a man aiding his own executioner, Glenn said, 'Yes. I have a result back from the labs on the DNA from the two cigarette butts I recovered at Shoreham Harbour. Remember, I reported that I saw someone who appeared to be watching the *Scoob-Eee* with interest last Friday morning?'

Grace nodded.

'Well, the national database people at Birmingham say it's a perfect match to someone they have recently put on the database at the request of Europol. He goes under two different names. Here he calls himself Joe Baker, but his real name is Vlad Cosmescu – he's Romanian.'

Grace thought for a moment. Joe Baker. The man who owned the black Mercedes he had clocked on his early-morning run. A coincidence, or more?

'That's interesting,' Bella Moy said. 'His name just popped up last night – pimping two girls, recent arrivals from Romania.'

'Clearly the Man of the Moment,' Grace said, sliding

some papers out of a brown envelope. 'The wizards in our fingerprint department managed to pull a clear set of dabs off an outboard that had been submerged in the sea using some equipment they're trialling – and they got a match from Europol this afternoon. Guess who?'

'Our New Best Friend, Vlad the impaler?' ventured DS Batchelor.

'Right on the money!' Grace said.

'Are we going to bring him in?' Norman Potting asked. 'They're all villains, these Romanians, aren't they?'

'That's very racist,' Bella said acidly.

'No, it's just a home truth.'

'What grounds do you want to arrest him on, Norman?' Grace said. 'Smoking a cigarette? Dropping an outboard motor in the sea? Or for being a Romanian?'

Potting lowered his eyes and made an indecipherable grumbling sound.

'Did the *Scoob-Eee* have an outboard, Glenn?' E-J asked.

'I didn't see one, no.'

'Do we know where this man, Baker/Cosmescu, lives?'

Bella replied, 'He's been a part of the brothel scene for some years, Roy. We should be able to track him down fairly easily.'

'Do you want someone to interview him?' DI Mantle asked.

'No, I think we'll just log him as a Person of Interest. I don't think we should talk to him at this stage. If he's up to anything it will just alert him. We might think about putting surveillance on him.' He looked down at his notes. 'OK, so how are we are we doing on the *actions*?'

'We've had two DCs out going round all suppliers of PVC sheeting in the area. Nothing so far,' said David Browne.

'Nick and I covered twelve brothels last night,' Bella Moy said, reaching for a Malteser.

'You must be shagged out, Nick!' Norman Potting said.

Nicholl blushed and gave a half-hearted smile. Grace suppressed a grin. Potting had been quieter than normal in recent days, which he imagined was due to the man's marriage problems. It was a relief. Potting was a good detective, but on a couple of recent cases when they had worked together Grace had come perilously close to having to fire the DS for his offensive remarks.

Turning to Bella, he asked, 'And? Anything?'

Glancing at Nick Nicholl for confirmation, she replied, 'Nothing, beyond Cosmescu. We didn't find any girls who seemed in distress.'

'Good to know that our brothels are such happy places,' Grace commented sarcastically.

'We'll carry on today,' she said.

Glancing at his notes again, Grace turned to Potting. 'Anything from your man in Romania?'

'I had an email from Ian Tilling an hour ago. He's following up a lead tonight. I may have some information by the morning.'

Grace made a note.

'Good. Thank you. How about people who were on a transplant list but dropped off?'

'I've been working on that all day, Roy,' Potting said. 'I suspect we're on a hiding to nothing there. First thing we've got against us is the Hippocratic Oath – good old patient confidentiality. Second thing is the way the system works. These transplant lists aren't cut and dried. I spoke to a helpful liver consultant at the Royal South London, one of the main liver transplant hospitals. He told me they have a weekly meeting, every Wednesday at midday, when they review the list. Because there is such a shortage of donors they change priorities from week to week, according to urgency. We're talking about hospitals all over the UK. We'd have to go to court on every individual to get their records. What we need is a medical insider on our team.'

'What kind of insider?' Grace asked.

'A tame transplant surgeon whom medics would trust,' said Potting. 'Someone who might have an overview.'

'I have something that may be of interest,' Emma-Jane Boutwood said. 'I've been trying to find disaffected transplant consultants or surgeons on the web. Someone who's openly critical of the system and has gone public.'

'Openly critical in what way?' DI Mantle quizzed.

'Well – for instance, a surgeon who doesn't think it is unethical to buy human organs,' the young DC said. 'And I've found someone – his name is Sir Roger Sirius – and he pops up on several different links.'

She looked at Grace, who nodded encouragement for her to continue.

'A number of things about Sirius are interesting. He trained under one of the pioneers of liver transplant surgery in the UK. Then he was the senior consultant at the Royal South London Hospital for some years. He actively campaigned for a change in the organ donor laws – advocating an opt-out system – meaning that people's organs would automatically be harvested on death unless they had requested otherwise. It's the system they have in Spain, for instance. Now, where it gets even more interesting, is that he took early retirement from the Royal after a row about this. Then he went abroad.'

She stopped and looked at her notes.

'He appears on some websites involving Colombia – which is a country heavily involved in human organ trafficking. It seems he worked out there for a while. Then he pops up in Romania.'

'Romania?' Grace said.

E-J nodded, then went on, 'He's into a big lifestyle. Flies his own helicopter, flash cars, and a huge mansion in Sussex, near Petworth.'

'Interesting,' DI Mantle said. 'About Sussex.'

'Four years ago he went through a very acrimonious and expensive divorce – and he's now married to a former Miss Romania. That's all I have so far.'

There was a long silence, then Grace said, 'Good work, E-J. I think we should go and have a chat with him.'

He thought for a moment. From his limited experience of senior medics, they tended to be upmarket, pompous people. Guy Batchelor, who'd had a public school education, might be the kind of person a man like Sir Roger Sirius would feel comfortable with. It also fitted with what Batchelor had been working on.

He turned to the DS. 'Guy, this is the terrain you were actioning. I think you should go with E-J.'

'Yes, chief.'

'Tell him we are investigating three bodies we believe are connected with an organ trafficking ring and ask him if he could give us his wisdom about where to look for such people. Flatter him, massage his ego – and watch him like a hawk. See how he reacts.'

Then he turned back to his notes. 'The phone number I was given from Germany. Who's working on that?'

One of the researchers, Jacqui Phillips, raised a hand. 'Me, Roy. I obtained an address in Patcham and the name of the subscriber. But there was something else, which I gave to DI Mantle.'

Picking up from this, Lizzie Mantle said, 'It was good

observation, Jacqui. The house owner is a Mrs Lynn Beckett. Jacqui spotted that's the same surname as one of the crew members of the *Arco Dee* dredger which found the first body. It was myself and Nick who took the original statements from the crew members, so we went back this afternoon, when it was in harbour, discharging its cargo. We got it confirmed that this Lynn Beckett is the former wife of the chief engineer, Malcolm Beckett. One of his fellow crew members told me that he's quite depressed at the moment, because his daughter is ill. He wasn't sure exactly what the problem is, but it was something to do with her liver.'

'Liver?' Grace echoed.

She nodded.

'Did you find out anything else?'

The DI shook her head. 'No. Malcolm Beckett was very guarded – in my view, too guarded.'

'Why?'

'Because I think he had something to hide.'

'Such as?'

'He kept saying that his daughter lived with his ex-wife and he rarely saw her, so he didn't really know what was wrong with her. That didn't ring true to me – as a parent. Nor did he pass the Detective Superintendent Grace *eye* test.'

Grace smiled.

'Perhaps we should put in for a phone tap, Roy?' David Browne said.

'I don't think we have enough to get one at this stage, but I think we've enough to warrant a monitoring of calls to that number.'

'Presumably this Lynn Beckett has a mobile too,' Guy Batchelor said.

'Yes, someone needs to get on to the mobile phone companies, see what they've got registered to that name and address.' He looked at his notes again. 'Tomorrow, I'm flying to Munich and back in the evening, so DI Mantle will be taking over command until I return. Any questions?'

There were none until after the briefing had ended, when Glenn Branson caught up with Roy Grace as he headed along the network of corridors back towards his office. They stopped in front of a diagram that looked like a spider's web, pinned to a red felt notice-board which was headed COMMON POSSIBLE MOTIVES.

'Yo, old-timer,' he said. 'This trip to Munich – it wouldn't be anything connected with Sandy, would it?'

Grace shook his head. 'God, no. I have an appointment with the organ broker woman – I'm posing as a customer. And while I'm over there my LKA friend is going to slip me some files – on the QT.'

On the diagram behind Glenn's head Grace read the words, DESIRE, POWER, CONTROL, HATE, REVENGE.

Glenn stared hard at him. 'Are you sure that's the only reason for your visit? It's just – you know – you and I haven't talked about Sandy in a while, and now you're going to the place were there was a reported sighting of her.'

'That sighting was a red herring, Glenn. You know what I really think?'

'No, you've never told me what you really think. Got time for a drink?'

Grace looked at his watch. 'Actually I've got to swing by the house to pick up some clothes, but I've got half an hour's stuff to do in my office first. Where do you fancy?'

'The usual?'

Grace shrugged. The Black Lion was not his favourite

pub, in a city that was filled with great watering holes, but it was convenient and had its own car park. He looked at his watch again.

'Meet you there at a quarter to eight. But one drink only.'

*

When Grace arrived, ten minutes later than he had said, Glenn was already seated at a quiet corner table, with a pint in front of him, and a tumbler of whisky on the rocks, with a jug of water on the side, for Grace.

'Glenfiddich?' Branson said.

'Good man.'

'I don't know why you like that stuff.'

'Yeah, well, I don't know why you like Guinness.'

'No, what I mean is that Glenfiddich isn't the *purist* single malt, right?'

'Yep, but I like it best of any I've ever drunk. You have a problem with that?'

'You ever see that film *Whisky Galore*?'

'About the shipwreck off the Scottish coast – with a cargo of whisky?'

'I'm impressed. You do actually impress me sometimes. You aren't a complete cultural ignoramus. Even though you have rubbish taste in clothes and music.'

'Yep, well, I wouldn't want to be too perfect.' Grace grinned. 'Anyway, how are you? What's happening with Mrs Branson?'

'Let's not even go there.' Glenn shook his head. 'It's a fucking train crash, OK?' He raised his glass and drank. Then, wiping the froth from his mouth with the back of his hand, he said, 'I want to hear about you and Munich – and Sandy?'

Grace picked up the tumbler and swirled the ice cubes around. Johnny Cash's 'Ring of Fire' was twanging out of the pub's speakers.

'Now, that's real music.'

Branson rolled his eyes.

Grace took a sip, then put the glass down.

'I think Sandy's dead – and that she's been dead for a long time. I've been a fool for holding out hope. All it's done is to lose me years of my life.' He shrugged. 'All those mediums.' He sipped some more whisky. 'You know, a lot of them said the same thing, that they could not get through to her – meaning that she was not in spirit – like, the spirit world.'

'What does that signify?'

'If she's not in the spirit world – i.e. dead – then she must be alive – in their rationale.' He drank some more, and saw to his surprise that he had drained the glass. Lifting it up, he said, 'That was a double?'

Glenn nodded.

'I'll get one more – just a single – keep me legal. Another half for you?'

'A pint. I'm a big guy – I can take more than you!'

Grace returned with their fresh drinks and sat down, noting that Branson had drained his first pint in his absence.

'So you don't believe these mediums?' Branson asked. 'Even though you've always had a belief in the paranormal?'

'I don't know what to believe. It'll be ten years next year that she's been gone. That's long enough. She's either physically dead or at least dead to me. If she is alive and hasn't made contact in nine years, she's not going to.' He fell silent for a moment. 'I don't want to lose Cleo, Glenn.'

'She's well fit. Great lady. I'm with you on that.'

'If I don't let go of Sandy, I will lose Cleo. I'm not going to let that happen.'

Glenn touched his friend's face gently with his balled fist. 'Good man, that's the first time I've ever heard you talk like this.'

Grace nodded. 'It's the first time I've felt like this. I've given instructions to my solicitor to start the process to have Sandy declared legally dead.'

Staring at him intently, Glenn said, 'You know, mate, it's not just the legal process, it's the mental one that's the most important, yeah?'

'What do you mean by that?'

He tapped the side of his head. 'It's believing it – in here.'

'I do,' Roy Grace said, then smiled wryly. 'Trust me, I'm a copper.'

81

Dr Ross Hunter sat on the edge of Caitlin's bed, while Lynn was downstairs, fussing up a cup of tea for him.

The chaotic room was stuffy and airless, and thick with the rancid smell of Caitlin's perspiration. He could feel the clammy heat coming off her as he stared through his half-moon tortoiseshell glasses at her deeply jaundiced face and the heavy dark rings around her eyes. Her hair was matted. She lay under the bedclothes, propped up against the pillows, wearing a pink dressing gown over her nightdress, with her headphones hanging around her neck, and the small white iPod lying on top of her duvet, alongside a paperback about Jordan's life and several fluffy bears.

'How are you feeling, Caitlin?' he asked.

'I've been sent glitter,' she mumbled, her voice barely audible.

'Glitter?' He frowned.

'Someone sent me glitter, on Facebook,' she mumbled, only semi-coherently.

'What exactly do you mean by *glitter*?'

'It's like, you know, a Facebook thing. My friend Gemma sent it. And I've been poked by Mitzi.'

'OK.' He looked bemused.

'I got sent wheels by Mitch Symons – you know – so I can get around more easily.'

The doctor peered around the room, looking for wheels. He stared at the dartboard on the wall, with a purple boa hanging from it. At a saxophone case propped up against a wall. Then at a tiny toy horse on wheels, standing amid the shoes scattered all over the carpet.

'Those wheels?' he said.

She shook her head. 'No,' she mumbled, and windmilled her right hand, as if trying to tease a thought out from inside her head. 'It's a sort of Facebook thing. To get around. They're sort of virtual.'

Her eyes closed, as if she was exhausted from the effort of speaking.

He bent down and opened his medical bag. At that moment Lynn came back in with the tea and a digestive biscuit lying in the saucer.

He thanked her, then turned his attention to Caitlin.

'I just want to take your temperature and blood pressure, is that OK?'

Still with her eyes shut she nodded, then whispered, 'Whatever.'

*

Ten minutes later he walked back downstairs, followed by Lynn. They went into the kitchen and sat down at the table. She knew what he was going to say before he opened his mouth, just from the worried set of his face.

'Lynn, I'm very worried about her. She's extremely ill.'

Feeling her eyes watering, Lynn was tempted, desperately tempted, to open up and confide in him about what she was doing. But she could not predict how he would react. She knew he was a man of the deepest integrity and that, whether or not he believed in the course she was taking, he could never condone it. So she just nodded, silently and bleakly.

'Yes,' she gulped, her heart heaving. 'I know.'

'She needs to be back in hospital. Shall I phone for an ambulance?'

'Ross,' she blurted. 'Look – I . . .' Then she shook her head and sank her face into her hands, trying desperately to think clearly. 'Oh, God, Ross, I'm at my wits' end.'

'Lynn,' he said gently. 'I know you think you can look after her here, but the poor girl is in a lot of discomfort, quite apart from danger. She's raw all over her body from scratching. She has a high temperature She's going downhill very quickly. I'm shocked how she's deteriorated since I last saw her. If you want the brutal truth, she's not going to survive here, like this. I spoke to Dr Granger about her earlier. A transplant is her only option and she needs one very urgently, before she gets too weak.'

'You want her back in the Royal?'

'Yes. Right away. Tonight, really.'

'Have you ever been there, Ross?'

'Not for some years, no.'

'The place is a nightmare. It's not their fault. There are some good people there. It's the system. The National Health management. The government. I don't know where the blame lies – but it's a living hell to be there. It's easy for you to say she should be in hospital, but just what does that mean? Sticking her in a mixed ward, with confused old people who try to climb into bed with her in the middle of the night? Where you have to fight to find a wheelchair to move her around? Where I'm not supposed to be with her, to comfort her, after eight-thirty at night?'

'Lynn, they don't put children into adult wards.'

'They have done it. When they were overcrowded.'

'I'm sure we can see that it doesn't happen again.'

'I'm so damn scared for her, Ross.'

'She'll get a transplant quickly now.'

'Are you sure? Are you really sure, Ross? Do you know how the system works?'

'Dr Granger will make sure of it.'

She shook her head. 'I'm sure Dr Granger means well, but he doesn't know his way around their bloody system any more than you do. They meet once a week, on Wednesdays, to decide who gets a transplant that week – assuming a matching liver becomes available. Well, it's now Thursday night, so the earliest we'd get a green light would be next Wednesday. Almost a whole week. Is she going to survive another week?'

'She won't survive here,' he said bluntly.

She reached out and gripped his hand, and through a flood of tears she said, 'She has a better chance here, Ross, believe me. She does. Just don't ask. Please just don't sodding ask.'

'What do you mean by that, Lynn?'

She was silent for a moment. Then she said, 'I'll get her back to the Royal the instant you have a liver for her. Until then, she stays here. That's what I mean. OK?'

'I'll do what I can,' he said. 'That's a promise.'

'I know you will. Just so long as you understand, I'm her mother, and I will do what *I* can.'

82

Fat snowflakes were falling as Ian Tilling parked his clapped-out Opel Kadett on an empty stretch of street, just a couple of hundred yards from the front entrance of the Gara de Nord. As usual when he turned off the ignition, the engine rattled on, continuing to turn over, coughing and firing for several seconds before finally quitting.

He climbed out, along with Andreea and Ileana, and slammed the door. He liked Ileana. She was a committed carer, totally dedicated to helping the deprived of Bucharest. She had a pretty face, even with her predatory, aquiline nose, but, almost as if to deliberately deter admirers, she kept her fair hair fiercely combed back into a matronly bun, wore unflattering glasses and dressed in functional rather than feminine clothes.

On more than one occasion when they had worked together, he had thought about how stunning she could look with a makeover. He had also been amused by how persistently the randy Subcomisar Radu Constantinescu had attempted to get her to come for a drink with him, and how adroitly she had rebuffed him on each occasion.

Sometimes there were prostitutes out along the street here, but to his disappointment there were none tonight. This was where they had been hoping to find the girl called Raluca. With Ileana leading, they walked up the steps in the icy night air, and into the cavernous, gloomy interior of Bucharest's mainline railway terminus. Almost immediately, Ian noticed a gaggle of street kids over to their left. A hundred yards further on, beneath the feeble sodium glow of the overhead bulbs, a small group of policemen stood smoking and sharing a joke.

'Those are friends of Raluca, over there,' Ileana said to him quietly, jerking her gloved thumb at the group.

'OK. Let's take them something.'

Followed by the two girls, he walked across the deserted concourse, past the closed METROPOL café, and an old, bearded man, in a woollen hat, ragged clothes and gumboots, swigging a bottle of spirits, who had been there, sitting on the ground with his back against the wall, in this same location, in those same clothes, for as long as he could remember. He sidestepped and dropped a five lei note on to the small group of coins spread out in front of the man and received a cheery wave for his troubles.

In the echoing silence, Tilling heard the clanking of a train's wheels, steadily picking up speed, departing from a nearby platform, and his eyes mechanically flicked up to the departures and arrivals board. The confectionery stall was about to close for the night, but Ian persuaded its surly proprietor to allow him to purchase an armful of chocolate bars, biscuits, crisps and soft drinks, which they then lugged over, in several bulging plastic bags, to the street kids.

He knew a few of them. A tall, thin boy of about nineteen, called Tavian, wearing his blue woollen hat with ear flaps, and military camouflage jacket over a windcheater and several layers beneath. He held a sleeping baby, wrapped up tightly in a blanket. Tavian always smiled – whether it was his nature or because he was permanently smashed on Aurolac, Tilling did not know, but suspected the latter.

'I have some presents for you!' the former English police officer said, in Romanian, holding out the bags.

The group grabbed them, jostling each other to peer inside, then digging into the contents. No one thanked him.

Ileana turned to another girl in the group, a Romany of indeterminate age, dressed in a pink day-glo shell-suit top and shiny green bottoms, with a scarf wound around her neck.

'Stefania,' she said, in Romanian. 'How are you?'

'Not so good,' the girl said, ripping open a packet of crisps. 'The weather's shitty, no? It's a really bad time. Nobody has money to give to beggars. Where are the tourists? Christmas is coming, right? Nobody has money.'

A tall, sullen youth, with a small moustache, wearing an embroidered woollen hat, a black fleece and grimy jeans, and gripping the neck of a plastic carrier, doubtless containing Aurolac, began ranting about how the *turkeys* – their slang for the police – were treating them recently. Then he peered into one of the bags Stefania was holding open and pulled out a chocolate bar.

'They don't leave us alone. They just don't leave us alone.'

'I'm looking for Raluca,' Ileana said. 'Has anyone seen her tonight?'

The group shot each other glances. Although it was clear they knew her, they all shook their heads.

'No,' Stefania said. 'We don't know any Raluca.'

'Come on, she was here with you last week. I spoke to her with you all!' Ileana said.

'What has she done wrong?' another girl asked.

'She's done nothing wrong,' Ileana reassured her. 'We need her help. Some of you street kids are in real danger. We wanted to warn you about something.'

'Warn us about what?' the sullen youth with the moustache said. 'We are always in danger. No one cares about us.'

Ian Tilling asked, 'Have any of you been offered jobs abroad?'

The youth gave a sneering laugh. 'We're still here, aren't we?' He broke off a slab of chocolate and crammed it into his mouth. Chewing, he said, 'You think we'd still be here if we were offered a way to get out?'

'Who is this man?' A strung-out-looking girl at the back of the group pointed at Ian Tilling, suspicion in her voice.

'He's a good friend to us all,' Ileana said.

Andreea pulled the e-fit photographs of the three dead teenagers in Brighton out of one of her anorak pockets.

'Can you all please look at these and see if you recognize any of them?' she asked. 'It is very important.'

The group passed them round, some looking carefully, some indifferently. Stefania studied them for the longest and then, pointing at the face of the dead female, queried, 'Is that Bogdana, possibly?'

Another girl took the photograph and studied it. 'No, I know Bogdana. We sheltered together for a year. That's not her.'

They handed them back to Ileana.

'Does anyone know a boy called Rares?' Ian Tilling asked. He held up the close-up of the tattoo.

Again they all shook their heads.

Then, suddenly, Stefania stared past him. Tilling turned around and saw a girl of about fifteen, with long, dark hair, clipped up, wearing a leather jacket, a leather miniskirt and knee-length shiny black boots walking towards them, looking furious. As she got closer, he saw she had a black eye and a graze on her opposite cheek.

'Raluca!' Ileana said.

'Fucker!' Raluca said angrily, addressing all of them and none of them. 'Do you know what this man wanted me to do in his truck? I won't tell you. I told him to go to hell and he hit me. Then he pushed me out into the street!'

Ileana stepped away from the group, put an arm around Raluca and led her a short distance across the concourse, out of earshot of the others. She examined her eye and the graze for a moment and asked her if she wanted to go to hospital. The girl refused vigorously.

'I need some help, Raluca,' Ileana said.

Raluca shrugged, still brimming with anger.

'What help? What help does anyone give me?'

'Listen to me a minute, please, Raluca,' Ileana implored, ignoring the comment. 'You told me, some weeks ago, that you had heard of a woman who was offering kids jobs abroad, with an apartment? Yes?'

She shrugged again, then conceded that she had.

Ileana showed her the photographs. 'Do you recognize any of these?'

Raluca pointed at one of the boys. 'His face – I've seen him around, but I don't know his name.'

'This is really important, Raluca, believe me. Last week, these Romanian kids were found murdered in England. All their internal organs were taken. You must tell me what you know about this woman who offers the jobs.'

Raluca blanched. 'I don't know her, but – I . . .' Suddenly she looked very frightened. 'You know Simona, and Romeo, her friend?'

'No.'

'I saw Simona, just a couple of days ago. She was really happy. She was telling me about this woman who has offered her a job in England. She is going to go – she had a medical . . .' She stopped abruptly. 'Oh shit. You have a cigarette?'

Ileana gave her a cigarette, took one herself and pulled out her lighter.

Raluca inhaled, then blew the smoke out quickly.

'A medical?'

'This woman told her she needed – you know – to check on her health. To get the travel documents.'

'Where is she?'

'She lives with her guy, Romeo, and a group, under the street, by the heating pipe.'

'Where?'

'I don't know exactly. I know the sector. Only that, she told me.'

'We need to find her,' Ileana said. 'Will you come with us?'

'I need money for my drugs. I don't have time.'

'We'll give you money. As much as you could earn tonight. OK?'

Minutes later they were hurrying towards Ian Tilling's car.

83

The Airbus was on its landing approach, steadily sinking through the clear, but bumpy sky. The seat-belt lights had just pinged on. Grace checked his seat was upright, although he hadn't touched it during the flight. He had been concentrating on the notes a researcher had prepared for him on liver failure, and planning what he wanted to get out of his meeting, later this morning, with the German organ broker.

They were twenty-five minutes later than scheduled, due to air traffic control delays at take-off, which was a sizeable dent in the preciously short time he had here. From his window seat, he peered down. The snowy landscape looked very different from the previous time he had come here, in summer. Then it had been a flat, colourful patchwork quilt of farmland, now it was just a vast expanse of white. There must have been a recent heavy dump, he thought, because even most of the trees were covered.

The ground was looming closer, the buildings getting bigger with every second. He saw small clusters of white houses, their roofs covered in snow, then several thin copses and a small town. More clusters of houses and buildings. The light was so bright he regretted, for a moment, not bringing sunglasses.

It was strange how time changed everything. Not long ago he had come here, to Munich, with real hope that he might find Sandy, finally, after close friends had been sure they had spotted her in a park. But now all those emotions had gone, evaporated. He could honestly say to himself that he no longer had any feelings towards her. He really felt, for the first time, that he was in the final stages of laying all the complexities of his memories of her to rest. The darkness and the light.

Grace heard the clunk of the landing wheels locking beneath him and felt a sudden prick of apprehension. For the first time in so, so long, he really had something to live for. His darling Cleo. He did not think it would be possible to love a human being more than he loved her. She was with him, in his heart, in his soul, in his skin, his bones, his blood, every waking second.

The thought of anything bad happening to her was more than he could bear. And for the first time in as long as he could remember, he felt nervous for his own safety. Nervous of something happening that might prevent them from being together. Just when they had found each other.

Such as this plane crash-landing them all into oblivion.

He'd never been a nervous flier, but today he watched the ground coming steadily closer, thinking of all the things that could go wrong. Overshooting. Undercarriage collapsing. Skidding off. Colliding with another plane. Bird strike. Power failure. He could see the runway now. Distant hangars. Lights. The mysterious markings on the runway and signs at the edge that were like a secret code for pilots. He barely even felt the wheels touching down. In a perfectly judged landing, the plane went seamlessly from flying to taxiing. He heard the roar of the reverse thrust, felt the braking pulling him forwards against his seat belt.

Then, over the intercom system, a hostess with a soft, friendly, guttural accent welcomed them to Franz Josef Strauss International Airport.

*

The rear door of the taxi opened and the woman alighted, her chic dark glasses shielding her eyes from the wintry glare. She paid the driver, giving him a small tip, and, towing her wheeled overnight bag, headed off into the departures hall of the domed terminal building.

An attractive woman in her late-thirties, she was dressed smartly and warmly in a long camel-hair coat over suede boots, a cashmere shawl and leather gloves. After years of dyeing her hair brown and keeping it cropped short, she had recently let it lighten of its own accord, and it was almost back to her natural, fair, not-quite-blonde colour. She had read in a magazine that when a woman is seeking a new man, she will often change her hair. Well, that was right in her case.

She went across to the Lufthansa section and joined the queue for the Economy check-in desks for Miami, a city she had last visited fifteen years ago, in a former life.

The woman behind the counter went through the routine questions with her. Had she packed her own bags? Had her bags been out of her sight? Then she handed her back her passport, her ticket and her frequent-flier card.

'*Ich wünsche Ihnen ein guten Flug*, Frau Lohmann.'

'*Danke.*'

She spoke perfect German now. That had taken a while, because, as everyone had correctly told her, it was a difficult language to learn. Towing her bag, she followed the signs to the gate, knowing from all her many experiences at this airport that it was a long journey.

Riding up the moving staircase, her phone rang. She pulled it out of her handbag and brought it to her ear.

'*Ja, hallo?*'

The voice at the other end was crackly and indistinct. It was her colleague, Hans-Jürgen Waldinger, calling her from his Mini Cooper on a bad line. She could barely hear him. Stepping off the top of the escalator, pulling her bag over the lip and raising her voice, she said again, '*Hallo?*'

Then the line went dead. She walked along a short distance, following the signs for the Departure Gate in zone G, heading towards the first section of the moving walkway that could take her to the hall. Then her phone rang again. She answered.

Hans-Jürgen, barely audible for the crackling, said, 'Sandy? Sandy?'

'*Ja*, Hans!' she said, and stepped on to the walkway.

*

Eight hundred yards away, at the arrivals section of zone G, Roy Grace, clutching his thick briefcase, and approaching from the opposite direction, stepped on to the parallel carriageway of the same moving walkway.

84

To Glenn's relief the sea was calm, or at least about as calm as the English Channel was ever going to get. Even so, the powerboat was still pitching and rolling quite enough in the gentle swell. But so far he felt fine. The breakfast of two boiled eggs and dry toast that Bella had recommended was still safely inside his digestive system rather than becoming part of the boat's colour scheme, and he hadn't yet experienced any attack of the roundabouts that had done for him on his last voyage.

It was a cold but glorious day, with a steely-blue sky and bottle-green sea. A gull circled low overhead, on the scrounge and out of luck. Glenn breathed in the rich smells of salt and varnish, and the occasional waft of exhaust fumes, and watched a jellyfish the size of a tractor tyre drift past, deciding he was very happy not to be one of the team going into the water, despite all their protective clothing. He had never experienced any desire to jump out of an aeroplane, or to explore the bottom of the ocean. He'd figured out, a long time ago, that he was definitely a terra-firma kind of a guy.

The tiny red smudge in the distance grew closer as they powered steadily further out to sea, at a diagonal angle to Brighton's long seafront, on the exact course he and Ray Packham had charted. As they approached closer still, the smudge sharpened into focus and he saw it was in fact a triangle of bobbing pink marker buoys, which the Specialist Search Unit team had placed there yesterday evening.

At the helm, PC Steve Hargrave – Gonzo – throttled back, and their speed dropped from eighteen knots to less than five. Glenn gripped the handrail in front of him, as the sudden loss of motion pushed him forwards. This boat, a thirty-five-foot Sunseeker, was a much more upmarket vessel than the *Scoob-Eee*. It had been chartered in a hurry from a local nightclub owner and was a proper gin palace, with leather chairs and padding all around, teak decking, an enclosed bridge and a luxurious saloon down below, not that any of those on board were using it other than as a storeroom for some of their kit.

Arf, in the SSU team uniform of black baseball cap, with the word POLICE across the front, red windcheater, black trousers and black rubber boots, removed the microphone of the ship-to-shore radio from its cradle and spoke into it.

'Hotel Uniform Oscar Oscar. This is Suspol Suspol on board MV *Our Current Sea*, calling Solent Coastguard.'

He heard a crackled response. 'Solent Coastguard. Solent Coastguard. Channel sixty-seven. Over.'

'This is Suspol,' Arf repeated. 'We have ten souls on board. Our position is thirteen nautical miles south-east of Shoreham Harbour.' He gave the coordinates then announced, 'We are over our dive area and about to commence.'

Again the crackly voice. 'How many divers with you, Suspol, and how many in the water?'

'Nine divers on board. Two going in.'

Gonzo pushed the twin throttle levers into neutral. Tania, standing beside him, made some adjustments on the controls to the right of the Humminbird scanner screen.

Glenn looked at the display on the left of the screen: *98 ft. 09.52 am. 3.2 mph.*

'If you watch now, Glenn, we should just be coming

over,' Tania said, pointing at what looked like a straight, black tarmac road, divided by a white line, running vertically down the centre of the screen. On either side of it was a bluish tinted moonscape.

'There!' she called out excitedly.

In the left-hand lane of the black section he saw clearly a boat-shaped shadow, even darker, about half an inch long.

'You think that's her? The *Scoob-Eee*?' he asked.

'There's one way to find out,' Arf said. 'Coming in with us?'

A flaccid, murky-looking object drifted past. Glenn wasn't immediately sure if it was another jellyfish or a plastic bag.

'Nah, think I'd better stay on deck and keep a lookout for pirates. But thanks all the same.'

Arf pointed at the sea. 'If you change your mind, there's plenty of room down there.'

85

'Someone told me your father used to play tennis for Sussex, E-J,' Guy Batchelor said. 'I'm a bit of a player myself – well – used to be – but not that kind of standard. What's his name?'

'Nigel. He played for the under-sixteens – but he hasn't played seriously for years. He could probably drink for Sussex now. Or, more likely, talk for Sussex.' She grinned.

'Gift of the gab?'

'You could say.'

They were heading west, away from the village of Storrington, with the softly undulating South Downs to their left. She peered at the map on her knees.

'Should be the next right.'

They turned into a narrow country lane, barely wider than the car and bounded by tall hedgerows. After a quarter of a mile, Emma-Jane directed him to turn left, into an even narrower lane. Police cars, Batchelor thought, were going to be the last vehicles on the planet without SatNav – and the ones that needed it the most. He was about to comment on that to E-J when he heard a muffled call-sign on his radio. Although he was driving, he lifted it to his ear, but it was a request for assistance in a different part of the county, not remotely near them.

'Should be coming up on the left,' Emma-Jane said.

He slowed the blue unmarked Mondeo down. Moments later they saw a pair of imposing wrought-iron gates between two pillars topped with stone balls. Written in gold letters on a black plate was the name, THAKEHAM PARK.

They pulled up in front of the gates, under the cyclops gaze of a security camera mounted high up. On the opposite pillar was a yellow sign, with a grinning face, beneath which was written the legend SMILE, YOU ARE ON CCTV.

The young DC climbed out and pressed the button on the speakerphone panel beneath. Moments later, she heard a crackly, broken-English, female voice.

'Hello?'

'Detective Sergeant Batchelor and Detective Constable Boutwood,' she announced. 'We have an appointment with Sir Roger Sirius.'

There was a sharp crackle from the speakerphone, then the gates began to open. She climbed back into the car and they drove through, along a tarmac drive, lined by mature trees on either side, which wound steadily for about half a mile up an incline. Then a huge Jacobean mansion came into view, with a circular driveway in front, in the grassed-in centre of which was a lily pond.

Several cars were parked in front of the house including, Guy recognized, a black Aston Martin Vanquish. To their right, on a large concrete circle in the middle of a mani-cured lawn, sat a dark blue helicopter.

'Seems like there's money in medicine!' he commented.

'If you are in the right area of it,' she retorted.

'Or maybe the *wrong* area,' he corrected her.

Emma-Jane did not even bother trying to count the number of windows. This place must have twenty or thirty bedrooms – maybe more. It was on the scale of a stately home.

'I think we chose the wrong career,' she said.

He drove slowly around the pond and pulled up almost

directly in front of the grand front door. 'Depends what you want out of life, doesn't it? And the moral code by which you choose to live.'

'Yes, I suppose so.'

'Have you ever met Jack Skerritt?'

'A few times,' she said. 'But only briefly.'

Jack Skerritt was the Chief Superintendent of HQ CID – the most senior detective in Sussex. And the most respected.

'I had a drink with him a couple of years ago,' Batchelor said. 'In the bar at Brighton nick, when he was Commander of Brighton and Hove. We were talking about what coppers earned. He told me he was on seventy-three thousand pounds a year, plus a couple of grand more in allowances. *That might sound a lot,* he said, *but it is less than a school headmaster earns – and I'm in charge of the entire city of Brighton and Hove.* He then said something I'll never forget.'

She looked at him inquisitively.

'He said, *In this job, the riches come from within.*'

'That's nice.'

'And true. Being a copper, doing this job, makes me feel like a millionaire, every day of my life. I never wanted to be anything else.'

They climbed out of the car and rang the doorbell.

Moments later the huge oak front door was opened by a slight, unassuming-looking man of about seventy. He had a trim figure, a kindly, bird-like face, with a small, crooked nose and alert, wide blue eyes filled with curiosity. His thinning head of hair was grey, going on white, and tidy, and he was dressed in a beige cardigan over a gingham shirt, with a paisley cravat around his neck, rust-coloured corduroy trousers, which looked like they were used for gardening, and black leather slippers. The only hint from his appearance that he was a rich man was the faint, but distinct, glow of a tan.

'Hello,' he said in a cheery, cut-glass voice that belonged in a 1950s film.

'Sir Roger Sirius?' Batchelor asked.

'That's me.' He held out a slender, hairy hand, with long, immaculately manicured fingers.

The detectives shook hands with him, then Batchelor pulled out his warrant card and held it up. Sirius gave it only the most cursory of glances and stepped aside with a theatrical wave of his hand.

'So, do come in. I'm intrigued to know how I can be of help. Always fascinated by you chaps. Read a lot of crime novels. I quite like *The Bill*. Ever watch it?'

Both officers shook their heads.

'*Morse*. Used to like him. Didn't care too much for that John Hannah in *Rebus*, but thought Stott was a lot better. D'you watch them?'

'Don't get a lot of time, sir,' Batchelor said.

They followed the distinguished transplant surgeon across a grand oak-panelled hall. It was filled with antique furniture, as well as several gleaming suits of armour. On the walls was a mix of antique swords, firearms and oil paintings, some of which were portraits, some landscapes.

Then they entered a magnificent study. The walls in here were panelled in oak, too, and hung with certificates evidencing the surgeon's qualifications. All around were framed photographs of him with numerous famous faces. One was Sirius with the Queen. In another, at a black-tie function, he was with Princess Diana. Others showed him with Sir Richard Branson, Bill Clinton, François Mitterrand

and the footballer George Best. Batchelor peered at that photograph with particular interest – Best, famously, had had a private liver transplant.

The two police detectives sat on a studded red leather sofa, while a raven-haired beauty, whom Sirius introduced as his wife, brought them coffee. Sirius was briefly distracted by his BlackBerry buzzing, and Batchelor and E-J used the opportunity to exchange a brief glance. The surgeon was clearly a complex character. Modest in appearance and manner, but not in ego – nor in his taste in women.

'So, how can I help you?' Sirius asked, after his wife had left the room, settling down into an armchair opposite them, across the oak chest that served as a coffee table.

Guy had already rehearsed this with E-J on the way over. Suddenly he was feeling badly in need of a cigarette but knew, from the fresh smell of the room and the total absence of ashtrays, that he had no chance. He would have to sneak one later, something he had become used to these days.

Watching the surgeon's eyes carefully, he said, 'This is a very beautiful house, Sir Roger. How long have you lived here?'

The surgeon reflected for a moment. 'Twenty-seven years. It was a wreck when I bought it. My first wife never liked it. My daughter loved it here.' His eyes went misty, suddenly. 'It's just a shame that Katie was never able to see it finished.'

'I'm sorry,' E-J said.

The surgeon shrugged. 'A long time ago, now.'

'You've been quoted many times in the press over your views on the UK organ donor system,' Guy Batchelor went on, still watching his face intently.

'Yes,' he agreed, nodding vigorously, instantly animated by the subject. 'Absolutely!'

'We thought that you might be able to help us.'

'I'll do my best.' He leaned towards them and, looking even more bird-like, smiled eagerly.

'Well,' Emma-Jane cut in almost on cue, 'it's true, isn't it, that around 30 per cent of patients in the UK who are waiting for a liver transplant will die before they get one?'

'Where did you get that figure from?' he asked with a frown.

'I'm quoting *you*, Sir Roger. That was what you wrote in an article in the *Lancet* in 1998.'

Frowning again, he said defensively, 'I write a lot of stuff. Can't remember it all. Particularly not at my age! Last I heard, the official figure is 19 per cent – but, as with everything, that depends on your criteria.' He leaned forward and picked up a silver milk jug. 'Either of you take milk?'

'Can't remember it all. Particularly not at my age.' But *you still hold a private helicopter licence, so your memory can't be that crap*, Guy Batchelor thought to himself.

When he had sorted their coffees out, the DC asked, 'Do you remember the article you wrote for *Nature*, criticizing the UK organ donor system, Sir Roger?'

He shrugged. 'As I said, I've written a lot of articles.'

'You've also worked in a lot of places, haven't you, Sir Roger?' she pressed. 'Including Colombia and Romania.'

'Gosh!' he said, with what looked like genuine excitement. 'You chaps have certainly boned up on me!'

Batchelor handed the three e-fit photographs of the dead teenagers across to the surgeon.

'Could you tell us if you've ever seen any of these three people, sir?'

Sirius studied each of them for some moments, while Batchelor watched him, intently. He shook his head and handed them back.

'No, never,' he said.

Batchelor replaced them in the envelope.

'Is it just coincidence that you chose those two countries to work in? The fact is that they are high on the list of known countries involved in human trafficking for organ transplantation.'

Sirius appeared to think carefully before answering. 'You've both clearly done your homework on me, but I wonder – tell me something. Did your research show up that my darling daughter, Katie, died just over ten years ago, at the age of twenty-three, from liver failure?'

Shocked by this revelation, Batchelor turned to E-J. She looked equally taken by surprise.

'No,' he said. 'I'm sorry – sorry to hear that. No, we didn't know that.'

Sirius nodded, looking sad and bleak suddenly.

'No reason why you should. She was one of those 30 per cent, I'm afraid. You see, even I couldn't get around the donor system we have here in this country. Our laws are extremely rigid.'

'We are here, Sir Roger,' Emma-Jane said, 'because we have reason to believe some members of the medical profession are flouting those laws in order to provide organs for people in need.'

'And you think I may be able to help you to name them?'

'That's what we are hoping,' she said.

He gave a wan smile. 'Every few months you read on the Internet about some chap or other who gets drunk in a bar in Moscow and wakes up minus a kidney. These are all urban myths. Every organ supplied for donor surgery in the UK is governed by UK Transplant. No hospital in the UK could obtain an organ and transplant it outside this system. It's a complete impossibility.'

'But not in Romania or Colombia?' Batchelor asked.

'Indeed. Or China, Taiwan or India. There are plenty of places you can go to get a transplant if you have the cash and are willing to take a risk.'

'So,' Batchelor went on, 'you don't believe there is anyone in the UK who is doing such things illegally?'

The surgeon bristled. 'Look, it's not just a question of removing an organ and popping it into a recipient. You'd need a huge team of people – a minimum of three surgeons, two anaesthetists, three scrub nurses, an intensive care team and all kinds of specialist medical support staff. All of them medically trained, with all the ethics that go with the territory. You're looking at around fifteen to twenty people. How would you ever stop that many from talking? It's a nonsense!'

'We understand there might be a clinic in this county doing just this, Sir Roger,' Batchelor pressed.

Sirius shook his head. 'You know what? I wish there was. God knows, we could do with someone bucking the system we have here. But what you are talking about is an impossibility. Besides, why would anyone take the risk of doing this here, when they could go abroad and obtain a transplant legally?'

'If I can ask a delicate question,' Batchelor said, 'with your knowledge, why did you not take your daughter abroad for a transplant?'

'I did,' he said, after some moments. Then, venting sudden, surprising fury, he said, 'It was a fucking filthy hole of a hospital in Bogotá. Our poor darling died of an infection she picked up in there.' He glared at the two officers. 'All right?'

*

Half an hour later, in the car heading back towards Brighton, Emma-Jane Boutwood broke the several minutes of silence between them that had persisted since they left Sir Roger Sirius, as both of them gathered their thoughts.

'I liked him,' she said. 'I felt sorry for him.'

'You did?'

'Yes. He's clearly very bitter about the system. Poor guy. What an irony to be one of the top liver transplant surgeons in the country and then to lose his daughter to liver disease.'

'Tough call,' Batchelor responded.

'Very.'

'But it also gives him a motive.'

'To change the system?'

'Or to buck it.'

'Why do you say that?'

'Because I was watching him,' Batchelor said. 'When he was looking at the e-fit photos, he said he didn't recognize any of them. Right?'

'Yes.'

'He was lying.'

86

To the casual – and occasionally not-so-casual – observer, some men could instantly be pigeonholed. From their combination of a brutal haircut, muscular physique, badly fitting suit and strutting walk, they were unmistakably either coppers or soldiers in civvies. But, despite his close-cropped hair and his very busted nose, Roy Grace cut a suave figure that gave few clues about his occupation.

Dressed in his Crombie coat, navy suit, white shirt and quiet tie, and carrying his bulging briefcase, he could have been a company executive or an IT man on a business trip, or perhaps a Eurocrat, or a doctor or an engineer, heading to a conference. Anyone glancing at him might also have noticed his authoritative expression, the few small frown lines of worry and the slightly blank gaze, as if he was deep in thought, as he strode along the moving walkway.

Roy felt strangely nervous. The trip was straightforward. His old friend Kriminalhauptkommissar Marcel Kullen was collecting him from the airport, and taking him straight to the offices of the organ broker, whom he would see alone. So long as he was careful and didn't screw up, it would be fine. One quick, cunning meeting and then back to England.

Yet his stomach was unaccountably full of butterflies. That same nervous excitement he used to feel when going on a date, and he was at a loss to understand why. Perhaps it was his brain reminding him of his expectations last time he had come to Munich. Or was it just tiredness? He had slept badly for several nights running now. He never really got a decent night's rest during any murder inquiry he was running, and this one, in particular, seemed to have so many moving parts. And, on top of that, he badly wanted to impress the new Chief Constable.

Checking his watch, he quickened his pace, overtaking several people, then found his path blocked by a harassed-looking mother with a pushchair and four small children. The end of this walkway section was coming up, so he waited for a minute or so to reach it, then stepped around the family and hurried on to the next section.

He passed, on a stand to his right, a crimson Audi TT – a later model than Cleo's – with big signs around it in German. He could not read them, but assumed the car was being advertised as a prize. He could do with winning a car, he thought, to replace his wrecked Alfa. For sure, the insurance company bastards were going to come up with a derisory offer that might just about enable him to replace it with a second-hand moped.

Next, he passed a bar, followed by a Relay news stand and bookstore, then an empty departure gate. Faces on the opposite side of the walkway glided past, all ages, half of them talking on mobile phones.

He glanced at a beautiful young redhead, in a fur-trimmed leather coat, looking like a million dollars, who was heading towards him. Saw her big, classy handbag and wheeled suitcase, and wondered if she was a model, or a supermodel, or whatever they were called these days. He'd always had a thing for redheads, but had never actually dated one.

Strange, he thought. Before his relationship with Cleo had begun, he would have looked longingly at that girl, but now he didn't lust after anyone, except for Cleo herself. This redhead was one of the few women he had even glanced at twice in recent months. As the walkway continued moving him forward, he again reflected how lucky he was, just how incredibly lucky, to love this amazing woman.

Four Japanese businessmen, talking intently, swept past in the opposite direction. His nerves were jangling even more. Screaming at him. He could almost feel a crackle of static in the air. Had the flight affected him?

Then two camp men in their twenties, wearing almost matching leather jackets, were heading towards him, holding hands. One had a shaven head, the other, blond spikes. He strode on and they shot past. Then the walkway track ahead of him was blocked by a large gaggle of teenagers, all with rucksacks, who were clearly off on some adventure.

Suddenly, gliding towards him, on the parallel walkway some distance ahead of him, her face blocked by an elderly couple who stood as motionless as statues, he saw a flash of light brown hair that reminded him of Sandy.

It was like a punch in the stomach.

He stood transfixed.

Then his phone pinged with an incoming text. He glanced down at the display for a split second.

*

Hans-Jürgen's call disconnected abruptly again, as if he had gone into a tunnel. Why did the stupid guy always pick the places with the worst signal reception to call her from? It drove her nuts at times. Except, of course, she knew how to control her anger, so that nothing ever did *truly* drive her nuts any more – not like the way stuff used to.

Anger management was all part of the mental rebirth process of the International Association of FreeSpirits. The Scientologists operated the 'Clear', under their universal banner, THE BRIDGE TO TOTAL FREEDOM. The organization she had deserted them for offered similar mental regeneration, but through a less aggressive – and expensive – process.

Sandy was still a novice, but she was pleased, this morning, as she stepped off the end of the first stretch of the moving walkway and crossed the short distance to the next, passing a shoe-shine and a small bar, that the initial flare of temper she had felt at Hans-Jürgen's call had been instantly extinguished, like the flame of a match in the wind.

That was one of the things her new masters were teaching her: to be a FreeSpirit was to be a flame in the wind, but not one that was attached to the wick of a candle or the top of a matchstick. Because if you needed a crutch to survive, when that crutch was gone, so were you. Extinguished.

You needed to learn to burn free. That way you could never be extinguished. Every FreeSpirit sought, one day, to become a free-floating flame in the wind.

She stared at the passing humanity on the opposite walkway. People chained to their BlackBerry emails, their iPhone keypads, their departure times, their financial worries, their guilt. Their stuff. They didn't realize that none of it mattered. They didn't realize that she was one of the few people on this planet who knew how to set them free.

She singled out one of the faces. A truly sad-looking man, tall and bendy, with a bad comb-over, wearing Porsche sunglasses and one of those Mandarin-collared leather jackets that were covered in motoring badges, and were designed to give off the impression that you were something important in the world of motorsport.

I could free you, she thought.

Beyond him was a group of teenagers, with backpacks, noisily teasing each other. Then her phone rang again.

Fumbling to answer it with her gloves on, she dropped it on the floor and instantly knelt down to retrieve it.

*

When Roy Grace looked up again from the display of his phone, the woman had gone.

Did I imagine it? he wondered. An instant ago, he was sure he had seen a woman's hair, the same distinct, fair colour of Sandy's hair, behind the grim-faced oldies heading rapidly towards him.

He glanced down at the display again and pressed the key to open the text message:

> *Yo, old-timer. At sea. Haven't thrown up yet. How u doing?*

He composed a reply, then sent it:

> *Me neither.*

Out of curiosity, he looked behind him. The woman with the same colour hair as Sandy had reappeared, standing behind the elderly couple, receding into the distance.

Again he felt that punch in his stomach. He turned, squeezed past a tall, irritated-looking man in a trench coat, and half walked, half ran a few steps back against the direction of the walkway. Then he wormed his way through a cabin crew group, all in uniform and towing their luggage.

Then he stopped.

Stupid.

Come on, man! Pull yourself together!

A few months ago, he might have continued to run after her, just in case . . .

But today he turned round and began, instead, threading a path back through the cabin crew, saying some of the few words of German he knew. '*Entschuldigung. T'schuldigung. Danke!*'

87

The four of them had been up all night and were cold, wet through and exhausted. On top of that, Raluca was strung out and getting increasingly agitated. She needed money, now, to go to her dealer, she told Ian Tilling.

None of the three Romanians knew what he meant when, venting his frustration, and ignoring Raluca for a moment, Tilling banged the table-top in the smoke-filled café and shouted out, 'This is like looking for a fucking needle in a haystack!'

But they got the drift.

They were in a café, inside a corrugated-iron shack, one of a row that included a butcher's and a mini-mart, adjoining a rubbish-strewn dirt road that was one of the main suburban arteries of Bucharest, running through Sector Four. The snow was doing a good job of tidying the street up by covering the litter.

Tilling munched hungrily on a massive, dry bread roll that had some kind of meat in the centre – he had no idea what it was. It was dead and had the consistency of leather, but it was protein. He was wired from caffeine. Ileana, Andreea and Raluca, all barely awake, were smoking. Their task was almost impossible. In a city of two million people, as many as ten thousand lived outside of society. Thousands, mostly young people, whose common currency was silence and suspicion.

For the past fourteen hours, they had scoured the sector's shanties along the steam pipe network and they'd crawled down so many holes in the road they had lost count. But so far, nothing. No one knew Simona. Or, if they did, they were not saying.

He yawned, his tiredness bringing back memories. He'd forgotten the sheer exhaustion that came, at times, with the territory of being a police officer. The days – and nights – when you had to keep going, running on adrenalin, fuelled by the scent of progress.

It was one of the best feelings in the world.

'Please, Mr Ian, I must go now,' Raluca said.

'How much do you need?' Tilling asked her, pulling out his battered wallet.

Rubbing her thumbs anxiously together, rocking backwards and forwards on her chair and eyeing the wallet intently, as if scared it might disappear if she stopped looking at it, she said, 'One hundred and forty lei.' Then she picked her cigarette from the ashtray and drew hard on it.

Ian was constantly staggered at the amount of money heroin addicts needed for their fixes. This was more than she could earn in a week in a menial job. Little surprise she was a hooker. Apart from stealing or fraud, there wasn't any other way she could earn that kind of money.

Almost beyond hope – but not beyond caring – as he riffled through the banknotes, Tilling called the proprietor over. He was an elderly, bearded man, wearing a grimy apron over brown overalls, who had lived through and survived Ceauşescu, and who seemed to have found a level of contentment with his lot, somewhere behind the resigned sadness of his expression. The former British police officer asked him whether he knew of any street kids living close by.

He knew plenty, he replied, who didn't? Some of them

came in, late afternoon, just before he closed, to scrounge any leftovers, or stale bread he was about to throw away.

'Do you ever see a young girl and a young man together?' Tilling asked. 'He's about sixteen, she's about thirteen, but they probably look older.' Those who lived on the streets aged fast.

There was a faint glimmer in the man's eyes, which they all picked up on.

'The girl is called Simona,' Raluca said. 'And the boy, Romeo.'

'Romeo?' He frowned.

Raluca, animated by the sight of the money, suddenly said, 'You would recognize him. He has a withered left hand, short black hair, big eyes.'

The proprietor's recognition seemed to deepen. 'This girl with him, she has long hair? Long brown hair? Wears a multicoloured tracksuit thing – always the same?'

Raluca nodded.

'They have a dog? Sometimes, they bring the dog in here. I find bones for him.'

'A dog!' Raluca became even more animated. 'A dog! Yes, they have a dog!'

'Some days they come here.'

'Always when you are closing?' Tilling asked.

'Depends.' He shrugged. 'Different times, some days. Other days I don't see them. I prefer customers!' He laughed at his own joke. Then he said, 'Crazy me, I'm forgetting. The girl, she was in here this morning. She asked me for a bone, for a special bone. She said she was going away and she wanted to give a bone to the dog as a goodbye present.'

'Did she say where she was going?' Tilling asked, panic rising inside him.

'Yeah, I think on a cruise around the Caribbean,' he said. Then he smiled again. 'I ask, she didn't tell me. Just, she said, "Away".'

'Do you have any idea where they live?'

He opened his arms in a shrug. 'Close. Somewhere near to here, I think. On the street, under the street, I don't know.'

Tilling looked at his watch. It was just gone midday. Raluca wasn't going to be functioning well soon, without her fix, and he needed her to identify Simona and, equally importantly, to talk to her. Simona and Romeo were more likely to believe a friend than himself. But if he gave Raluca the cash, she might disappear, get her day's supply and then crash out somewhere.

'Raluca, I'll drive you to your dealer. OK? Then we come back and search.'

Raluca looked hesitant. Then she glanced out of the window, at the increasingly bleak snowscape, and nodded.

Tilling paid and they left. The temperature seemed to have dropped further in the brief time they had been inside. You could not survive in this kind of weather on the street. If Simona and Romeo were close by, as the man suggested, they would almost certainly be underground, near a section of the heating pipe.

But there were hundreds of holes in the streets leading down into subterranean dwellings for the homeless. And already, they had only a few hours of daylight left.

88

Somewhere in the centre of every major city he had visited, there was always one street that stood out from the rest. The kind of street where Roy Grace knew, without looking through the windows at the price tags – if indeed the items even had price tags – that he could not afford to shop.

He was entering such a street now.

'Maximilianstrasse,' Marcel Kullen informed him, as they bumped over tramlines, turning into a grand, wide avenue that was lined on both sides with handsome, formal, neo-Gothic buildings. Some had colonnaded fronts, others had marble pillars, and most, at street level, had gleaming shop windows beneath elegant canopies. Grace clocked some of the names: *Prada*, *Todd*, *Gucci*.

Even the German detective's elderly but immaculate grey BMW felt a little out of place here, amid the kerbside parade of chauffeured limousines, Porsches, Ferraris, Bentleys and greenly fashionable little Minis, Fiat Cinquecentos and Smarts, most of them gleaming despite the filthy grey, ankle-deep slush.

Seated on the front passenger seat, Grace clutched the pile of phone records that the Kriminalhauptkommissar, true to his word, had promised him. Although anxious to get stuck into them, he had politely maintained conversation with Kullen during the thirty-minute drive in from the airport.

The tall, good-looking German filled him in on how his wife and kids were doing, and despite Grace's protestations that he was no longer interested in looking for Sandy, Kullen gave him an update on all the efforts made by his bureau at the Landeskriminalamt to find any trace of her – to no avail.

They passed on their right the imposing front of the Four Seasons hotel, then Kullen made a U-turn and pulled over, outside a posh café with an enticing window display of cakes, and a clientele that seemed to consist exclusively of women in long fur coats. Some were seated outside in the colonnade, smoking.

The German detective pointed at a brass doorbell panel on a marble pillar and the door next to it.

'There is the company,' he said. 'Good luck. I will wait for us.'

'You don't need to do that. I can take a cab back to the airport.'

'You were very kind when I was in England. Now I am – how you say – at your service?'

Grace grinned and patted him on the arm.

'Thank you. I appreciate it.'

'And perhaps afterwards, we have time for a little lunch – and I think maybe there will be things we need to talk about.'

'I hope so.'

As he climbed out of the car into the bitterly cold air, a fleck of sleet tickled Grace's cheek. He took his briefcase from the back seat, then walked up to the entrance door and looked at the names on the panel: *Diederichs Buchs GmbH. Lars Schafft Krimi* and then, the third one down, *Transplantation-Zentrale.*

His nerves seemed to have settled since leaving the airport, and he was feeling quite relaxed as he pressed the bell, if a little tired from his early start. Immediately a bright light shone in his face from a small lens above the panel. A female German voice asked his name, then told him to come to the third floor.

Moments later the door release clicked. He pushed it and stepped into a narrow hall, plushly carpeted in red, with a burly security guard behind a desk, who requested Grace to sign his name in a register. He wrote *Roger Taylor* and faked a signature beneath. Then the guard pointed him to the old-fashioned cage lift. He rode it up to the third floor and stepped out into a large, sumptuously appointed reception area, carpeted in white. A number of scented white candles were burning, filling the air with a pleasant aroma of vanilla.

A young woman, chicly dressed with short black hair, sat behind an ornate, antique desk.

'*Guten Morgen*, Herr Taylor,' she said, with a cheery smile. 'Frau Hartmann will see you shortly. Please take a seat. May I get you something to drink?'

'Coffee would be great.'

Grace sat on a hard white sofa. On a glass table in front of him was a stack of the company's brochures. On the walls were framed photographs of happy-looking people. They ranged in age from a small child playing on a swing to an elderly, smiling man in a hospital bed. No captions were needed. They were all clearly satisfied customers of Transplantation-Zentrale.

He picked up one of the brochures and was about to start reading it when a door opened behind the secretary and out stepped a strikingly handsome and confident-looking woman. She was in her early to mid-forties, he guessed, with beautifully groomed, shoulder-length blonde hair, wearing a slinky black trouser suit, shiny black boots and several big rocks on her fingers, including her wedding one.

'Mr Taylor?' she said, in a warm, guttural accent, striding towards him in a cloud of her own perfume, with her hand outstretched. 'Marlene Hartmann.'

He shook it, feeling the bite of her rings cutting into his flesh.

She stood for a moment, staring at him with bright, inquisitive grey eyes, as if appraising him. Then she gave him what appeared to be a smile of approval.

'Yes,' she said. 'It's nice that you came here to see me. Please come to my office.'

Her mixture of considerable physical beauty and sexiness, combined with an element of professional coldness, reminded him of Alison Vosper. This woman definitely had a hard, *don't mess with me* edge to her.

She ushered him through into a room that made him realize, for the first time, just how similar Cleo's and Sandy's taste in furniture was. This could be a room that had been decorated by either of them. It was carpeted in white and the walls also were in the purest white, relieved only by a triptych of white abstract paintings in black frames. There was a curved black lacquered desk, on which sat a computer terminal and some personal artefacts, a few fine plants and, strategically placed around the room, tall, abstract sculptures rose from plinths. In several places, white scented candles were burning here too, the same vanilla, but it was almost drowned out by the pungency of the woman's perfume. He liked it, but it smelled masculine to him.

In front of the desk there were two high-backed upright chairs that looked as if they had come from a museum of modern art, and he sat down, as bidden, in one of them. It was marginally more comfortable than it looked.

Marlene Hartmann sat opposite him, behind her desk,

opened a leather-bound notepad and picked up a black fountain pen.

'So, first would you please tell me, Mr Taylor, how Transplantation-Zentrale may be of assistance to you? And perhaps, first, how it is you have heard of us?'

Being careful not to fall into an elephant trap, Grace said, 'I found you on the Internet.'

From the way she nodded, approvingly, the answer seemed to satisfy her. '*Gut.*'

'The reason I've come to see you is that my nephew – my sister's son – who is eighteen years old, is suffering from liver failure. My sister is afraid that he will not get a transplant in time to save his life.'

He paused as the assistant brought him a cup of coffee and a jug of what he thought was milk but, when he poured, realized was cream.

'You are based where, Mr Taylor?'

'In Brighton, in Sussex.'

'You have a system, I think, in your country that is – how do you say it in English? – a little arborary. No, *arbitrary.*'

'You could say that,' he agreed enthusiastically, doing all he could to bond with this woman and gain her trust.

Then, leaning across her desk towards him, she placed her elbows on the surface, interlocked her finely manicured hands and cradled her chin on them, peering, almost seductively, deep into his eyes.

'Tell me, does your nephew have chronic or acute liver failure?'

Suddenly, to his horror, Grace found himself completely thrown. The bloody researcher had not differentiated between the two for him. *Acute* seemed the obvious answer to him. *Acute* smacked of urgency. *Chronic*, he knew, meant a disease that you lived with for years.

'Acute liver failure,' he replied.

She noted this down. Then she looked up at him. 'So, what time frame do you think your nephew has?'

'A month, maybe,' he replied. 'After that he may not even be strong enough to cope with transplant surgery.'

'He is in which hospital?'

'He has been treated at the Royal South London, but at the moment he's back home.'

'And what is the condition that the boy has?'

'Auto-immune hepatitis,' he said. 'This is now causing severe cirrhosis.'

She marked this down, too, with a grimace, as if to show she understood the severity.

'Can you tell me what service your company is able to provide?'

'Well,' she said, 'we are approaching the Christmas holiday period, so I think we need to move quickly. Normally the transplant and aftercare are effected at a clinic somewhere within comfortable reach of the recipient's home. If budget is a problem, there are certain cheaper alternatives, to have the operation in China, India and one or two other countries, for example.'

'What is the price for a liver transplant in the UK?'

'Do you know what is the blood grouping of your nephew?'

'AB negative,' he said.

Her eyes flickered and the faintest frown appeared on her face. 'Not so common.'

'I know.'

'Our price for a liver is three hundred thousand euros. We need 50 per cent in advance, before we start to look, and 50 per cent on delivery, before the transplant takes place. We guarantee to find a matching liver within one week of receipt of the deposit.'

'Even a rare blood group?'

'Of course,' she said, confidently.

'So, with my nephew living in Brighton, in Sussex, in England, where would the transplant operation take place?'

'Brighton is a nice city,' she said.

'You've been there?'

'Brighton? *Ja*, sure. With my husband, we made a tour of England.'

'So, you have a facility near to Brighton?'

'We have many facilities around the world, Mr Taylor. That you have to trust us on. In some we have the facility for liver and kidney transplants, in some heart and lung, and in some all four. I can give you references who are very satisfied with our service. People who would not be alive today without what we do. But there is no pressure. In your country, a thousand people die each year because they are unable to obtain an organ for the operation which could have saved them. Yet one million, two hundred and fifty thousand people a year die in road accidents around the world. At Transplantation-Zentrale we are merely the facilitator. We are giving comfort to the families of loved ones who have died suddenly and tragically, by creating a use for their organs – in saving the lives of others. In doing this, you see, it gives some kind of purpose to each loved one's death. You understand?'

'Yes. Which do you do in Sussex?'

'Liver and kidneys.' She looked at him quizzically. 'You carry an organ donor card yourself?'

He blushed. 'No.'

'You and most of the world. Yet, if you wake up

tomorrow with kidney failure, Mr Taylor, you will be grateful that someone else did.'

'Good point. Tell me something, is there anyone in the Brighton area who has used your services, who I could talk to?'

'You will understand our client confidentiality.'

'Naturally.'

'I will check our records and, if there is someone in your area, I will contact them and see if they would be willing to talk to you.'

'Thank you. Can you tell me which clinic you would use?'

She looked evasive. 'I'm sorry, but that will depend on theatre availability. We won't make a decision until closer to the time.'

'A private facility or a National Health one?'

'I don't think your National Health would be very cooperative, Mr Taylor.'

'Because this is illegal?'

'If you want to call saving your nephew's life *illegal*, then yes. Correct.' She looked at her watch. 'I have a plane to catch, so I am sorry – because you arrived late, we have to make this meeting short. Perhaps you want to think about what I have said? Take our literature home with you? We never do a hard sell here. Why? Because, simply this. Always there are desperate people – and always there are organs. It is nice to meet you, Mr Taylor. You have my email and my phone number. I am available 24/7.'

*

Marlene Hartmann's limousine was waiting outside and she was anxious to get off to the airport – her schedule was tight. But she sat at her desk until she saw, on the CCTV camera, that Roy Grace had left the building, then she downloaded two of his photographs from the camera to her mobile phone and texted them to Vlad Cosmescu in Brighton, asking him if he could identify this man, urgently.

Mr Roger Taylor, you are a liar, she thought to herself.

After ten years as an international organ broker she knew her market pretty well. She knew the way the system worked in the UK. If you were a patient suffering from *acute* liver failure, you would instantly be put on the liver transplant list and you would be hospitalized. You would not be well enough to be at home.

Roger Taylor, if that was his real name – and she thought not – had fallen at the first hurdle. Who was he? And why had he come to see her? She suspected from the man's demeanour and the kinds of questions he was asking, that she already knew the answer.

Then, as she stood up to leave, her phone rang and her day suddenly got worse.

89

With the calm weather and the wide, empty expanse of the English Channel all around them, diving conditions – regardless of the near-freezing water temperature – were about as good as it got. Compared to a weed-infested lake or a murky canal booby-trapped with discarded shopping trolleys, barbed wire and chunks of jagged metal, today was, in the slang of the Specialist Search Unit, a *Gucci* dive.

But on the two monitors relaying video images from the diver's camera, there was just a grey blur.

Jon Lelliott – better known as WAFI – assisted by Chris Dicks, nicknamed Clyde, had positively identified the wreck as being the *Scoob-Eee*. And he had found a body in the prow cabin that he was bringing to the surface now.

The rest of the team, accompanied by Glenn Branson, who was feeling a little wobbly but a lot better than on his last sea voyage, peered over the deck rail at the increasing mass of bubbles breaking the surface around the yellow, blue and red coils of the air and voice supply line, and the four ropes on which the buoyancy bag had been lowered. Moments later the masked head of WAFI appeared, accompanied seconds later by a body breaking the surface in a maelstrom of bubbles.

'Oh shit!' Gonzo exclaimed.

Branson turned away after one quick look, now struggling to hold down his breakfast.

WAFI pushed the body, which, supported by the air

bags, was floating high in the water, towards the side of the boat.

Then several members of the team, clumsily aided by Glenn Branson, hauled on the ropes, pulling the heavy, waterlogged body up the side of the Sunseeker, over the deck rail.

The marine architect who had designed this craft had in his mind, most likely, that the rear sundeck would be adorned by wealthy playboys and beautiful, topless floozies. He probably never envisaged the sight that now greeted the SSU team and the hapless Detective Sergeant.

'Poor sod,' Arf said.

'Definitely Jim Towers?' Tania Whitlock asked him.

Although in charge of the Specialist Search Unit, the sergeant had been with the team for less than a year and did not know all the local harbour faces as well as some of her team.

He nodded grimly.

'Definitely,' Gonzo confirmed. 'I've been working with him for about five years. That's Jim.'

The man's body was bound, up to his neck, with grey duct tape. His head poked above it, with just a single strip across his mouth. A small crab skittered across the tape, and Arf ducked down, grabbed it and threw it back overboard.

'Fuckers,' he said. 'I hate them.'

Glenn could see why.

The heavily bearded lower part of the dead man's face was intact. But some of the flesh from his cheeks and forehead, and the muscle and sinews beneath, were gone, leaving patches of bare skull. One eye socket had been picked clean. The other contained the remnants of the white of an eye, reduced to the size of a raisin.

'Don't think I'll be ordering the crab and avocado starter for a while,' quipped Glenn, trying to put on a brave face.

'Anyone here fancy being buried at sea?' Juice enquired. There were no takers.

90

Vlad Cosmescu was a worried man. He sat at his desk with his computer in front of him, no longer enjoying the view out across the Brighton seafront. Every half-hour or so he checked the latest online news on the local paper, the *Argus*.

He had been smarting ever since that phone call last week.

You've screwed up.

For years this city had been a great gig for him. Awash with money and girls. Providing him with the cash to keep his handicapped sister in a nice home. And the income to keep him in a lifestyle he could once only have dreamed of.

He did not like to be told he had *screwed up*.

He had always been obsessively careful. Gaining the trust of his employees. Steadily building up his business empire here. The massage parlours. Escort agencies. The lucrative drug deals. And, more recently, the German connection. The organ trade was the best business of all. Every successful transplant put tens of thousands of pounds in his pocket. And from there, straight into his Swiss bank account.

If he had learned one thing about his adopted country, it was that the police were focused on the trafficking of drugs. Everything else took a back seat. Which was OK by him.

Everything had worked just fine. Until Jim Towers.

Maybe the boatman had made a genuine mistake in putting those bodies in a dredge area. But he did not think so. Towers had tried to screw him – whatever his motive. Morality? Blackmail?

Suddenly his phone pinged with an incoming text.

It was from his biggest source of money, Marlene Hartmann, in Munich.

Like himself, to make it harder for the police to monitor her, she acquired a new pay-as-you-go mobile phone each week.

The text said: *Do you know this man?*

Two photographs were attached. He opened them. Moments later, he was reaching for a cigarette.

When he had first set up shop here, he had made it his business to learn the face of every police officer who might be interested in him. He had followed the career path of this particular detective, thanks to the *Argus* newspaper, for several years, watching his rise up the ranks.

He dialled her number. 'Detective Superintendent Roy Grace from Sussex CID,' he informed her.

'He has just been in my office.'

'Maybe he needs an organ?'

'I don't think so,' she said humourlessly. 'But I think you should know I just received a phone call from Sir Roger Sirius. The police went to interview him at his home just now, this morning.'

'What about?'

'I think it was just a fishing trip. But we should put Alternative One into operation right away. Yes?'

'Yes, I think so.'

Fishing trip. The words make him squirm.

'I'm bringing everything forward. Please be on standby,' she ordered.

'I am ready.'

She terminated the call with her usual abruptness.

Cosmescu lit his cigarette and smoked it nervously, thinking hard, going over the list for Alternative One in his mind. He did not like it that the police had been to see the surgeon and the organ broker – and on the same day. Not good at all.

Then he was distracted by a news item that suddenly appeared in front of him.

CHANNEL TRAWL PRODUCES FOURTH BODY, the headline shouted.

He read the first few lines of the story. A police diving team, searching for the missing Shoreham-registered fishing boat, *Scoob-Eee*, recovered a body from its wreckage.

Futu-i! he thought. *Oh shit, oh shit, oh shit.*

91

Lynn sat at her work station, her throat tight with anxiety. The tuna sandwich she had brought in for her lunch lay in front of her, with one small bite taken from it, along with her untouched apple.

She had no appetite. Her stomach was full of butterflies and she was a bag of nerves. Tonight, after work, she had a date. But the butterflies were not the kind she used to have, all excited, before going to meet her boyfriend as a teenager. They were more like dark, trapped, dying moths. Her date was with the odious Reg Okuma.

Or more specifically, so far as she was concerned, it was with his promised £15,000 in cash.

But, from all his innuendo over the phone earlier this morning, he was clearly expecting more than just a quick, happy-hour cocktail.

She closed her eyes for a moment. Caitlin was worsening by the day. Sometimes, it seemed, by the hour. Her mother was sitting with her this morning. Christmas was looming. Marlene Hartmann had guaranteed a liver within one week of receipt of the deposit, and she had that now. But regardless of the organ broker's promises – and all the references which had checked out reassuringly – the reality was that a lot of activities shut down over Christmas, and the wheels of those that did not turned at a slower pace.

Ross Hunter had phoned her earlier today, imploring her to get Caitlin into hospital.

Yeah, to die, right?

One of her colleagues, a lively, friendly young woman called Nicky Mitchell, stopped by and put a sealed envelope on her desk.

'Your secret Santa!' she said.

'OK, right, thanks.'

Lynn stared at the envelope, wondering who it was in the office she would have to buy an anonymous gift for. Normally she would have enjoyed doing that, but now it was just another hassle.

On the big screen on the wall ahead of her the words, CHRISTMAS BONUS! were flashing, surrounded by little Christmas trees and spinning gold coins. The bonus was over £3,000 now. There was a feeling of money everywhere in this office. If she cut half her colleagues open, she was sure cash would pour from their veins instead of blood.

So much damn money. Millions. Tens of millions.

So why the hell was it proving so hard to find that last fifteen thousand for the German broker? Mal, her mother, Sue Shackleton and Luke had all been brilliant. Her bank had been surprisingly sympathetic, but with her overdraft already exceeded, her manager told her he would need to go to head office for approval and he was not confident he would get it. Her only real option was to try for a bigger mortgage, but that was a process which would take many weeks – time she did not have.

Suddenly her mobile phone rang. The number was withheld. She answered surreptitiously, not wanting to get a reprimand for taking a personal call.

It was Marlene Hartmann, her voice terse and a little agitated. 'Mrs Beckett, we have identified a suitable liver for your daughter. We will perform the transplant tomorrow afternoon. Please be ready with Caitlin, with bags packed,

at midday tomorrow. You have the list I sent you of everything you will need to pack for her?'

'Yes,' Lynn said. 'Yes.' But her mouth was so dry with
nerves and excitement, barely any sound came out. 'Can
you – can you tell me – anything about the – the donor?'

'It is coming from a young woman who was in a motor
accident and is now brain dead on life support. I am not
able to tell you more.'

'Thank you,' Lynn said. 'Thank you.'

She hung up, feeling dizzy and sick with excitement –
and fear.

92

It was too cold to search on foot, so they sat in Ian Tilling's Opel, peering through the holes they rubbed in the condensation on the windows as the car slithered along the slushy streets close to the café. It was just after half past four and the light, beneath the grim snow clouds, was fading rapidly.

They had already stopped and investigated several holes in the road, but so far none of them appeared to have been occupied. Backtracking, they once more passed the mini-market, the café, the butcher's, then an Orthodox church covered in scaffolding. Two large dogs, one grey, one black, were busily ripping open a garbage bag.

Raluca, on the back seat, calm now after her fix, suddenly stiffened and leaned forward. Then she shouted excitedly, 'Mr Ian! There, over there, see! Stop the car!'

At first all he could see in the direction she was pointing was a wide strip of wasteland, with several derelict cars, and a cluster of drab, high-rise tenement buildings, with dozens of satellite television dishes littering the outside walls, like an infestation of barnacles.

He pulled over abruptly, bumping through a rut, then sliding to a halt. Behind him an ancient truck gave him a furious blast of its horn and thundered past, missing ripping off the side of the car by a whisker.

Raluca pointed through the windscreen at three figures who had emerged from a jagged hole in a patch of concrete. Because of the light and the covering of snow it was impossible to tell whether it was the edge of the road or the pavement. Close to the hole, Tilling saw a makeshift kennel, fashioned from a section of collapsed fencing. A dog lay inside it, chewing on something, impervious to the weather. A short distance away, its engine running, thick vapour rising from its exhaust pipes, was a large black Mercedes.

One of the trio was a tall, elegant woman, wearing a fur hat, long dark coat and boots. She was gripping the hand of a bewildered-looking brown-haired girl who was dressed in a woollen hat, a blue puffa over a ragged, multicoloured jogging suit and trainers, hopelessly inadequate footwear for this snow. The third person was a boy, in a hooded top and jeans, also wearing trainers, who just stood by the hole, watching them, looking lost.

The woman was guiding the girl towards the car. The girl turned her head forlornly and waved. The boy waved back and called out something. Then the girl turned and waved at the dog, but the dog wasn't looking.

The wind was whipping the snow into a blizzard.

'That's her!' screamed Raluca. 'That's Simona!'

Ian Tilling threw himself out of the car, the snow stinging his face like buckshot. Andreea hurled herself out of the passenger door, followed by the others in the rear.

Another truck thundered past, dangerously fast, and they had to wait. Then, sprinting through the slush, Tilling yelled as hard as he could, 'Stop! Stop!'

The woman and the girl were more than fifty yards ahead and right by the car.

'Stop!' he yelled again. Then, to the boy, 'Stop them!'

Hearing his voice, the woman glanced round, hastily pulled open the rear door of the car, pushed the girl in and threw herself in after her. The Mercedes pulled away before the rear door was even closed.

Tilling continued to sprint after it for another hundred

yards or so, until he fell flat on his face. Clambering to his feet, puffing, he began running back to his Opel, calling out for Raluca, Ileana and Andreea to get back in. Then he stopped by the boy and saw he had a withered hand

'Was that Simona?'

He said nothing.

'Simona? Was that Simona?'

Again the boy said nothing.

'Are you Romeo?'

'Maybe.'

'Listen, Romeo, Simona is in danger. Where is she going?'

'The lady is taking her to England.'

Tilling swore, ran over to his car, climbed in and accelerated, following the direction the Mercedes had taken.

Within a few minutes he realized they had lost it.

But then he had another thought.

93

Already she was missing Romeo and Artur. The sad expression on the dog's face when she had given him that bone. As if he knew, and could sense they were parting forever.

She had promised Artur she would be back one day. Put her arms around his mangy neck and kissed him. But he looked at her as if he did not believe it. As if there were goodbyes and *goodbyes*, and he understood the difference. The dog carried the bone off into his makeshift kennel without looking back at her.

The dog she could live without, she realized. The dog was a survivor and would be fine. But she could not live without Romeo. Her heart was crying out for him. Tears rolled down her cheeks as she pressed Gogu, the small, mangy strip of fake fur that was the only possession she carried with her, to her cheeks.

In the back of the black limousine, with its darkened windows, and the rich smells of leather and the German woman's perfume, she had never felt so alone in her life. The woman talked constantly on her mobile phone, and occasionally looked anxiously out of the rear window into the darkness. They were driving slowly, on a slushy, salted road, in stop–start traffic. And every few minutes she stared at the neck of the man who was driving.

The man with his hair cropped to a light fuzz. With the tattoo of a snake, its tongue forked as if striking, rising out of the right side of his white shirt collar, which she had seen a couple of times when the woman had put on the interior lights, to make notes in her diary.

She shivered. Scared of him despite the fact the woman was here with her, looking after her.

He was the driver for the man who had saved her from the police at the Gara de Nord and then raped her, who had tried to have sex with her as he drove her back home. The man she had bitten and hurt.

In the mirror she caught his eyes, repeatedly glaring at her. Giving her a signal that he was not yet finished with her. That he had not forgotten. She tried to stop looking at the mirror, but every time she weakened, his eyes were there, fixed on her.

She wished she had hurt him more. Bitten his damn thing right off.

Finally, the woman ended her call.

'When will Romeo come?' she asked forlornly.

'Soon, *meine Liebe*!' The woman patted her cheek with her leather gloved hand. 'You will be together again very soon. You will like England. You will be happy there. You are excited?'

'No.'

'You should be. A new life!'

Quietly, to herself, Marlene Hartmann was thinking, *In fact, three new lives.*

It was a shame to waste the heart and lungs, but she had no one matching in the UK on her books, and she did not want to take the risk of delaying, in the hope of a suitable recipient turning up. Not with the police poking around, and those organs would not survive long enough out of the body to be transported overseas. As with a liver transplant, it was best, if at all possible, to have the donor and recipient close to each other, for the least possible

PETER JAMES

delay between death and transplantation. The girl was too small for them to be able to do a split liver, but one on its own was quite profitable enough.

Kidneys had a reasonable shelf life, up to twenty-four hours if properly kept. She had buyers for Simona's kidneys lined up and waiting, one in Germany, one in Spain. In other countries she would have sold the girl's skin, eyes and bones, but the margin was low on these and it was not worth the trouble to export them from England. She would clear 100,000 euros' profit on the two kidneys, and 130,000 net after costs on the liver.

She was very happy.

94

Come on, come on, come on! Damn traffic! Damn fucking traffic!

Ian Tilling drove on his horn, but it made no difference. During the evening rush hour the whole centre of Bucharest and its suburbs turned into one joined-at-the-bumper grid-lock. Tonight the snow had made things even worse, extending the rush hour well into the night.

The only consolation was that the car with Simona in it would be stuck in this too.

Damn you, you lazy bastard, Subcomisar Radu Constantinescu, Tilling thought, yet again wiping condensation off the inside of the windscreen, staring at the red blur of tail lights from a stretch Hummer limousine in front of him. For forty minutes he had been repeatedly trying the mobile and direct office lines of the one powerful Bucharest police officer that he knew. Both phones rang on interminably, neither answered nor going to voicemail. Had the man already left the office for the day? Was he in a meeting? Taking the world's longest shit?

Almost certainly, he reckoned, the German woman would be taking Simona to one of Bucharest's two international airports. The more likely, which he had tried first, was the larger one, Otopeni. But they were not there. Now he was battling towards the second airport. He desperately needed to get hold of the Subcomisar, and have them picked up, or at least prevented from leaving the country – if the officer would even agree.

The traffic inched forward and halted again, and he braked sharply, almost rear-ending the Hummer. He was running low on petrol and the temperature gauge was rising to a dangerously high level. He dialled Constantinescu's number again and, to his surprise and relief, this time it answered on the first ring. He heard the police officer's gravelly voice.

'Yes?'

'It's Ian Tilling. How are you?'

'Mr Ian Tilling, my friend, Member of the British Empire for services to the homeless of Romania! How can I be of help?'

'I need a very urgent favour.'

Tilling heard a sharp sucking sound and realized the man was probably lighting a new cigarette from the stub of the previous one. He explained the situation as quickly and succinctly as he could.

'You have the German woman's name?'

'The English police told me Marlene Hartmann.'

'I don't know this name.' He suddenly broke into a racking cough. When he had finished, he asked, 'And the name of the girl?'

'Simona Irimia. I believe she may be part of the same group as three kids you were going to run checks on for me, do you remember? I was hoping you might be able to identify her for me.'

'Ah.'

To his dismay, Tilling heard a drawer sliding open. The drawer he had seen the police officer open and shut on his last visit to his office. The drawer into which the Subcomisar had shoved the three e-fits and sets of fingerprints Tilling had asked him to circulate. He had clearly forgotten about them, like most other stuff that was low priority for him.

'Marlene Hartmann, you spell this for me, Mr Important Man?'

Tilling patiently spelled it. Then, assisted by Raluca, gave him a detailed description of Simona.

'I phone the airport right away,' Constantinescu assured him. 'These two, together, should not be hard to find, either at the ticket desk or passport control. I will ask the airport police to arrest the woman on suspicion of human trafficking, yes? You are on your way there?'

'I am.'

'I phone you back with the name of the police officer to contact when you get there, OK?'

'Thank you, Radu. I really appreciate this.'

'We have drink soon, to celebrate your *gong* – yes?'

'We'll have several!' Tilling replied.

*

As the Mercedes headed further away from the city, the traffic thinned out. Marlene Hartmann turned once again to look out of the rear window. To her relief, the headlights of a vehicle that had been behind them for the past forty minutes were fading into the snowy distance.

Simona rested her face against the cold glass of the window, hugging Gogu to her cheek, watching through the snow as the buildings slowly gave way to a vast, dark, empty, translucent landscape.

Marlene Hartmann settled back in her seat, opened her laptop and began to check through her emails. They had a long drive through the night ahead of them.

95

Roy Grace made it back from Munich just in time for the 6.30 p.m. briefing.

He entered the room hurriedly, reading the agenda as he walked, and trying not to spill his mug of coffee.

'Successful trip, Roy?' Norman Potting said. 'Sorted the Krauts out? Got them to understand who won the war?'

'Thank you, Norman,' he said, taking his seat. 'I think they know that these days.'

Potting raised a finger in the air. 'They're devious buggers. Like the Nips. Look at our car industry! Every other car is German!'

'NORMAN, thank you!' Grace raised his voice, feeling tired and tetchy after his long day, which was far from over, and trying to finish reading the agenda before everyone had settled down.

Potting shrugged.

Grace read on in silence as more people shuffled in, then he started.

'Right, this is our sixteenth briefing of Operation Neptune. We have another body, which may or may not be linked to this operation.' He looked at Glenn. 'Would our reluctant fisherman like to talk us through it?'

Branson smiled grimly. 'Seems like we found poor old Jim Towers. Because he's bound up head to foot, it's impossible to see if he has had surgery, so we'll have to wait for the PM. There's no one available tonight, it's being done in the morning.'

'Has he been formally identified?' Lizzie Mantle said.

'From a gold bracelet and his watch,' Branson replied. 'We decided not to let his wife have a look at him. He's not a pretty sight. Remember that face, underwater, in *Jaws*? The one that popped through the hole in the hull, with its eyeball hanging out, and scared the shit out of Richard Dreyfuss? He looks like that.'

'Too much information, Glenn!' Bella Moy said in disgust, changing her mind about popping a Malteser into her mouth.

'What do we know, so far?' Grace asked.

'The boat was scuttled – it wasn't in a collision.'

'Any possibility it could have been suicide?'

'Difficult to scuttle your own boat when you're trussed up like a mummy in gaffer tape, chief. Unless he had a secret life as an escapologist.'

There was a titter of laugher.

Grace smiled too, then said, 'For the immediate time being, the investigations will be done by this team. DI Mantle will head a dedicated group investigating this, and will decide whether a separate murder inquiry needs to be set up – to some extent dependent on what the post-mortem tells us.'

He looked at her.

'Yes,' she replied. 'I'd want you to be part of this team, Glenn, as you've already met Towers's wife – widow.'

'Sure.'

'We need to handle the press carefully on this one,' Grace said. 'Again, let's wait and see what we learn from the post-mortem.'

'I agree,' DI Mantle said.

Branson said, 'I'm increasingly unhappy about Vlad Cosmescu. The DNA tests on the cigarette butts prove he was at Shoreham Harbour. Then the outboard—'

'It's *evidence* that he was there, Glenn,' Roy Grace corrected him. 'But not *absolute proof*. Someone else could have dropped them. You – everyone –' he paused to look around his team – 'we all need to be aware that if you say that something *confirms* or *proves* something, there is a big danger that in court you could be picked to pieces by a smart brief, who'll accuse you of misdirecting the jury. The word to use is *evidence*, OK? Never say *proved* or *proof*. It's the fast-track way to lose a case.'

Almost everyone nodded.

'So what else do you have on him, Glenn?'

'We know he's a Person of Interest to Europol and Interpol, in several inquiries they have running into human trafficking and money laundering.'

'But no charges, and no convictions against him, on record?'

'No, Roy.'

'The Channel's not turning out to be a very good hiding place, is it?' Bella Moy commented. 'If you want to hide a body or an engine, you'd do better to plonk it in the middle of Churchill Square. At least someone might nick it for you!'

'I'd like to pull him in for questioning, get a search warrant, go through his residence, get his phone details,' Branson went on.

'Because of a couple of dog-ends at Shoreham Harbour and an abandoned outboard motor?' Grace quizzed.

'Because he was *watching* the *Scoob-Eee* through binoculars. Why was he doing that? It's an old fishing boat, what was so special about it – before the dead teenagers were hauled up on to it? I have a hunch about this man, Roy.'

'Is the boat salvageable?' Grace asked.

'Yes, but it would be a big operation, and extremely

expensive. I went through it with Tania Whitlock. I think you'd have a hard time selling the cost to ACC Vosper.'

'If your hunches are right, you're going to need evidence he was on that boat – someone who saw him, or something forensic, or something belonging to him.'

Branson looked pensive. 'Perhaps they could dive on it again and do a thorough search.'

Grace thought for some moments. 'Do you have any ideas on what his involvement might be, Glenn?'

'No, chief, but I'm certain he has a connection. And I think we should move on him quickly.'

'OK,' Grace agreed. 'Get a search warrant, but you'll need to beef up the application a bit. Then see if he'll talk voluntarily – you might get more out of him that way than if you arrest him and he gets silenced by a brief. Take someone interview-trained. Bella.' He looked at DI Mantle. 'OK with you, Lizzie?'

The Detective Inspector nodded.

Grace glanced at his watch, doing a quick calculation. By the time Branson had filled in the search warrant paperwork, then found a magistrate to sign the warrant, it would be at least ten, if they were lucky. Thinking back again to his own sighting of Cosmescu's Mercedes sports car, he said, 'The man's a night owl – you might have a long wait for him.'

'Then we'll just have to make ourselves comfy in his pad in the meantime!' Branson said.

'God help his CD collection,' Grace replied.

Branson had the decency to look embarrassed.

'When you do catch up with him,' Grace said, 'I think you'll find him hard work. He's been around in the vice world of this city for a decade without being nicked once. You don't do that unless you know how to play the game.'

Then he glanced back at the agenda.

'Yesterday we established a Mrs Lynn Beckett, whose phone number I was given by our German police contacts, has a daughter suffering from liver failure.' He tapped the photocopied wodge. 'These are phone call logs from the German company I went to see today, Transplantation-Zentrale. I'm not meant to have them, officially, so we'll have to handle them a bit delicately, but that won't hinder us.'

He sipped his coffee, then went on.

'I've found nine outgoing calls to Lynn Beckett's landline number, and four incoming calls received from it, in the past three days, and a further two outgoing calls to her mobile phone.'

'Do you have any recordings of the calls, Roy?' Guy Batchelor asked.

'Unfortunately not. They have similar privacy laws to us. But they're working on authorization, which should come through any time now.'

'Probably different in Adolf's day,' mumbled Potting.

Grace shot him daggers, then said, 'I met with a woman called Marlene Hartmann, head of the German organ broking firm, Transplantation-Zentrale, in Munich this morning. They're doing business in England right under our noses! We need to find very urgently where they are operating here. This flurry of activity with Mrs Beckett indicates something's brewing and—'

Potting's mobile phone suddenly rang, playing the *Indiana Jones* theme tune. Blushing, he glanced at the display, then stood up, muttered, 'This might be relevant – Romania!' and stepped out of the room.

'And we probably have very little time to find where they are doing this,' Grace continued. 'I've been making some calls around the medical world, trying to understand exactly what would be needed for an organ transplant facility, whether temporary or permanent.'

'A large team, Roy,' Guy Batchelor said. 'When we were interviewing Sir Roger Sirius, he said –' he paused to flip a couple of pages back through his notebook – 'you'd need a minimum of three surgeons, two anaesthetists, a bare minimum of three scrub nurses, and a 24/7 intensive care team including several trained in transplant aftercare.'

'Yes, in total fifteen to twenty people,' Grace said. 'And they need a minimum of one fully equipped operating theatre and a full intensive care unit.'

'So we have to be looking at a hospital,' Nick Nicholl said. 'Either a National Health or a private one.'

'We can rule out the National Health. It would be virtually impossible to get an illegal organ like a liver through the system,' said DI Mantle.

'How sure are we of that?' Glenn Branson asked.

'Very sure,' Lizzie Mantle said. 'The system is pretty watertight. To slip an organ through the system, an awful lot of people would have to know about it. If it was just one person, that might be different.'

Branson nodded pensively.

'I think we're looking at a private hospital or clinic,' Grace said. 'There must be drugs specific to human organ transplants – we need to identify what those are, who makes them and supplies them, and then take a look at the private hospitals and clinics they're sold to.'

'That's going to take time, Roy,' DI Mantle said.

'There can't be that many drugs, or suppliers of them, and not that many end users,' Grace said. He turned to the researcher, Jacqui Phillips. 'Can you make a start on that right away? I'll get you some more helpers, if you need it.'

Norman Potting came back into the room. 'Apologies,' he said. 'That was a colleague of my contact in Bucharest, Ian Tilling.'

Grace signalled for him to continue.

'He is attempting to tail a young Romanian woman – a teenager called Simona Irimia – who, he believes, is in the process of being trafficked, imminently, possibly tonight or tomorrow, to the UK. His colleague has emailed me a set of police photographs of the person he believes to be her – taken when she was arrested for a shoplifting offence two years ago – when she gave her age as twelve. I'm just printing them out now. Can you give me a couple of minutes?'

'Go ahead.'

Potting went out of the room again.

'If DS Batchelor and DC Boutwood are right in their suspicions of Sir Roger Sirius, we should consider surveillance on him. If we follow him he might lead us to the hospital or clinic,' DI Mantle said.

Grace nodded. 'Yes, excellent point. Do we know what manpower the DIU have available?'

'They have a major op on,' Mantle replied. 'So it might be tricky.'

The Divisional Intelligence Unit was the covert surveillance arm of the CID. They focused mainly on drugs, but increasingly their work involved human trafficking as well.

Potting returned after a few minutes and distributed several copies of the Romanian police photographs of the front, right and left profiles of Simona around the inquiry team.

'According to Ian Tilling, this girl was collected earlier today from her home by a German woman who was taking her to start a new life in England. Some life, I'd say. *Someone else's* new life, from what it sounds.'

'Pretty girl,' commented Lizzie Mantle.

'She'll look less pretty when she's a canoe,' said Potting.

Canoe was crude police jargon for a body during a post-mortem after all the internal organs had been removed.

From an envelope, Grace pulled out several photographs of Marlene Hartmann, taken with a long lens, and passed them around.

'These are also from my LKA friends in Munich. Do you think this might be the woman, Norman?'

Potting peered at them intently. 'She's a looker, Roy!' he said. 'Can see why you went to Munich!'

Ignoring the comment, Grace said tersely, 'Christmas is coming up fast. In my experience, people tend to want to get business concluded well in advance of the Christmas break. If this girl is coming in tonight, or tomorrow, to be killed for her organs, then I think we can assume that will happen fairly quickly after she gets here. We need more information on this Lynn Beckett woman. We've enough, from what Norman's given us, to get a phone tap sanctioned, in my view.'

The criterion for obtaining a phone tap order was evidence that a human life was in immediate danger. Grace was confident he could demonstrate that.

'We need a signature from the ACPO and either the Home Secretary or a Secretary of State,' DI Mantle said.

The duty Acting Chief Police Officer rotated between the Chief Constable, the Deputy Chief Constable and the two Assistant Chief Constables.

'It's Alison Vosper this week,' Grace said. 'Won't be a problem. She's up to speed on everything.'

'How fast can you get a Secretary of State to move?' Bella Moy asked.

'The system's speeded up a lot recently. London will take the instruction on a phone call now.' He glanced at his watch. 'We should have consent and a tap on her lines live before midnight.'

'This woman and the young girl might already be here now, sir,' Guy Batchelor said.

'Yes, she might. But I think we should still keep a lookout at ports of entry. Gatwick's the most likely, but we need to cover Heathrow too – make sure that's on our radar – and the Channel Tunnel and the ferry ports. I'll call Bill Warner at Gatwick, get him to watch all incoming flights from Bucharest and other points of departure they might use.' He was silent for a moment. 'I'm afraid we've got a long night ahead of us. I don't want another body turning up dead tomorrow.'

96

Normally, Lynn disliked the winter months, because that meant leaving the office in the dark. But tonight, with Reg Okuma parked just down the street, she was glad it was dark, even though the car was clearly illuminated by the street lighting. She could hear the music pounding out of its boom-box speakers when she was still fifty yards away from it, along with the burble from its drainpipe-size exhausts.

It was an old, 3-Series BMW, in what appeared to be a shade of dark brown the colour of dung, but at least it had blackened windows. The engine was running, presumably, she thought, to provide the power for the amplifier.

The door swung open for her and she hesitated for a moment, wondering if she was making a terrible mistake. But she was desperate for the cash he had promised to bring. Glancing around to check no one from work had seen her, she slipped into the front passenger seat and hastily pulled the door shut.

The interior of the car was even more horrible than its exterior. The bass of the speakers, pounding out some abysmal rap song, physically shook her brain. A pair of furry dice, hanging from the interior mirror, were shaking too. There was a string of blue iridescent lights across the top of the dash that she thought for a moment might be an attempt at Christmas decorations, but which she then realized was there because Reg Okuma thought it was cool.

And the dense reek of the man's cologne was even more overpowering than the music.

The pleasant surprise was the car's occupant.

Lynn always tried to form mental images of her clients, and the one she'd had of Reg Okuma, which was a cross between Robert Mugabe and Hannibal Lecter, was a long way off the mark now that, in the glow of the street lights and the blue iridescents, she could see him clearly for the first time.

In his late thirties, she estimated, he was actually good-looking, with an air of strength and confidence about him that reminded her of the actor Denzel Washington. Lean and wiry, with a buzz-cut dome, he was fashionably dressed in a black jacket over a black T-shirt. His fingers were adorned with too many rings, a loose, chunky, gold-link bracelet hung on one wrist and the other sported a watch the size of a sundial.

'Lynn!' he said, with a big smile, attempting clumsily to kiss her.

She pulled away, equally clumsily.

'All day I have been hard, thinking about you. Are you juicy, thinking about me?'

'Did you bring the money?' she asked, glancing out of the window, terrified one of her colleagues might walk past and spot her.

'It's so vulgar to talk about money on a romantic date, don't you think, my beautiful?'

'Let's drive off,' she said.

'Do you like my car? It is the 325 i.' He emphasized the *i*. 'It is the fuel-injection version. It is very fast. It's not a Ferrari, right? Not yet. But that's going to happen.'

'I'm happy for you,' she said. 'Shall we go?'

'I need to look at you first,' he said, turning and staring at her. 'Oh, you are even more beautiful in the flesh than in my dreams!'

Then, mercifully, he moved the gear lever and the car shot forward.

She looked behind her and saw a canvas bank bag, grabbed it and put it on her lap. Moments later she felt his strong, bony hand on her thigh.

'We are going to have such beautiful sex tonight, my pretty one!' he said.

They stopped behind a long queue of cars at the New England Hill lights. She peered into the bag and saw bundles of £50 notes, held by elastic bands. A lot of them.

'It's all there,' he said. 'Reg Okuma is a man of his word.'

'Not from my past experience,' she said, emboldened by the fact there were cars in front of them and behind them. She took out one bundle, which she counted quickly: £1,000.

His hand moved further up her thigh.

Ignoring it as they crept slowly forward, she counted the bundles. Fifteen.

Then suddenly he was pressing right up between her legs. She clenched her thighs and pushed his hand away, firmly. There was no way she was going to sleep with Okuma. Not for £15,000. Not for anything. She just wanted to take the money and get out of here. But even in her desperate state, she knew it was not that simple.

'We are going to a bar,' he said, 'my sweet Lynn. Then I have booked a romantic table. We will have a candlelit dinner, and then we will make the most beautiful love.'

His fingers pressed harder inside her.

The lights changed to green and they crossed, turning left, up the hill. She gripped his hand, removed it and placed it on his own thigh.

'You make me feel so sexy, Lynn.'

*

Twenty minutes later they were seated on the outside terrace of the Karma bar, on the boardwalk of Brighton Marina. Despite the fierce glow of the gas heater above them, she was freezing. Reg Okuma puffed on a huge cigar and she sat, huddled in her coat, sipping a whisky sour, which he had insisted she would like – and actually she did. She would have liked it a lot more, though, if they had been inside.

A couple of other tables were also occupied by smokers, otherwise the roped-off terrace was deserted. Below them, in the watery darkness of the Marina basin, yacht rigging clacked and clanked in the biting wind.

'So, my beauty,' he said, lifting his glass to his lips, 'tell me more about you.'

'First tell me how you know that my daughter is ill,' she said frostily, keeping up her guard.

He puffed on his cigar and she caught a whiff of the rich, dense smoke. She liked the smell which reminded her of her father at Christmas, when she was a child.

'Beautiful Lynn,' he said, in a rich, chiding voice. 'Brighton and Hove may be a city, but you know, in reality, it is just a small town. I was dating a teacher at your daughter's school. One night I was picking her up, and I saw you. I thought you were the most beautiful woman I had ever seen. I asked her who you were. She told me about you. That made me desire you even more. You are such a caring person. There are not enough caring people in the world.'

97

Everyone drove on the left in Cyprus. Which made the country a ready marketplace for fencing stolen British cars. Of course, there were other countries as well, but Cyprus was the most lax at checking up on them. Provided you did a good job of filing off the numbers from the chassis and engine block, and replacing them and the documentation with good forgeries, you weren't going to have a problem. Vlad Cosmescu had long known, from some of his acquaintances in this city, that if you wanted a car to disappear without trace, the most efficient method was to send it to Cyprus.

He was not a sentimental man, but watching his beloved black SL 55 AMG Mercedes being driven into a container, under the glare of the arc lights on the busy quay of Newhaven Harbour, gave him a twinge of regret. He took a last drag on his cigarette, then tossed it on the ground. A few yards from where he stood, a crane hoisted another container up in the air and swung it towards the deck of a ship. A horn beeped as a driver wove a fork-lift truck through the chaos of crates, containers, people and vehicles.

England had served him well and he'd had a good run in Brighton. But to survive in life, just like in gambling, you had to discipline yourself to quit while you were ahead. With the discovery of the wreck of the *Scoob-Eee* and the recovery of Jim Towers's body, at the moment he was ahead by only a very small margin.

Just one more day and then he would be out of here. One last job to take care of. Tomorrow night he would be on a plane to Bucharest. He had a nice pile of cash tucked away. Lots of opportunities open to him. Maybe he would stay in Europe, but there were several other places that took his fancy: Brazil, in particular, where everyone said the girls were beautiful, and many of them were interested in working in the sex trade abroad. Somewhere warm definitely appealed. Somewhere warm with beautiful girls and nice casinos.

The English had an expression for it. How did it go? Something like *The world is your oyster*.

But maybe marine connotations were not entirely appropriate.

98

Later they walked back along the wind-blown, almost deserted boardwalk, towards the multistorey car park. Fuelled by three whisky sours and half a bottle of wine Lynn was feeling mellow. And sad for Okuma. He had never known his father. His mother had died of a drugs overdose when he was seven and he'd then been brought up by foster parents who had sexually abused him. After them had followed a series of care homes. At fourteen, he'd joined a Brighton street gang, the only people, he said, who had given him any sense of self-worth.

For a while he'd made money as a runner for a local drug dealer, then, after a spell in an approved school, had got himself into the Business Studies course at Brighton Poly. He'd married, fathered three children, but, a few months after graduating, his wife had left him for a wealthy property dealer. Since then he had decided that the only way to achieve any kind of status was to make a large amount of money. That's what he was trying to do now. But so far his life had been a series of false starts.

A few years ago he had concluded that it was hard to amass big money, quickly, through legitimate business enterprises, so he had taken to scamming the system.

'All business is a game, Lynn,' he said. 'Right?'

'Well – I wouldn't go that far.'

'No? I understand how collection agencies work. You make your big money on what you can get back from debts that are already written off. That's not a game?'

'Bad debts ruin companies, Reg. They put people out of work.'

'But without entrepreneurs like me, the businesses would never start in the first place.'

She smiled at his logic.

'But, hey, we should not be talking shop on a romantic date, Lynn.'

Despite her haze of alcohol, she remained totally focused on her mission. Tomorrow morning she had to transfer the balance of the funds to the account of Trans-plantation-Zentrale. Whatever that took.

Okuma had his arm around her shoulders. Suddenly he stopped and tried to kiss her.

'Not here!' she whispered.

'We go back to your place?'

'I have a better idea.'

She dropped her hand down, against his zipper, and gave his erection a provocative squeeze.

*

Back in his car, in the darkness of the half-empty car park, she pulled his zipper right down and slipped her fingers inside.

Within a few minutes, it was all over. With a tissue, she dabbed a few places where he had squirted on her blue overcoat.

He drove her home, meek as a lamb.

'I'll see you again soon, my beautiful one!' he said, sliding his arm around her shoulders.

She popped the door handle, clutching the canvas bag tightly. 'That was a nice evening. Thank you for dinner.'

'I think I love you,' he said.

From the relative safety of the pavement, she blew him

a kiss. Then, feeling sick inside, and more than a little drunk, she hurried into the house, her brain a maelstrom of confused emotions. She went into the downstairs toilet, shut the door and knelt with her face over the bowl, thinking she was going to throw up. But after some moments she felt calmer.

Then she ran upstairs and into Caitlin's room. It was sweltering hot and smelled of perspiration. Her daughter was asleep, iPod headset plugged into her ears, the television off. Was it her imagination, or the light, she wondered? Caitlin's colour seemed to have gone an even deeper yellow since this morning.

Leaving the door ajar, she went into her own bedroom, took off her overcoat, placed it inside a plastic dry-cleaning bag and, feeling sick again, squashed it into the bottom of her wardrobe.

Downstairs, in the sitting room, Luke was sound asleep, with a repeat episode of *Dragons' Den* that she had seen playing on the television. Grabbing the remote, she turned the sound right down, worried that it would disturb Caitlin, then went into the kitchen, poured herself a large glass of chardonnay and downed it in one go. Then she went back into the sitting room.

Luke woke with a start as she came in. 'Hi! How was your evening?'

Lynn, the wine rushing straight to her head, felt her face reddening. It was a good question. *How was her evening?*

She felt dirty. Guilty. Dishonest. But at this moment, she did not care. Looking down at the canvas bag full of banknotes, she said quietly, 'It was fine. Mission accomplished. How's Caitlin?'

'Weak,' he said. 'Not good. Do you think—?'

She nodded.

'Tomorrow?'

'God, I hope so.'

For the first time ever, she hugged him. Held him tight. Held him like the lifeline he now truly was.

And felt the drop of his tears on her face.

Then they both heard a terrible scream from upstairs.

99

Shortly after midnight the doorbell rang. Lynn sprinted down the stairs and opened the door. Dr Hunter stood on the front step, dressed in a suit, shirt, tie and overcoat, holding his black bag. He looked tired.

For an instant, she wondered incongruously about his suit – had he put it on just for this visit, or had he been on call all night?

'Ross, thank God you're here. Thank you. Thank you for coming.'

She had to struggle to resist hugging him in gratitude.

'Sorry it took me a while. I was dealing with another emergency when you rang.'

'No,' she said. 'No. Thank you for coming. I really appreciate it.'

'How is she?'

'Terrible. She keeps screaming out with stomach pains and crying.'

He strode up the stairs and she followed him into Caitlin's bedroom. Luke stood there, looking bewildered, holding Caitlin's hand. In the dim glow of the bedside light, perspiration was pouring down her face. There were scratch marks all over her neck and arms.

'Hello, Caitlin,' the doctor said. 'Tell me how you are feeling?'

'Actually, you know what?' She spoke in a breathless rasp. 'Not great actually.'

'Do you have an acute pain?'

'I'm in so much pain. Please – please stop the itching.'

'Where exactly is the pain, Caitlin?' he asked.

'I want to go home,' she gasped.

Ross Hunter frowned. 'Home?' Then he said gently, 'You are home.'

She shook her head. 'You don't understand.'

'It's OK,' Lynn intervened. 'She's talking about where we first lived. Winter Cottage.'

'Why do you want to go there, Caitlin?' he asked.

She stared at him, opened her mouth as if to answer, then appeared to have difficulty in breathing for some moments.

'I think I'm dying,' she gasped, then she closed her eyes and let out a long, dreadful moan.

Ross Hunter gripped her wrist, checking her pulse. Then he stared into her eyes.

'Can you describe the pain in your tummy?'

'Awful,' she gasped, her eyes still closed. 'It's burning. I'm burning.'

She suddenly thrashed, twisting from right to left, then back, like some crazed animal.

Lynn switched on the overhead light. Caitlin's face, and now her eyes too, which sprang open, were the colour of nicotine.

Inside, Lynn was burning too. Her whole insides felt as if they were being twisted into a tourniquet.

'It's OK, darling. Angel, it's OK. It's OK.'

'Can you show me where it hurts exactly?'

She opened her nightdress and pointed. Ross Hunter placed his hand there for a few moments. Then he peered closely at her eyes. Then, telling Caitlin they would be back in a few moments, he took Lynn's arm and led her out of the room, closing the door.

Luke was standing, ashen, on the landing.

'Is she going to be all right?' he asked.

Lynn nodded at him, trying to give him reassurance, but wanted a few moments in private with the doctor.

'Would you mind fetching me a glass of water, Luke?'

'No – er, sure. Yes, of course, Lynn.' He disappeared downstairs.

'Lynn,' Ross Hunter said, 'we need to get her into hospital right away. I'm extremely concerned at her condition.'

'Please, Ross, can we just wait until tomorrow? Tomorrow afternoon? She does have moments when she seems really strong – then she relapses. She'll be OK for a little longer.'

He put his finely manicured hands on her shoulders and stared hard at her.

'Yes, she might rally every now and then, for a short while, when she gets a build-up of strength, but don't be fooled. Those are her very last reserves she uses up, every time that happens. Lynn, you need to understand that without emergency medical treatment, she might not survive until tomorrow afternoon. She's suffering almost total liver failure. Her body is being poisoned by her own toxins.'

Tears began streaming down Lynn's face. She felt giddy, felt his firm hands steadying her as she swayed. *Got to be strong*, she thought. *Come all this way. Got to be really strong now.* The German woman was coming to collect her at midday. Just a few hours' time. *Have to hang on till then.*

She stared back at him, determinedly. 'Ross, I can't, not tonight.'

'Why on earth not? Are you mad?'

'I can't let her go into hospital to die. That's what's going to happen. She's just going to die in there.'

'She won't die if she gets immediate treatment.'

'But she will die without a new liver, Ross, and I don't have any faith they are going to find her one.'

'It's her only chance, Lynn.'

'I can't tonight, Ross. Perhaps tomorrow afternoon?'

'I don't understand your reluctance.'

Luke was coming up the stairs with the water. She took it gratefully from him, then he stayed, listening. She could hardly tell him to go away.

'I want you to give her something yourself, Ross.'

'I'm not a liver specialist, Lynn.'

'You're a fucking doctor, for Chrissake!' she snapped at him. Then she shook her head at herself. 'I'm sorry – I'm sorry, Ross. But you must be able to give her something. I don't know, some boost for her liver, something to stop the damn pain, something to perk her up, a shot of vitamins or something.'

He pulled his mobile phone out of his pocket. 'Lynn, I'm going to call an ambulance.'

'NO!'

Her sudden vehemence startled him. For some moments they both just stared at each other, in a kind of Mexican stand-off.

Then he gave her a strange look.

'Is something going on, Lynn? That I don't know about? Are you planning to take her abroad, is that it? To get a transplant in China?'

She stared back at him without responding, wondering whether she dared to take him into her trust, caught Luke's eye, willing him to keep silent.

'No,' she said.

'She wouldn't survive the journey, Lynn.'

'I – I'm not taking her abroad.'

'So why do you want to delay her going into hospital?'

'Just don't ask me, Ross, OK?'

He frowned deeply. 'I think you'd better tell me what's going on. Are you seeing some alternative practitioner? A faith healer?'

'Yes,' she said, suddenly short of breath with nerves, the word jetting out. 'Yes. I – I have someone—'

'They could see her in hospital, surely?'

Lynn shook her head vigorously.

'Do you understand how much you are endangering Caitlin's life, doing this?'

'And what the hell has your damn system done for her so far?' Luke suddenly said, simmering with rage. 'What's your bloody National Health done for her? Drag her in and out of hospital for years, putting her on the transplant list and getting all her hopes up, finding her a liver, then deciding instead to give it to some fuck-wit alcoholic so he can have a couple more years in the boozer? What do you want to do – send her back up to that hell-hole so more people can promise her a liver she's never going to bloody well get?'

He turned away, dabbing his eyes with the backs of his fists.

In the silence that followed, Lynn and the doctor stared bleakly at each other.

Sniffing, she said, 'He's right.'

'Lynn,' Ross Hunter said gravely, 'I'll give her a strong shot of antibiotics and I'll leave you some tablets to give her every four hours. They'll help reduce the infection which is causing her the pain. If I give her an enema, that will help too by reducing the protein build-up in the bowel. She should really be on a fluid drip – you need to get a lot of liquid down her.'

'What sort?'

'Glucose. She needs a lot. And you have to get her to eat, as much food as she can get down her.'

'This will work, will it, Ross?'

He looked at her sternly. 'If you do all those things, hopefully she will rally for a while. But what you are doing is dangerous and you're only buying a short amount of time. Do you understand?'

She nodded.

'I'll come back tomorrow afternoon. Unless there's a dramatic improvement, which I don't think we're going to see, then I'm sending her straight to hospital. All right?'

She threw her arms around him and hugged him.

'Thank you,' she whispered, tearfully. 'Thank you.'

100

Pulling his coat on, Glenn Branson left Bella Moy sitting in the warmth of the unmarked police car, crossed the narrow street behind the Metropole Hotel and once more rang the bell marked 1202, *J. Baker*. Then he stood outside the tower block in the icy wind, waiting for any sound to come down the speaker system.

Yet again, silence.

It was now just after four in the morning. In his pocket was the search warrant that had been signed at eleven last night by Juliet Smith, a senior magistrate he had always found helpful. Since then they had maintained a vigil here through the long night, only driving off for two brief periods.

The first had been to visit one of Cosmescu's known haunts, the Rendezvous Casino in the Marina, but the manager told them, with some regret in his voice, that unusually Mr Baker had not been there for a few days. The second had been to get bacon sandwiches and coffee from the Market Diner, one of the city's few all-night cafés.

He got back into the car shivering, slamming the door gratefully against the elements. The smell of greasy bacon lingered.

Bella looked at him wearily. 'I think it's time to wake up the caretaker,' she said.

'Yup, seems very selfish to be the only ones appreciating this beautiful night,' he said.

'Very selfish,' she agreed.

They climbed out, locked the doors, then walked back across to the front door. Glenn pressed the button marked Concierge.

There was no response. After a few moments he tried again. About thirty seconds went by, then there was a sharp crackle, followed by a voice with a strong Irish accent.

'Yes, who's that?'

'Police,' Glenn Branson said. 'We have a search warrant for one of your flats and need you to let us in.'

The man sounded suspicious. 'Police, you say?'

'Yes.'

'Fek! Just be giving me a minute, will ya, to get some clothes on.'

A short while later the front door was opened by a strong-looking, shaven-headed man of about sixty, with a broken, boxer's nose, wearing a sweatshirt, baggy jogging bottoms and flip-flops.

'Detective Sergeant Branson and Detective Sergeant Moy,' Glenn said, holding up his warrant card.

Bella produced hers too and the Irishman squinted at them in turn with suspicion.

'And your name is?' Bella asked.

Folding his arms defensively, the concierge replied, 'Dowler. Oliver Dowler.'

Then Glenn produced a sheet of paper. 'We have a search warrant for Flat 1202 and we've been ringing the occupant's bell regularly since just after eleven last night, with no response.'

'Well, now . . . 1202?' Oliver Dowler said with a frown. Then he raised a finger and gave a cheery smile. 'I'm not surprised you're getting no answer. The occupant vacated the premises yesterday. You've just missed him.'

Glenn cursed.

'Vacated?' Bella Moy queried.

'He moved out.'

'Do you know where he's gone?' Glenn asked.

'Abroad,' the concierge said. 'Fed up with the English climate.' Then he jabbed his own chest. 'Just like me – I got two more years to go, then I'm retiring to the Philippines.'

'Do you have a forwarding address or a phone number?'

'Nothing at all. He said he would be in touch.'

Glenn pointed upwards. 'Let's go to his flat.'

The three of them rode the lift and stepped straight out into the penthouse.

True to Oliver Dowler's word, Cosmescu had indeed vacated the place. There was not one piece of furniture left. No carpet, rug, not even any rubbish of any kind. A couple of bare light bulbs hung from their flex, and a few down-lighters burned starkly. There was a strong smell of fresh paint.

They walked through each of the rooms, their footsteps echoing. The whole place looked as if it had been profes-sionally cleaned. In the kitchen, Glenn opened the fridge and freezer doors. Inside they were bare. As was the dish-washer. He checked the inside of the washing machine and tumble dryer in the utility room and those were empty too.

There was nothing that either Glenn Branson or Bella Moy could see, in this cursory inspection, that gave any clue as to the previous occupant, or indeed that there had ever been one. There weren't even any shadows on the walls from where pictures or mirrors might have been removed.

Branson rubbed his finger down one pale grey wall, but however recent the paint might have been, it was now dry.

'Did he rent this flat or own it?' Bella Moy asked.

'He rented it,' the concierge said. 'Six-monthly renewa-ble lease, unfurnished.'

'How long has he been here?'

'About the same as me. Ten years I been here, next month.'

'So his lease just expired?' Glenn Branson said.

Dowler shook his head. 'Not at all. He's paid up for about three months still.'

The two detectives frowned at each other. Then Glenn handed him a card.

'If he gets in touch with you, will you contact me, please? We need to speak to him very urgently.'

'He said he would be dropping me a line or an email, with a forwarding address, like for the bills and stuff.'

'Can you tell us anything about him, Mr Dowler?' Bella asked.

He shook his head. 'In ten years I never had a conversation with him. Nothing. Very private.' Then he grinned. 'But I saw him a few times with some lovely ladies. He had a good eye for women, he did.'

'What about his car?'

'Gone too.' Then he yawned. 'Will you be needing me any more tonight? Or shall I leave you to be getting on with your search?'

'You can leave us. I don't think we'll be very long,' Glenn said.

'No,' the concierge said with a grin, 'I don't think that you will.'

After he had departed Glenn smiled at something. 'Got it!'

'What?' Bella enquired.

'Who the concierge reminds me of, the actor, Yul Brynner.'

'Yul Brynner?'

'*The Magnificent Seven.*'

She looked puzzled.

'One of the greatest movies ever made! Also had Steve McQueen, Charles Bronson, James Coburn.'

'I never saw it.'

'God, you've led a sheltered life!'

From the crestfallen look on her face, he realized he'd touched a raw nerve.

101

At 7.45 a.m. in the cramped conference room of the Specialist Search Unit, Tania Whitlock was briefing her team on an operation none of them was enjoying.

Post-mortem tests on Brighton drug dealer, Niall Foster, who had fallen to his death from a seventh-floor flat, had concluded that the blow to the side of his head was caused by a heavy, blunt object which had struck him before he fell, and not, as had originally been believed, by one of the metal railings on which he had landed, head first.

From the bevel-mark imprints on his skull, and metallurgy analysis from fragments in the hair, the pathologist believed the murder weapon might well be an antique brass table lamp – which Foster's distraught girlfriend said was missing from his flat.

Spread out in front of Tania was a crude map of a large open space to the south of Old Shoreham Road, adjoining Hove Cemetery – the Hove Domestic Waste and Recycling Depot. The whole team would be spending their entire Saturday searching through eighteen tons of rat-infested rubbish for this object. Last time they'd had to search this dump, a couple of months ago, several of them suffered headaches for days from the methane rising from the decomposing rubbish. None of them was looking forward to this return visit.

*

In the breaking dawn sky above the SSU building, the pilot of a four-seater Cessna was radioing Shoreham Tower.

'Golf Bravo Echo Tango Whiskey inbound from Dover.'

The little airport was unlit, so only operated between the hours of sunrise and sunset. This plane would be one of the morning's first arrivals.

'Golf Bravo Echo Tango Whiskey, Runway Zero Three. How many passengers?'

'I'm solo,' the pilot said.

*

As Sergeant Whitlock showed the next section on the grid that her team members were to cover, they were all concentrating hard. None of them heard the drone of the light aircraft coming in low overhead, circling to make its landing approach to Shoreham Airport's runway 03.

Private aircraft and helicopters came and went here all the time. As there were no international flights, there was no Border Control presence, or any Customs either. Incoming flights from abroad were meant to radio a request for a customs officer and a border control agent to attend, and to remain in their aircraft until both had cleared them. But that normally meant a long delay, often with no officers arriving anyway, so pilots sometimes took a risk and did not bother.

Certainly the pilot of the twin-engined Cessna was not intending to radio them. The flight plan he had filed last night was from Shoreham to a private airstrip near Dover and then back. He had omitted to include, on the plan, a minor detour across the Channel to Le Touquet in France and back – which he had made with his transponder switched off. For cash payments of the size that he was receiving for this trip, he was always more than happy to make omissions in his flight plans.

He taxied along the three-deep line of parked aircraft towards his parking space, happy to hear that there were several more incoming aircraft stacking up, which would keep the crew in the tower occupied. He turned in, manoeuvring his plane to the same angle as the others, then put on the parking brake and throttled back the engines. He looked around carefully for signs of anyone who might be taking an interest in them, then switched off both ignitions.

As the propellers spun down, the aircraft vibrated less and less and the noise diminished. The pilot removed his headset, turned to the beautiful, blonde German woman directly behind him and said, 'OK?'

'*Sehr gut,*' she said, and began unbuckling her harness.

He raised a cautioning hand. 'We have to wait a little.' He peered anxiously out again, then turned to the tired-looking teenage girl, dressed in a smart white overcoat, on the seat behind the woman. 'Enjoyed the flight?'

The girl didn't understand English, but she picked up the gist of what he had said from his tone and nodded nervously. He unbuckled himself and reached over to help her out of her safety harness. Then he signalled for her to stay, climbed out and jumped down, leaving the door slightly ajar.

Marlene Hartmann welcomed the blast of cold, fresh air, even though it was laced with the smell of kerosene. Then she yawned and gave Simona a smile. The girl smiled back. A pretty little thing, Marlene thought. In another country, in different circumstances, life could have been good for her. She yawned again, longing for a cup of coffee. It had been a long, long night. By road to Belgrade, then a late flight to Paris, then a taxi at four in the morning to Le Touquet. But they were here. And she was happy with the plans.

Yes, after the visit from the police officer yesterday, it would have been more sensible to abort. But then she would have lost a good customer. She did not think the Detective Superintendent could move this fast. Everything would be done before he even knew it and by tonight she would be back in Germany.

Another plane was coming in to land and the pilot, standing outside, heard the roars of several different aero engines, including the clatter of a helicopter, and saw a convoy of three aircraft taxiing out towards the runways. Plenty to keep the tower occupied. This was always a good time of day, still a little bit of darkness and numerous distractions, including the vehicles of airport workers arriving.

The white van was parked a few hundred yards along, beside the perimeter fence. He stared at it, then pulled out his handkerchief and blew his nose.

Behind the wheel of the van, Vlad Cosmescu was watching. This was the signal.

He started the engine and put the van into gear.

102

Lynn Beckett sat, bleary-eyed from a sleepless night, her heart thudding, hunched over her kitchen table, sipping a cup of tea. She had lain in bed for hours, tossing and turning, shaking her pillows to try to get them comfortable, and getting up, obsessively, every twenty minutes or so to check on Caitlin, help her to the loo, ensure she drank glucose water and took the antibiotic tablets. The combination Ross Hunter had prescribed, probably aided by the jab, seemed to be working. Caitlin's pain had subsided and the itching was a little less bad.

For a long time after the doctor's visit, she had remained downstairs with Luke. They had downed a bottle of Sauvignon Blanc and smoked their way through an entire packet of Silk Cut, sharing the last cigarette between them.

Now her head was pounding, her lungs were raw and she felt terrible. Luke had finally fallen into a deep slumber in the chair beside Caitlin's bed.

The television was on. She stared at the 9 a.m. news, but she had no interest in it. Nor in the programme on helicopter rescues that followed. She had no interest in anything, at this moment, except for the phone call she was waiting for from Marlene Hartmann.

Please call. Oh, please God, call.

She did not know what she would do if the German woman did not make contact. If she had simply conned them out of the money. She had no Plan B.

Then, suddenly, the landline phone rang.

She answered it before it had completed the first ring. 'Yeshello?'

To her relief, it was Marlene Hartmann. 'How are you today, Lynn?'

'Yesfine,' she gasped.

'Everything is good. We are here. You will be ready for collection?'

'YesIwill.'

'The payment is in order? You have the balance ready?'

'Yes.' She swallowed.

Her bank manager had already queried the first transfer she had made, and she had given him a lame reason that she was buying an investment property in Germany, from a one-off-payment final divorce settlement from her ex-husband, following an inheritance he had received.

'You will see us later. The car will arrive for you as scheduled.'

She hung up before Lynn could thank her.

The car was scheduled for midday. Less than three hours.

She was so wound up with stress, fear and excitement, she could hardly think straight.

103

Shortly after the 8.30 a.m. briefing Roy Grace was sitting at the work station in MIR One, on the phone to one of the two detectives who were on surveillance outside Sir Roger Sirius's house. They had been there since shortly before midnight and reported that no one had left the house and the helicopter was still on its pad in the grounds. He was in an irritable mood, and while he talked, one of the phones in the room warbled on, unanswered. He clapped his hand over the mouthpiece and shouted for someone to answer it. Someone did, rapidly.

Every Secretary of State had either been abroad or out at dinner somewhere last night. It had been after midnight before one – the Home Secretary himself – had signed the phone-tapping consent, and it was after two in the morning before it was up and running on Lynn Beckett's home and mobile phone lines.

Grace had grabbed three hours' sleep at Cleo's house and been back here since six. He was running on Red Bull, a handful of guarana tablets Cleo had given him, and coffee. He was very concerned that the only real lead they had at this moment was the transplant surgeon, Sir Roger Sirius – and no certainty that he was involved, or would give them anything.

He was also concerned about the news from Glenn Branson of Vlad Cosmescu's disappearance. Was that connected with his visit to the German organ broker yesterday?

Had he been rumbled by Marlene Hartmann? Had he panicked her team into aborting their plans and making a fast retreat? The all-ports alert, not only to watch for the German woman accompanied by a young girl arriving, but to watch for a man answering Vlad Cosmescu's description leaving, had so far yielded nothing.

Ports of entry and departure would forever be a policing problem on an island like Great Britain, with miles of open coastline and numerous private airports and landing strips. Sometimes you would get lucky, but the resources to monitor everyone arriving on and departing from these shores were beyond any budget the police force had. It didn't help that the Home Office, in its enthusiasm to comply with government budget cuts, had scrapped passport controls for people leaving the UK. In a nutshell, unless someone positively identified them, the UK law enforcement agencies hadn't a clue who was here and who wasn't.

The post-mortem on Jim Towers would now be under way and Grace was anxious to get down to the mortuary to see whether there were any early findings from the pathologist to link his death to Operation Neptune – and of course to see Cleo, who had been asleep when he had arrived at her house and when he had left.

As he stood up and pulled his jacket on, telling the other members of his team where he was going, yet another phone was warbling on, unanswered. Was everyone deaf in here today? Or just too plain exhausted after the long night to pick up the receiver?

He got as far as the door before it stopped. As he turned the handle, Lizzie Mantle called out to him, holding up the receiver.

'Roy! For you.'

He went back over to the work station. It was David Hicks, one of the phone surveillance operatives.

'Sir,' he said, 'we've just picked up a call on Mrs Beckett's landline.'

104

'I'm like ... I've got to be at this workshop thing at ten,' Luke mumbled, staggering into the kitchen as if he was sleepwalking. 'Do you think it would be OK if I went?'

'Of course,' she said to his left eye, the only visible one. 'Go. I'll call you if anything develops.'

'Cool.'

He went.

Lynn hurried upstairs, a million things that she had to do between now and midday swirling in her head, and with Luke gone – God bless him – she could think more clearly.

She had to go through the checklist from Marlene Hartmann of Transplantation-Zentrale.

Had to get Caitlin up, washed, packed.

Had to get herself packed.

It took her a while to rouse Caitlin, who was in a deep sleep from the medication Dr Hunter had given her. She ran a bath for her and then started packing overnight bags for each of them.

Suddenly, the doorbell rang.

She looked at her watch, panic gripping her. Surely not now? The German woman had said *midday*, surely? It was only just gone ten o'clock. Was it the postman?

She hurried downstairs and pulled open the front door.

A man and a woman stood there. The man was about forty, with close-cropped fair hair, a small, slightly flattened nose and piercing blue eyes. He was dressed in an overcoat, navy suit, white shirt and a plain blue tie, and was holding up a small, black leather wallet with something printed inside it, and his photograph. The woman was a good decade younger, blonde hair pulled up in a bun, wearing a dark trouser suit with a cream blouse, and held up a similar black wallet.

'Mrs Lynn Beckett?' he asked.

She nodded.

'Detective Superintendent Grace and DC Boutwood of Sussex CID. Would it be possible to have a word with you?'

Lynn stared at them in shock. She felt as if she had been dropped into the plunge pool of a sauna. The floor beneath her feet felt unstable. The police officers were in her face, right up close to her, so close she could almost feel the warmth of the Detective Superintendent's breath. She stepped back, in a red mist of panic.

'It's – er – it's not really a very convenient time,' she gasped.

Her words sounded disembodied, as if someone else was saying them.

'I'm sorry, but we do need to speak to you right away,' the Detective Superintendent said, stepping forward, his face coming closer, intimidatingly closer, again.

She stared wildly, for a moment, at each of them in turn. What the hell was this about? The money she had taken from Reg Okuma, she thought, with sudden terror – had he reported it?

She heard her disembodied voice say mechanically, 'Yes, right, come in, please come in. It's cold, isn't it? Cold but dry. That's a good thing, isn't it? Not raining. December's often quite a dry month.'

The young woman DC looked at her sympathetically and smiled.

Lynn stepped back to let them in, then shut the front

door behind them. The hallway seemed smaller than ever and she felt crowded by the two police officers.

'Mrs Beckett,' the Detective Superintendent said, 'you have a daughter called Caitlin, is that correct?'

Lynn's eyes shot upstairs. 'Yes.' She struggled to get the word past the lump in her throat. 'Yes. Yes, I do.'

'Forgive me if I'm being a little forward, Mrs Beckett, but as I understand it, your daughter is unwell with liver failure and in need of a transplant. Is that correct?'

For some moments, she said nothing, trying desperately to think clearly. Why were they here? Why?

'Would you mind telling me what you are doing here? What is this about? What do you want?' she asked, shaking.

Roy Grace said, 'We have reason to believe that you may be attempting to buy a new liver for your daughter.'

He paused and they stared at each other for a moment. He could see the fear in her eyes.

'Are you aware that, in this country, that would be a criminal offence, Mrs Beckett?'

Lynn shot a glance upstairs, afraid that Caitlin might overhear, then ushered the two officers through into the kitchen and shut the door.

'I'm sorry,' she said. 'I have absolutely no idea what you are talking about.'

'Shall we sit down?' Grace said.

Lynn pulled up a chair facing the two detectives across the table. She considered offering them tea, but decided against, wanting to get shot of them as quickly as possible.

With his coat still on, Roy Grace sat opposite her, with arms folded.

'Mrs Beckett, during the past week there have been a large number of telephone calls exchanged between your home and mobile phone numbers and a company in

Munich called Transplantation-Zentrale. Could you tell us why you made those calls?'

'Transplantation-Zentrale?' she echoed.

'They are a firm of international organ brokers. They obtain human organs for people who need transplants, such as your daughter,' he said.

Lynn shrugged defensively. 'I'm sorry, I've never heard of these people. I know my daughter's boyfriend has been very upset about my daughter's treatment from her hospital in London.'

'Upset about what exactly?' Grace asked.

'The way they run their fucking transplant waiting list.'

'Sounds like you're upset too,' he said.

'I think you'd be upset if it was your daughter, Detective Superintendent Grace.'

'So it hasn't crossed your mind to try to look beyond the UK for a suitable liver?'

'No, why should it?'

Grace was quiet for a moment. Then, as gently as he could, he asked, 'Would you deny that you had a phone conversation with a lady called Frau Marlene Hartmann, who is the chief executive of Transplantation-Zentrale, at five past nine this morning? Less than one hour ago?'

Suddenly, despite all her efforts to think clearly, she felt herself losing it. She was shaking uncontrollably. *Shit, oh shit, oh shit.* Wide-eyed, she stared at him.

'Have you bugged my bloody phone?'

Above her, she heard the sound of water gurgling out of the bath.

The Detective Superintendent slipped his hand into his coat pocket and retrieved a brown envelope. Carefully, from inside it, he pulled out a photograph and laid it on the table for Lynn to see.

It was a photograph of a girl in her early to mid-teens. Despite looking grubby, she had a pretty face, with Romany features and complexion, lank brown hair, and was wearing a blue, sleeveless puffa over a ragged, multicoloured jogging top.

'Mrs Beckett,' he went on, 'I expect you have been told that your daughter's liver is coming from someone who has been killed in a car accident.'

He paused, watching her eyes closely. She said nothing.

'Well,' he continued, 'that's actually not the case. It is coming from this Romanian girl. Her name is Simona Irimia. So far as we know she is still alive and healthy. She has been trafficked to England and will be killed so that your daughter can have her liver.'

Suddenly, Lynn's world felt as if it was crashing down all around her.

105

Simona sat on a lumpy mattress in the back of the swaying, lurching van, with Gogu on her lap. One moment they were accelerating, the next braking hard, on a twisting, switch-back road. For most of the journey she kept her hands pressed flat on the ribbed, metal floor, trying to grip and stop herself from being thrown around.

A blue metal toolbox lay near her, along with a wheel brace, a coiled blue rope and some wide rolls of tape. The stuff clattered and clanked and slid about each time they went over a bump. It had been hours since she had last eaten or drunk anything – before they had got on board that little plane. She was desperately thirsty and the stench of exhaust fumes was making her feel sick.

She wished Romeo were here, because she always felt safe with him, and she would have had someone to talk to. The German woman had ignored her for most of the long journey, either working on her laptop or speaking on her phone. Now, seated in the front, she was engaged in a serious-sounding conversation with the driver of the van, a tall, craggy-faced, expressionless Romanian with jet-black hair slicked back, wearing a blouson jacket over jeans, and with a chunky gold bracelet hanging from his wrist.

Every now and then the woman raised her voice, and the driver either fell silent or argued back – at least, it sounded like he was arguing, in whatever language it was they were speaking.

There were no windows here in the back and Simona

could see only by craning her neck and looking forward between the seats, out of the windscreen. They were driving through well-kept countryside. She could see mostly trees, hedges and just the occasional farm building or house.

Suddenly, they were braking sharply. Moments later they turned in between two tall brick pillars. A grid clattered beneath them, then they were heading up a long, winding driveway. Simona saw several signs on posts, but she was unable to read what they said:

PRIVATE PROPERTY

NO PARKING

NO PICNICKING

STRICTLY NO CAMPING

In the distance she saw lush green hills beneath a grey sky. They wound past a large lake, then a vast area beyond it, to their left, of beautifully tended grass. Some of it was mown shorter than other parts and she saw several craters that were filled with what looked like sand. She wondered what they were, but didn't dare interrupt to ask.

They entered a long, straight avenue of overhanging trees, with the verges covered in fallen leaves, then the van braked sharply again suddenly, slowing to a crawl. They went over a sharp bump, then speeded up again. After three more sharp bumps, Simona could see, ahead of them, a huge grey house, with gleaming cars parked randomly around the driveway in front, and in orderly rows along the side. She felt a beat of excitement. This place looked so beautiful! Was this where she would be working?

She wanted to ask the German woman, but she was talking on her phone again now, and sounding very cross about something.

The van drove under an archway, then halted at the rear of the house. The driver switched off the engine and climbed out, while the woman continued her phone argument, her voice getting louder and more agitated.

Moments later, the driver opened one of the rear doors of the van. He gripped Simona's hand as she scrambled out and, to her surprise, he continued holding her hand, gripping it hard, despite her effort to free it, as if worried she might run away.

She tugged hard, feeling a flash of resentment at him, but his grip was like iron and his face showed nothing.

The German woman climbed out, ended her call and clicked her phone shut. Simona caught her eye. Normally the woman smiled at her, but there was no smile now, or even a hint of acknowledgement. She just stared through her coldly, as if Simona did not exist.

She must be very angry about her phone call, Simona thought.

A nurse came out of the house, through a door almost beside the van. She was a big, muscular-looking woman, with a broad frame, stubby neck and arms the size of hams. Her greying hair was cropped short, like a man's, and gelled into spikes. For some moments, she scrutinized the teenager as if she were an object on display in a shop. Then her rosebud lips, far too tiny for the size of her fleshy face, formed into a faint smile.

'Simona,' she said stiffly, in Romanian, 'you come with me.'

She held out her hand and gripped Simona's. The driver finally let go of her other hand. The nurse pulled Simona so hard she stumbled, and as she did so, the comforter she was clutching fell to the ground, and remained there, as she was dragged inside the house.

'Gogu!' Simona cried out, turning her head back desperately. 'Gogu!' she called again, trying to break free. 'Gogu!'

But Marlene Hartmann quickly followed her in, slamming the door shut behind them.

Outside, Vlad Cosmescu saw the strip of mangy fur lying on the ground. He knelt and picked it up. Then, distastefully holding the grimy object by his fingertips, he deposited it in a nearby wheelie bin.

Next, he reversed the van into one of the garages in a row across the yard and pulled down the door, hiding it from view. Just as a precaution.

106

Struggling desperately hard to maintain her composure at the kitchen table, Lynn stared at the photograph of the pretty, scruffy-looking girl that lay in front of her.

Scare tactics, she thought. *Please God, let it be scare tactics.*

Marlene Hartmann was a decent woman. It was impossible to believe, for an instant, that what the Detective Superintendent had just told her was true. Impossible. Impossible. Impossible.

Her hands were shaking so much she moved them off the table on to her lap. Gripped them tightly together, out of sight. *Impossible!*

She had to get through this. Had to get these people out of her house, so she could call the German woman. She felt a lump in her throat choking her voice. Took a deep breath to calm herself, the way she had been taught at work when dealing with a difficult or abusive client.

'I'm sorry,' she said, looking up at each of them in turn. 'I don't know why you're here or what you want. My daughter is on the transplant priority list at the Royal South London Hospital. We are very happy with all that they are doing and we are confident that she will be getting her liver very shortly. There is no reason at all why I should be looking elsewhere.' She swallowed. 'Besides I – I don't – I wouldn't know – know – where to begin – to look.'

'Mrs Beckett,' Roy Grace said levelly, staring hard at her, 'human trafficking is one of the most unpleasant crimes in this country. You need to be aware just how seriously the police and the judiciary view this activity. One gentleman in London recently had a sentence for human trafficking increased by the Court of Appeal to *twenty-three* years.'

He paused to let this sink in. She felt as if she was going to throw up at any moment.

'Human trafficking involves a multitude of criminal offences,' he went on. 'I'm going to list them for you: unlawful immigration, kidnap and false imprisonment, just for starters. Do you understand? Any person in this country who attempts to buy a human organ here or abroad is open to being charged with conspiracy to traffic, and with being an accessory. These carry the same custodial sentences as actual trafficking itself. Am I making myself clear?'

She was perspiring. Her scalp felt as if it was shrinking around her skull.

'Very clear.'

'I have sufficient information to arrest you now, Mrs Beckett, on suspicion of conspiracy to traffic a human organ.'

Her head was swimming. She could barely even focus on the two of them. She had to hold it together somehow. Caitlin's life depended on her, on getting through this. She stared down again at the photograph, desperately trying to buy time, to think clearly.

'Where would that leave you, if I arrest you?' the police officer asked. 'Where would that leave your daughter?'

'Please believe me,' she said desperately.

'Perhaps we should talk to your daughter?'

'No!' she blurted. 'No! She's too – too ill – too ill to see anyone.'

She stared desperately at the young woman detective and saw a fleeting glimpse of compassion in her eyes.

There was a long silence, suddenly broken by the crackle of the Detective Superintendent's radio phone.

He stepped away from the table, pulled it to his ear and spoke into it.

'Roy Grace.'

The male voice at the other end said, 'Target One's on the move.'

'Give me thirty seconds.'

Grace jabbed a finger at DC Boutwood, and pointed at the door. He turned back to Lynn.

'Think very carefully about what I just said.'

Seconds later both detectives had gone, deliberately leaving the photograph behind. The front door slammed behind them.

Lynn sank back down at the table and buried her face in her hands.

Moments later she felt a pair of hands on her shoulders.

'I heard that,' Caitlin said. 'I heard everything. There's no way I'm going to have that liver.'

107

The wrought-iron gates swung open and a black Aston Martin Vanquish rumbled slowly forward between the stone pillars, nosing cautiously out of the blind entrance. Then, with a blast of thunder from its tail pipes, it turned right and accelerated hard. Immediately, the gates began to close again.

The driver would have noticed nothing different in the wooded country lane this morning from any other day. The two rural surveillance experts were well concealed. One was inside the hedgerow, the other, in camouflage clothing, was halfway up a conifer, and their vehicle was parked down a Forestry Commission track a quarter of a mile away.

DS Paul Tanner, inside the hedge, had a clear line of sight and, despite the tinted glass and the car's black interior, clocked the driver's silver hair.

Roy Grace, standing on the pavement outside Lynn Beckett's house, radioed him back.

'What information do you have?'

'Index Romeo Sierra Zero Eight Alpha Mike Lima, sir. Heading east.'

From Guy Batchelor and Emma-Jane Boutwood's debriefing after their interview with the liver surgeon, Grace knew this was Sir Roger Sirius's car. He also knew that these two Divisional Intelligence Unit surveillance officers were badly needed for another surveillance job on a major drugs operation that was currently taking place in Brighton today. A shortage of police manpower was a constant problem in the city.

'Good work,' he said. 'Stay in situ for another thirty minutes in case he returns. If he doesn't, then stand down.'

'Stand down after thirty minutes, sir, yes, yes.'

Grace ended the contact and called the Incident Room, instructing them to put an immediate ANPR out on the car and to see if the police helicopter was available.

A network of Automatic Number Plate Recognition cameras covered many major arteries across the UK. Any number plate fed into the system would, in theory, enable a car to be tracked every few miles – so long as it stuck to main roads. Once the car pinged a camera or was spotted by an alert police officer, the helicopter would be sent to the area, and with luck follow the car, unseen, from the air.

Then he turned to DC Boutwood and nodded back towards Lynn Beckett's house.

'What did you think?'

'You're right, she's up to something. Are you going to arrest her?'

He shook his head. 'It's not her I want. She's a bit-part player. Let's see what she does now – where she leads us.'

'You don't think she might abort?'

'My guess is she's going to make a few phone calls.'

He unlocked the doors to their Hyundai. Before climbing in, he raised a discreet finger of acknowledgement to the driver and passenger of the green Volkswagen Passat that was parked a short distance down the road.

108

'Hello! Don't you read the fucking newspapers? Have you been living under a stone for the last two weeks, Mother?'

Mother?

When the hell had she last called her Mother? Lynn wondered desperately, panic-stricken as a result of the police officers' visit. The nightmare she was living was getting darker every second.

'Like, we're in the middle of the biggest organ-trafficking scandal of the century and somehow you kind of don't know about it?'

Lynn stood up, pushing the kitchen chair back behind her, and faced her daughter, astonished and delighted by how much stronger she seemed this morning. But also a little alarmed; Caitlin was almost hyper.

'Yes, that's right, I, like, kind of don't know about it. OK?'

Caitlin shook her head. 'That's so totally not *OK*. OK?' Then she scratched each of her arms in turn furiously.

'The police are lying, angel,' she said. 'There is no trafficking scandal, it's just a wild theory.'

'Yeah, right. Three dead bodies turn up in the Channel, missing their vital organs, and all the newspapers and TV news programmes and radio programmes are lying.'

'Those bodies have nothing to do with your transplant.'

'Sure,' Caitlin said. 'So why did the cops come round?'

Lynn was floundering, she knew. She could hear the desperation in her own voice, and another voice inside her head screaming at her, as she glanced back down, almost reluctantly, at the photograph on the table: *WHAT IF DETECTIVE SUPERINTENDENT ROY GRACE WAS TELLING THE TRUTH?*

The photograph of the girl's face burned into her brain. Burned into the backs of her eyelids, so that even when she blinked she could still see her.

It wasn't possible. No one would do that. No one would kill a child for – for money – for another child – for – for . . . ?

For Caitlin?

Would they?

How she wished Malcolm was here at this moment. She needed someone to share this with, to talk this through with. Terror was coming at her from every direction.

Twenty-three years in prison.

You need to be aware quite how seriously the police and the judiciary view this activity.

She had not thought about it. Beating the system, yes, using an organ from an accident victim, that was all. There was nothing wrong with that, surely to God?

Killing a child.

Killing that girl.

The money was gone. Half of it. Would she ever get it back? Shit, she didn't want it back. She wanted a damn liver.

The policeman had to be lying.

There was one quick way to find out. She picked up her mobile phone, opened the address book, then scrolled to Marlene Hartmann's name.

She was about to press the dial button when she stopped.

Realizing.

Realizing just how dumb that would be. If the organ broker knew that the police were on to her, she would probably abort the operation and flee. Lynn could not take that risk. Caitlin had perked up since Dr Hunter's booster, but that was not going to last. She had bought time from him, by promising she would allow Caitlin to be admitted to hospital this afternoon.

Barring a miracle, she was certain that if Caitlin went back into the Royal she would not come out again. There was no way she could let this all fall apart now.

'Hello? Hello? Hello, Mother? Mum? Anyone home?'

Lynn looked at her daughter with a start. 'What?'

'I asked you, why did the cops come round?'

Then, to Lynn's shock, Caitlin's body suddenly sagged and she lurched sideways. Lynn grabbed her just in time to stop her falling, gripping her tightly.

For an instant, her daughter looked at her in total confusion.

'Darling? Angel? Are you OK?'

Caitlin's eyes seemed unfocused. Looking as if she were surprised by what had happened, she whispered, 'Yes.' Her skin seemed even more yellow than last night. Whispering again, so that Lynn had to put her ear to her mouth to hear, she said, 'Why did they come? The cops?'

'I don't know.'

'Are they going to bust us?'

Lynn shook her head. 'No.'

Caitlin's voice gained a little strength. 'They seemed pretty desperate, you know? That's a desperate thing, right? To lay that photo of the child on us. Unless it's true, of course.'

She stared hard at her mother, her eyes suddenly focusing sharply again.

'They're probably under pressure about those bodies. Maybe they are getting desperate for a result. They'll try anything, resort to anything.'

'Yeah, well, we're pretty desperate too.'

Despite all she was feeling, Lynn smiled, then threw her arms around Caitlin and held her, hugging her closer and more tightly than she had ever hugged her before.

'God, I love you, my darling. So much. So much. You are everything to me. You're the reason I get up in the morning. You're the reason I get through work. You're my life. Do you know that?'

'You should get out more.'

Lynn grinned, then kissed her on the cheek. 'You're so horrible to me.'

'Yeah.' Caitlin was grinning too. 'And you're so fucking *possessive*!'

Lynn pushed her gently away and held her at arm's length.

'You know why I'm so possessive?'

'Because I'm beautiful, smart, intelligent and would have the world at my feet if it wasn't for one small problem, right? God gave me a liver from the wrong box.'

Lynn broke down in tears. Tears of joy. Tears of sadness. Tears of terror. Hugging Caitlin tight again, she whispered, 'They lied. *He* lied. Don't believe him. The detective lied. Just believe *me*. Angel, darling, just believe *me*. I'm your mum. *Just believe me.*'

Caitlin hugged her back, with all her feeble strength. 'Yeah, OK, I believe you.'

Then suddenly Caitlin turned away, making a retching sound. Breaking free of her mother's arms, she stumbled over to the sink. Lynn caught up with her, gripping her arm to prevent her from falling.

Then Caitlin threw up violently.

To her utter horror, Lynn saw it was not vomit that was spattering the sink and the tiled splash-back and the draining board. It was bile specked with bright red blood.

As she cradled her heaving, choking daughter, she knew then, in that moment, that she did not care about anything else. Did not care if Detective Superintendent Grace was telling the truth. Did not care if that girl he had brought the photograph of had to die. Did not care who had to die. If she needed to, she would kill them herself, with her own bare hands, to save the life of her child.

109

Simona sat on a chair in a small, windowless room, crying and drinking a glass of Coca-Cola. The room reminded her of the prison cell she had spent a night in when she and Romeo had been arrested a couple of years ago for stealing from a shop. The same smell of disinfectant. There was nothing in here except cupboards full of medical supplies. She was so hungry her stomach was aching.

'I want Gogu,' she sniffled.

The big Romanian nurse, who had gripped Simona's arm so hard it was now bruised and hurting, stood with her arms folded in front of the door, watching her drink.

'I dropped him outside.'

'I'll fetch it later,' the nurse replied.

Simona felt a little better about that and nodded appreciatively. She stared at her glass, then back at the woman.

'Please may I have something to eat?' she asked for the third time in the quarter of an hour or so that she had been here. 'Anything?'

'Drink,' the woman commanded.

Obediently, Simona drank some more. Maybe when she had finished this second glass, then she would get something to eat, and the woman would get Gogu for her.

'What kind of work will I be doing here?' she asked.

The nurse frowned. 'Work? What kind of work?'

Simona smiled dreamily. 'I would like to do bar work!' she said. 'I would like to learn to make drinks. You know, fancy drinks. What do they call them? *Cocktails!* I think that would be nice work, to make drinks and talk with people. I would think they have a nice bar here in this hotel, don't they?' Seeing the continued frown, she added hastily, 'But of course I don't mind what work. Anything. I could clean. I'm happy to clean. I'm just happy to be here. I will be even happier when Romeo comes! Do you think that might be soon?'

'Drink,' the woman replied.

Simona drained the glass. Then she sat in silence, while the woman continued to stand, with her arms folded, like a sentry.

After a few more minutes, Simona began to feel sleepy. She had a sudden wave of giddiness, then lost focus on the woman. Lost focus on the walls, on the cupboards. They were sliding past in front of her eyes, faster, then faster.

The nurse stood impassively, watching as Simona's eyes closed and she fell sideways on to the floor and lay still, breathing hard.

She then hoisted the girl over her shoulder, carried her out a short distance along the corridor into the small pre-op room and laid her on the steel trolley. Then she removed all her clothes, checking greedily that Simona had no valuables on her. Sometimes, street vermin like this girl secreted stolen valuables in their bodies, hoping to get cash for them in England.

Hastily pulling on a rubber glove before anyone else came in, she checked inside the girl's mouth, then carefully probed her vagina and anus. Nothing! Useless little bitch.

Then, on her intercom phone, she called the anaesthetist and told him, barely masking the disgust in her voice, that the girl was ready.

110

Roy Grace was just walking back in through the door of MIR One when *Romeo Sierra Zero Eight Alpha Mike Lima* pinged an ANPR camera. The information was radioed through to him immediately. He stopped in front of the crowded work station and wrote down the information. Sir Roger Sirius's Aston Martin was heading north from the Washington roundabout on the A24.

Instantly he called the Air Operations Unit and requested Hotel Nine Hundred, the police helicopter, airborne. They estimated seven minutes' time to be over the roundabout, which was four miles north of Worthing and eight miles from their base at Shoreham Airport.

He did a quick calculation. Hotel Nine Hundred's maximum ground speed, depending on any head or tail winds, was about 130 mph. The A24 at this point was largely fast, open dual carriageway, but Sirius was unlikely to want to risk being pulled over for speeding. Assuming he was travelling at 80 mph and continuing on this road, the helicopter should have the car in sight in about fifteen minutes.

Assuming he had not turned off on to a minor road.

Although the sky was overcast this morning, there was a high cloud ceiling, giving the chopper plenty of visibility. Raising his hand in acknowledgement at a couple of his team members who were trying to get his attention, he walked over to the map that had been pinned up on the whiteboard. It showed Sussex and parts of its neighbouring counties, with the positions of Lynn Beckett's and Sir Roger

Sirius's houses ringed in red. Ringed in purple were the locations of all the private hospitals and clinics in the area. There were a large number, including sports injuries clinics, diagnostic centres and skin clinics, and Grace knew that most of them could be ruled out as too small to house the kind of facilities they were looking for.

He quickly found the A24 and the roundabout, then traced his finger up the road northwards. There were any number of places the car could be heading to. The conurbations of Horsham or Guildford were possibilities, but Grace's hunch was that a private clinic with the kind of facilities needed for transplants, and all its support staff, would more likely be concealed somewhere in the countryside.

He glanced at his watch, anxiously waiting for the car to ping another ANPR camera, or for word from the chopper, and regretting his decision to keep the rural surveillance team outside Sirius's gates rather than have them follow the car.

He did not know how much time they had, but from the call they had intercepted, Lynn Beckett and her daughter were due to be picked up shortly. His guess was that they had a few hours, at most.

They had not intercepted any calls since his visit and he considered that a bad sign. It meant she wasn't panicked by his visit and was still going ahead. It was, of course, possible she had another phone, a pay-as-you-go one that didn't show up on her records, but if that had been the case, she would surely have used that instead of her landline earlier, wouldn't she? Or her daughter's phone, assuming she had one.

Wherever she or Sirius went, and he was certain it was going to be to the same place, he was going in hard. During the night he'd been assembling the units and he had all the vehicles and crews on standby. Fortunately, so far it had been a quiet morning in Sussex and he had the full team he needed.

'Sir!' Jacqui Phillips, one of the researchers, called to him.

He went across to her. Yesterday he had tasked her with listing all manufacturers and wholesale suppliers of operating theatre materials, instruments and drugs in the country. But as she showed him now, it was an impossibly long list. One that would take weeks to work through.

Next, Glenn Branson wanted him. The DS had some feedback from the all-ports alert they had put out and the photographs of Marlene Hartmann and Simona they had circulated. There had been a number of potential sightings during the night and early morning, including a mother and daughter from Romania who had been held by Gatwick police for an hour, before being cleared, and another couple with a young girl, from Germany, who had been interrogated after arriving by Eurostar.

'I think we have to assume she's already here now,' Grace said.

'Want me to cancel the alert?'

'Give it another hour, just in case,' he said.

His radio crackled again. Another ANPR had been pinged by Sirius. He was still on the A24 – this time heading past Horsham, still travelling north. Grace glanced at his watch again. Sirius was going like the wind. At this rate, he would shortly be out of the county and into Surrey, which meant the police there would need to be informed of their pursuit.

He radioed the helicopter and relayed this information, asking where they were.

The observer replied they were just approaching Horsham themselves. Within seconds of ending the call, Grace's radio crackled again and he heard the observer's excited voice.

'We have contact with Romeo Sierra Zero Eight Alpha Mike Lima! In slow traffic approaching roadworks, still proceeding northbound on A24.'

Grace went back to the map and made a wide east, west and north arc from the car's position. There were seven purple rings within that arc, all existing clinics.

But ten anxious minutes later, the helicopter reported that the Aston Martin was still travelling north. If it kept on this route, Grace thought, staring at the map again, feeling vexed, it would soon reach the M25 London orbital road.

'Where the hell are you bloody going?' he said out loud.

None of the twenty-two members of his inquiry team in this room at the moment, hunched in front of their screens, or with phones to their ears, or poring over printouts, had any better idea than he did.

111

Lynn was in her room, zipping shut her overnight bag, when the doorbell rang.

The sound shrilled through her veins. Shrilled through her soul. She froze in total, blind panic.

Was it the police again?

Then she stepped across to the window and peered cautiously down. Outside was a turquoise and white Streamline taxi estate car.

Relief flooded through her. She had not been expecting a taxi, but that was fine, that was good, she realized as her thoughts clarified. A taxi! Yes, very good! A taxi meant that Marlene Hartmann had nothing to hide. A taxi was open. If she was happy for them to be picked up in a taxi, then everything had to be absolutely fine.

Sod you and your damn scaremongering, Detective Superintendent Grace, she thought. Then she rapped hard on the window. The driver, a man in his forties in a bomber jacket, who was standing outside the front door, looked up and Lynn signalled to him that they were coming.

Then she carried hers and Caitlin's bags downstairs with a sudden burst of optimism in her heart. It was going to be all right. It was going to be fine. Everything would be brilliant. She was going to give Caitlin the best Christmas ever!

'OK, darling!' she called out. 'This is it!'

Caitlin was sitting at the kitchen table, cradling Max on her lap and stroking him, staring at the face of the Romanian girl in the photograph. The glass of glucose water and the antibiotic pills from Ross Hunter lay untouched in front of her.

'Have you done Max's food and water, darling?' Lynn asked.

Caitlin looked at her blankly.

'Darling?'

Suddenly, Lynn's optimism dipped as she saw the confusion in her daughter's face.

'Don't worry, I'll do it!'

She quickly filled up the water bowl, topped the food up in the dispenser, lifted Max gently from Caitlin's arms, gave him a nuzzle and a kiss and set him down.

'Guard the house, Max, OK! Remember what you're descended from!'

Normally Caitlin would grin whenever she said that. But there was no reaction. Lynn touched her arm gently.

'OK, angel, drink up and take your pills, and let's rock and roll.'

'I'm not thirsty.'

'It'll make you feel better. You can't eat anything this morning, before the op, remember?'

Reluctantly, Caitlin drank. Holding the glass, she half stood up, then crashed back down heavily in the chair, slopping some of the liquid over the rim.

Lynn stared at her for a moment, panic rising again. She held the glass, helping Caitlin get the rest of the fluid and the pills down, then she ran outside and asked the taxi driver to help her.

Two minutes later, with their luggage in the boot, Lynn sat holding Caitlin's hand in the back of the cab as it pulled away.

*

A hundred yards behind them, the green Volkswagen Passat radioed that Target Two was on the move and read out the index of the taxi.

From his desk in MIR One, Grace ordered them to follow and keep them in sight.

*

'Where are we going?' Lynn asked the driver.

'It's a surprise!'

She caught his grin in his mirror.

'What do you mean?'

'I'm not allowed to tell you.'

'What?'

'It's all a bit cloak and dagger. James Bond stuff.'

'*Die Another Day*,' murmured Caitlin, through half-closed eyes. She was now scratching her thighs, harder and harder and harder.

They turned left into Carden Avenue, then left again on to the London Road, heading south towards the centre of Brighton.

Lynn looked at the driver's ID card mounted on the dash. Read his name. *Mark Tuckwell.*

'All right, Mr Bond,' Lynn said. 'Are we in for a long journey?'

'Not this part of it. I—' He was interrupted by his phone ringing. He answered curtly, 'I'm driving. Call you back in a bit.'

'Want to give me any clues?' Lynn asked.

'Chill, woman!' Caitlin murmured.

Lynn sat in silence as they headed down towards Preston Circus, then turned right at the lights and went up New England Hill, under the viaduct. Then they turned sharp left. Moments later they crested the hill and began descending, down towards Brighton Station. The driver stopped at a junction, then carried on down the hill and suddenly pulled over sharply and halted by a row of bollards recently installed to prevent cars dropping off here.

A short man, about fifty years old, in a cheap beige suit, with greasy hair and a beaky nose, hurried over and opened Lynn's door.

'You come with me,' he said in broken English. 'Quickly, quickly, please! I am Grigore!' He gave a servile, buck-toothed smile.

Staring at him in bewilderment, Lynn said, 'Where – where are we going?'

He almost yanked her out of the car in his agitation, with an apologetic smile, into the bitterly cold noon air.

The taxi driver removed their bags from the boot.

None of them noticed the green Passat driving slowly past.

*

In the Incident Room, Grace's radio beeped.

'Roy Grace,' he answered.

'They're getting out at Brighton Station,' the surveillance officer informed him. 'In the wrong place.'

Roy was thrown into total confusion. *Brighton Station?*

'What the fuck?' he said, thinking aloud.

There were four trains an hour to London from there. Romeo Sierra Zero Eight Alpha Mike Lima was still heading towards the M25. All his theories about a clinic in Sussex were suddenly down the khazi. Were they going to a clinic in London?

'Follow them on foot,' he said, in sudden total panic. 'Don't lose them. Whatever you do, don't sodding lose them.'

*

With Grigore holding one bag and Lynn holding the other, dragging a stumbling Caitlin between them, they hurried across the concourse of Brighton Station. Every few seconds the man threw a nervous glance over his shoulder.

'Quick!' he implored. 'Quick!'

'I can't go any bloody quicker!' Lynn panted, totally bewildered.

They hurried beneath the clock suspended from the glass roof, past the news stall and the café, then along, past the far platform.

'Where are we going?' Lynn asked.

'Quick!' he replied.

'I need to sit down,' Caitlin said.

'In minute you sit. OK?'

They stumbled out into the drop-off area beside the car park exit, past several waiting cars and taxis, and reached a dusty brown Mercedes. He popped open the boot, hefted their bags in, then opened a rear door and manoeuvred Caitlin inside. Lynn clambered in on the far side. Grigore jumped into the driver's seat, started the car and drove like a demon away from the station.

*

The surveillance officer, DC Peter Woolf, stood and watched in horror, sensing his promotion prospects disappearing down that ramp, and frantically radioed his colleague in the Passat to get round to the car park exit.

But the Passat was stuck on the far side of the station in a queue of frustrated drivers, waiting for the imbecile in an articulated lorry that was blocking the entire street to complete his reversing manoeuvre.

112

Marlene Hartmann anxiously paced her office on the ground floor of the west wing of Wiston Grange, one of the six clinics that Transplantation-Zentrale quietly owned around the world. Most of the pampered clientele who came here for its spa, as well as surgical and non-surgical rejuvenation facilities, were wholly unaware of the activities that went on behind the sealed doors, marked PRIVATE NO ACCESS, to this particular wing.

There was a fine view towards the Downs from her window, but whenever she came here she was normally too preoccupied to notice it. As she was today.

She looked at her watch for the tenth time. Where was Sirius? Why were the mother and daughter taking so long?

She needed Lynn Beckett here to fax instructions to her bank to authorize the transfer of the second half of the funds. Normally she would wait for confirmation that the cleared funds were in her account, in Switzerland, before proceeding, but today she was going to have to take a risk, because she wanted to get the hell out of here as quickly as possible.

Sunset was at 3.55 p.m. Shoreham Airport closed then for landings and take-offs. She needed to be there for half past three at the latest. Cosmescu would be coming with her, with the remains of the Romanian girl. The team she left behind would be fine, looking after Caitlin. Even if the police did find out it was this place, by the time they turned up the operation would be completed and they would struggle to recover evidence. They might not be happy, but they could hardly cut Caitlin open to check if she had any new organs.

She left her office and walked through into the changing room, where she gowned up in surgical scrubs, boots and rubber gloves. She then opened the door to the operating theatre and entered, nodding acknowledgement to Razvan Ionescu, the Romanian transplant specialist, the two Romanian anaesthetists and the three Romanian nurses.

Simona lay naked and unconscious on the table, beneath the brilliant glare of the twin octopus overhead lights. A breathing tube had been inserted down her throat, connected to the ventilator and the anaesthetic machine. An intravenous cannula in her wrist, connected to a pump fed from a drip bag hanging from a pole beside the table, kept her under with a continuous infusion of Propofol. Two more pumped in fluids to keep her organs well perfused, for maximum quality.

On the flat state-of-the-art computer screen on the wall was a steady readout of her blood pressure, heart rate and oxygen saturation levels.

'*Alles ist in Ordnung?*' Marlene Hartmann asked.

Razvan stared at her blankly. She forgot he spoke no German.

'You are ready?' she said, in Romanian this time.

'Yes.'

She looked at her watch again. 'You want to harvest the liver now?'

Despite his experience, Razvan said, 'I would prefer to wait for Sir Roger.'

'I'm worried about time,' she replied. 'You could make a start with the kidneys. I have orders from Germany and Spain for these.'

Suddenly her radio beeped. She answered and listened for a moment. Then she said, 'OK, super!'

Mrs Beckett and her daughter would be here in twenty minutes.

113

An embarrassed DC Woolf radioed in a somewhat sheepish report that Whiskey Seven Nine Six Lima Delta Yankee was a total loss. The brown Mercedes, containing Lynn and Caitlin Beckett, had given them the slip.

Great, Roy Grace thought, seated at his cramped work station in MIR One. *How fucking great is that?*

All he could do now was hope to hell it pinged an ANPR camera.

A phone was ringing, unanswered. They were being deluged with calls at the moment, following all the media publicity, and were struggling to keep up. Even so, there were twenty-two people in this room and only a dozen of them were on the phone, the rest were reading, or typing.

'Can someone answer the sodding phone!' he called out.

Then Grace glanced down at the post-mortem report on Jim Towers, which had just landed on his desk. The cause of death was asphyxiation caused by water inhalation. Hypoxia and acidosis, resulting in cardiac arrest. Cutting through Nadiuska De Sancha's pages of technical notes, he now knew that the *Scoob-Eee*'s skipper had drowned. All the man's internal organs were intact.

But even so, despite the difference from the three dead teenagers, Grace's instincts told him these deaths were connected. He would need to make a decision about whether to argue the case for having the wreck of the *Scoob-Eee*, now officially a crime scene, recovered. But he hadn't time to start getting his head around that now.

He tapped out a command on his keyboard to bring up a mapping screen. Moments later, from their on-board transponders, he had the positions of the police helicopter and the two cars that were tailing Sirius's Aston Martin. They were only a few miles south of the M25 now. At least with the number of ANPR cameras there, it would be easy to keep track of him.

Then a call came through from the Control Centre. Whiskey Seven Nine Six Lima Delta Yankee had just been spotted on the A283, west of Brighton.

He jumped up with excitement and dashed over to the map. Then he frowned. The purple circles closest to the vehicle's position were Southlands Hospital, in Shoreham, a National Health hospital which had already been marked as unlikely, and a health and beauty spa, Wiston Grange, also marked as unlikely. However, more significantly, this road led to the same roundabout at Washington, just north of Worthing, from where Sirius's car had headed up the A24.

Returning to his work station, he phoned Jason Tingley, the Division Intelligence Unit inspector, and asked if by chance he had a surveillance unit in the Washington area. But Tingley replied apologetically that he hadn't.

Ten minutes later, there was still nothing from the car.

Which meant, almost certainly, he was wrong about the direction. All he could hope was that an alert patrol officer spotted it.

Another phone was ringing on, unanswered. *Answer it, for fuck's sake, someone!* he thought.

To his relief, someone did.

His nerves were becoming increasingly frayed. Alison Vosper wanted an update and Kevin Spinella from the *Argus* had left four messages, wanting to know when the next press conference would be held.

He pulled up a police map of Sussex on his screen and stared at it, wondering desperately what he might be missing.

Then, suddenly, the police observer in the helicopter radioed him, updating him. The Aston Martin was pulling into a petrol station.

Grace thanked him. Seconds later, one of the unmarked units radioed him, informing him they had pulled up at adjoining pumps and requesting instructions.

'Stay with him,' Grace responded. 'Do nothing. Just fill up too, or pretend you're filling up.'

'Stay with him, yes, yes.' There was a crackle, then, 'Sir, Target One emerging from vehicle. Except, sir, it's not a him, it's a *her*.'

'What?'

'It's a woman, sir. Long dark hair. Five-ten, late twenties.'

'Are you sure?' Grace retorted.

'Umm – it's a woman, sir, yes, yes.'

Grace suddenly felt as if a plug had been pulled inside him. 'A woman with long brown hair? But – she had grey hair half an hour ago!'

'Not any more, sir.'

'You're kidding me!' he said.

'I'm afraid not, sir.'

'Stay with her,' Grace said. 'I want to know where she's going.'

Next, he instructed the helicopter to head down to the Washington roundabout and watch for the Mercedes. Then he sipped some stone-cold coffee and closed his eyes for a few moments, tapping his fist against his chin, deep in thought.

Was the woman in the Aston just on an innocent journey somewhere, or was she a decoy? Had DS Tanner, an
experienced surveillance officer, made an error? That was a
big difference in hair colour to get wrong. The car probably
had darkened windows, but the law forbade heavy tints in
the front windows.

Moments later his radio beeped and he got his answer.

It was the surveillance officer at the petrol station.

'Sir, I just got a glance inside the car while she went to
pay. There's a short grey wig lying on the passenger seat.'

Grace thanked him and told him to continue following
her. Then he ended the call.

Shit, he thought. *Shit, shit, shit.*

Immediately, he radioed Paul Tanner.

The rural surveillance expert was apologetic. He
informed Grace that he and his colleague had remained in
situ for thirty minutes after the departure of the Aston
Martin, as instructed. But they were now heading into
central Brighton, urgently required for a drugs surveillance
operation.

Grace thanked him, then turned to Guy Batchelor and
asked him to call Sirius's home number, to see if the man
was there.

Two minutes later, the Detective Sergeant informed him
that Sirius had left home a short while ago.

Grace listened despondently. He just couldn't believe
he'd allowed himself to be so completely and utterly duped
– and so simply. It wasn't what his team expected of him.
Nor was it what he expected from himself.

He should have arrested Lynn Beckett earlier today,
when he'd had the chance. At least that might have contained the situation. Except, of course, it would have caused

panic and he'd almost certainly have blown any chance of catching the people red-handed. God, hindsight was so easy!

Think, he willed himself. *Think, man, think, think, think.*

An unanswered phone was warbling again. He was finding it hard to concentrate with this damn, incessant ringing. A light was blinking on the panel on the phone in front of him. In frustration he pressed the button and answered it himself.

'Incident Room,' he said.

On the other end of the line was a nervous-sounding woman. In her thirties or forties, he guessed. She said, 'May I please speak to someone involved with the three bodies that were – were – found in the Channel? Is it Operation Neptune? Is that right?'

She sounded as if she was probably a time waster, but you could never be sure. His policy was always to be polite and listen carefully. 'You're speaking to Detective Superintendent Grace,' he said. 'I'm the Senior Investigating Officer on Operation Neptune.'

'Ah,' she said. 'Right. Good. Look, I'm sorry to trouble you – but I'm worried. I shouldn't be making this call, you see – I've sneaked out in my break.'

'OK,' he said, picking up his pen and opening his notebook on a blank page. 'Could you let me have your name and your contact number?'

'I – I saw on a Crimestoppers' advertisement that – that I could be anonymous.'

'Yes, certainly, if you'd prefer. So, how do you believe you can help us?'

'Well,' she said, sounding even more nervous, 'this may

be nothing, of course. But I've read – you know – and seen on the news – the – er – the speculation that these poor young people might have been trafficked for their organs. Well, the thing is, you see . . .' She fell silent.

Grace waited for her to continue. Finally, he prompted her, a tad impatiently. 'Yes?'

'Well, you see, I work in the dispensing department of a pharmaceutical wholesaler. For quite a long time now we've been supplying two particular drugs, among others, to a cosmetic surgery clinic in West Sussex. Now the thing is, I don't understand why this clinic would need these particular drugs.'

Grace started becoming more interested. 'What kind of drugs?'

'Well, one is called Tacrolimus.' She spelled it out and he wrote it down. 'The other is Ciclosporin.' He wrote that down, also.

'These drugs are immunosuppressants,' she continued.

'Which means they do what, exactly?' he asked.

'Immunosuppressants are used to prevent rejection by the human body of transplanted organs.'

'Are you saying they don't have any application in cosmetic surgery?'

'The only application is for skin grafts, to prevent rejection. But I very much doubt they would be using the quantity we've been supplying for the two years that I've been here now if it was just for skin grafts. I know quite a lot about that area, you see, I used to work in the burns unit at East Grinstead,' she said, suddenly sounding proud and less nervous. 'There's another drug as well that we supply to this clinic that I think might be relevant.'

'Which is?'

'Prednisolone.' Again she spelled it out. 'It's a steroid – it can have a wider application, but it has a particular function in liver transplants.'

'Liver transplants?'

'Yes.'

Suddenly, Roy Grace's adrenalin was surging. 'What's the name of this clinic?'

After some hesitation, the woman's voice dropped and she sounded nervous again. Almost whispering, she said, 'Wiston Grange.'

114

The driver's English was limited, which suited Lynn fine, as she wasn't in any mood for chatting. He'd informed her his name was Grigore, and every time she glanced at his rear-view mirror, she saw him grinning at her with his crooked, glinting teeth. Twice on the journey he made a brief phone call, speaking in a foreign language Lynn did not know.

All her attention was on Caitlin, who, to her intense relief, seemed to rally a little again during the course of the journey – thanks perhaps to the glucose fluid or the antibiotics, or both. It was Lynn who was the hopeless bag of nerves at this moment, barely even noticing where they were heading, as they travelled along the A27 west of Brighton, passing Shoreham Airport, then along the Steyning bypass. The sky was an ominous grey, as if reflecting the darkness inside her, and flecks of sleet were falling. Every few minutes the driver briefly flicked the wipers on.

'Will Dad come and see me?' Caitlin asked suddenly, her voice sounding weak. She was scratching her stomach now.

'Of course. One of us will be with you all the time until you are back home.'

'*Home*,' Caitlin said wistfully. 'That's where I'd like to be now. *Home*.'

Lynn nearly asked her which *home*, but decided not to go there. She already knew the answer.

Then, looking frightened and vulnerable, Caitlin asked, 'You'll be there during the operation, won't you, Mum?'

'I promise.' She squeezed her daughter's weak hand and kissed her on the cheek. 'And I'll be there when you wake up.'

Caitlin gave a wry smile. 'Yeah, well, don't wear anything embarrassing.'

'Thanks a lot!'

'You haven't brought that horrible orange top?'

'I haven't brought that horrible orange top.'

*

A little over half an hour after leaving Brighton Station car park, they turned in through a smart, pillared gateway, past the sign which read WISTON GRANGE SPA RESORT, then they drove on up a metalled driveway, through rolling parkland and over a series of speed humps. After a short distance Lynn saw a golf course to their left and a large lake. Ahead were the Downs, and she could make out the cluster of trees that formed Chanctonbury Ring.

Caitlin was silent, her eyes closed, listening to music on her iPod, or asleep. Lynn, sitting in funereal silence, did not want to wake her until the last moment, hoping sleep might help conserve her strength.

God, please let me have made the right decision, she prayed silently.

It had been OK until the police officers' visit this morning. She had known until then that she was doing the right thing, but now she didn't know what the *right thing* was any more.

Finally, jerked by a speed hump, Caitlin's eyes opened and she stared around, bewildered.

'What are you listening to, darling?' Lynn asked.

Caitlin did not hear her.

Lynn stared at her daughter with such affection she thought her heart would burst. Stared at the bilious yellow colour of her skin and her eyes. She looked so damn frail and vulnerable.

Stay strong, darling. Just for a little while longer. Just a few more hours and then everything is going to be fine.

She looked through the windscreen for some moments at the place looming up ahead, a big, ugly, stately pile of a house. The central part looked, to Lynn, as if it was Victorian Gothic, but there were a number of modern annexes and outbuildings, some sympathetic to the style, others just bland, modern prefabs. She saw a circular driveway ahead, lined with cars, flanked by a car park on either side, but the driver turned off at a sign marked PRIVATE, drove through an archway along the side of the house and into a large rear courtyard, bounded on one side by what she presumed had once been the mews stables and on another by a row of ugly lock-up garages.

They pulled to a halt beside an unpretentious back entrance. Before Lynn had climbed out of the Mercedes, a massive beefcake of a woman emerged from the door, wearing a white nurse's tunic and gym shoes.

Grigore sprang around to open Caitlin's door, but, with considerable effort, she slid over to her mother's side, following her out unaided.

'Mrs Lynn Beckett, Miss Caitlin Beckett?' The woman's formal voice and broken English accent made it sound like an interrogation.

Lynn nodded meekly, holding an arm around her daughter, and read the woman's name tag: Draguta.

She looked like a dragon, she thought.

'You will follow me, please.'

'I bring your bags,' Grigore said.

Lynn gripped Caitlin's hand as they followed the woman along a wide corridor with white tiled walls which smelled strongly of disinfectant, passing several closed doors. Then the woman stopped at a locked door at the end and punched in a security code.

They walked through into a carpeted area, with pale grey painted walls, which had the feel of an office suite, then the woman stopped at a door and knocked.

A female voice from the other side called out, '*Reinkommen!*'

Lynn and Caitlin were ushered into a large, plush office, and the nurse closed the door behind them. Marlene Hartmann rose up from behind a bare desk to greet them. Behind her was a window giving a panoramic view across towards the Downs.

'*Gut!* You are here! I hope you had a pleasant journey – please sit down.' She pointed to the two armchairs in front of the desk.

'We had an interesting journey,' Lynn said, a hard knot in her stomach and her throat feeling so tight she could barely get the words out. Her legs were shaking.

'*Ja.* We have problems.' Marlene Hartmann nodded seriously. 'But I have never let a customer down.' She smiled at Caitlin. 'All is good, *mein Liebling*?'

'I'd quite like the surgeon to have Feist playing during the operation. Do you think he'd sort of like do that?' Caitlin asked quietly.

She sat, scratching her left ankle, hunched up on the chair.

'Feist?' The woman frowned. 'What is Feist?'

'She's cool. A singer.'

Now she started scratching her distended stomach.

The German woman shrugged. 'OK, sure, we can ask. I don't know.'

'There's kind of like one other thing I want to know,' Caitlin said.

Lynn stared at her in alarm. She seemed to be having breathing difficulties when she spoke.

'Tell me?'

'This liver I'm getting – who is it coming from?'

Without any flicker of hesitation, the woman responded, 'From a poor little girl about your age who was killed in car accident yesterday.'

Lynn glanced anxiously at her daughter, signalling with her eyes not to probe further.

'Where was she killed?' Caitlin asked, ignoring her mother. Her voice suddenly sounded stronger.

'In Romania – outside a town called Brasov.'

'Tell me more about her, please,' Caitlin said.

This time, Marlene Hartmann shrugged defensively. 'I'm afraid I have to protect donor confidentiality. I cannot give you any more information. Afterwards, you may write, through me, to thank her family, if you wish. I would encourage this.'

'So it's not true what the police—'

'Darling!' Lynn interrupted hastily, sensing what was coming. 'Frau Hartmann is right.'

Caitlin was silent for some moments, looking around, her eyes searching as if they were having difficulty focusing. Then, speaking weakly, she said, 'If – if I'm going to agree to have this liver, I need to know the truth.'

Lynn looked at her, bewildered.

Suddenly, the door opened and the nurse called Draguta came back in.

'We are ready.'

'Please, Caitlin, you go now,' the broker said. 'Your mother and I have business to conclude. She will be with you in a few minutes.'

'So the photograph the police brought round – that's not true?' Caitlin persisted.

'Darling! Angel!' Lynn implored.

Marlene Hartmann looked at them both stonily. 'Photograph?'

'It was a lie!' Lynn blurted, close to tears. 'It was a lie!'

'What photograph is this, Caitlin?' the broker asked.

'They said she was not dead. That she was going to be killed for me.'

Marlene Hartmann shook her head. Her lips formed into a rigid, humourless line and there was astonishment in her eyes.

Very gently, she said, 'Caitlin, this is not how I do business. Please believe me.' She smiled warmly. 'I don't think your English police are happy with anyone doing something to – how do you say it? – *buck* their system. They would rather people died than obtain an organ by paying for it. You have to trust me on this.'

Behind them, the nurse said, 'Now you come, please.'

Lynn kissed her daughter. 'Go with her, darling. I'll follow you in a few minutes. I just have to make the final payment. I'll fax the bank while you're getting ready.'

She helped Caitlin to her feet.

Swaying unsteadily, her eyes looking very unfocused, Caitlin turned to Marlene Hartmann.

'Feist,' she said. 'You'll ask the surgeon?'

'Feist,' the German woman said, with a broad smile.

Then she took a step towards her mother, looking scared. 'You won't be long, Mum, will you?'

'I'll be as quick as I can, darling.'

'I'm frightened,' she whispered.

'In a few days' time you will not know yourself!' the broker replied.

The nurse escorted Caitlin from the room, closing the door behind them. Instantly, Marlene Hartmann's eyes narrowed into a glare of suspicion.

'What is this photograph that your daughter is talking about?'

Before Lynn could answer, the German woman's attention was diverted by the sudden clatter of a helicopter, low overhead. She leapt up from her chair, ran across to the window and looked out.

'*Scheisse!*' she said.

115

Back in the tiled corridor, the nurse ushered Caitlin into a tiny changing room with a row of metal lockers and a solitary hospital gown hanging on a peg.

'You change,' she said. 'You put clothes in locker 14. I wait.'

She closed the door.

Caitlin stared at the lockers and swallowed, shaking. Number 14 had a key with a rubber wrist-band sticking out of the lock. It reminded her of public swimming baths.

Swimming scared her. She did not like being out of her depth. She was out of her depth now.

Feeling giddy, she sat down, harder than she had intended, on a wooden bench and scratched her stomach. She was feeling tired and lost and sick. She just wanted to stop feeling sick. To stop itching. To stop feeling scared.

She had never felt so scared in her life.

The room seemed to be pressing in on her. Squeezing her. Crushing her. Spinning her around with it. Thoughts came into her head, then went. She had to be quick, to try to grab them before they faded.

Things were being hidden from her. By everyone. Even by her mother. What things? Why? What did everybody know that she did not know? What right did anyone have to keep secrets from her?

She stood up and tugged off her duffel coat, then sat back down, hard, the room spinning even faster. Her stomach was hurting again. She felt as if a thousand mosquitoes were biting her all at once.

'Fuck off!' she gasped suddenly, out loud. 'Just fuck off, pain.'

Fighting the giddiness, she stood up again, then opened the locker and was about to put her coat in, when she hesitated. Instead, she laid it down on the bench seat and opened the door.

The corridor was deserted.

She stepped out unsteadily, closing the door behind her, checked both directions warily, her vision a little blurry, and walked a short distance to her right. On her left she saw a door. A sign on the outside read STRICTLY NO ADMISSION WITHOUT STERILE CLOTHING. She squinted at it until she could read it clearly.

Then she opened it and stumbled through into a narrow, windowless room that looked like it was a store for medical supplies. There was a steel gurney on wheels, which she bumped into, banging her thigh, a floor-to-ceiling cupboard with glass doors, the shelves stacked with surgical equipment, a row of oxygen cylinders on the floor, one of which she knocked over, cursing, and several pieces of electrical monitoring equipment. At the far end was a door with a circle of glass in it, like a porthole. Caitlin made her way across to it.

And froze.

Through it, she could see into a very high-tech-looking operating theatre. It was crowded with people attired in green surgical scrubs, elasticized hats, white masks and flesh-coloured gloves. Most of them were standing around a brightly illuminated steel table, on which lay a naked girl, who looked prepped for surgery. From all the time she had spent in hospital herself, and hours of watching her favourite medical dramas, *House* and *Grey's Anatomy*, she knew what quite a lot of the apparatus connected to the girl was. The endotracheal breathing tube. The nasogastric tube, the central lines cannulated into her neck, the cardiac monitor pads on her chest, the cannulated arterial and peripheral lines, the PiCCO monitor, the pulse oximeter, the urinary catheter.

An elderly-looking man was holding a scalpel, talking to a younger man, tracing lines on the body with a gloved finger, where he was clearly about to make incisions.

Even though the girl's face was distorted and inert, Caitlin recognized her instantly.

It was the Romanian girl in the photograph the two detectives had brought to the house this morning.

The girl that the German woman said had been killed in a car crash in Romania yesterday. Surely, Caitlin thought, her view of the girl improving as someone moved aside, if you were in a car accident bad enough to kill you, there would be marks on your body, wouldn't there? Cuts, bruises, abrasions, at the very least.

This girl just looked as if she was asleep.

Caitlin squeezed her eyes shut, then opened them again, trying to focus more sharply. She could not detect a mark on her body.

The words of the Detective Superintendent replayed in her head.

Her name is Simona Irimia. So far as we know she is still alive and healthy. She has been trafficked to England and will be killed so that your daughter can have her liver.

And now she realized he had been telling the truth.

The German woman was lying.

Her mother was lying.

They were going to kill this girl. Maybe she was already dead.

Suddenly, behind her, she heard a furious voice, shouting in broken English, 'What do you think you are doing?'

She turned and saw Draguta lumbering towards her.

Frantically, Caitlin pushed the door, but it would not budge. Then she saw the handle, yanked it open and stumbled in. Anger surged inside her. Anger, and hatred at all these people. At their masked faces.

'Stop!' Caitlin croaked, crashing through the two gowned figures immediately in front of her. She lunged at the surgeon and grabbed the scalpel from the startled man's hand, feeling it cutting into her fingers as she did so. 'Stop right now! You're evil!'

Then, standing between him and the younger man, she stared down hard, scrutinizing, in a few split seconds, every visible inch of the girl's body. There was no sign of any trauma injury at all.

'Young woman, please leave immediately,' the older man said, in a very posh voice muffled by his mask. 'You are contaminating the theatre. Give me that back at once!'

'Is she still alive?' Caitlin screamed at him, using every remaining ounce of her strength to power her voice.

Rows of meaningless waveforms travelled across the flat, wall-mounted screen just beyond the table. More symbols and numbers flickered on smaller screens on free-standing monitoring equipment behind the young girl's head.

'What the hell does this have to do with you?' he exploded, the visible parts of his face turning puce.

'Quite a lot, actually,' Caitlin said, breathing heavily. She jabbed her chest with her free hand. 'I'm meant to be getting her liver.'

There was a moment of stunned silence.

Draguta shouted a command for her to come out, as if she were shouting at a dog.

'She's alive, at this moment, yes,' the younger man said enthusiastically, as if this was something Caitlin wanted to hear.

She lunged forward, grabbed at the drip lines that were in Simona's arm with her left hand and jerked them free, then grabbed the ones out of the neck and tore at the cardiac monitor pads.

The surgeon seized Caitlin by her shoulders. 'Are you crazy, little girl?'

Caitlin responded by biting his hand, hard. The surgeon cried out in pain and she wriggled free, twisting, staring at pairs of eyes behind masks, all of them in shock, uncertain what to do. Then she saw the nurse marching towards her.

She raised the scalpel, holding it by the handle like a dagger, brandishing it at everyone, beyond caring.

'Get her off that table!' she said, her voice cracking. 'Get her off that table now!'

The entire theatre team stood motionless, staring at her in shock.

Except the big nurse, who pushed through, grabbed Caitlin's free arm and yanked her so hard she almost fell over. Then she jerked her back across the room to the door, Caitlin's trainers sliding on the tiled floor as she tried, with her failing strength, to resist.

'Let me go, you ugly fucking cow!' she hissed.

The nurse stopped to push open the door, then jerked Caitlin hard again. She stumbled forward, falling, and as she shot out her arm to cushion herself, the blade of the scalpel, still gripped tightly in her hand, sliced through the top of the woman's cheekbone, cleanly through her right eye and the bridge of her nose.

The woman let out a terrible howl, her hands shooting to her face, blood jetting in every direction. She staggered against someone, wailing like a banshee, and several of the team rushed over to help and to stop her falling.

In the commotion, no one noticed Caitlin stumbling out.

116

Marlene Hartmann was striding anxiously down the tiled corridor, her normal steely composure already shot to pieces, when she heard the screams. She broke into a run, then saw what looked like utter mayhem spilling out of the operating theatre.

She stormed through the supplies room and saw her theatre team frantically trying to restrain the massive nurse, who had blood gouting from her face and spurting all over her white tunic. She was lashing out with all her considerable strength and screaming hysterically as, blood-spattered, Sir Roger Sirius and two junior surgeons, the anaesthetists and the scrub nurses all wrestled with her. Simona lay on the operating table, wires and lines all around her, oblivious to everything.

'*Gottverdammt*, what is happening?'

'The girl went crazy,' Sirius said, panting.

Then, before he could say anything further, Draguta's meaty fist smashed into his cheek, sending him reeling backwards and crashing on to the hard floor.

Marlene ran over to him, knelt and helped him to his feet. He looked dazed.

'There's a police helicopter here!' Marlene yelled at him. 'We need to do a lock-down! Pull yourselves together! Do you understand?'

Draguta fell, with several green-gowned members of the team crashing down on top of her.

'I'm blind!' she screamed in Romanian. 'God help me, I'm blind!'

'Get her sedated!' commanded Marlene. 'Shut her up! Quickly!'

A junior anaesthetist grabbed a syringe, then scrabbled around on the trolley and picked up a vial.

One of the nurses said, 'We need to get Draguta to an eye hospital.'

'Where's the English girl? Caitlin? Where is she?'

Blank, dazed eyes stared at her.

'WHERE IS THE ENGLISH GIRL?' Marlene Hartmann shouted.

117

The roundabouts were getting worse. Caitlin, freezing cold, sleet tickling her face every few seconds, bumped against the wall, pushed herself away and almost fell over. It was an effort to move her feet. She dragged one, then the other. She was almost at the front of the building now. She could see a car park. Rows and rows of vehicles.

They came in and out of focus.

She stumbled through a flowerbed and nearly fell. Her iPod, dangling from a wire, tapped against her knee. She itched terribly.

They're going to be angry with me. Mum. Luke. Dad. Gran. Shit, they're going to be angry with me. Shit. Angry. Shit. Angry.

Above her was a terrible, loud, clattering roar.

She looked up, furiously scratching her chest. A few hundred feet above her head she saw a dark blue and yellow helicopter, like a huge mutant insect. And she saw the word POLICE along its side.

Shit. Shit. Shit. They were coming to arrest her for stabbing the nurse.

She pressed against the wall, gulping air, fighting for every breath. The wall was moving, swaying. She inched forward. Saw the circular driveway. The helicopter swept away, making a wide arc. Then she saw a taxi, the same turquoise and white colours as the one that had brought them here.

A woman in a fur coat and silk headsquare was standing

by the driver's door, paying the driver. Then she turned and walked towards the front door, towing her bag behind her. The driver was getting back into his cab.

Caitlin ran, stumbling, towards him, waving her arms.

'Hello!' she called. 'Hello!'

He did not hear her.

'Hello!'

He was getting back into the vehicle.

She grabbed the front passenger door and swayed again, hanging on to it with all her strength. Then she pulled it open. 'Please,' she gasped. 'Please – are you free?'

'I'm sorry, love, this is out of my area. I'm not allowed to pick up here.'

'Please – where are you going? Could you just give me a lift?'

He was a wrinkled man with white hair and a kind face.

'Where do you want to go? I have to get back to Brighton.'

'Yes,' she said. 'Yes, great, thanks.'

She half stumbled, half fell on to the front seat. The interior smelled strongly of the woman's perfume.

'Are you all right, love? You're bleeding.'

She nodded. 'Yes,' she gasped. 'Just – just shut my hand in a door.'

'I've got a first-aid kit – do you want a sticking plaster?'

Caitlin shook her head vigorously. 'No. No thanks. I'm fine.'

'Been having treatment here, have you?'

She nodded, desperately trying to keep her eyes open.

'Expensive, this place, I've heard.'

'My mother pays,' she whispered.

He leaned over and pulled her seat belt on for her, then clipped it into place.

She was almost unconscious by the time they reached the front gates.

'Are you sure you're all right?' he asked.

Nodding, she replied, 'It's tiring, you know, the treatments.'

'I wouldn't know,' he said. 'Not in my budget.'

'Budget,' she echoed weakly. Then, as her eyes closed, she felt the vehicle accelerate.

'You really sure you're all right?' he asked again insistently.

'I'm fine.'

Five minutes later, three police cars shot past in the opposite direction, roof spinners flashing, sirens wailing. Moments later, they were followed by another.

'Something's going on,' the driver said.

'Shit happens,' she murmured drowsily.

'Tell me about it,' he agreed.

118

Alarmed by the abrupt, panicky departure of the organ broker from the room, Lynn went over to the window to see what was causing the incessant, clattering noise. Her gullet tightened as she looked up at the circling helicopter and read the word POLICE.

It was circling low overhead, as if looking for something – or someone.

Herself?

Her stomach felt as if a drum of ice had been emptied into it.

Please, no. Please, God, no. Not now. Please let the operation go ahead. After that, anything.

Please just let the operation go ahead.

She was so tensed up, watching it, at first she didn't hear the sound of her phone ringing. Then she fumbled inside her handbag and pulled her phone out. On the display it read, *Private Number.*

She answered.

'Mrs Beckett?' said a woman's voice she recognized but could not place.

'Yes?'

'It's Shirley Linsell, from the Royal South London Hospital.'

'Oh. Yes, hello,' she said, surprised to hear from the woman. What the hell was she calling about?

'I have some good news for you. We have a liver which

may be suitable for Caitlin. Can you be ready to leave in an hour's time?'

'A liver?' she said blankly.

'It's actually a split liver from a large person.'

'Yes, I see,' she said, her mind spinning. *Split liver.* She couldn't even think what a *split liver* meant at this moment.

'Would one hour's time be all right?'

'One hour?'

'For the ambulance to collect yourself and Caitlin?'

Suddenly, Lynn felt boiling hot, as if her head was about to explode.

'I'm sorry,' she said. 'Pardon?'

Shirley Linsell patiently repeated what she had just said.

Lynn stood in numb silence, holding the phone to her ear.

'Hello? Mrs Beckett?'

Her brain was paralysed.

'Mrs Beckett? Are you there?'

'Yes,' Lynn said. 'Yes.'

'We'll have an ambulance with you in one hour.'

'Right,' Lynn said. 'Umm, the thing is . . .' She fell silent.

'Hello? Mrs Beckett?'

'I'm here,' she said.

'It's a very good match.'

'Right, good, OK.'

'Do you have some concerns you'd like to talk about?'

Lynn's brain was scrambling for traction. What the hell should she do? Tell the woman no thanks, that she was now sorted?

With a police helicopter overhead.

Where had Marlene Hartmann gone, almost running from the room?

What if the wheels fell off, despite the payment she had

made? Maybe it would be more sensible, even at this late stage, to take the offer of the legitimate liver?

Like the last time, when they had been bumped for some sodding alcoholic?

Caitlin would not survive if they got bumped again.

'Can we talk through your concerns, Mrs Beckett?'

'Yep, well, after the last time – that was a pretty damn tough call. I don't think I could put Caitlin through that again.'

'I understand that, Mrs Beckett. I can't give you any guarantees that our consultant surgeon won't find a problem with this one either. But, so far, it looks good.'

Lynn sat back down at one of the chairs in front of Marlene Hartmann's desk. She desperately needed to think this through.

'I have to call you back,' Lynn said. 'How long can you give me?'

Sounding surprised, the woman said, 'I can give you ten minutes. Otherwise I will have to pass it to the next person on the list, I'm afraid. I really think you would be making a terrible mistake not to accept this.'

'Ten minutes, thank you,' Lynn said. 'I'll call you. Within ten minutes.'

She hung up. Then she attempted to weigh the pros and cons in her mind, trying not to be influenced by the money she had paid over.

A certain liver here at this clinic, versus an uncertain liver in London.

Caitlin should be part of this decision. Then she looked at her watch. Nine minutes to go.

She hurried out across the carpeted area and through the door into the tiled corridor. Ahead on her right she saw a door ajar and peered in. It was a small changing room, with lockers and a bench seat. Lying on the seat was Caitlin's duffel coat.

She must be somewhere near, she thought. A short distance further along was another open door, to the left. She walked down and looked in, and saw a storeroom with a gurney on wheels and what looked like an operating-theatre door, with a glass porthole, at the far end.

She hurried across and peered through the glass. An unconscious, naked girl, not Caitlin, lay intubated on the operating table. Several masked people, in green scrubs, were heaving a huge, unconscious nurse, covered in blood, up off the floor. As they staggered around under her weight, Lynn saw, to her shock, it was the nurse, Draguta, who had taken Caitlin off.

She felt a sudden fear catching her throat. Something was terribly wrong. She pushed the door open and went in.

'Excuse me!' she called out. 'Excuse me! Does anyone know where my daughter is? Caitlin?'

Several of them turned to stare at her.

'Your daughter?' said a young man, in broken English.

'*Caitlin*. She's having an operation. A transplant.'

The surgeon glanced at the nurse, then back at Lynn. 'I don't think so,' he said. 'Not now.'

'Where is she?' she said, almost yelling at him, her fear rising. 'What's going on? Where is she?' She jabbed a hand at Draguta. 'What's happened?'

'I think you should speak with your daughter,' he said.

'Where is she? Please, where is she?'

He shrugged. 'I don't know.'

She glanced at her watch. Seven minutes left.

She turned and ran, panic-stricken, from the room, back out into the corridor, shouting loudly, 'Caitlin! Caitlin! Caitlin!'

She flung open a door, but it was just a laundry room. Then another, but it contained only an MRI scanner and was otherwise empty.

'CAITLIN!' she screamed desperately, running further along the corridor, then outside into the deserted yard and the freezing air. She looked around frantically, shouting again, 'CAITLIN!'

Choked with tears, she went back in and ran along the corridor into the office suite, throwing open door after door. There were just offices. Startled administration staff looked up from their work stations. She opened another door and saw a small back staircase. She sprinted up it and at the top saw a heavy fire door with the words STERILE AREA. STRICTLY NO UNAUTHORIZED ADMITTANCE across it.

It was unlocked and she went through into what felt, and smelled like a hospital corridor. There was another door ahead, with a hand-cleansing unit, on the wall outside. Ignoring that, she opened the door and stepped in.

It was a small intensive care ward. There were six beds, three of them occupied, one by a long-haired man in his early forties, who might have been a rock singer, another by a boy of about Caitlin's age and the third by a woman, in her late fifties Lynn estimated. All three were intubated with endotracheal and nasogastric tubes and plumbed into a forest of drip and monitoring lines from the battery of equipment surrounding each bed.

Three nurses, in the same white uniform as Draguta had been wearing, stared up at her with suspicion from behind the central station.

'I'm looking for my daughter, Caitlin,' she said. 'Have any of you seen her?'

'Please leave,' one said in broken English. 'No admission.'

She backed out quickly, checked for more doors, saw one and pulled it open. It was a canteen and sitting room. She ran across and checked another door, but that opened on to an empty bathroom. Then she looked at her watch again.

Less than five minutes.

Surely they could give her a little more time? She had to be here.

Had to.

She dialled Caitlin's mobile phone, but it went straight to voicemail. Then she stumbled back down the stairs, through the office suite and out of another door. She ran along a short passageway, then pushed open another door and suddenly found herself in the vast, marble-floored entrance lobby of the spa.

There were people all around. Three women in white towelling dressing gowns and throw-away slippers were peering at a display of jewellery in a showcase. A man, similarly attired, was signing a form at one of the reception desks. Near him a woman in an elegant coat with a silk headsquare, her wheeled suitcase beside her, appeared to be checking in.

She swept the entire room with her eyes in just a few seconds.

No Caitlin.

Then the two halves of the electric front door slid open with a sharp hiss. Six solid and determined-looking police officers all wearing body armour entered.

She turned and ran.

119

'The far end!' Marlene Hartmann said to Grigore. 'Down the end of the golf course, just past the eighth tee, there's another exit. The police won't know about it. It takes us out on to a lane. We can keep away from the main road for several miles. I know it works. I'll direct you.'

She sat in the back of the brown Mercedes, hands gripping the top of the passenger seat, anxiously looking all around her, breathing heavily, cursing. Cursing the damned Beckett woman and her little bitch daughter. Cursing the police. Cursing the panicky surgeon, Sirius.

But mostly cursing herself. Her stupidity in thinking she could get away with this. Greed. It was like gambler's folly. Not knowing when to quit.

In front of her, Vlad Cosmescu was silent. He was having similar thoughts. Always at the roulette table – well, almost always, anyway – he knew when to quit. To walk away. To go home.

He should have gone home last night. Then it would have been fine. Back home to Romania. He didn't owe this woman anything. She just used him, the way everyone used him. The same way he used them. That was how the world worked, to him. Life wasn't about loyalty, it was about survival.

So why was he here?

He knew the answer. Because this woman had a spell on him. He wanted to conquer her, wanted to sleep with her. He thought that by being brave it would attract her.

He swore silently. For ten years he had made money and kept free of the law.

Stupid, he thought. *Just so stupid.*

The car slewed and bumped over a mound, then, to the fury of two male golfers, drove straight over a green, between the balls they were waiting to putt out. Marlene clung on as the car dipped steeply, its suspension bottoming out, her head striking the ceiling as the car bounced.

'*Scheisse!*' she said, but not from pain.

It was the sight of the white police van that was squarely parked across the rear exit to Wiston Grange, ahead of them, that made her swear.

'Turn!' she commanded Grigore. 'We try the front.'

'Maybe we are better on foot?' Cosmescu said, as Grigore braked sharply, sliding the car around on the grass.

'Oh sure, with the helicopter up there? No chance!' She peered out of the side window, craning her neck up.

Then Grigore let out a yell and jabbed his finger over his shoulder. Marlene turned and, to her horror, saw a police Range Rover on their tail, lights flashing and gaining rapidly.

'Want me to try?' Grigore said. 'I drive fast?'

'No, stop. Don't say anything. I'll speak. I'll try to bluff. Stop the car! *Halten!*'

Grigore obliged. The three of them sat in numb silence, for an instant, Marlene thinking hard.

Another police car was racing towards them. It pulled up nose to nose with the Mercedes, blocking them, its siren dying away. And as she looked at the occupants of the front seat, her heart sank even further.

The driver was a black officer she had never seen before, but his front seat passenger was someone she had very definitely met before. In her office in Germany.

Yesterday.

Now he was out of his car and walking towards her, his unbuttoned overcoat open and flapping in the breeze. Several uniformed officers in stab vests materialized from the Range Rover and stood close behind him.

'Good afternoon, *Mr Taylor*,' she greeted him coolly, as he opened her door. 'Or would you prefer I call you *Detective Superintendent Grace*?'

Ignoring her comment, and unsmiling, he said, 'Marlene Eva Hartmann, I'm arresting you on suspicion of trafficking human beings for organ transplantation purposes.' He cautioned her and said, 'Step out of the car, please.'

He gripped her wrist and held on as she climbed out, then nodded to one of the uniformed police officers, who stepped forward and handcuffed her. 'Just hold her here for a moment,' he instructed the PC, then he opened the front door and addressed Cosmescu.

'Joseph Baker, otherwise known as Vlad Roman Cosmescu, I'm arresting you on suspicion of the murder of Jim Towers.' Grace then cautioned him.

As Cosmescu was being handcuffed, Grace walked around to the driver's side and opened the door. The man was staring at him bug-eyed and shaking. 'So who are you?' he asked.

'Me, Grigore. I the driver.'

'You have a last name?'

'A what?'

'Grigore? Grigore what?'

'Ah. Dinica. Grigore Dinica!'

'You're the driver, right?'

'Yes, just taxi driver, like taxi driver.'

'*Taxi* driver?' Grace pushed, brushing a fleck of sleet from his face. His radio crackled but he ignored it.

'Yes, yes, *taxi*. I only driving taxi for these people.'

'You want me to nick you for driving an unlicensed taxi, on top of what I'm about to charge you with?'

Grigore stared at him blankly, perspiration popping on his brow.

Telling Glenn Branson to arrest the man on suspicion of aiding and abetting human trafficking, Grace turned back to the woman.

Before he could speak, she said, 'Detective Superintendent Grace, may I recommend that next time you pretend to be a customer interested in some services, you should be better briefed.'

'If you're so well briefed yourself, how come you're nicked?' he retorted.

'I have done nothing wrong,' she said adamantly.

'Good,' he said. 'Then you're lucky. English prisons are horribly overcrowded at the moment. I wouldn't recommend a stay in many of them, especially the women's ones.' He brushed more flecks of sleet from his face. 'Now, Frau Hartmann, do you want us to do this the easy way or the hard way?'

'What do you mean?'

'We have a search warrant signed for these premises, which is on its way – it'll be here in a few minutes. You can give us the guided tour, if you like, or leave us to find our own way around.'

He smiled.

She did not smile back.

120

Lynn ran through a seemingly never-ending succession of rooms with a bewildering array of signs and names. Some she checked out, some she ignored. She didn't bother with the sauna, or the steam room, or the aromatherapy room. But she peered into the yoga classroom, the Ayurvedic Centre, several treatment rooms, then the Rainforest Experience Zone.

Every few moments she looked over her shoulder for any sign of the police officers. But they were not following her.

Out of breath and disoriented by the geography of the place, she stumbled on. She was feeling clammy and jittery, a sign, she recognized through her distress, that she was low on sugar.

Darling. Caitlin, darling. Angel, where are you?

As she ran, she dialled Caitlin's mobile for the third time, but it again went straight to voicemail.

The ten minutes were up. She stopped and, panting, dialled Shirley Linsell and pleaded for a few more minutes, giving a half-truth that she had taken her to a spa and she had wandered off. Reluctantly, the Royal's transplant coordinator agreed to another ten minutes. But that would be it.

Lynn thanked her profusely, then stood still, her heart thumping, thinking desperately, worried out of her wits.

Please appear, Caitlin, please, please, please.

This place was too big. She was never going to find her without help. Trying to get a grip on her bearings, she ran back, following the signs to the front lobby, and arrived quicker than she had expected. One police officer was standing by the front door, as if guarding it, and the others had disappeared.

She went through the door which was marked PRIVATE. NO ADMITTANCE, back into the office suite area, opened the door to Marlene Hartmann's room and went in.

And froze in her tracks.

The German woman, her arms in front of her, hand-cuffed together, was looking sullen but dignified. Behind her stood two uniformed police officers. Beside her stood a tall, bald black man in a raincoat and, standing at her desk, riffling through papers, was the detective superintendent who had visited her earlier this morning. He turned his head to look at her and his eyes widened in recognition.

'Brought your daughter here for a treat before her operation, have you, Mrs Beckett?'

'Please, you have to help me find her,' she blurted.

'Do you have a good reason for being here at Wiston Grange?' he responded sternly.

'A good reason? Yes,' Lynn said, venomously, suddenly angered at his attitude. 'Because I want to look good at my daughter's funeral. Is that enough of a reason?'

In the silence that followed, she covered her face with her hands and began sobbing. 'Please help me. I can't find her. Please tell me where she is.' She looked at the German woman through her blurry eyes. 'Where is she?'

The broker shrugged.

'Please,' Lynn sobbed. 'I have to find her. She's run off somewhere. We have to find her. They have a liver for her at the Royal. We have to find her. Ten minutes. Just have ten minutes. TEN MINUTES!'

Roy Grace stepped towards her, holding up a sheet of paper, his face hard.

'Mrs Beckett, I am arresting you on suspicion of conspiracy to traffic a human being for organ transplantation purposes, and on suspicion of attempting to purchase a human organ. You do not need to say anything but it may harm your defence if you do not mention when questioned something which you later rely on in court.'

Lynn could see what the sheet of paper was now. It was the fax she had sent, just a short while ago to her bank, instructing them to transfer the balance of the funds to Transplantation-Zentrale.

Her legs felt weak suddenly. She balled her hands, pressing them against her mouth, sobbing hysterically. 'Please find my daughter. I'll admit to anything, I don't care, just please find her.'

She looked imploringly at the black man, who had a sympathetic face, then at the cold carapace of the German woman, then at the Detective Superintendent.

'She's dying! Please, you have to understand! We have a ten-minute window to find her, or the hospital will give her liver to someone else. Don't you understand? If she doesn't get that liver today, she will die.'

'Where have you looked?' Marlene said stiffly.

'Everywhere – all over.'

'Outside, also?'

She shook her head. 'No – I—'

'I'll call the helicopter,' Glenn Branson said. 'Can you give me a description of your daughter? What is she wearing?'

Lynn told him, then he brought his radio to his ear. After a brief exchange, he lowered it.

'They spotted a teenage girl who matches that description getting into a taxi about fifteen minutes ago.'

Lynn let out a shocked wail. 'A taxi? Where? Where was – where was it going?'

'It was a Brighton taxi – a Streamline,' Glenn Branson said. 'We should be able to find out, but it's going to take more than ten minutes.'

Shaking her head in bewilderment, Lynn said, 'Fifteen minutes ago, in a taxi?'

Branson nodded.

Lynn thought for a moment. 'Look – look, she's probably gone back to our house. Please let me go there. I'll come back – I'll come straight back, I promise.'

'Mrs Beckett,' Roy Grace said, 'you are under arrest, and you are going to be taken from here to the Custody Centre at Brighton.'

'My daughter is dying! She can't survive. She will die if she doesn't get to hospital today. I – have to be with her – I—'

'If you like we'll have someone go there and see how she is.'

'It's not that simple. She has got to go to hospital. Today.'

'Is there anyone else who can take her?' Grace asked.

'My husband – my ex-husband.'

'How can we contact him?'

'He's on a ship – at sea – a dredger. I – can't remember – what his hours are – when they're ashore.'

Grace nodded. 'Can you give us his phone number? We'll try him.'

'Can't I speak to him myself?'

'I'm sorry, no.'

'Can't I just make – I thought I could make – one phone call?'

'After you are booked in.'

She looked at both men in despair. Grace looked back at her with compassion but remained firm. She gave them Mal's mobile number. Glenn Branson wrote it on his pad, then immediately dialled it.

121

There were only two things to read in the room. One, pinned to a green door with a small window in it, said, NO MOBILE PHONES TO BE USED IN THE CUSTODY AREA. The other read, ALL DETAINED PERSONS WILL BE THOROUGHLY SEARCHED AS DIRECTED BY THE CUSTODY OFFICER. IF YOU HAVE ANY PROHIBITED ITEMS ON YOUR PERSON OR IN YOUR PROPERTY TELL THE CUSTODY OFFICER OR YOUR ARRESTING OFFICER NOW.

Lynn had read them both about a dozen times each. She had been in this grim room, with its bare white walls and bare brown floor, seated on the rock-hard bench that felt like it was made of stone for over an hour now, sustained by two small packets of sugar she had been given.

She had never felt so terrible in her life. None of the pain of her divorce came close to what she was experiencing inside her mind and her heart now.

Every few minutes the young police officer who had accompanied her here from Wiston Grange glanced at her and gave her a helpless smile. They had nothing to say to each other. She'd made her point over and over to him, and he understood it, but he could do nothing.

Suddenly his phone beeped. He answered it. After a few moments, during which he gave monosyllabic responses, he held the phone away from his ear and turned to Lynn. 'It's Detective Sergeant Branson – he was with you earlier, at Wiston?'

She nodded.

'He's with your ex-husband now, at your house. There's no sign of your daughter.'

'Where is she?' Lynn said weakly. 'Where?'

The officer looked at her helplessly.

'Could I speak to Mal – my ex?'

'I'm sorry, madam, I cannot permit that.' Then he suddenly pulled his phone closer to his ear and raised a finger.

Turning to Lynn, he said, 'They've got Streamline Taxis on the phone.'

He listened for some moments and then said, into the phone, 'I will relay that, sir, if you hold a moment.'

He turned to Lynn again. 'They've been in contact with the driver who picked up a young lady from Wiston Grange about two hours ago – answering to the description of your daughter. He said he was concerned about her state of health and wanted to take her to hospital, but she refused. He dropped her off at a farm in Woodmancote, near Henfield.'

Lynn frowned. 'What was the address?'

'Apparently it was just a track – that's where she insisted on getting out.'

And then the penny dropped.

'Oh Jesus!' she said. 'I know where she is. I know exactly where she is. Please tell Mal – he'll understand.' Fighting tears again, she sniffed, her voice jerky with sobs. 'Tell him she's gone *home*.'

122

Shortly after four o'clock, in the failing daylight, the sky was leaden with sleet and Mal needed to put the MG's headlamps on. The deeply rutted track, which was mostly mud peppered with flint stones, had a heavy coating of leaves from its overhanging trees, and he drove slowly, not wanting to ground his exhaust, or kick up dirt at the police car following behind him.

He was trying to think how many years it had been since he'd last come up here. They'd sold when Lynn and he divorced, but two years later he'd seen it was on the market once more, and had brought Jane up here in the hope of buying it again. But she took one look at it and rejected the idea flat. It was far too isolated for her. She said she would be terrified on her own.

He had to agree that she was right. You either liked isolation or you didn't.

They passed the main farmhouse, occupied by an elderly farmer and his wife, who had been their only neighbours, then drove on for another half-mile, past a cluster of tumble-down barns, a partially dismembered tractor and an old trailer, then wound on into the woods.

He was worried sick about Caitlin. What the hell mess had Lynn got into? Presumably it had to do with the liver she was trying to buy. He still had not told Jane about the money, but at this moment, that was a long way from his mind.

The police would not tell him anything, only that Caitlin

had run off and her mother was desperately worried about her failing health – and the opportunity of a liver transplant, which had come up and she was in danger of missing.

A ghostly slab of white shone ahead, as they approached a clearing. It was Winter Cottage, once their dream home. And the end of the track.

He angled the car so that the lights were fully on the little house. In truth, behind the ivy cladding was an ugly building, a squat, square two-storey affair, cheaply built in the early 1950s out of breeze blocks to house a herdsman and his family. In the farming slump of the late 1990s they'd been made redundant and the farmer had put the place on the market to raise some cash, which was when he and Lynn had bought it.

It was the position that had appealed to them both. Utter tranquillity, with a glorious view of the Downs to the south, and yet it was only fifteen minutes' drive to the centre of Brighton.

From the looks of it, the place was derelict now. He knew the couple of Londoners they'd sold to had big plans for the place, but they had then emigrated to Australia, which was why it had gone back on the market. It had clearly not been touched for years. Maybe no one else had come along with the cash or the vision. It certainly needed plenty of both.

He grabbed his torch off the passenger seat and climbed out, leaving the headlights on. The two police officers, DS Glenn Branson and DS Bella Moy, climbed out of their car too, each holding a switched-on torch, and walked up to him.

'Don't suppose you get many Jehovah's Witnesses around here,' joked Branson.

'That's for sure,' Mal said.

Then he led the way, along the brick path he had laid himself, up to the front door and around the side of the house, under a holly archway that was so overgrown all three of them had to duck to avoid the prickles, and through into the back garden. The brick path continued past a rotting barbecue deck, and then on, along the side of a lawn that had once been his pride and joy and was now just a wilderness, through an almost-closed gap in a tall yew hedge, into what Caitlin used to call her Secret Garden.

'I can understand why you needed to come with us, sir,' Bella Moy said.

Malcolm smiled thinly. He felt a tightening in his gullet as the beam of his torch struck the wooden Wendy house. Then he stopped. Nervous suddenly.

In a way, he was surprised it was still there, and in another way, he wished it wasn't. It was too much of a reminder, suddenly, of the pain of his split with Lynn.

The little house was made from logs and supported on stubby brick legs at each corner. He had rebuilt it himself as a labour of love for Caitlin. There was a door in the middle, with steps up to it, and a window either side. There was still glass in both of them, although the beam of his torch could barely penetrate the coating of dust through to the interior. He was pleased to see that the asphalt roof was still in place, although curling at the edges.

He tried to call her name, but his throat was too dry and nothing came out. Flanked by the two police officers, he walked forward, reached the steps, turned the wobbly handle and pushed open the door.

And his heart leapt for joy.

Caitlin was sitting on the floor at the back of the little house, all hunched up like a bendy doll, staring down into her own lap.

A tiny green glow came from her iPod, which rested on her thighs, and in the silence he could hear a refrain that went, *'One ... two ... three ... four ...'*

He recognized it. Feist. Currently one of her favourite singers. Amy liked her too.

'Hi, darling!' he said, trying not to dazzle her.

There was no response.

Something lurched inside him. 'Darling? It's OK, Dad's here.'

Then he felt a restraining arm on his shoulder.

'Sir,' Glenn Branson cautioned.

Ignoring him, he hurried across, dropping down on to his knees, putting his face up close to his daughter's.

'Caitlin, darling!'

He cupped her face in his hands and was shocked how cold she was. Stone cold.

He raised her face gently, and then he saw that her eyes were open wide, but there was no flicker of movement in them.

'No!' he said. 'No! Please, no! No! NOOOOOOOOO!'

Glenn Branson raised his torch, stared into her eyes, looking for any movement of the pupils or lids or lashes. But there was nothing.

Desperately, Mal laid Caitlin gently down, pressed his lips to his daughter's and started giving her the kiss of life. Behind him, he heard the voice of the female detective radioing for an ambulance.

He was still frantically trying to resuscitate Caitlin twenty minutes later, when the paramedics finally arrived.

123

Ten days later the kindly woman PC and the female translator walked Simona across the apron at Heathrow Airport, towards the British Airways plane.

Simona clutched Gogu tightly to her chest. The officer had rummaged through all the wheelie bins at Wiston Grange and recovered him for her.

'So, Simona, are you happy to be going home in time for Christmas?' the PC asked chirpily.

The translator repeated the question in Romanian.

Simona shrugged. She didn't know much about Christmas, other than that there were lots of people around with money in their bags and wallets, making it a good time to steal. She felt lost and confused. Shunted from place to place, room to room. She did not know where she was and did not want to be here any more. She just looked forward to seeing Romeo again.

She looked down at the ground, not knowing what to reply, and it still hurt to talk. It was from the breathing tube, they had told her, and it would get better soon.

She didn't understand why they had put the breathing tube down her, nor why she was being sent back now. The translator told her that bad people had planned to kill her and take her insides away. But she did not know if she believed her. Perhaps it was just an excuse to send her back to Romania.

'You'll be fine!' the PC said, giving her a final hug at the foot of the gangway. 'Ian Tilling has arranged for someone to meet you at Bucharest Airport and take you to his hostel – he has a place for you there.'

The translator repeated the assurance.

'Will Romeo be there?' she asked.

'Romeo is waiting for you.'

Simona climbed the steps forlornly, unsure whether to believe them.

Two stewardesses greeted her cheerily at the top, checked her boarding card, and led her to her seat, then helped to buckle her in. She stared in glum silence at the rear of the seat in front of her for most of the flight, clutching the passport document she had been told to present at the other end, and left her tray of food untouched. She just thought about Romeo constantly. Maybe he *would* be there. Maybe, when she saw him, things would be OK again.

Maybe they could find a new dream.

124

This had always been Roy Grace's favourite walk, underneath the chalk cliffs, east from Rottingdean. As a child it was almost a Sunday ritual with his parents, and recently, at least on those Sundays when he didn't have to work, it was becoming a ritual for himself and Cleo.

He loved the sense of drama, particularly on rough days, like this afternoon, when there was a blustery wind and the tide was high, and occasionally the sea surged right up the beach and sent spray and pebbles crashing over the low stone wall. And the signs that warned of the danger of falling rocks added to that drama. He loved the smells here too, the salty tang and the seaweed and the occasional whiff of rotting fish that would be gone in an instant. And the sight of cargo ships and tankers out on the horizon, and sometimes yachts, closer in.

Today was the last Sunday before Christmas and he knew he should be feeling free, and looking forward to some time off with the woman he loved. But inside he felt as churned up as the roiling, spuming, grey Channel water to his right.

They were both wrapped up warmly. Cleo had her arm comfortably looped through his and he wondered, suddenly, if they would still be doing this walk as wrinkly old people in fifty years' time.

Humphrey trotted along on his extended lead, holding a large piece of driftwood proudly in his mouth, like a trophy. A small brown dog bounded towards them, yipping, its owner some distance away yelling its name. Cleo broke free for a moment and knelt to stroke it. But it backed away nervously when Humphrey dropped the driftwood and growled. Hushing him, she took a step towards it and it bounded back again. They both laughed. Then, recognizing its name, it suddenly raced away.

'So, Great Detective, how do you feel?' she asked, placing her arm back through his.

'I don't know,' he said truthfully. He watched Humphrey struggling to pick up the wood again.

'Tell me?'

'Was it the Duke of Wellington who said that the only thing worse than losing a battle is winning one?'

She nodded.

'That's how I feel.'

'Something I don't understand,' she said. 'How were all those medical people kept silent for so long?'

'A surgeon in Romania earns 4000 euros a year. Other medical staff even less. That's how. They were all making a fortune at Wiston Grange, so they were happy as hell.'

'And tucked safely away in the countryside.'

'Most of them not able to speak English. So no gossiping with the locals. It was a smart set-up. Ship them in, let them all make a bundle, then ship them out again. They're members of the EU, so no cross-border work restrictions, no questions asked.'

'And Sir Roger Sirius?'

'Big money. And he had his own moral justification.'

They walked on in silence for a while.

'Tell me something, Grace – if that had been our child – that girl, Caitlin. What would you have done?' With her free arm she patted her belly. 'If it were to happen to this little person, sometime in the future?'

'How do you mean?'

'In the same circumstances, if our only option was to try to buy a liver to save our child, what would you have done – do?'

He shrugged. 'I'm a policeman. My duty is to enforce the law.'

'That's what scares me about you sometimes.'

'*Scares* you?'

'Uh huh. I think I would take a bullet for my child. And I think I would be capable of killing for my child. Isn't that what being a parent means?'

'You think I was wrong, doing what I did?'

'No, I suppose not. But I can understand why the mother did what she did.'

Grace nodded. 'In one of the philosophy books you gave me, I read something Aristotle said: The gods have no greater torment than for a mother to outlive her child.'

'Yes. Exactly. So how do you think that woman feels now?'

'Is a Romanian street kid's life less valuable than a middle-class Brighton kid's? Cleo, darling, I'm not God, I don't play God, I'm a copper.'

'Do you ever wonder if sometimes you are too much a copper?'

'Meaning?'

'Enforcing the law at any cost? Hiding behind the *human* cost? Are you so constricted by your policeman's view of the world that you can't see outside it?'

'We saved the life of that Romanian kid. That matters a lot to me.'

'Kind of, *job done, move on to the next*?'

He shook his head. 'No, never. That's not how I work – or feel – ever.'

She held him tighter. 'You're a good man really, aren't you.'

He smiled wistfully. 'In a shitty world.'

She stopped and stared at him, smiling that smile that he truly would die for. 'You make it a little less shitty.'

'I wish.'

EPILOGUE

Lynn stood in Caitlin's room, which had remained untouched for almost two and a half years. Now, amid all the mess of her daughter's things, there was a stack of cardboard boxes from the removals firm.

What the hell did she keep and what did she throw away? There wasn't much space in the tiny flat she was moving into.

With tears rolling down her cheeks, she stared around at the impenetrable tangle of clothes, soft toys, CDs, DVDs, shoes, make-up containers, the pink stool, the mobile of blue perspex butterflies, shopping bags and the dartboard with the purple boa hanging from it.

The tears were for Caitlin, not for this place. She wasn't sorry to be leaving. Caitlin had been right all along, in her way. It had been their *house* but not their *home*.

She walked through into her bedroom. The bed was piled high with the contents of her wardrobe and cupboards. On the very top was her blue coat, still in the plastic zipper where she had sealed it after her first 'date' with Reg Okuma. Although it was her favourite coat, she had felt it was sullied, and had never worn it again. But Reg Okuma was all in the past now. Denarii had been good to her after Caitlin died, and had promoted her to manager. That had enabled her to write off his debt and adjust his credit rating on the computer system. No one had been any the wiser.

She slung the coat over her arm, went downstairs and

out into the fine spring morning. Then she crammed it into the dustbin.

She was paying back Luke and Sue Shackleton from the money from the sale of the house. And some of Mal's money, and her mum's. There wouldn't be much left after that, but she didn't care. She needed to put the past behind her somehow.

And some of it nearly was. Her prison sentence, at any rate. Two years, suspended, thanks to an Oscar-winning performance by a barrister, or the luck of coming up in front of a judge with a heart – or maybe both.

The life sentence of grief for Caitlin was another thing. People said that the first two years were the worst, but Lynn was finding it didn't really get any better. Several nights a week she would wake, in a cold sweat, crying bitterly over the decisions she had made and for the beautiful girl she had lost.

She would curse and kick herself that the legitimate transplant for Caitlin had been so close and she'd blown it out of sheer panic, out of sheer stupidity.

And the only thing that would calm her down and comfort her was the purring of Max, the cat, on the end of the bed, and remembering the smile of her daughter and those words she used to say that would so annoy her.

Chill, woman.

ACKNOWLEDGEMENTS

This book is a work of fiction, as are all my Roy Grace novels. But it is a sad truth that three people die every day in the UK because there are not sufficient organs for transplant available. It is also sad and true that there are over a thousand children living rough in Bucharest – some of them third-generation street kids – and over five thousand adults, a legacy of Ceauşescu's monstrous regime. Some of these children do get trafficked for their organs.

There are many people who have given me so much help in creating this book, and without their immensely kind and generous support it would have been impossible to write with any sense of authenticity.

My first thank you is to Martin Richards, QPM, Chief Constable of Sussex, who has been immensely generous in his support for my work, and who has made so many helpful suggestions and opened so many avenues for me.

My good friend, former Detective Chief Superintendent David Gaylor, has, as ever, played an invaluable role, reading the manuscript as I go along, not just checking facts, but contributing constantly and wisely to every aspect of the story. I can genuinely say it would have been a much poorer book without his input.

So many officers of Sussex Police have given me their time and wisdom and tolerated me hanging out with them, as well as answered my endless questions, that it is almost impossible to list them all, but I'm trying here, and please forgive any omissions. Detective Chief Superintendent

Kevin Moore; Chief Superintendent Graham Bartlett; Chief Superintendent Peter Coll; Chief Superintendent Chris Ambler; DCI Adam Hibbert; DCI Trevor Bowles; Chief Inspector Stephen Curry; DCI Paul Furnell; Scientific Support Branch Manager, Brian Cook; Stuart Leonard; Tony Case; DI William Warner; DCI Nick Sloan; DI Jason Tingley; Chief Inspector Steve Brookman; Inspector Andrew Kundert; Inspector Roy Apps; Sgt Phil Taylor; Ray Packham and Dave Reed of the High-Tech Crime Unit; Sergeant James Bowes; PC Georgie Edge; Inspector Rob Leet; Inspector Phil Clarke; Sgt Mel Doyle; PC Tony Omotoso; PC Ian Upperton; PC Andrew King; Sgt Malcolm (Choppy) Wauchope; PC Darren Balcombe; Sgt Sean McDonald; PC Danny Swietlik; PC Steve Cheesman; PC Andy McMahon; Sgt Justin Hambloch; Chris Heaver; Martin Bloomfield; Ron King; Robin Wood; Sgt Lorna Dennison-Wilkins and the team at the Specialist Search Unit; Sue Heard, Press and PR Officer; Louise Leonard; James Gartrell; and Peter Wiedemann of the Munich LKA.

And I owe an extremely special and massive thanks to the terrific team at the Brighton and Hove Mortuary, Elsie Sweetman, Victor Sindon, Sean Didcott. And also to Dr Nigel Kirkham.

Two people gave me the most extraordinarily personal insights into the world of liver failure and transplants – Zahra Priddle and James Sarsfield Watson – both recent recipients of new livers. Both Zahra and James's wonderful family, Séamus Watson, Cathy Sarsfield Watson and Kathleen Sarsfield Watson added so much to this book.

I am indebted in my education into liver disease and related medical matters to the kindness of Professor Sir Roy York Calnes; Dr John Ramage; Dr Nick Vaughan; the wonderful Dr Abid Suddle of King's College Hospital, who really